SAILS
ON THE
HORIZON

SAILS
ON THE
HORIZON

A Novel of the Napoleonic Wars

Jay Worrall

RANDOM HOUSE TRADE PAPERBACKS

NEW YORK

2006 Random House Trade Paperback Edition

Published in the United States by Random House Trade Paperbacks,
an imprint of The Random House Publishing Group,
a division of Random House, Inc., New York.

RANDOM HOUSE TRADE PAPERBACKS and colophon are trademarks
of Random House, Inc.

Originally published in hardcover in the United States by Random House,
an imprint of The Random House Publishing Group,
a division of Random House, Inc., in 2005.

Library of Congress Cataloging-in-Publication Data
Worrall, Jay.
Sails on the horizon : a novel of the Napoleonic Wars / Jay Worrall.
p.   cm.
ISBN 0-345-47648-4
1. First Coalition, War of the, 1792–1797—Naval operations—Fiction.   2. Great
Britain—History, Naval—18th century—Fiction.   3. Great Britain. Royal Navy—
Officers—Fiction.   4. Quaker women—Fiction.   5. Farm life—Fiction.   6. England—
Fiction. I. Title.
PS3623.O77S35 2005
813'.6—dc22   2004052033

Printed in the United States of America

www.atrandom.com

2 4 6 8 9 7 5 3 1

Book design by Victoria Wong

To Chel Avery

FOREWORD

THE ERA OFTEN THOUGHT OF AS THE NAPOLEONIC WARS covers a period of roughly twenty-two years, from February 1, 1793, when Revolutionary France declared war on Britain, to June 18, 1815, the Battle of Waterloo. This was a titanic struggle—arguably the first worldwide war—between France, western Europe's most populous country, and Great Britain, the world's richest. Napoleon Bonaparte, whose personality and abilities came to dominate the period, does not become a prominent figure until about 1799.

It has often been said that this was a strangely unbalanced conflict: England paramount (though not unchallenged) on the seas; France an almost unrivaled land-based military force. In order for the French army to subdue Britain it had, of course, to cross the English Channel. In order to cross the Channel, France had to at least temporarily neutralize His Majesty George the Third's Royal Navy. To accomplish this, she would require the assistance of such other naval forces as were available from Spain, Denmark, and Holland.

Numerous nations and their colonial possessions were allied with one side or the other, not infrequently changing allegiances as a result of conquest, coercion, or choice. Of particular interest is Spain; a nominal ally of Britain at the outset of the conflict, she came under the dominion of France and switched sides in October 1796. This is important because, on paper, the Spanish possessed a powerful navy that if allowed to combine with the remnants of once-significant French naval forces would present very serious strategic problems to London. Thus on the morning of February 14, 1797, a Spanish fleet of about twenty-seven sail of the line is to be found sailing from Cádiz for the purpose of joining with the French at the port of Brest.

A NOTE ON
MEASUREMENTS AND VALUES

Money

IT IS NOT POSSIBLE TO DIRECTLY EQUATE THE PURCHASING power of currency between the late eighteenth and early twenty-first centuries. It has been suggested, however, that the value of an English pound in 1790 might be multiplied by a factor of seventy or eighty to give an approximate year-2000 equivalent. From pounds to American dollars the ratio might be 1:100 or 110. English pounds were divided into shillings, pennies, and farthings: twenty shillings to a pound; twelve pennies to a shilling; four farthings to a penny. A loaf of bread cost about four pence.

Distance

Units of measurement for distance at sea were not always standardized. The author has used:

1 league = 3 nautical miles = 5.6 kilometers
1 nautical mile = 6,076 feet (1.15 statute miles) = 1.9 kilometers
1 cable length = about 200 yards (1/10 of a league) = 185 meters
1 fathom = 6 feet (1/100 of a league) = 1.8 meters

Time

Time on British naval ships was measured in "watches" and "bells." The day officially began at noon and was divided into seven watches, five of four hours each and two of two hours:

Afternoon:	noon to 4 P.M.	Middle:	midnight to 4 A.M.
1st Dog:	4 P.M. to 6 P.M.	Morning:	4 A.M. to 8 A.M.
2nd Dog:	6 P.M. to 8 P.M.	Forenoon:	8 A.M. to noon
First:	8 P.M. to midnight		

The ship's bell was rung in cumulative half-hourly intervals during each watch, so that three bells in the afternoon watch is 1:30 P.M. and four bells in the middle watch is 2 A.M.

SAILS
ON THE
HORIZON

ONE

St. Valentine's Day, 1797
Eight leagues southwest of
Cape St. Vincent, Portugal

"THE F-FLAGSHIP'S SIGNALING AGAIN, SIR. 'ENGAGE THE enemy,' I think it says." The adolescent midshipman stood in an oversized jacket and flapping trousers at the top of the forward ladderway, squinting into the distance along the line of British warships, each laboring more or less one cable's length behind the other, pointed toward a gap between two large Spanish squadrons. He fairly danced with excitement.

"Thank you, Mr. Bowles. You may come down now," said Charles Edgemont, the second lieutenant aboard His Britannic Majesty's sixty-four-gun ship of the line *Argonaut*. At twenty-five, Edgemont's career in the navy had already spanned thirteen years, seven as a midshipman himself and six as a commission officer. His responsibility with the ship at quarters was the upper gundeck and its twenty-eight brightly painted black twelve-pounder cannon, neatly aligned on their carriages, fourteen to a side. The smallish and outdated *Argonaut*, captained by Sir Edward Wood, had taken her position as the last in the nearly mile-long fifteen-ship English line. Charles had watched as the fleet arranged itself into formation earlier in the morning and knew the order of battle. Leading the van was *Culloden,* seventy-four guns, under Captain Thomas Troubridge, and then the *Blenheim* and the *Prince George,* both grand ninety-eights. The flagship, *Victory,* with its hundred guns and Admiral Sir John Jervis, took station seventh in the line, near the center. The fleet sailed on an easy gray sea, through intermittent gray mist, under gray skies with a chill wind blowing steadily if moderately from the west. The *Argonaut's* crew had long since been ordered to quarters, the sails shortened, the topgallant masts struck down, and the courses brailed up in preparation for battle. Sand had been scattered on the wetted decks to improve footing and reduce the chance of fire. The guns were charged, double-shotted, primed, and run out, each of their six-man crews standing anxiously beside them.

"My G-God, there's a lot of 'em," Bowles reported, his voice breaking. "There must be near a score in the group awindward. T'other bunch alee ain't but about half that large." Billy Bowles was fourteen, a pimply youth with sallow skin and unruly hair, assigned to the gundeck. Charles had taken a liking to the boy but thought him too tender for a life in the navy. He was easily bullied by his messmates in the gun room and Charles had come across him bruised and reduced to tears more than once. "The *Culloden's* almost up to them," the boy bubbled on. "Can't be more than a mile and a half afar."

"Come down from that ladder and take your station," Charles said. "We'll be up to them soon enough."

"I see a four-decker, sir, and a bunch of three-deckers! Oh, my God."

Exasperated, Charles jumped to the ladderway and grabbed the apparently deaf midshipman by the back of his coat. "Look, the flagship's signaling again," the boy squealed. Charles looked down the line of ships until he saw the signal flags on *Victory's* halyards, repeated by the frigate *Niger* standing to windward: "Admiral intends to pass through enemy line." At the same moment he saw clouds of smoke erupt from the sides of the nearest Spanish warships, answered immediately by a broadside from *Culloden.* A moment later, the sounds of the great guns rumbled like distant thunder. "Get to your station," he said to the boy, pulling him down the ladderway. "You can watch through a gunport."

(4)

The roll of cannon fire slowly grew louder and more intense as the British line engaged the Spanish fleet in sequence and larger numbers from both sides became involved. It had been cold and foggy earlier in the morning and Charles had pulled on a woolen sweater under his uniform coat. Now he felt beads of clammy sweat under his arms. He began nervously drumming his fingers against his trouser leg. It came to him that, despite the span of time he had spent in the navy, he had never seen one of the great guns fired in anger. Through years of training and practice he knew well the mechanics of their operation, the bellowing roar so loud it could make the crew's ears bleed, and the recoil as the brutes leapt inward on screaming trucks with ample force to crush anyone in their way until jerked to an abrupt halt against their breechings. He had been told by others who had survived major fleet actions off Toulon or the Saints or on the Glorious First of June of the giddy jubilation that went with delivering a deafening broadside into an opponent and the horror of receiving the full weight of a well-delivered salvo. But by accident or fate or design, the *Argonaut* had not been present at those battles and Charles had not experienced it.

And now he would. He wondered how he would react. Some men, he had heard, rose in stature and determination as the world exploded around them in the din of battle. Others became paralyzed, unable to function, their only thought to protect themselves. The former were heroes, the latter cowards. It was as simple as that; everyone said so. He remembered—it had been hammered into him repeatedly at every level of his naval career—that, as an officer and a gentleman, it was his responsibility to set an example of coolness and courage before the men he commanded. He forced himself to stop rapping his fingers against his leg, deliberately rested one hand on his sword hilt, placed the other behind his back, and stood as apparently relaxed and indifferent to the approaching battle as he was able to manage.

"Silence, there," he snapped at a gun crew, some of whose members were clustered around a port, staring at the Spanish fleet and talking excitedly among themselves. "All of you, stand by your guns." Charles didn't really see anything wrong with the men looking through the gunports and discussing the oncoming battle, but Captain Wood would reprimand him sharply if he noticed any lack of discipline among the men under his charge. Charles had been reprimanded for apparent lack of smartness among his men before.

The devil of it was that he couldn't see what was happening. He caught occasional glimpses of Spanish warships through the forward gunports, including what he thought was the gigantic flagship, *Santissima Trinidad,* with 130 guns on four decks, the largest ship in the world. The now almost incessant cannon fire had grown decidedly louder, more immediately threatening, and a hint of spent gunpowder tainted the air. It was maddening not to be able to see anything of the progress of the battle, the positions of the fleets, or what damage had been done. He didn't want to climb the ladder to the upper deck; that would invite a rebuke from the captain for displaying undue curiosity and leaving his post. He also didn't want to gawk through a porthole like a common landsman.

"Mr. Bowles," he shouted.

"A-aye aye, sir," came a voice from close behind him.

"Mr. Bowles, get back up the forward ladderway and tell me what you see."

"Aye aye," the boy answered and cheerfully scurried away. After a moment he called down, "The *Culloden*'s almost through their line, sir. The *Victory* and the *Egmont* are just coming into range. There's still a ways afore us."

"Do you see any damage?"

Bowles paused before answering. "Hard to say, sir. There's s-so much s-s-smoke. Seems most everybody's masts are still standing, though."

"What are the Spaniards doing?"

"The bigger group, the one to windward, is sort of sliding to the north like. If they can, I think they'll run with the wind back to Spain. Can't tell what t'other bunch are doing. Kind of circling about, tacking like."

"Thank you, Mr. Bowles. Let me know if anything important happens." Of their own accord, Charles's fingers resumed their nervous tamping against his thigh.

A cheer broke out on the upper deck and was quickly shouted down by cries of "Silence, there," from one officer or another.

"A dago's lost a mast, I think," came Bowles's voice. "*Culloden* has hoisted a signal . . . 'Acknowledge,' I think."

"Acknowledge what?" Charles asked.

"Oh, I see," Bowles said after a pause. "The admiral telegraphed for *Culloden* to tack and come back at the Spanish. Only *Culloden* acknowledged and came about afore the flagship signaled. We're all supposed to tack in s-s-succession when we get through the Spanish line, it says."

Charles longed to climb the ladder and see with his own eyes, but he contented himself with asking, "How long till we're in range?"

"*Culloden's* around, and *Blenheim* and *Prince George*. There goes *Orion*. About two more ships and we'll be up to the first. Right after *Captain* and *Excellent*. Wait!" Bowles squealed with excitement. "The Spaniards, the smaller group what was milling about, they've all come up to where our boys were turning. They've shot some yards off *Colossus's* foremast! Her head won't swing. *Orion's* backed and covering her. Oh, my God! Here comes *Victory*. Oh, such a broadside she just gave. . . . "

"Lieutenant Edgemont!" the first lieutenant's voice boomed down from the quarterdeck. "A Spanish warship's approaching to starboard. You may fire as your guns bear."

"Aye aye, sir," Charles called back. At last he would be tried in battle. "Starboard guns, aim true for the waterline," he yelled to the captains of his gun crews. "Prepare to fire on my command." His spine tingled with anticipation and he felt sweat on his palms. He was about to be in battle, a real battle. At the forewardmost cannon he knelt down and peered along the thick black barrel out the gunport. Almost immediately the Spanish seventy-four, with all sails set and gloriously ornamented with red-and-gold paint, sailed into view on the opposite tack. She had already been considerably knocked about; she had several parted stays, holes in her courses, and her hull was scarred. As soon as he was satisfied that the gun would hit her he jumped back and shouted, "Fire!" a little louder than strictly necessary. The gun captain yanked on his lanyard. Instantly the cannon erupted with a thunderous bang and leapt backward against its restraining tackle. Since they were firing to windward, the smoke billowed back into the gunport, momentarily obscuring any view. Charles knelt by the second gun, stepped back, and again barked, "Fire!" At the same time he heard and felt the larger twenty-four-pounder cannon on the lower gundeck explode in a single broadside, heeling the ship with their recoil. The two ships were passing a good deal faster than he had anticipated, so he yelled, "Fire as you bear!" The remainder of his starboard cannon crashed inward as one, the wind filling the gundeck with the acrid smoke of burnt gunpowder, shrouding everything. As the air cleared, Charles saw that the Spaniard was now well astern and beyond the traverse of his guns. She had suffered little if any additional damage that he could detect. He let out a deep breath and was about to congratulate himself on his coolness under fire when he realized that his target had not discharged a gun in her haste to escape.

"Worm and sponge out," he ordered in an almost disappointed tone. "Load with cartridge. Load with shot and wad your shot." He continued the sequence of cleaning and charging the cannon, mechanically ending with, "Put in tompkins. House your guns. Secure your guns."

Where was the rest of the Spanish fleet? Despite the risk to his dignity, Charles knelt by a starboard gunport and peered out. The larger body to windward sailed briskly northward out of cannon range. A glance to larboard told a similar story. The smaller squadron—he counted eight ships of the line—was tacking across the rear of the British line, where they could rejoin their sister ships. Charles searched in vain to starboard and port for the other British warships. They had to be more or less dead ahead or still in the process of turning. He tried to figure how the fleet, still tacking into the wind in succession, well beyond the rapidly departing Spanish, would be able to reform and engage before the enemy could unite to form a unified line of battle or, more probably, flee safely back to Cádiz.

He had almost decided that the enemy was bound to escape, that Jervis's fleet could not possibly come about in time, when he heard the shouted order "All hands to wear ship" from the quarterdeck and the sounds of pounding feet as sailors rushed to the shrouds and braces. He looked at the young midshipman still standing near the top of the ladderway. "What the hell's going on, Bowles?"

"We've gotten a s-s-s-signal from the flagship," the boy answered shakily, his complexion a deathly white. "Our number. J-just our number. We're to wear and engage the enemy more c-c-closely."

Charles's mouth worked for a moment but no sound came out, certainly not a coherent question he could ask Bowles that would explain what he wanted to know. He bounded for the ladderway to see for himself. It immediately became clear. The main body of the Spanish fleet was already well to the north and clear of the British line. Very soon they would turn to the east, and, with the wind behind them, collect the smaller squadron to make all haste for Spain, escaping virtually intact. The *Argonaut* had already turned and he saw that she was now on a course to cross just in front of the main body. He looked desperately around for the rest of the British warships. The *Culloden, Blenheim, Prince George,* and the rest of the British van that had already tacked were adding sail after sail in pursuit of the Spanish rear. Others, which had been toward the rear of the British line, *Excellent* and *Captain* among them, had worn after *Argonaut* in response to a second, general signal from *Victory* to "Engage the enemy more closely," which still flew. None of them would reach the *Argonaut* anywhere near in time to support her in what she alone was in position to do: Stop or at least delay a Spanish squadron of perhaps a dozen and a half heavy men of war.

"We're the only ones who can reach 'em, you see, sir," said Bowles's small voice beside him.

"Yes." Charles almost swallowed the word. His eyes grew wide as he studied the onrushing mass of two- and three-decked warships, with the immense *Santissima Trinidad* somewhere near the center. All of them were larger and more heavily armed than the *Argonaut*—many were much larger and much more heavily armed. He put his hand on the boy's shoulder and felt him shaking. "It will be all right if we just do our jobs," he said gently, well aware that there was no truth in it.

Billy Bowles nodded slowly, never taking his eyes off the Spanish fleet.

"Get back to your station. There's no more time for gawking," Charles said, leading the boy back down to the gundeck.

"Are the portside guns loaded and primed?" he yelled out to the captains of the gun crews. "Report by number. Two?"

"Ready, sir," was the immediate reply.

"Four?"

"Loaded and primed, sir."

"Six?" And so it went to number twenty-eight, odd-numbered guns to starboard, even to port.

"Port side, loose your guns." The hands at each gun slipped the knots that bound the guns to ringbolts on the bulwark and deck.

"Out tompkins." The wooden plugs that kept sea spray out of the muzzles were removed.

"Run out your guns." The crews heaved on the side tackles, dragging the heavy beasts, trucks rumbling and squealing in protest, up snug against the ship's outer planking. The Spanish fleet, bows on and clouds of sail at their masts, could clearly be seen through the weather gunports. Charles counted four large ships of the line nearly abreast at the front of the mass.

"How d'we know which to aim for?" the captain of a nearby gun crew asked.

"Any one you like," Charles answered tersely. He felt a lump rise in his throat and jammed his hands in his pockets to keep them from fidgeting. He needed to do something to show his men that he was unconcerned.

"Mr. Bowles," he yelled.

"Aye aye, sir."

"Get below to the magazine and tell the gunner that we shall probably need more powder cartridges. All he can make."

"A-aye aye, sir."

"And, Mr. Bowles, on your way down please convey my respects to Lieutenant Bevan and say that I expect him to do better than last time, during practice, when he very nearly sank the ship's jolly boat."

Bowles looked at him and grinned. "He won't like that, sir."

"Sod him," Charles said cheerfully. "You can tell him that I said that, too." Daniel Bevan, a Welshman, the third lieutenant and Charles's closest friend on the *Argonaut,* commanded the lower gundeck. The two men were much the same age and Charles Edgemont was the senior officer by a matter of only one and a half weeks.

As soon as Bowles had gone, he bent and looked through a gunport. The Spaniards were nearly in range, head-on, their bow waves bright curls of white against dark bows. Two of the leading ships were three-deckers, one of over a hundred guns. The others were seventy-fours at least, and all of them had their guns run out on both sides. Typical of the

Spanish, he thought. They could only use one broadside. Didn't they know which one?

At that moment another midshipman, with fine, almost delicate features and attired in a perfectly tailored uniform, appeared at Charles's elbow. Charles knew him but not well and had taken something of a dislike to him from the day they were introduced. His name was Winchester something. He was eighteen or nineteen and, it was said, soon to stand for lieutenant. He was also said to be the son of a well-connected and wealthy barrister from York. Charles thought him excessively and unjustifiably confident, lacking in discipline and the rudiments of politeness to his betters, or at least those who outranked him. Winchester something was assigned to the quarterdeck, he knew, and acted as the captain's messenger. Well, Charles thought with some satisfaction, he was going to get more than he bargained for today.

"Captain's compliments, Lieutenant Edgemont," the midshipman announced coolly. "Hold your fire until captain's orders. He wants the first broadside to make a statement."

"Thank you," Charles answered. After touching his hat the young man left to carry his message to the lower gundeck.

A series of bangs broke the silence. Several of the Spanish warships had opened with their bow chasers as they rushed onward. He watched a ball skip across the waves in a series of diminishing splashes until, its energy nearly spent, it hit with a dull thunk against the *Argonaut*'s side and sank to the bottom of the sea.

"Beg pardon, sir," Bowles's voice said breathlessly beside him, "but Lieutenant Bevan sends his compliments and says you can shove . . ."

"*Fire!*" came the order from above, shouted so loud it made Charles jump.

"All together, fire!" he yelled quickly, and both main and lower gundecks exploded instantaneously with a deafening noise that made his ears ring. Billows of smoke swept back in through the open ports but were soon cleared away by the wind. One of the leading seventy-fours had her foremast and bowsprit dragging over her side and her mainmast from the tops up swaying as to soon follow. "Reload fast as you can. Fire at will," he yelled. The second salvo was slightly ragged, as some crews were quicker than others at sponging out, ramming in cartridge and ball, priming, hauling the guns out by brute force, and sparking the powder.

Through a break in the smoke he saw the smaller of the three-deckers, the *San Nicolás,* he thought, an eighty-four, heave to and present her broadside. Almost at once she spoke in a bellowing roar and the ship was lost in a cloud of her own making with orderly rows of orange tongues stabbing through. The *Argonaut* shuddered from numerous impacts the length of her hull. The bulwark between the number four and six guns imploded in a horrific spray of splintered wood, upsetting the six gun and killing or wounding most of its crew. "Right that gun and put it back into action," Charles found himself shouting. "And find someone to get the wounded below." The *Argonaut* fired her increasingly drawn out broadside again.

A second salvo from the three-decker was slow in coming by English standards, but equally determined. Several balls passed straight through the gundeck with terrifying crashes, hurling swarms of jagged shards of oak. Charles barely noticed when a twelve-year-old powder boy passing in front of him whispered, "Oh, mother," and sank to the deck with a splinter the size of a sword through his chest.

The Spanish roundshot smashing through the *Argonaut*'s timbers were unbelievable in their power, their destructiveness, and the randomness of their violence. One man of a cannon's crew, or two or three if they happened to be aligned one behind the other, would be scythed into pieces while another standing a foot to the side would only be stupefied into insensibility by the percussion of the passing ball. Arms, legs, heads were abruptly ripped away or left dangling by thin strips of flesh. The unceasing, deafening roar of the great guns as they belched flame and lurched inward, the shriek of enemy shot passing through the deck unseen in the thickening smoke and crashing against frame and timber or clanging against guns, and the screams of the injured and moans of the dying numbed all sensibility.

Charles stood rooted in place on the edge of panic, stunned by the din and violence clearly heard but only dimly seen in the choking, swirling smoke. His mind shut out all but the most elemental thought, flinching at every crash, struggling to resist the urge to flee when there was nowhere to flee to, struggling to fight back against the enemy without and the horror within. Over and over he bellowed, "Keep firing! Hit 'em hard! Keep firing!" at the gun crews struggling at their weapons, as if the words would give him courage while men and boys died all around.

Another gun overturned with a sound like a ringing bell. One exploded while being loaded, with terrible effect. Dead and dying lay sprawled here and there, but mostly along the center of the deck, where they had been dragged. Others had already been dumped overboard. Great ragged holes in the sides of the ship admitted smoke and additional daylight. Streams of bright-red blood ran in zigzag patterns across the deck as the ship rolled from side to side. Charles lost all sense of time as the gun crews loaded, ran out, and fired their cannon as quickly as they could, over and over again. The powder boys hurried across the deck with fresh cartridges and returned without pause to the magazine for more. Repetitive and frenetic, the great guns bellowed again and again and again. All the while Spanish balls crashed through the *Argonaut*'s hull or existing fractures, destroying anything in their path. Time lost meaning, as did life or death. There remained only the absorbing moment of firing the guns and being fired upon, destroying and being destroyed. Even the death and destruction around him lost meaning, and only the mechanical and repetitive act of reloading and firing the fewer and fewer serviceable cannon retained any coherence.

"By your leave, sir," a nearby voice insisted. The speaker had to repeat himself at least twice to get Charles's attention. It was Winchester, his perfect blue-and-white uniform torn across the front and stained with black powder and red blood.

"What do you want?" Charles snapped, unreasonably irritated at the intrusion.

"You're needed on the quarterdeck."

For a moment Charles thought the midshipman was smirking at him, but then saw that the boy was badly shaken and struggling to control himself. He had to stop to let the words penetrate. He started to say that it would be inconvenient just now, he was busy. "All right, I'll be there in a moment," he managed.

"Please, it's urgent, sir," Winchester insisted. "Captain Wood and the first are dead. You're in command now."

Charles heard the words, but his mind refused to accept them. They didn't make sense. Nothing made any sense except that most of his men on the shattered gundeck were dead or bleeding their lives away and screaming in agony. Two cannon nearby went off almost together, causing him to start.

"The captain's dead?" he said stupidly.

"Yes, sir, and the first," Winchester insisted desperately. "You're in command."

Charles looked at the carnage around him. Six of the port-side cannon were still manned by some remnants of their crews. "Do you know how to manage these guns?" he asked, desperately trying to clear his mind.

"Yes, sir," Winchester replied without hesitation. Charles doubted it but he had no choice.

A flood of questions began to penetrate. What was the state of the ship? Bad, he knew, but how bad? How many Spanish warships were still firing into the *Argonaut*? What condition were they in? Where was the rest of the British battle fleet? And if the captain and the first, and God knows how many others, were dead, he would have to reorganize the remaining officers and warrants. How many were left, how many of the crew? Only two things were certain: He had to do something quickly, and he would need help.

"Get word to Lieutenant Bevan below," he ordered Winchester, "and have him meet me on the quarterdeck. You'll have to keep both gundecks working until I say otherwise." As soon as the midshipman started toward the partly shattered ladderway, Charles saw young Billy Bowles crouched in a corner, staring at him with terror-filled eyes. He couldn't leave him there; the boy could be court-martialed and hanged for cowardice if some other officer saw him.

"Come on, Billy," he said softly. "I need your help on the quarterdeck." The child meekly rose and followed him.

The first thing Charles saw when he reached the deck was an unnatural expanse of sky. Both the mainmast and foremast and all their yards and sails were gone. The mainmast, he saw, had been shot off about three feet above the deck; its huge trunk lay half over the starboard side in a tangle of rope and tackle. The foremast had snapped about eight feet up and its stump stood like some obscene heathen monument. Of the foremast itself, its sails and rigging, there was no sign. The mizzen seemed more or less intact, although a number of its stays and braces had been shot away. In the waist a disorganized collection of seamen with axes swarmed over the wreckage of the mainmast, hacking at the rigging and struggling to free the ship from its drag. The quarterdeck itself was a shambles and nearly empty. The decking, holystoned pristine smooth and white earlier that morning, was gouged by long furrows and lay covered with broken and splintered wood, a profusion of tangled snakes of rope and loose tackle, pieces of dislodged hammocks and clothing, blood, bodies, and pieces of bodies. There were gaping sections where the railing and hammock netting had been shot away; all the quarterdeck carronades were dismounted, damaged, or missing. The ship's wheel and compass housing were smashed to rubble, with the master and all four of his mates lying dead nearby. Charles recognized the body of Captain Wood on his back near the port-side rail, one leg bent unnaturally underneath. Blood covered his shirt where a Spanish musket ball had found him. Hudgins, the first lieutenant, lay partly on and partly off one of the gratings he had been standing on when a ball cut him in half. Charles heard Bowles sob and turned in time to see the boy throw up on the deck. He took the boy's arm, led him to an overturned bucket, and sat him down on it.

A dozen marines in their red coats and pipe-clayed belts stood behind what remained of the port railing, firing their muskets under the command of a young marine lieutenant who mechanically called out their orders: "Load cartridge . . . load ball . . . ram home . . . rammers out . . . cock your arms . . . shoulder arms . . . aim . . . fire . . . load cartridge . . ." as if it were a parade drill. A greater number of redcoats lay writhing or still on the deck in an untidy line behind them.

Looking over the railing, he saw that the *Argonaut* had exacted a heavy toll in exchange for the damage she'd suffered. The two leading Spanish seventy-fours were both dismasted and badly battered, drifting helplessly leeward. The *San Nicolás,* her foremast and bowsprit hanging in a tangled ruin half in the sea, lay broadside-on opposite them. She still fired sporadically from this gun or that, but there were numerous and large holes in her side and several upward-pointing cannon muzzles indicating dismounted guns. A better-organized broadside from the *Argonaut's* gundecks sounded. Charles watched as the *San Nicolás's* mainmast shuddered and fell in a slow graceful arc, snapping stays and braces as it descended. It crossed Charles's mind that perhaps Midshipman Winchester did know something about how to manage the guns.

Behind and just to the north of the *San Nicolás* seemed to be the main body of the Spanish fleet. It was hard to tell—all Charles could see were masts and sails and smoke. A number of them had apparently become entangled behind the leading men of war when they were confronted and slowed by the *Argonaut*. Others, he could see, were working their way around the obstruction in order to flee, and some had already done so. The smaller Spanish lee squadron was hull down to the east with all sail set and disappearing fast. Of the British he could see little but two ships of the line, probably *Barfleur* and *Britannia,* both some way off. He guessed from the sound of cannon fire that some had finally gotten in behind and were engaging the Spanish rear.

Lieutenant Bevan appeared from the ladderway, his familiar stocky form and face dark with burnt gunpowder. "Oh, my God, Charlie," he said, surveying the wreck of the ship.

"Collect that party midships," Charles said quickly, "and finish clearing the mainmast away. Then scab on some sort of spar for a foremast. We've got to get steerageway."

"Aye aye," Bevan said. As he turned to leave, he noticed Bowles sitting on his bucket with his face in his hands, sobbing in great heaves. Bevan looked at Charles quizzically.

"You never saw that, Daniel," Charles said. "If anybody asks I'm going to say that he did his job as well as he could. It was just more than he was able to deal with, is all."

Bevan nodded wordlessly and left.

A Spanish frigate, small among the men of war but deadly with a broadside of twenty guns, crept around the bow of the *San Nicolás* under topgallants and jibs close enough that Charles could see her captain, a short, wiry man in a brilliant red-and-blue uniform, shouting orders. He watched with a helpless feeling as she crossed the *Argonaut's* undefended stern, her gunports open and her cannon waiting. "No, please don't," Charles breathed. The Spaniard's broadside came in a tearing crescendo, sending ball after ball screaming the length of *Argonaut's* decks. Without the time or wit to flinch, Charles felt the concussion of a passing shot and saw Billy Bowles, struggling to stand, dissolve into a mist of gore. He swore savagely as the black-hulled ship backed her mainsail, methodically ran out her guns, and fired again. The *Argonaut* shuddered as iron shot smashed timbers, upset the few remaining gun carriages, killed, and maimed. Charles's fear turned to rage at the gratuitous slaughter. It was pointless, cruel, uncalled for. The ship was already crippled. She had no way to defend herself. After a third murderous salvo, the frigate smartly filled her sails and fled to the east. Her name, etched in gold leaf across her stern, was *Santa Brigida*.

"I'll sink you, you son of a bitch! I'll see you in hell," he screamed at the departing form, but the words rang hollow, even in his own ears. He was powerless to do anything, impotent.

After a moment he tried to calm himself. He had to think. The *Argonaut* had to gain control of her rudder if she was to have any hope of survival. He made his way as quickly as he could over the littered deck to the lieutenant of the marines with his sharpshooters. "My compliments, sir," he said, trying to steady himself. "I want you to take your men belowdecks to the tiller ropes. When I send an order down to turn to starboard, for example, I want you all to pull the tiller over the right, if you were facing forward, that is."

The lieutenant drew himself up to his full height. "Cease fire," he snapped at his men. To Charles he said disdainfully, "I know port from starboard, sir. But the tiller and its ropes ain't my responsibility. Shooting dagos is."

"I'm making it your responsibility, Lieutenant," Charles growled. "At present I command this ship. I am giving you a lawful order that you disobey at your peril."

The lieutenant hesitated. "I don't know. It ain't my—"

Charles cut him off. "If you don't like it, you can bloody well complain to the Admiralty. In the meantime, if we don't get some goddamned steerage soon, none of us will live to see England again. Take your men to the fucking tiller room." The lieutenant stared at him wide-eyed for an instant, then nodded, collected his men, and marched them off in the direction of the aft ladderway.

Out of the corner of his eye, Charles noticed another Spanish three-decker edging around from behind the *San Nicolás*'s bow for a clear shot at the *Argonaut. My God, when will it stop?* He recognized her as the *San Josef,* 112 guns. She towered over the *San Nicolás* and from the *Argonaut* looked like a mountain, masts seemingly reaching to the clouds. She was about halfway clear when her forward guns fired. The roundshot and grape ripped through the marching marines. The young marine lieutenant died instantly along with about half of his charges.

The mizzenmast, already much weakened, snapped with a loud crack at deck level and came crashing forward, braces, stays, yards, blocks, tackle, and all. Charles barely had a chance to duck before something heavy and solid swung down on the end of a rope and hit him a glancing blow to the side of his head. In a stunning blaze of pain, he dropped like deadweight to the deck. Instinctively, he scrambled to his feet on unsteady legs, tripped over a line, and fell again. The second time he gingerly pushed himself to a sitting position, where he struggled to penetrate the wool that seemed to have filled his brain. The huge *San Josef* was nearly clear, looming over *Argonaut*'s stern—beautiful, terrifying, and ready to finish off his crippled ship.

Charles stared, holding his breath as one by one the three decks of cannon were run out. He vaguely noted that *San Josef*'s mizzenchains had fouled themselves on the *San Nicolás*'s catheads by the bow. It hardly mattered. In an instant she would unleash at least fifty guns, including the thirty-six-pounders on her lower deck, and blast the beaten *Argonaut* to matchwood. He could hear his heart pounding in his chest and his hands began to shake uncontrollably. After a moment that seemed unending he exhaled and then breathed in again. He waited. Inexplicably, the massive thing neither fired nor moved nor even attempted to free herself from her sister. There was a brief commotion on her upper deck and what sounded like musket shots, but he couldn't see what it was. Then *San Josef* hauled down her colors. Charles stared, dumbfounded. After a moment a slight figure in a British naval commodore's uniform appeared at the quarterdeck railing, yelled something Charles couldn't make out, and waved his hat.

Charles struggled to stand, but it took too much effort. He eased himself back down, wiped clear some blood that had run into his eye, and waved back.

TWO

CHARLES TRIED TO WILL HIS SENSES TO WORK. A THROB-bing, splitting pain burned in the left side of his head above the temple, and for an instant he wondered if he were dead or alive. Had he really seen a British naval officer at the railing of the *San Josef,* or had he imagined it? There was no one there now. He had to be alive; it wouldn't hurt so badly if he were dead. At least he didn't think so.

In stages he became aware of the increasingly distant and isolated exchanges of cannon fire as at least some British warships pursued the scattered rear of the fleeing Spanish fleet. So he was alive and the commander of the *Argonaut,* or what remained of her. He tried to guess at the damage the ship had sustained. That she had been cruelly battered there was no question. Not a mast was standing, and he sensed from the sluggish way she rolled that she had taken on a great deal of water. *Christ, his head hurt!*

"Well, this is a fine way to spend St. Valentine's Day," Daniel Bevan's familiar voice sounded behind him. "Decided to sit down and take the rest of the day off, I see."

Charles half-turned and smiled thinly at his friend. The movement brought a fresh stab of pain. He tentatively raised a hand to the area just above his ear to feel for the wound. "How bad is it? The ship, I mean."

"Oh, it's bad, very bad, Charlie," Bevan said, kneeling beside him.

He brushed Charles's hand away and with both of his own carefully tilted his head to examine the injury. "We're dismasted, without steerage, and sinking. But look at the bright side; it could be worse."

"How? Ow!" Charles chirped. It felt like Bevan was poking at the side of his temple with a boarding pike.

"Hold still, you sissy. It would be worse if we'd already sunk, of course. Then you'd have to learn how to swim." Bevan released Charles's head and stood. "You'll live to fight another day, Charlie. The Admiralty will be awfully sorry to hear it, though."

Charles began shaking again, partly as a reaction to the intensity of the battle and partly from the cold that seemed to seep into his bones. Bevan removed his uniform jacket and draped it around his friend's shoulders. "Come on," he said, pulling Charles to his feet. "The admiral may come to visit, and we can't have him find you sitting on your duff, bleeding all over the deck. It ain't professional." Charles stood unsteadily and leaned on Bevan's broad shoulders for support. The tangled remains of the nearly destroyed ship were more evident from an upright position—*his* ship. He was responsible. "Oh, Lord," he muttered, "the navy's going to have my arse for this."

"No, they're not," Bevan said earnestly. "You'll be a hero. The navy always loves a long butcher's bill. Shows you take your work seriously." He led Charles over to a raised hatch cover and helped him sit on it. "All right, Charlie, you stay here. I'm going to fetch someone to come and fix you up."

"Wait." Charles grabbed Bevan's arm. "How many?"

"Don't know yet; we still have to count. The numbers will be high, though. But that's what happens when you throw a tiny sixty-four in front of the whole Spanish navy." Bevan gently pulled himself away and left to find someone to fetch the ship's surgeon. Charles watched a party of sailors forward attempting to rig shearlegs so they might sway up a spar and lash it as a jury replacement to the stump of the former foremast. The midshipman he had left in charge of the gundecks—Winchester something, he remembered—seemed to be directing the effort. He noted that the younger man was working alongside the seamen, even grabbing a line and heaving on it himself. Most officers, especially midshipmen, relied on orders backed up by very real threats of punishment to get the men to do their duty. His attention was diverted as parties of crewmen appeared here and there, clearing wreckage and starting repairs. Four marines, probably all that were left, systematically moved across the deck from one body to the next, separating the dead from the still living. Some they dragged unceremoniously to a central location midships; others they lifted onto litters and carried below. He could hear the incessant clanking of the ship's pumps as they labored to keep the *Argonaut* from sinking.

After a short time Bevan reappeared with the surgeon, a grizzled figure with a deeply veined nose, and an equally dissolute assistant who doubled as the ship's barber. They wore long aprons, now far more red than white, and their hands and arms were likewise splattered with fresh blood. Both men smelled strongly of rum, and Charles had a clear idea of what they were doing while the battle was in progress.

"This won't hurt a bit, sir," the surgeon said, roughly tilting Charles's head to the side and sponging a dank, vile liquid that stung like fire over his wound. "Hold still, you've got a nasty cut there." The assistant produced a mug of frothy shaving soap and a straight-edged razor. He tilted Charles as far over to the side as he would go without falling, daubed soap liberally from ear to crown and into one eye, and began scraping at Charles's temple with the blade.

From this position Charles heard Bevan say, "Look bright, Charlie. We have visitors." Charles opened his unsoaped eye, and, from his position bent double sideways, he saw the ship of the line *Excellent* heave to and back her sails on the *Argonaut*'s lee side. Her gig was already in the water and pulling across. Charles recognized the gray-haired, slightly rotund form of Cuthbert Collingwood, the *Excellent*'s captain, in the bows. Collingwood was a senior post captain with a long and distinguished record. Bevan quickly left to greet him.

"Let me up, damn it," Charles demanded. "I can't see anyone like this."

"It'll be just a minute longer, sir; not half a minute," the surgeon replied, forcing Charles's head lower still. "All we have to do is sew you up. Don't you worry, you won't feel nothing." The stab of a very large, very dull needle into the flesh on the side of his head would have made him jump if the barber/surgeon's mate hadn't anticipated it by clamping Charles in a headlock. "God damn, you whoreson sodomite, let me up!"

he demanded, to no avail. He heard more than saw ("Keep your head down, you puppy, we're almost there.") Captain Collingwood come aboard and bellow, "Who's in charge here? Where's Captain Wood?"

"Captain Wood is dead, sir," Bevan's voice answered smartly. "Lieutenant Edgemont is in command. This way if you please."

"Please, let me up," Charles begged. He saw Collingwood's shoes and white-stockinged legs in front of him. "No, no, stay as you are, sir," he heard Collingwood say warmly. "Don't even think about moving on my account. I only came to convey my compliments on your stand against the Spaniards, sir, my very best compliments. Truly a heroic stand. Our success in arms today is due in no small measure to you. And your health, sir, are you badly injured?"

"He's as fit as a fiddle, sir," the surgeon answered. "Only a scratch. Be as frisky as a newborned colt tomorrow. That is, if the mortification don't set in. You mark my words." He jerked a final knot in the sutures, nodding to his assistant to release his hold. Charles straightened and shot the two of them a killing look. Then he turned to Collingwood. "You are too kind, sir," he managed, half-rising. "I, we, were only doing our duty. We had no choice."

"Sit, sit," Collingwood said, motioning impatiently with his hands. "No choice but to do your duty, of course. England expects no less. Your modesty becomes you." Collingwood paused and looked around at the desolation around him. "What assistance can I offer? Men, supplies—you have only to ask."

The surgeon applied a poultice and then began winding a long, once-white bandage around his patient's head. Charles used the diversion to think as rapidly as he could. He hardly knew where to start. On the other hand, he didn't want to appear unable to manage his ship. "I'd be very grateful for any support," he said carefully. "I'm sure our able surgeon here is overwhelmed and would welcome help."

"I'll see to it immediately," Collingwood responded, half-bowing. "You're sure that's all? You're sure?" When Charles nodded, he said, "Yes, well, I must return; I have matters to attend to on my own ship. I'll have our doctor sent over as soon as he's free. Again, my heartiest congratulations on your success, Mr. Edgemont. The navy needs more officers like yourself, and you may rest assured that I will mention it to the admiral."

He started to depart, then momentarily turned back. "Oh, yes, I almost forgot. The *Excellent* has taken possession of your two prizes. We will be more than happy to send them on for you."

"Prizes?" Charles said. "What prizes?"

"The two Spanish seventy-fours, of course, the *San Ysidro* and *San Antonio.* They struck to you, did they not?"

"I don't know, sir," Charles answered. "I was too busy to notice."

"Well, I noticed," Collingwood said warmly, "and I'll personally see you get credit for them. Good day to you, sir."

As *Excellent's* gig pulled away, Bevan turned to Charles and said, with a sense of awe in his voice, "Well, fancy that—Collingwood himself."

Before Collingwood's barge had returned to the *Excellent*, Charles saw a second boat approaching *Argonaut's* entry port. After a moment, two elegantly dressed naval officers, one about Charles's age and wearing the single epaulette of a naval commander, the other somewhat older and shorter with a commodore's stripe on his sleeve, climbed up onto the deck. Charles recognized the slight, almost delicate-featured older man immediately as the one who had waved to him from the deck of the *San Josef.* He did not know who the man was, but sensed that he was someone unusually significant when he heard Bevan's sharp intake of breath beside him.

"Who?" Charles asked softly as the two men crossed toward them.

"Captain Nelson," Bevan whispered, standing rigidly erect. Charles immediately struggled unsteadily to his feet. He had heard of Nelson; everyone had. Some said he was the most aggressive and brilliant captain in the British navy. Others, and Charles had heard it often from less successful officers, his own Captain Wood among them, were of the opinion that much of Nelson's fame was empty talk, inspired by the man himself to enhance his own reputation.

The two men quickly crossed the quarterdeck and stopped in front of Charles. "At last we meet in person," the commodore said with genuine warmth. "I am Horatio Nelson, and this is my friend, Commander Edward Berry. I beg to know your name, sir." The voice was calm, slightly high-pitched, authoritative.

"Lieutenant Charles Edgemont, sir, second on the *Argonaut* and acting commander," Charles said with a tentative bow. "And this is Lieutenant Daniel Bevan, third and acting first."

"Your servant, sir," Bevan managed, touching his hat smartly.

"Captain Wood?" Nelson inquired.

"Killed by a sharpshooter, sir," Charles replied.

"Pity," Nelson said, "but, just between us, not all that much of a loss. Wood was a bit shy when it came to battle, if you ask me. Still, he met his end like a man. Your wounds are not serious, I trust?"

"No, sir. I'll be fine, thank you."

Nelson looked Charles straight in the eye and extended his hand. When Charles took it, the commodore said, "I came to congratulate you on your victory, Mr. Edgemont. It was most impressive and nobly won. I greatly admire such a display of tenacity and sheer bullheaded determination. I couldn't have done more in your situation myself. If all England's officers showed such selfless courage as you have displayed today, we would have no fear of any enemy."

"Thank you, sir, we were just doing our duty," Charles answered, emphasizing the "we" in an attempt to include Bevan.

"Nevertheless," Nelson continued, his eyes keen, "uncommon heroism such as you have displayed must be recognized. If I may say so, I have some influence with the admiral, and I will press my recommendations to him on your behalf with as much determination as you have shown toward the Spanish fleet this day. England needs every fighting captain she can find."

"Thank you, sir," Charles managed, swallowing hard. He knew he hadn't done anything heroic or determined, but he was afraid that saying so would just be taken for false modesty. Searching for the right words, he came up with, "On behalf of *Argonaut's* officers and men, I am most grateful."

"And one more thing," Nelson continued. "I was blessed this afternoon with the boarding of both the *San Nicolás* and *San Josef.* By rights *San Nicolás* is yours. She was already much reduced when I reached her, and in fact she surrendered as soon as our guns came to bear. We only boarded her in order to use her forecastle to reach the *San Josef.* You may count her as a prize to the *Argonaut* with my heartiest approval."

"Thank you, sir," Charles said. He couldn't think of anything else to add.

"Duty calls," Nelson concluded with a second round of handshakes, this time including Bevan, and a bow. "I salute you, sir, and look forward to serving with you in the future." Commander Berry likewise shook both their hands and briefly offered his own congratulations. Then the two men were gone.

Charles sat heavily back down on the hatch cover with a rising sense of anxiety. His superiors clearly thought he had done something out of the ordinary. What would happen when someone discovered he hadn't?

"A few more visitors like this and we'll own half the Spanish navy," Bevan beamed, not sounding anxious at all.

Charles laughed weakly. Prize money. By God, he hadn't thought about prize money. Even with a lieutenant's share, three Spanish ships of the line would bring a pretty penny.

"You're a certifiable hero, Charlie," Bevan said, turning to leave. "But one of us has to keep the old *Argonaut* from going under. I should get back to work."

"Just a minute," Charles said. "How badly damaged is she, Daniel?"

"Well," Bevan answered, turning serious, "we've been hulled more than a few times; don't know how many holes yet, but the carpenter and his crew are working on them now. We're down by the head, and there's about six feet of water in the well. I've got every man available on the pumps, and we're almost holding our own. As the holes are plugged one by one, we'll start to make some headway. You know about the helm and the masts. All in all, we're in pitiful shape."

"The dead and wounded? How many do you reckon?"

"I'm not sure yet, exactly. I'd guess about four score killed outright, and maybe a hundred and a quarter or more wounded. A fair proportion of those will die soon, of course."

Charles considered this. *Argonaut* had lost more than a third of her complement. But there were still enough to patch and man the ship if they didn't have to fight her. "Two things," he said carefully. "Heave the guns overboard; they're no good to us now and the reduced weight will give us some grace with the pumps. You may also start the water if necessary. And, second, you and I are the only commission officers. What do you think about promoting one of the senior midshipmen to acting lieutenant?"

Bevan looked doubtful. "Can you do that? You're just a lieutenant yourself. And it's not going to help to appoint some young yahoo who doesn't know a spinnaker from a spade." Bevan, Charles knew well, had a low opinion of all the *Argonaut*'s midshipmen.

"Well," Charles said seriously, "I don't know if I can or not, but I'm going to. What do you think about—what's his name, the one who was in charge of the guns at the end—Winchester something, I think."

"Stephen Winchester? I don't see him getting his hands dirty."

"Who would you recommend?" Charles asked.

Bevan's face assumed a pained expression as his mind ran down the list of potential alternatives. "All right," he said at length. "I suppose he can't sink the ship all by himself."

The talk turned to other tasks necessary to restore a sense of purpose and routine to the running of the ship. Charles sent word to have the galley lit so the ship's company could be fed. The watch list had to be reorganized to compensate for their reduced numbers and to ensure that the pumps would continue to be manned while the most critical repairs were being made. And it all had to be done without exhausting the crew.

Darkness shaded the eastern horizon when Bevan left to oversee the reorganization and repair of the ship. Feeling slightly more fit, Charles pushed himself slowly off the hatch cover and got to his feet with the idea of looking around to reassure himself that everything that needed doing was being attended to. He heard a loud splash as the first of the cannon was levered over the side. A third ship's boat—he immediately recognized it as the admiral's barge—pulled smartly from behind the bows of the captured *San Josef* and headed for the *Argonaut*'s side. A solitary officer, who Charles knew was the flag lieutenant on the *Victory*, climbed the side steps. He stayed only long enough to ascertain whether *Argonaut* would be serviceable to sail or be towed in the morning, and to deliver an envelope. Charles responded that he was confident the ship would be fit to be towed in the morning, but not ready to sail, even under the most limited jury rig, until the afternoon.

"Thank you, sir," the flag lieutenant said, saluting. "I will report your situation to Admiral Jervis." He offered his own congratulations and after a few pleasantries returned to his boat.

Charles inspected the envelope and was surprised to see that it was addressed to *"Lieutenant Charles Edgemont, Commanding,* HMS *Argonaut."* He broke the seal and read:

HMS *Victory*
February 14th, 1797

Sir,

The fleet sails for Lisbon at four bells in the morning watch. If you are unable to sail under your own power, the frigate *Niger,* Captain Edward Foote commanding, will be alongside to take you under tow.

I expect your fullest report in writing and in person the inst. we reach port.

Your servant, &c,
J. Jervis

Charles folded the letter and put it in his jacket pocket. He felt tired and hungry now and his head still stung painfully. So the *Argonaut* was officially his. The admiral must have learned of his identity from Collingwood or Nelson. He, and he alone, was responsible for every one of the almost five hundred men still alive aboard her, for seeing that the repairs were carried out efficiently and competently, and for getting her to Lisbon, tow or no tow. There were no such things as excuses in the navy, not for a senior post captain, and certainly not for a junior lieutenant who hoped to keep his commission. For a moment he wished for the return of Captain Wood, cold, aloof, and autocratic in life, now laid out in his cabin. Wood had made it seem the easiest and most natural thing in the world to command a ship of the line, and Charles began to glimpse some of the pressure that made him the seemingly harsh and distant man he had been.

Would he become the same, frigid and aloof, should he ever come to command one of His Majesty's warships? More important, would he ever have the abilities and judgment that the position required? Deep in his heart, Charles knew there was doubt. During his years in the navy he had experienced all of the many complex operations, from setting sails to arranging the holds, that were required to keep a large line-of-battle ship and her crew at sea for months at a time and to fight her when necessary.

But could he be responsible for all of them at once, balancing one crisis against another? Would he have the instinct to know when to order the sails taken in just before a sudden squall or to judge the exact moment to cut across an enemy's bow and rake her? It was all well and good for Nelson and Collingwood to congratulate him for *Argonaut*'s heroic stand, but he hadn't been in command then. Besides, he knew he had been frightened half out of his wits during the battle, with the ship being pounded and men dying all around him. He should have struck the colors, surrendered the ship the moment he'd come on the quarterdeck. That would at least have saved the deadly raking by the Spanish frigate.

He bristled at the recollection of the *Santa Brigida*'s repeated broadsides into the *Argonaut*'s unprotected stern. If he ever did command a ship of his own, he would very much like to meet with her again. But to have any hope of striking back at the Spaniard he would need a ship to command. To have even the slightest chance of gaining such a command, he had to see to it that *Argonaut* reached Lisbon safely. He decided that he had better see for himself what damage she had suffered and what progress was being made to repair it. The most important thing in his life at that moment was that she be at least fit enough to be towed at dawn the next morning.

A little unsteadily at first, he made his way belowdecks, bending deeply so as not to hit his head on the low deck beams above, and headed aft. In the cramped, dimly lit tiller room, he found two men threading a three-inch cable painfully through several sets of blocks and pulleys. The cable would then be fished up through a chase to the upper deck, wound around the axle of the newly replaced helm, and fed back down into the tiller room, run through a second, identical set of blocks and pulleys on the other side, and reattached to the tiller head. "How long till the helm is rigged?" Charles asked the seaman nearest him.

"Not too long, sir," the man answered, glancing over his shoulder. "As soon as I get this here pulley-block set"—he grunted and strained with his arms and shoulders at something over his head in the darkness—"we'll send the cable topside. Maybe an hour, maybe an hour and a half, and she'll be good as new."

"Thank you, er—" Charles began, but couldn't recall the man's name or even if he had ever known it.

"Smith, sir, Todd Smith, carpenter's mate. And this here's Jimmy Bowan," he nodded at the seaman farther back in the shadows.

"Thank you, Smith and Bowan," Charles said. "I'm sure the helm is in good hands. Carry on."

"Thank ye, sir," Todd Smith answered while Jimmy Bowan shouted, "Goddamn you fishmonger's doxie's poxed whore's arse; get through there!" He was trying to bend the heavy, stiff cable through the eye of the block. "Sorry, sir," he added, nodding in Charles's direction.

Charles grinned to himself and started forward in search of the ship's carpenter to find out about the progress patching the shot holes in the hull. The unceasing sounds of the chain pumps rattled loudly in the dark, confined space between decks. He came upon numbers of hands, some hurrying on one errand or another, others in small gangs, carrying tools, timbers, or lengths of cable of various thickness, or other objects urgently needed for repairs. Everyone knew by now that Captain Wood had been killed, and how and where and what he looked like when he was dead. Firsthand reports, rumors, conjecture, and pure fiction all moved like lightning belowdecks. And every member of the crew now knew who Charles was—"The second who were the new captain. You know, the taller one what 'as dark hair like, not t'other one"—even if he didn't know half of their names. Every one of them, when they came upon him, stopped with a surprised look at seeing him, then knuckled a fist to his forehead or nodded respectfully if his hands were full, and waited for him to pass. Yesterday they would have hurried around him with the briefest nod and a quick, "By your leave, sur."

Charles passed through the lower gundeck. Here the wounded were laid out on the floor or in hammocks hung from the deck beams. The numbers shocked him. Even with the added space once occupied by the great guns, the deck seemed to be filled with prone or seated men, some still, others writhing in pain. Incoherent babble, cries for mothers or sweethearts, moans, and occasional screams competed in the thick, foul-smelling air. Charles recoiled from the sight of the blood-sodden bandages and shortened stumps where arms or legs had been removed. He hurried through the mass as quickly as he could, picking his way carefully around the injured men and stepping over those he could not avoid. Their presence, the reminder of the human cost of the battle paid in pain, limbs, and lives, unsettled him. It wasn't that he saw his own mortality in their injuries—like most young men, he thought himself immune to crippling wounds or death—but he felt awkward to be whole in their presence and inadequate to do anything for them.

"Lieutenant, Lieutenant," a weak voice implored as Charles passed. He stopped and looked at the faces to see who might be calling him.

"Here, sir, it's me, Johnson." Charles recognized the pale figure lying under a bloody cover on the deck as the captain of a gun crew under his command during the battle. He knelt by the man, noticing from the shape of the blanket that Johnson had had a leg removed just above the knee.

"How are you, Johnson?" Charles said as cheerfully as he could manage.

"Oh, I'll be fine, sir," Johnson answered a little uncertainly, as if it were something he wanted to believe. "I wanted to ask ye about the fight; how we did."

Charles raised his voice so others around them might overhear. "We did ourselves proud. The Spaniards have run for home with their tails between their legs. *Argonaut* herself got three prizes: two seventy-fours and the *San Nicolás,* a three-decker. There'll be plenty of prize money to go around." He heard pitiful murmurs as the wounded closest by passed his words on.

"That's truly wonderful, sir," Johnson said. "We really gave it to them."

"Yes," Charles said, starting to rise, "we really did."

Johnson's hand grabbed Charles's sleeve. "Ye're hurt, sir. Are ye all right?"

Charles touched the bandage over his injury. "Just a knock on the head," he said grinning. "It's nothing. You and the others down here are the ones who did the hard part. You're all heroes in my book."

"Thank ye, sir," Johnson said, letting go of his arm. "Thank ye kindly."

The ship's surgeon was in the midshipmen's wardroom, which had been taken over for use as a surgery. The long dining table had become an operating platform for two patients at a time, head to foot. The surgeon and his well-remembered mate were working with a third man, noticeably less disreputable in appearance, who was introduced as *Excellent*'s surgeon. There was a name attached, but Charles didn't catch it. He told his own surgeon that he wanted a full report on the dead and wounded first thing in the morning. The man nodded and said, "O' course, sir," picked up a bloodied bone saw, and turned toward a seaman with a shattered arm on the table. Charles fled.

He finally found the master carpenter, several of his mates, and a number of other seamen on the orlop deck just forward of the mainmast. Here there was ample evidence of damage from the Spanish guns. Most of it had been crudely patched with hammocks or partly unraveled pieces of sailcloth saturated in tar, wadded up, and jammed into the shot holes with scraps of wood nailed over them. Larger repairs were reinforced with shoring, wedged and nailed against the deck or ceiling beams or any other convenient anchor. Water ran in small rivers down the inner planking below the patches, but in far less quantity than had gushed in through the open holes.

The carpenter, a stout, ruddy man who spoke in a broad Irish brogue, reported that all the more serious damage to the hull had received attention, but some of the patches would have to be reinforced or redone before the ship could get under way. The worst of the damage, he went on, was forward, where several ribs had been stove in. "They've been braced every which way," he said, "but they won't hold in heavy weather."

"Enough to get us towed to Lisbon?" Charles asked. "If the wind holds, it should only be two days or so."

"Aye, if the sea don't get up too much." The carpenter scratched his chin thoughtfully with the claw of his hammer before continuing. "I don't know if she's worth fixing proper, to go to sea again, like. I never seen her this bad, and I been on the ol' girl near on thirty years as mate and carpenter. She's too old and slow, like me. For sure they'll send her to the breaker's yard."

"But she won't sink between here and Lisbon?" Charles wanted to be certain. He didn't care much about what happened to her afterward.

"Probably not," the carpenter said thoughtfully. "Now, when Captain Wood—ain't it a shame he copped it?—were in command, he took real good care to see that nothing happened to her. Hardly had a scratch in all his years. Now he dies and see what happens."

"Thank you," Charles said, the irony not lost on him, and started to leave.

"It's a crying shame, I say. I remember—"

"Thank you," Charles said again and disengaged himself from the man and his crew. He made for the forward ladderway when he heard word being passed that dinner was available on the upper gundeck for the starboard watch. His stomach growled. He made his way to the galley, two decks above, sat himself at the cook's table, and gobbled down a large helping of the biscuits, peas, and salt pork prepared for the crew. The cook protested repeatedly that such food wasn't fit for the *Argonaut's* commander and that he would prepare a proper meal from the captain's stores and have it served to him in the captain's dining room along with after-dinner coffee.

"Coffee," Charles finally said between mouthfuls. "I'm going topside. You may send up a large mug of coffee as soon as it's ready."

Charles wiped his mouth on the sleeve of his uniform jacket, noticing anew that it was still discolored by blood and filth, pushed himself away from the table, and went to see about the rigging of the foremast. On reaching the forecastle, he saw that it had grown quite dark under a moonless and starless sky. By the light of several lanterns, he noticed that a tall, foot-thick spar had been raised and securely scabbed to the stump of the old foremast. Two bosun's mates were busy securing stays and shrouds in the dimness above and preparing to hoist a yard so that at least the forecourse and the forestaysail could be set. Charles noticed Midshipman Winchester standing near the port rail, organizing the lowering of the shearlegs upon which the jury-rigged foremast had been lifted. A boy arrived from the galley, gingerly holding a tin mug of steaming-hot coffee.

"Thank you kindly," Charles said, taking the mug and savoring the strong bitter-smooth liquid. "Now hurry back and bring me a second cup."

The boy looked at him questioningly, but when Charles repeated, "A second cup. Now. Hop," the child turned and departed at a run.

"Mr. Winchester," Charles called, taking a careful sip, "a word with you, please." Stephen Winchester turned, said something to a man beside him, and approached.

"May I say I'm sorry about your injury, sir," Winchester said touching his hat.

"It's a little tender," Charles answered. "Probably hurt like hell in the morning."

"Probably, sir," Winchester replied and fell silent.

Charles found the curt reply irritating. He had expected something warmer in response to his opening. The one he got seemed smug bordering on overconfident. Perhaps he had been mistaken about Winchester's readiness to assume greater responsibilities. Still, he had come this far, so he pressed on. "I wanted to tell you that I appreciated your handling of the cannon earlier this afternoon. I didn't know you'd had experience in guns."

"Thank you, sir. To tell the truth, I hadn't much. I asked one of the gun captains, the oldest one I could find, what to do. He, Higgins, I think, told me."

Charles thought that showed uncommon presence of mind in such a chaotic situation. He could think of few other midshipmen who would have done anything other than blunder ahead to cover their ignorance. "You've done a tolerable job with this foremast as well," he said, nodding at the spar.

Winchester's face broke into an unexpected smile. "This is the first time I've been able to set up a mast and rig it on my own, as it were." Then he quickly added, "Sir."

The second cup of coffee arrived from the galley. Charles offered it to Winchester, who blew on it and then drank a little too much so that it burnt his mouth. In that moment Charles sensed that what he had taken for excessive confidence, even arrogance, in the younger man came from an effort to mask his nervousness or sense of inadequacy in the presence of his superiors. Charles could remember feeling similar emotions during his own years as a junior officer. He came to a decision. "How old are you?" he asked.

"Eighteen," Winchester answered, competing flickers of curiosity at Charles's question and pain from his burnt tongue crossing his face. "I'll be nineteen in April."

"How long have you been rated midshipman?"

"Since I first came into the navy, just before I turned thirteen, sir."

"You've been at sea all that time?" It was not uncommon for children of twelve, or even considerably younger, especially from well-connected families, to be entered onto a ship's books but not actually serve until they were much older. It helped them get promotions requiring seniority without their having to do anything inconvenient or dangerous, like actually going to sea.

"Yes, sir, my father thought I needed to see the world—and discipline."

Charles sensed a note of resentment in the young man at the mention of his father. "You know we're short of officers," he said. "There's only Lieutenant Bevan and myself." Winchester nodded his comprehension without speaking.

"In my capacity as acting commander, I would like to raise you up to acting lieutenant. It will mean more work and more responsibility."

Winchester blinked, then quickly nodded his head. "Thank you, sir. I'll do my best," he said, a small show of emotion crossing his face.

"I'll put it in my report to the admiral and recommend that it be fixed permanent if you do well. But I don't really know if I have the authority to promote you, even to acting status. And, of course, I don't know whether the admiral will confirm it."

"It's all right, sir," Winchester responded with feeling. "I just appreciate your confidence."

"Well, that's settled," Charles said. "When you're finished with the foremast here, you might try the same job with the mizzen. There's not enough standing to lash it to, so you're going to have to pull the stump and reset the new spar on the keel."

"Yes, sir," Winchester said. "I've already sent a party to knock the wedges loose. We're moving the shears aft now."

"Good," Charles said, and, because he could think of nothing else, he turned and walked a little way off to an unlit part of the deck, then stopped and watched thoughtfully for a few moments as Winchester resumed his work with the rigging.

"Pass the word for Lieutenant Bevan," he said to a passing seaman. "Tell him I'll be on the quarterdeck."

"Aye aye, sir." The man knuckled his forehead and departed. Charles could hear the call—"Lieutenant Bevan to the quarterdeck, pass the word"—echo the length and breadth of the ship.

As he made his way aft, Charles observed that much of the clutter and wreckage that had littered the ship had been cleared away. The salvaged ropes and cables from the fallen rigging were neatly coiled and stacked along the center of the deck, and the ship's wheel had been restored, with two seamen standing ready beside it.

"You sent for me, sir?" Bevan said as he entered the circle of light from a lantern hanging from the poopdeck railing above the quarterdeck. Charles immediately noticed the term "sir" instead of "Charlie," which had been more normal between them. He thought Bevan looked tired and strained.

"Yes," Charles said. "How goes it?"

"Oh, we're making progress," Bevan said, relaxing marginally. "There's still a thousand things to see to."

"The frigate *Niger* will be alongside soon," Charles said. "She's to take us in tow to Lisbon in the morning. Her captain is"—he had to fish in his pocket for the Admiral's letter—"Edward Foote. I want whichever officer is on duty when he comes to say that we'll be ready to ship the cable at dawn."

Bevan frowned and his natural good humor began to wear thin. "Whichever officer, sir? I'm the only other naval officer on this barely floating mound of kindling."

"I've promoted Winchester to acting lieutenant," Charles said quickly. "He can take the middle or the morning watch, whichever you want, and we'll work out a regular rotation after that. I don't want you staying up all night just to look over his shoulder. We talked about that."

"Oh, yes, it slipped my mind," Bevan said, wiping a hand across the stubble on his cheeks. "That'll help."

"Daniel," Charles asked in a softer tone, "have you eaten since breakfast?"

"No, not yet. Haven't had time."

"Well, I want you to get something in you. And I want you to talk with Winchester and arrange about sharing the work with him. And I want you to get some sleep tonight. Lord knows it will be little enough."

"All right, Charlie, you're the captain," Bevan said, his humor returning. "But have you ever thought how it would be if I was a week senior to you on the lieutenants' list instead of the other way around?"

"The mind shudders," Charles answered with a smile. "Now, off with you, beginning with a good meal. I have to go and write a report to Sir John Jervis; he made a point of it."

"Good luck, Charlie, sir," Bevan said over his shoulder as he started forward. "Mind that you spell my name correctly."

With Bevan gone, Charles made his way down to his cabin—scarcely more than a closet with a cot in it and a little room to hang his uniforms in—to find pen, ink, and paper and to begin organizing what he would put into his report to the admiral. It soon became clear that the cabin would not do. There was nowhere for him to sit except on the cot, and nothing for him to write on. Too many people were passing back and forth through the shattered remains of the officers' wardroom for any privacy, so he decided to go to the captain's day cabin, where there was a desk and chair and all the room he could want. And the captain certainly didn't need it anymore.

The marine private guarding the door snapped to attention as Charles approached, then stepped aside and opened the door for him. An overhead lamp lit the room, and the first thing he saw was Captain Wood's hastily made coffin on the floor near the smashed stern galley windows. He pushed away any qualms about working in a room with a dead man in it, crossed to the desk, and sat down. After unstopping his ink bottle, laying out his paper, and nibbling on the end of his goose quill, he began to write:

HMS *Argonaut*
Off Cape St. Vincent
Midnight, Feb. 14, 1797

Sir,

I have the honor to report that at about 1:30 this afternoon the *Argonaut,* as ordered, engaged the Spanish fleet off Cape St. Vincent. We came into conflict with an unknown number of Spanish warships of which we were fortunate enough to disable three before the battle ended. They were the *San Ysidro,* 74 guns, the *San Anto-*

nio, 74 guns, and the *San Nicolás,* 84 guns. I wish to state strongly that throughout the engagement the entire ship's company performed their duties with exceptional dedication and courage under the most adverse of circumstances.

It is my sad duty to report that in the course of these encounters Captain Sir Edward Wood was killed, as was the First Lieutenant, Thomas Hudgins. The ship's master, George Peabody, and her purser, Darcy Adkins, were also fatally injured. A complete list of the dead and wounded is attached.

The *Argonaut* sustained severe damage in the course of the battle, including the loss of all her masts and her helm, and was holed more than twenty times below the waterline. Thanks to the selfless and capable efforts of Lieutenant Daniel Bevan and Midshipman Stephen Winchester (whom I have provisionally appointed to acting lieutenant), repairs completed at the time this is written are sufficient to make her seaworthy to be towed to Lisbon on the morning of the 15th.

Your servant, sir,
Lieutenant Charles Edgemont,
Acting Commander

Charles pushed the paper away from him and slouched back in Captain Wood's chair. It slightly annoyed him that the events of such a tumultuous and deadly day could be summed up in three short paragraphs. Finally the tension and the weight of his responsibilities began to seep away. The pain in his head was manageable, but his limbs seemed too heavy to move. His eyelids drooped.

"'Ere, sir." A voice presented itself so unexpectedly beside him that he started. The voice belonged to Timothy Attwater, whom Charles knew to be Captain Wood's elderly steward. Attwater deftly placed a large crystal goblet full of deep, deep red liquid on the desk in front of him. "Drink this. The captain, 'e had a tote every night afore 'e went to bed. 'E won't mind."

"What is it?" Charles asked, lifting the glass to the light.

"Claret, sir. It's good for the blood, and it relaxes you. The captain swears—swore—by it."

Charles tasted the wine and savored the soothing, numbing sensation as it wound its way to his stomach. "Would you have a glass with me, Attwater? I hate to drink alone."

"Oh, no, sir. I couldn't. I never did nothing like that with the captain."

"You will now. Get yourself a glass and a chair and sit down with me. I'm not leaving unless you do." Attwater did as he was told, with crossed expressions of pleasure and trepidation on his wizened face.

The two sat in the large cabin in complete silence, sipping their wine. When Charles drained the last drops from his glass, he carefully placed it on the desk and slowly rose to his feet. He felt unbelievably relaxed and a little light-headed. "I'd best get back to my quarters before I fall asleep on the floor," he said, turning toward the door. "Would you pass the word to Lieutenant Bevan to have me wakened at dawn?"

"Oh, no, sir," Attwater said, looking alarmed. "I mean, yes, I'll call you at dawn, but no, sir, you can't go to your lieutenant's berth. You're the captain now. I've made up the bed for you with fresh linens and a clean nightshirt. You can't go back there with the others. It ain't fitting."

Charles opened his mouth to argue that if he was the captain he could sleep wherever he damn well pleased, decided he didn't have the energy to prolong the argument, and said, "Fine." He allowed the steward to help him out of his blood-caked clothes and into an oversized nightshirt—Captain Wood had been a man of rather generous girth. Attwater led him into the sleeping cabin with its soft bed, warmed by a pan of hot coals brought from the galley. It was a hanging bed, suspended from the ceiling and swaying with the roll of the ship. Charles climbed carefully in and lowered himself gratefully between the heated sheets. Before he could form a coherent worry about the state of his ship, he fell into bottomless sleep.

WHEN HE AWOKE to a pounding pain in his head, Charles was conscious of two things: He couldn't recall where he was, and the *Argonaut* was under way. "Attwater!" he yelled, remembering that much.

"Yes, sir." The door to the cabin opened and the steward carried in a basin of steaming water for him to wash in. "There's shaving things on the dressing table. 'Ere's a towel. Your breakfast will be ready as soon as you've dressed, sir. I took the liberty of sending for your uniforms from your old quarters."

"Not now," Charles said, hurrying past him. "The ship's under way and I need to be on the quarterdeck." Before Attwater's mouth could find words, Charles hurried out the door, past the very startled marine sentry, and up onto the quarterdeck, where the wind instantly caught the tentlike nightshirt, billowing it around his thighs.

"Ah, Venus rises," Bevan said to Winchester in an aside loud enough to be heard in any corner of the deck.

"I sent word to be woken at dawn," Charles snapped, his face dark with anger. The effect was largely lost because most of those present were distracted by the sight of him fighting to keep the nightshirt from flying up over his waist.

"Never got it," Bevan said, failing to suppress a smile. "But you're just in time. Look what's about to happen."

Charles looked. He saw the *Niger* immediately ahead with all plain sail aloft, and the gracefully dipping arc of the fifteen-inch cable connecting the two ships. *Argonaut* herself had fore and mizzen staysails set, as well as the forecourse and a very peculiar-looking mizzen sail.

"Not that," Bevan said, pointing to starboard—"that." Charles looked over the lee rail. The entire fleet, *Niger* and *Argonaut* excepted, was in a perfect line-astern formation behind *Victory*, which was rapidly overhauling them. Each ship was flying *Argonaut*'s number from her signal halyards, and their yards and shrouds were covered with sailors. As *Victory* came abreast, she fired a slow salute while her crew cheered and waved their hats and then she sailed past. The next in line, *Blenheim*, did the same, and then *Orion*, and so it went. Coincidental with the *Orion*, Attwater appeared with a clean uniform, which Charles hurriedly changed into on the deck. It didn't occur to him till later that every glass in the fleet was probably trained on him while he dressed.

After Attwater buttoned his uniform jacket and was brushing some lint off his shoulders with a small whisk, Charles said sternly, "I told you to have me called at dawn."

"Sorry, sir," Attwater responded guilelessly. "I did call you, sir, but you didn't seem like you wanted to get up just yet. I went and asked the lieutenant if you was needed on deck, and 'e said 'e didn't see why. So I left you be."

Charles didn't know where to focus his anger, which quickly began to drain away.

"Actually," Bevan said, "my words were, you'd never been any use on deck before, so I couldn't see why we'd need you now. And Lieutenant Winchester here looked after the shipping of the cable and making it fast to the bitts with never a hitch. Also, with the bang on the head you've had, we all thought you could do with the sleep. Everything's fine. Be easy."

Charles turned to Attwater. "In the future," he said slowly, emphasizing each word, "when I say I want to be called at dawn, it doesn't mean whisper through the door and tiptoe away. It means I want to be got up and out of bed by any means necessary. Is that clear?"

"Yessir," Attwater responded evenly, "I got it now."

Charles nodded, unsatisfied but not knowing what else to say. He decided on, "You may bring me some coffee."

Around nine-thirty the surgeon and his mate appeared, waving a piece of paper. "What's that?" Charles snapped as they approached.

"It's the report you asked for," the surgeon replied. "The butcher's bill—the dead and wounded, sir."

"Thank you," Charles said, relieved that they weren't planning to do anything to him. "What does it say?"

"Four score and seven killed outright," the surgeon intoned emotionlessly. "One hundred thirty-two wounded. Maybe two score seriously. Twelve of them died during the night."

"Thank you," Charles said again, sobered. Ninety-nine dead so far and there would be more, he was sure. And for this he was honored by the fleet. "You may go."

The surgeon hesitated, looking at him expectantly. "We have to change the dressing on your head, sir."

"You touch my head and I'll run you through with a sword," Charles snarled. "Go away."

"Now, do be serious, sir. It's just the dressing. We only have to unwind the old one, slap on a little physic, and wrap on a new one. It might go bad if we don't."

Charles hesitated. On a signal from the surgeon, his mate pulled up a stool and pushed Charles down onto it. "Just you sit still, it won't take a minute. Won't hurt a bit." As the surgeon was winding the new and somewhat cleaner bandage around Charles's head he said, conversationally, "When are we going to have the service?"

"Service for what?" Charles asked.

"The burial for the dead, of course. We have to have a service with words and all."

Charles tried to focus his mind on it. *Argonaut* carried no parson, and Captain Wood had neither encouraged nor discouraged attendance at the brief Bible readings held most Sundays. The last church service he could remember attending was his sister's christening when he was nine years old. He'd always considered himself as nominally Church of England when he thought of it, which was rarely. He had, however, been present at numerous burials at sea, and he knew generally what to do. He turned to Bevan. "Have the pulpit rigged and the dead brought on deck. Not Captain Wood; we'll carry him to Lisbon. Have all hands called aft at six bells."

He found a Bible in Wood's cabin, and at six bells he stood solemnly at the pulpit, said a short speech about remembering shipmates who'd made the last sacrifice, and then read the dog-eared sections from the book. He signaled to Winchester to have the first plank tilted over the rail. The drummer began his roll, one of the few remaining marines fired his musket into the air, and the bundled figure of a man, sewed into his own hammock and with two twelve-pound roundshot at his feet, slid off the board and plunged into the sea. The act was repeated to the solemn roll of the drum and the diminutive volleys innumerable times. When it came to the smaller form of Billy Bowles, Charles watched with a lump in his throat until it sank out of sight. He spent the remainder of the day distant and uncommunicative. That night he slept poorly and awoke twice to find himself sitting bolt-upright in a cold sweat, with images of the ship's side exploding inward and men being hideously mangled all around him. After the second episode he rose, dressed, and spent the rest of the night pacing back and forth on the quarterdeck.

THE VICTORIOUS BRITISH fleet sailed grandly between Lage Point and Calha Point, past the now single-turreted Belim Castle (the other turret had been shot off by a British frigate during another war, when the two countries had been adversaries, two decades earlier) and up the Tagus estuary into Lisbon harbor, prizes and *Argonaut* in tow. There was much celebration, flying of flags, and firing of salutes to and from the forts overlooking the harbor entrance. No sooner had *Victory* let go her anchor than signals ran up her halyards with *Argonaut*'s number and the command "Captain report on board."

Charles was ready. He had arranged to borrow the *Niger*'s gig—all *Argonaut*'s boats had been beaten to scrap in the battle. He wore his best full-dress uniform and had his report and hat tucked under his arm; he had to carry the hat because it wouldn't fit over the heavy bandage wrapped around his head. He'd also noticed while shaving that the side of his face below the wrapping had turned a nasty yellowish color and was very tender to touch. The gig fairly skipped across the anchorage toward the flagship, with four strong hands pulling hard and a bosun at the tiller while Charles fidgeted nervously in the sternsheets. Sir John Jervis had a fearsome reputation among the junior officers of the fleet. Charles had been briefly introduced to him months ago at a reception on board *Victory*, but he doubted the admiral would remember him. He remembered Jervis as a stocky, white-haired man who walked with a limp and talked in a growl. The weathered face and hard eyes bespoke a penchant for blunt speech and a sense of strict discipline that he exercised on himself as well as the officers and men who served him.

"*Argonaut*," the bosun yelled as the gig hooked into *Victory*'s mainchains, indicating that a ship's captain was about to come on board. Charles jumped for the side steps and climbed as best he could to the entry port on the ship's side. He was piped aboard by three smartly dressed, white-gloved sideboys and immediately welcomed by the flag lieutenant, the same person who had delivered the admiral's letter to him the day of the battle.

"You look awful," the lieutenant said, shaking Charles's hand. "How's the head?"

"I'll probably survive the injury," Charles answered. "I don't know if I'll survive Jervis, though."

"Don't worry. He's in a good mood this morning, and he'll stay that way if we don't keep him waiting. Come along." The lieutenant led

Charles past the twin marine sentries to Jervis's office, knocked once, and opened the door. He gestured Charles inside and closed the door behind him.

Admiral Sir John Jervis sat in his shirtsleeves behind a large, ornate, and hopelessly cluttered desk, scribbling something on a sheet of paper. Without looking up he gestured for Charles to sit on a small wooden chair opposite him. After a moment he laid his pen down and lifted his eyes. "Lieutenant Edgemont, isn't it? How's your head?"

"Yes, sir. Fine, sir," Charles answered, stammering slightly on both *sirs*. Then for something to do he presented his report and laid it on the desk. "You requested this, sir."

Jervis nodded, picked up the paper, and read it through, glancing at the attached list of killed and wounded with raised eyebrows. "Tell me what happened. Not the whole thing, just your part in it," he said, laying the report on top of a pile of papers on the corner of his desk.

"Sir, my station at quarters is the main gundeck," Charles began hesitantly, "where I remained throughout the battle until I was informed that the captain and the first had been killed." Once begun, his speech came more easily. "I then turned the guns over to Midshipman Winchester and called for Lieutenant Bevan, the only other remaining officer, to meet me on the quarterdeck. At that time we were still fighting the *San Nicolás,* but the issue had been largely decided."

"I see," Jervis said. "So I am to understand that you assumed command long after the battle had commenced and shortly before it concluded."

Charles swallowed hard and said, "Yes, sir."

"The *Argonaut* was dismasted, with no wheel, and generally sinking when you came onto the quarterdeck. Is that true?"

"Very nearly," Charles said. "We still had our mizzen—at least for a few moments."

"Yes," Jervis showed a small smile. "The *San Josef*'s appearance must have come as rather a nasty shock. My question is, why didn't you strike?"

"It hadn't occurred to me, sir," Charles answered slowly. "I'm not saying that I'm some kind of hero who would go down with his ship against overwhelming odds. I mean that I hardly had enough time to consider it.

Besides, after the mizzenmast fell I had no flag to strike and nowhere to strike it from. If the *San Josef* had fired a second broadside into us, I might have found something, though."

Jervis nodded slowly. "That's the correct answer. I'll have no officers thoughtlessly throwing their crews' lives away for some foolish gesture." Charles didn't think he was expected to reply to this, so he said nothing.

Jervis sat silently for a moment, absently fingering a paper on the desk in front of him. Finally he glanced down at it, then looked up at Charles. The steady, unblinking gaze made Charles want to squirm, but he held himself rigid.

"What are you, an American subject, doing in the King's Navy?" Jervis asked unexpectedly.

"I'm not an American," Charles answered quickly. "I am English. My family lives in Cheshire."

"It says here," Jervis held up the page and Charles could see it was a leaf from the *Argonaut's* muster book, "that you were born in Philadelphia."

"Yes, sir. That's true; I was born in the colonies. My father had a tea-importing business there. But I was born before the rebellion. After the troubles began, when I was about five, he moved us back to the family estate in Cheshire. I've lived most of my life there, sir, when not at sea, that is."

"I see," Jervis answered, his expression softening. "That's entirely different. A loyal Tory family. We can have no Jonathans, cousins or otherwise, as officers in the king's service. A dastardly ungrateful lot, those Americans."

Charles sat uneasily, knowing that he had left his admiral less than fully informed. It was true that his father left Pennsylvania for Cheshire with his American-born wife and their children after the beginning of the Revolution. But not because he was a true-blue Englishman; in fact, he had been actively sympathetic to the rebel cause, as was his wife. He had left only because his own father had written asking him to, owing to the unexpected death of the eldest brother in a riding accident. Charles's father, the second son, was needed to manage and eventually inherit the Edgemont family estate.

"Both Nelson and Collingwood," Jervis continued, "have put it to me in the strongest terms that I raise you in rank to commander because of their misperceptions of your role in the battle."

"Yes, sir, I know," Charles said, coming quickly back to the present. "Both of them visited the *Argonaut*. I tried to tell them I'd done nothing exceptional, but they insisted." His heart sank. He knew full well that a number of lieutenants would be promoted to commander or even captain following the Battle of St. Vincent. There were promotions after every successful fleet action. Now it appeared he had talked himself out of his.

"Quite," Jervis said drily. "Lieutenant Edgemont, I am going to promote you to commander, provisionally of course. The Admiralty will have to confirm it, but they can hardly refuse."

Charles sat stock-still. "Thank you sir, I—"

"Don't thank me, son," Jervis cut him off. "I'm doing you no favors. For every officer like Nelson who is promoted young and goes from glory to glory, there are ten who become overconfident, overaggressive, or complacent. Up to now you have had what can fairly be described as an unspectacular career. You've hardly been mentioned in Captain Wood's dispatches, except once for indiscipline."

Charles opened his mouth to speak, but Jervis raised his hand. "That's past. Nelson has insisted you be given a frigate. Lord knows why, but I'm going to recommend you be assigned to the *Louisa*. She's currently under renovation at the Plymouth yards. She's the smallest frigate that the Admiralty has available; twenty-eight guns, mostly long twelves. I shall be interested to see what you can do with her."

"I'm very grateful sir," Charles managed.

"I imagine you are," Jervis observed. "Is there anyone you wish to bring with you from the *Argonaut*? I can't promise anything, but I will request it."

"I'd like Lieutenant Bevan and Mr. Winchester, sir." Charles hesitated, wondering how far to push his luck. "And I hope you will approve Winchester's promotion. He's behaved very ably since I made him acting lieutenant."

"Has he?" Jervis's eyebrows rose. "Wonders will never cease. His father will be pleased. He writes to me incessantly. I will consider it. Now, I have a favor to ask of you."

"Me, sir?"

"Yes. I'd consider it a personal favor for you to take Wood's servant, Timothy Attwater, with you. He served under me back in fifty-nine and I'd be unhappy if he were put on shore against his wishes."

"Of course," Charles answered without thinking.

"Good, that's settled," Jervis said. "I'm sending you to London on the morning tide with my complete report. Please take Attwater along. I recommend you employ him as your steward—that's what he's best at." Charles nodded and wondered what he was getting himself into. "Your orders will be sent around to the *Argonaut* this evening."

Jervis rose from behind the desk and extended his hand. "Congratulations, Commander Edgemont. Work hard and learn from your mistakes and I am confident you will be a credit to the King's Navy. Oh yes, I nearly forgot." He opened a drawer in his desk, came up with a small card, and handed it to Charles. "This is a reputable prize agent in London, a Mr. Edwards of Threadneedle Street. I recommend him to you. He will see to the condemning of *Argonaut's* prizes before the Admiralty Court, the investment of your money, and that sort of thing. It should come to quite a piece."

"I'm most grateful sir, thank you," Charles said, looking at the card and feeling its texture between his fingers.

"Good luck," Jervis said, sitting down and immediately leafing through some papers on his desk, "and good day."

IF SOMEONE ASKED Charles an hour later how he got from the *Victory* back to the *Argonaut,* he probably could not have said whether he was rowed or if he had walked across the waves.

"Well?" Daniel Bevan asked Charles the moment he set foot on board.

"Well, what?" Charles said, grinning broadly.

Bevan made a loud hooting sound and hugged his friend tightly, actually lifting him off the deck. "We're to have a frigate, a small frigate," Charles said as soon as the air came back into his lungs. "A twenty-eight, long twelves."

"A twenty-eight is as big as you could get?" Bevan said, his face still lit with joy.

"You missed the 'we' part," Charles said by way of an answer. "You're to be my first."

"Sweet Jesus, *Captain* Edgemont," Bevan considered. "This day will probably go down in history as the beginning of the decline of the once-great British navy. 'Except for his selfless and hardworking first lieutenant,' they'll write someday, 'it would have been much worse.'"

"I asked for Winchester, too, and to have him confirmed. He'd be the second."

Bevan considered this seriously and nodded. "Do you think they will? He's worked like a dog these past days. And capably, too. What he doesn't know he asks or figures out." Winchester had evidently risen in Bevan's estimation.

"I think they will. Jervis apparently knows his father, or at least has heard from him."

"Well," Bevan said happily, "this calls for a celebration. Do you think you can borrow *Niger*'s gig again? We'll take Winchester."

"I have all the wine we could want from the captain's stores," Charles offered.

"Ah, but in Lisbon they have women—fine black-haired, black-eyed women."

Charles couldn't argue with that.

THREE

Joshua Turnbull, commander of the brig *raven*, welcomed Charles aboard in the damp gray light just before dawn. Charles brought with him onto the cramped vessel his single sea chest, Admiral Jervis's reports on the English victory off Cape St. Vincent, and his newly acquired steward, Timothy Attwater. He arrived with a pounding headache after a serious night of celebratory debauchery in the lower parts of Lisbon with Daniel Bevan and Stephen Winchester, which he now deeply regretted. *Raven* pulled her stream anchor and set sail for London almost as soon as his unsteady legs gained her deck.

Bevan and Winchester he left behind. They were to stay with the battered *Argonaut* on her slow journey to Plymouth, most likely for the breaker's yard, after she'd been made seaworthy enough in Lisbon for the journey. Afterward, they'd all agreed to meet at Charles's family home in Cheshire before returning to sea in his new command.

Commander Turnbull, a kindly, awkward-looking man with a face like a jackass, insisted that Charles ("the hero of St. Vincent, and wounded to boot") take his cramped cabin for the duration of the voyage. He would be more than happy, Turnbull said, to shift his things to his lieutenant's almost minuscule quarters, and the lieutenant could mess with the midshipmen. Charles noted that *Raven*'s only lieutenant did not look pleased at this, but remained stoically silent.

For Charles the weeklong journey in the tiny brig stood in stark contrast to his years aboard the *Argonaut*. For the first time in his career, he had no responsibilities and was left to his own devices, except when he was at dinner with Turnbull, or in what served as the wardroom, or with others of the ship's officers and warrants in their leisure time. He was asked the same unending questions about the battle and *Argonaut's* part in it, and he happily gave the same answers over and over again.

He found Turnbull a confident and friendly man who discussed the everyday workings of his ship in an open, give-and-take manner with his officers and even the crew, and addressed everyone by their first name. If he wanted a sail trimmed or a change of course, there were no shouted orders or bosuns swearing and swinging their starters. Rather, Turnbull would seek out the appropriate warrant and say something like, "Dickie, the wind's picking up. Do you think your lads could take in a reef on the topsail?" The suggestion was always acted on as if it were an order and the sail quickly shortened. With the task done and the topmen back on deck, Turnbull would usually follow up with a comment loud enough to be heard by all concerned, as, "Aye, she's riding much easier now. Well done." Charles looked hard for any sign of slackness or lack of discipline among the crew and found none. The *Raven* was a smart, polished, well-run ship, and it obviously didn't take the lash to make her so.

CHARLES SAT NEXT to Commander Turnbull in the sternsheets of *Raven's* cutter as two seamen leapt ashore to steady the craft against the Whitehall Steps in London. Another seaman had already been set running toward the Admiralty building to announce the arrival. Charles pulled his boat cloak up to his chin to ward off the cold rain-flecked wind in the last of the evening light, then rose and stepped carefully out onto the landing, followed by *Raven's* commander.

"Well, this is as far as I can take you, Commander Edgemont," Turnbull said, extending his hand. "I've taken pleasure in your company and I wish you well."

"I thank you for both a pleasant and a speedy voyage," Charles answered, shaking it. "I can't remember when I've enjoyed myself more."

"You have everything you need? Admiral Jervis's reports?" Turnbull asked. Before he could respond, Turnbull continued, "Ah, here comes your escort." He nodded toward a detachment of approaching marines.

"Yes, everything," Charles answered, patting the thick dispatch case under his cloak. "Wish me luck."

"Which of you is Lieutenant Edgemont?" the marine sergeant inquired while his men drew up in rigid attention. At the response, "I'm Edgemont," Charles was unceremoniously marched directly across to the Admiralty courtyard and through the large double doors. He had never been inside the ornate, high-ceilinged building before and stood somewhat in awe to find himself at the very seat of British naval power. Clerks and messengers hurried around him, while senior captains and admirals standing in small clusters in the hallways paused in their conversations to look curiously at the young lieutenant with his bandaged head, weathered uniform, marine escort, and dispatch case.

"St. Vincent?" one of the admirals, a short, pugnacious-looking man with the red sash of the Order of the Bath across his chest, spoke out, guessing at the subject of Charles's dispatches.

"Yes, sir," Charles answered, touching his forehead as he was hurried past.

"Damn good show, young man. Capital victory. That'll teach those papish heathens who rules the seas," the admiral called. There were echoed shouts of "Hear, hear" and "Well done, Lieutenant" and "A noble thrashing" from around the room. The marines halted with a loud stamp and handed him to a rather dowdy clerk, who walked him down a corridor and without knocking entered what must be the First Lord's office. The First Lord of the Admiralty, George Spencer, the second earl of Spencer, rose from behind the largest desk Charles had ever seen to personally greet him and receive the reports he carried. Charles felt as though he were shaking hands with God.

"Lieutenant Edgemont of the *Argonaut,* is that right?" Spencer asked.

"Yes, your Lordship," Charles answered.

"Admiral Jervis indicated in his preliminary correspondence, directly after the victory, that he would be sending you along. Please sit down," he said, gesturing toward a chair. "The sun is well over the yardarm; would you prefer port or sherry? And tell us of your experiences in the battle."

———

IN ALL, CHARLES spent a busy week in London, sharing a pair of rooms with Attwater in a boardinghouse in Haymarket. He visited an infinitely more competent physician than the *Argonaut*'s to have his sutures removed and to have a smaller, less cumbersome dressing applied to replace the turbanlike winding employed by *Argonaut*'s surgeon. A tailor who catered to naval officers measured him for two uniforms suitable for a newly made ship's commander in His Majesty's Navy, with a single gold-fringed epaulette proudly perched atop the left shoulder. During the evenings he was invited to so many dinners and gatherings to celebrate the victory that he had to refuse most of them. All the attention left him a little bewildered, and the repeated references to him as "the hero of St. Vincent" made him uncomfortable. On the other hand, he told himself, a free meal was a free meal, the food and drink were good, and he vastly enjoyed the attentions of young women in their fashionable gowns who hung on his every word as he described how the *Argonaut* had single-handedly forced three Spanish ships of the line to strike.

Charles's exposure to these women, though delightful, was also awkward. He had spent almost all his adolescent and adult years at sea. His principal interactions with women, and these were rare, were confined to ladies he encountered at various ports of call: ladies of a singularly basic and commercial inclination. He became acutely conscious that he had none of the easy talk or social graces with which to steer a conversation from a naval battle to a more personal discussion of other shared interests. In fact, he thought, he had very little idea what respectable women expected from him or how he might relate to them.

It was also during this time that his nightmares returned. The deafening roar of the cannon, the cloying smoke, the deaths, and a paralyzing, terrifying helplessness replayed itself most nights. The dreams were more than unsettling. He did not know what to make of them except that they must be the result of his own moral weakness and lack of courage. He spoke to no one about them.

After several days in the city he called on Mr. Edwards of Threadneedle Street, which he learned was practically adjacent to the Bank of England and just up from the Stock Exchange. "T. Edwards, Agent and Counselor," read a small, brightly polished brass plaque beside the doorway.

An elegantly liveried servant responded to his bell. Charles stated his name and presented the card Jervis had given him. The servant ushered him into a foyer lit by an impressive candelabra and disappeared into the depths of the house. A moment later, a short and somewhat plump man in his late thirties or early forties appeared.

"Commander Edgemont, this is indeed a pleasure. I have heard something of your successes off St. Vincent. I am Thaddeus Edwards," he said, extending one hand and gesturing toward an inner parlor with the other. "Tea, or something stronger?"

"Tea would be fine," Charles answered a little nervously, glancing at the exquisite furnishings and hangings in the room. The two men talked about inconsequential things until the tea had been poured and the maid departed.

"Now, how may I help you?" Mr. Edwards asked. "I assume that it was Sir John who gave you my card."

"Admiral Jervis, yes. He suggested that you might represent me in the matter of prizes taken at Cape St. Vincent that will presently be up for condemnation before the Admiralty Court."

"I see," Mr. Edwards said, removing a small notebook and pencil from his jacket pocket. "And which prize do you speak of?"

Charles hesitated, then said, "The Spanish warships *San Ysidro, San Antonio,* and *San Nicolás.*"

Mr. Edwards's eyebrows shot up. "Two seventy-fours and an eighty-four? Are any of these prizes in dispute?"

"No, sir. I don't believe so," Charles answered.

"And you were the officer commanding when they were taken?"

"I think so, I'm not sure," Charles said. He explained how he came to be in command of the *Argonaut,* how the three Spanish warships were actually boarded, and his conversations with Collingwood, Nelson, and Jervis. "Perhaps the captain's share would go to Captain Wood's estate," he concluded.

"No, I don't think so," Mr. Edwards said, scribbling some figures in his notebook. "The Admiralty won't want to do that. They'll want a living hero, not a dead one. In any case, Wood had a reputation as something of a reluctant warrior." Charles suddenly understood why Jervis's first signal to engage the enemy had specified the *Argonaut* and only the

Argonaut. Wood couldn't possibly evade such a direct order, and Jervis would know that the other captains needed no such encouragement.

Mr. Edwards wrote a number on a fresh page, tore it off, and handed it to Charles. "If everything you have told me is true, and if there are no complications at court, this is the minimum amount I think you may expect to receive."

Charles looked at the number and his eyes widened. He knew about prize money of course, but had little experience with it. During his time on her, *Argonaut* had not been involved in any naval battles or even the capture of commercial shipping. He tried to calculate the one-quarter share that was the ship's captain's due in his head, couldn't get it exactly, but knew that it was a very large sum.

"No, no," Mr. Edwards spoke, reading his thoughts. "I've already done the division. That is the amount that would go to you personally."

"Oh," Charles answered, unable to pull his eyes off the string of digits. "It's a great deal of money."

"The fortunes of war," Mr. Edwards responded affably, then spent some time explaining how the Admiralty court functioned, what his role as an agent was, his fees, the bewildering array of banking and investment options that Charles had before him, and the services Mr. Edwards's firm could offer in those areas. In the end Charles signed a contract naming Thaddeus Edwards as his sole agent and received in turn a check for two thousand pounds—roughly ten years' salary for a junior naval commander—as an advance on the sums he would receive from the court. Charles left the Threadneedle Street house with manufacturing companies, toll-road and canal-building projects, land acquisition, insurance, shipping and trade, and an assortment of other opportunities tumbling between his ears.

A final visit to the Admiralty confirmed his promotion to commander and that he would be given the *Louisa.* She would be ready for sea at the Plymouth Naval Yards around the end of April or early May. His orders would be delivered when appropriate. The next day, Attwater in tow, he boarded the post coach for Chester and home.

THE LARGE COACH bounced and swayed unmercifully as its six horses pounded along the ancient Roman road that was now the King's Highway between Birmingham and Chester. Charles sat facing forward next to the starboard window, opposite the fitfully snoring form of his steward. They had changed horses in Whitechurch and soon crossed from Shropshire into his native Cheshire at the village of Grindley Brook. The passing scene of small hamlets, patchwork fields surrounded by ancient hedgerows, extensive woods, and pasture for dairy cattle grew increasingly familiar as the coach rattled onward. When the heights of Brown Knowl came into view, and Bolesworth Castle beyond, his sense of anticipation grew with every turn in the road. He was almost home. It had been six years since he had last seen his father (Charles's mother had died when he was eleven, which was one of the reasons he had been sent to sea at the age of twelve), or his brothers or sisters, or slept in his own bed. He wondered if anything had changed in his absence, if his father had made any improvements to the property, or if there might be any other significant transformations in the community. He especially looked forward to seeing his father again and seeing the pride in his face when he told him he had been made commander and would have his own ship.

Late in the afternoon the coach changed horses at the crossroads at Bruxton, the last change before the final run into Chester. Two miles beyond Bruxton, Charles called for the coachman to halt at the hamlet of Handly, where he and Attwater descended and had their luggage passed down.

Charles looked up and down the high road, acutely disappointed as the coach clattered away. His first day in London he had written of his arrival in England and plans to come home, and he'd expected his father, or someone from home, to meet the coach. He searched the nearly empty street and the few half-timbered, thatch-roofed cottages crowded close on either side, but saw no one he recognized. There was a small horse-drawn farm cart plodding along in his direction, with a well-dressed if unfamiliar young woman on its front bench. That was all. Charles briefly wondered what such a woman was doing in such a shabby cart, then dismissed the thought and searched up and down the roadway again.

As the cart drew near, the young woman suddenly gave a loud shriek and leapt to the ground, her petticoats flying. "Charlie! It's you," she squealed in delight as she ran. Charles stood dumbfounded at the onrushing apparition and braced himself for the unavoidable collision as she flung herself on him, kissing his face and cheeks. "Charlie, you don't recognize me, do you?" she said with shining eyes after disengaging herself to the extent of grasping one of his arms in both hers and hugging it against her rather ample bosom.

"Ellie?" he said tentatively; then, "Hi, sis," and grinned. She'd been ten when he saw her last: skinny, flat-chested, and unremarkable. It hadn't really occurred to him that she would have aged at all, much less into the animated, auburn-haired beauty before him. To reinforce his assertion that he had recognized her, he added, "You've grown."

"So have you," she answered, looking up at him; then, seeing his bandage, "Oh, you're hurt."

"It's nothing," Charles said, touching the side of his head. "It's nearly healed." They stood together for a moment, neither knowing what to say first, until Attwater discreetly cleared his throat.

"Come," Charles said, "I'll introduce you to my steward and we can go home." Attwater was already loading their sea chests into the wagon. Introductions were made, and the older man gave the young woman his best imitation of a courtly bow. In the fading daylight the rickety wagon set off behind an aged, sway-backed mare for the two-mile ride to Tattenall. Charles took the reins and sat on the bench in front with his sister, Attwater and their luggage in the bed behind.

"How is everyone at home? Where's Father?" Charles asked as he fruitlessly encouraged the mare into a little more motion.

"Oh, you don't know," Ellie answered, putting her hand on his arm. "We wrote to you. Father died months ago."

Charles's heart seemed to stop. "Died?" he repeated as if he didn't understand. "Father?"

"Oh, I'm sorry," Ellie answered. "He'd been ill for some time, but didn't want anyone to worry you about it. We wrote to you immediately after."

A great emptiness enveloped him. He'd always seen his father as an anchor, a figure larger than life, strict, reliable, constant, but with a twinkle in his eye and a ready laugh. Someone who would always be there if Charles needed him. He couldn't imagine him being gone. "Oh,

God," he said. "No, I didn't know." His father would have been pleased that Charles had participated in a major sea battle and been raised in rank because of it. He'd looked forward to telling him about his adventures and luck. He had wanted his father to see him as a success, and now he couldn't.

"We wrote to you immediately after he passed," Ellie repeated defensively.

Charles tried to compose himself. He didn't want to distress his sister. "Mail at sea can take a long time, if it gets there at all," he said with forced cheerfulness. "How are things at home?"

"It's just John and me now," Ellie responded. "John's a little overwhelmed, I think." John Edgemont, the oldest at thirty-one and unmarried, would be the head of the household now. Charles had two other older brothers, both with the army in India, and an older sister who'd married a solicitor and moved to Liverpool, where she was steadily producing children.

A question stuck in Charles's mind, but he didn't know exactly how to put it. "How come you didn't meet me with the carriage? Why this old cart?"

Ellie sat silent for a moment. "We haven't a carriage anymore. It was sold along with almost all the horses and other things. Most of the servants were also let go."

"Why?" Charles asked. The family income derived from land. Edgemont Hall was an estate of some two thousand acres, the arable parts of which were let out in lots to crofters, small farmers, and herdsmen, who paid their rents in kind. It was an arrangement that had provided the Edgemont clan with a comfortable and largely unchanged living for centuries.

"I don't know," Ellie said stoically. "When Father died, we found that there was no money, only debts, lots of debts. John inherited, of course. He had to sell things and cut costs to keep the land. I think he said that it had to do with the tenants leaving or something."

Presently the wagon clattered through the village of Tattenall in the failing light, with its dimly lit cottage windows and the welcome smell of wood cooking fires. A little past the old square-towered church and the market square, they turned up the drive toward Edgemont Hall. The house was brightly lighted on the ground floor, and John Edgemont, a large, florid man with a receding hairline, immediately came out to greet them. Charles thought his brother looked old, and his face was lined with care. The money problems he'd inherited from their father probably contributed to that. John embraced Charles with a great bear hug and then set him down. "I read about St. Vincent in the *Gazette*. I want to know everything," he said warmly. "But not until you've had a chance to settle in." Charles introduced Attwater, who said, "How d'you do, squire," and bowed.

At dinner, served by the lone remaining maid, the talk was about Charles's years on the *Argonaut*, the places he had been, and the battle off Cape St. Vincent. He told and retold the story of his part in the battle and of his conversations afterward, especially with Nelson, as if he didn't quite believe it himself. After the dishes were cleared he made his way upstairs to his old room, where Attwater helped him prepare for bed.

"Have you eaten?" Charles asked.

"Yes, sir, I had dinner in the kitchen."

"Have you found a place to sleep?"

"Oh, yes, sir. There's plenty of room in the servants' quarters." With that Attwater blew out the lamp and closed the door behind him.

CHARLES FOUND HIMSELF awake before dawn the next morning. He dressed in rough civilian clothing that had been set aside for him, found an old broadcloth jacket, and slipped quietly from the house. The early light filtered shyly through low gray clouds as he walked soberly around the grounds, noting how the house and other buildings had fallen into disrepair. Inside the stable he found only the aging mare that had pulled them from Handley. Outside, he stopped to remember how foreign it had all seemed when his family first arrived from Philadelphia, and when he had played with his brothers in that large elm tree and how that path led to the pond where he had once built a raft that sank under him. And there was a hedgerow he and his father had spent a full day planting together; it was now overgrown and untended. They were largely warm memories of a pleasant time and place. Presently he turned from the house and started down the lane toward the village.

Almost immediately he saw a figure emerge from a wood on the left.

A bent, elderly man looked up and down the way, then froze on seeing Charles and quickly moved the limp forms of two hares behind his back.

"Mornin', governor," the man said, bowing and lifting his hat apprehensively as Charles approached. One arm and its bounty remained mostly hidden.

Charles thought he recognized the stooped figure as someone from his childhood and struggled to place him. "Good morning. Tate, isn't it?"

The man gave a toothless grin and nodded. "Ye remembered, sir. I doubted ye would. Ye wa' only belt-high then."

Robert Tate had been in the employ of Charles's father and managed the stables on the Edgemont estate. He had taught Charles to ride and a few other things besides, animal trapping being one of them. "Had a profitable morning?" he asked, nodding at the arm Tate still held behind his back.

"Aye, fair to tolerable," Tate answered, bringing out his catch without a hind of remorse that he had clearly been caught poaching. "And ye, young master Charles, how do ye find life asea?"

They talked in a friendly, intimate way, standing in the lane for a time recalling younger days in both their lives. Tate had mostly retired from his stable manager's position years before Charles's father died and the horses were sold, but he still lived in a small cottage on the estate.

"I must be getting on home, sir. The missus will be wondering," the old man said finally. "Take care in the navvy. I ken it's a hard life."

"How is Betsy?" Charles asked. He remembered her as a large, good-hearted woman, frequently found in the Edgemont kitchen, who usually had a secret sweet or a piece of pie for him whenever he appeared.

"Oh, not very spry, sir. But still herself, if ye takes my meanin'. She gets nervous if I'm away too long."

"Well, remember me fondly to her. You take care, too, Tate. And mind no one catches you with those hares."

"Aye, sir," Tate grinned. "Never ye worry. I'm as deft as ever I wa'."

The men parted with a handshake and Charles continued on toward the village. As he came closer, he saw that a few of the crofters' cottages stood empty, with their doors ajar, and there were occasional pigs rooting in untended fields. Other fields were newly plowed, ready for the spring planting of barley, corn, and oats. Above most of the cottages he saw the smoke of cooking fires from chimneys as families began to start the day. Here and there individuals emerged sleepily outside to collect firewood or to take care of more personal business. Those that noticed him stared curiously. A few nodded in greeting or touched their foreheads and he nodded or waved in return. After a time Charles turned and started home in a contemplative mood, noticing the hazy greens of early spring growth beginning on the tips of the birch trees.

He found his brother at the kitchen table, with Attwater by the stove. The maid, a stick-thin, graying, middle-aged woman who had been with the family for as long as Charles could remember, stood nearby with a stern look on her face, her arms folded across her chest. Apparently there had been a discussion about who would do the cooking and Attwater had prevailed. John sat looking pained and slightly flustered while the older man tinkered with the flue on the stove to try to get some of the smoke out of the room.

"Your man can be very stubborn," he said as Charles seated himself at the table.

"Yes, I've learned that it's best not to argue with him." Then to Attwater Charles said, "I didn't know you could cook. What's for breakfast?"

"Eggs and coffee, sir. 'E says there ain't no—isn't no bacon," Attwater responded, beaming. "I fetched the eggs from the coop down the lane. The coffee's from your stores."

"We don't have a hen coop," the maid said acidly. "He stole them from the Bridgetons. They'll have to be paid."

"Fine," Charles said absently, his mind on what he'd seen that morning and Ellie's talk of money problems the day before. He turned to his brother. "How bad is it?" he asked. "Ellie mentioned something about Father's debts."

John looked uncomfortable. "It's not your problem," he said quickly. "We'll be all right given a little time."

"How much time?" Charles asked. John's shoulders slumped in a gesture of resignation. "Father accumulated a fair amount of debt over the past several years. Some of it was from speculating on corn prices, some was borrowing for the upkeep of the house, other things. He tried raising the crofters' rents to pay the interest. When the price of feed fell, he had to borrow more. He was very ill toward the end, probably from the worry. I suspected something was wrong but didn't really learn how wrong until after he died."

"And now?" Charles asked, watching his brother carefully. He wanted to help, he was certainly able to help, but the offer had to be made tactfully.

John steepled his fingers and pressed them against his chin. "I've mortgaged the property, paid off some of it, and renegotiated the rest. Still, there are payments coming due that I may not be able to cover." He looked directly at Charles. "I can't raise the rents any higher. Some are leaving as it is. I may have to sell part of the land."

"How much do you need?" Charles asked.

John eyed him skeptically. "It's not your problem," he repeated.

"Still," Charles persisted, "how much? I came into some money as a result of St. Vincent. I will happily give or lend you whatever you want."

Attwater placed plates piled high with a yellowish mess, somehow both gooey and charred, that might have been cooked eggs in front of each of the men, then added two lumps of dark bread and steaming mugs of strong-smelling coffee. "We don't have almost no coffee left," he announced.

"You can go into the village and get some," Charles said, still watching his brother.

John stared incredulously at the plate in front of him before turning to Charles. "Fifty pounds is due at the end of the month," he said finally. "I can probably pull together twenty. Would the balance be too much for you?"

"I think I can do that," Charles said. "What's the total amount owing?"

"It's an awful lot. Almost a thousand pounds. But I'm not asking—"

"You'd have to sell a lot of land," Charles observed.

"It's worse than that. Land prices are down. There's a number of nearby estates up for sale already, including the Howell land on the other side of the village—the old hall, crofts, pastures and all. My God, if father had left any money, I'd buy the lot."

"All right," Charles said, several thoughts competing, "how about I give you the thousand pounds and say about a hundred extra to fix up the house and outbuildings. I'll lend it to you if you like, but I don't care when you pay me back."

John sat up straight in his chair. "Can you do that?"

"Actually, I can do it fairly easily," Charles answered. "But I may want to ask a favor of you in return."

"Anything. What?"

"I don't know yet. But rest comfortably, I'll think of something." Actually, Charles did have the beginnings of an idea.

At that moment Ellie entered, sleepily and prettily, into the kitchen. Attwater promptly placed an overflowing plate of egglike substance on the table in front of her, her own bread, and a mug of coffee. "I don't drink coffee," she said immediately, "and I can't possibly eat all this— whatever it is. I'll be as fat as a cow."

"Of course you can, miss," Attwater said cheerfully. "It'll put 'air on your chest."

With that image fixed firmly in his mind, Charles rose from the table, grabbed his jacket, and left the room, patting his sister on the head as he went. "Great thick mats of hair," he said as he disappeared out the door.

That morning he saddled the aging mare and rode through Tattenall to look at the Howell land and buildings. He spent a great deal of time, given the horse's plodding, swaying gait, traversing the narrow cart-paths that connected the crofters' plots. At the boarded-up manor house, larger but in worse repair than Edgemont, he dismounted and carefully inspected everything he could see from the outside. Once a handsome and well-proportioned structure, it was now covered with vines and tending to decay. The owners had died, and the eldest son lived in London—preferring cash, John had told him. Charles let his idea simmer the rest of the day. That evening he wrote a long letter to Thaddeus Edwards in London.

The next morning, at Attwater's bread-and-mounds-of-eggs breakfast, Charles announced that he wished to borrow the horse and wagon for a trip into Chester. Attwater would accompany him.

"What are we going to the city for?" Attwater asked a little grumpily. Charles suspected he was enjoying himself in the quiet of the country, with his new role as butler, cook, and head servant all rolled into one.

"I want to open an account at the bank and buy a few things," Charles answered.

"We need coffee," Attwater promptly stated. "They ain't, aren't got none in the village."

"Things and coffee," Charles agreed equitably.

"What sort of things?" Ellie asked, poking at the top of her pile of egg.

"It will be a surprise. Who knows?" Charles answered.

He and Attwater took the well-worn track back to Handley to the King's Highway, not because it was shorter, but because it was easier on the horse and cart. Eight miles and three hours later they crossed the ancient six-arched stone bridge over the River Dee, through the newly rebuilt Bridgegate piercing the walls, and into the city. The Dee was the traditional boundary between northern Wales and northwestern England, and Chester derived some of her commerce from the trade between the two. Most of the rest was seaborne trade with Ireland, particularly leather goods and linens. He went to a banking establishment near the cathedral and presented Mr. Edwards's check. The manager came out immediately, and within half an hour Charles was back in the street with an account at the bank and a fair amount in cash. He took Attwater to a sixpenny ordinary for lunch and afterward to the stockyards adjacent to the city. There, after much inspecting and haggling, he purchased a dappled gelding as a present for Ellie, two young matched chestnut mares, and a magnificent, heavily muscled dark-brown stallion of seventeen hands. Another stop got him a sturdy four-wheeled country carriage for the mares, rather prettily got up in black-and-green paint, and the location of a nearby saddlery. By midafternoon he left Attwater with ample money to purchase whatever he thought necessary in the way of supplies for the house. He also entrusted to him the gelding and mares, the carriage and the cart, and instructions that he should take his time shopping, sleep the night at an inn, and return to Tattenall in the morning, with the nag and cart tethered behind the carriage and the gelding to the cart.

After some concern voiced by Attwater about who would make breakfast (quickly dealt with), Charles lifted himself onto the stallion's broad back and tapped his flanks. The animal started quickly forward, incredibly quickly compared to the old mare and cart, and it took a time before he felt in control of the beast. The two made for Eastgate Street at a brisk pace, then for the Dee bridge and the highway beyond. Charles felt immensely pleased with himself and the turns in his life as he moved down the great road, the horse trotting impatiently beneath him. From time to time the stallion would snort loudly and shake his mane as if wanting to run.

Near Hatton, Charles left the highway for a more direct and less-used track toward Tattenall through the rolling wooded countryside. Feeling more confident, he allowed the stallion to break into a canter along the empty byway, then gave him his head. As if thankful to be free of the stockyards, the animal immediately lengthened his stride to a full gallop. The trees and brush by the roadway rushed past in an exhilarating blur. Charles leaned close over his neck to urge the stallion on. They jumped a small stream without breaking stride and started at a tearing pace around a blind bend in the road with high trees on either side, when he suddenly saw a horse and cart with a startled brown-and-white form on its bench directly in their path. He jerked the stallion's reins and saw the cart horse rear wildly as he flashed past, brushing his leg painfully on the cart's side. There was a sharp feminine exclamation and then a crash as the cart overturned. He pulled the stallion to a halt and turned its head to start back. The stallion reluctantly agreed, breathing heavily and snorting as he did so.

The wagon lay on its side in the road, its driver a jumble of brown dress, white shawl, and petticoats sprawled beside it. Appalled at what he'd done, Charles rode to the wagon, dismounted, and knelt by what turned out to be a young woman in some distress. She had pushed herself to a sitting position and was holding her left arm tenderly in her lap, her bonnet badly askew.

"Are you hurt?" Charles asked stupidly.

The girl looked at him with eyes narrowed in anger and pain. "Thou wilt please see to Maggie," she said sharply, jerking her head toward the gray mare. The horse lay kicking on her side, prevented from rising by the harness and shafts of the overturned wagon. Charles rose and heaved the cart onto its wheels, then took the mare by her bridle and helped her stand. She was scraped on one side and seemed to be favoring her right foreleg. He stroked the mare's muzzle to reassure her, then ran his hand down her leg, feeling for a break. The stallion also meandered over to see if anything interesting might be happening and introduced himself by giving Maggie a playful nip on her mane. Charles led his horse across the road and tied his reins firmly to a bush.

"Your mare is a little bruised. I don't think anything's broken," he said, returning to the girl. "How about you?"

She raised her head and glared at him with moist eyes. "Thou hast broken my arm." She clutched her forearm against her chest and lowered her head, rocking back and forth. Charles studied her for a moment while he tried to decide what to do. She was a severe-looking young woman, he decided, with pinched features, about seventeen or eighteen. She wore a simple brown dress without collar, ribbons, or lace, now muddied and torn on the side where she fell, a similarly dirtied woolen shawl, and a bonnet that had slipped over toward one side of her head. She had on brightly polished black leather shoes over white stockings. She was no crofter or herdsman's daughter, he thought; her dress and shoes were too finely made. But the drab clothing and absence of any finery seemed to rule out her father being some sort of merchant or landowner.

"I'm very sorry. It was entirely my fault," he said, trying to get her to look at him.

Her head shot up. "Yes, it wert thy fault. Thou wert very, very reckless, racing along like that. Thou couldst have murdered someone."

"All right," Charles said evenly. "Let me see your arm."

"Don't thou touch me," she said fiercely, but fresh tears came to her eyes. "It pains me terribly. I think it's broken."

"Let me see," Charles insisted. He brushed some dirt off her shoulder. "Come on. It's not going to do you any good to sit there holding it until it becomes really painful."

Reluctantly she relaxed her hold on the injured limb and moved it a small way from her body.

"This may hurt a little," he said, running his hand as gently as he could over the sleeve covering her arm. He'd done this or watched it done dozens of times on board ship, where broken and cracked bones were commonplace. She nodded wordlessly and fixed her eyes on him so intently that he felt self-conscious as he worked his way from her wrist along her arm. When he was halfway to the elbow, she gave a sharp cry and he relaxed his grip.

He'd felt the place where the bone, the smaller of the two in the forearm, was broken and partially displaced. "I'm going to sit you on the back of your wagon," he said soberly. "There's no point doing what we're going to have to do down here in the dirt."

"Is it really broken?" she said tensely. "I heard something go snap when I fell."

"Yes, it's broken," Charles said. He put one arm behind her shoulders and the other under her knees and lifted her off the ground, setting her upright with her legs hanging over the back of the wagon bed.

"What art thou going to do?" she asked through tightly clenched teeth.

He breathed in deeply, trying to find his nerve. He knew he was about to cause her considerable pain, more than he already had, and he didn't relish it. "I'm going to set it and then fasten a splint so it won't move around." He avoided her eyes.

"Will it hurt?"

Charles nodded. "It's going to hurt very badly for a short time. You're going to have to be brave and hold as still as you can. It won't take long."

He noticed that she was still watching him intently, as if debating whether she could trust him. Their eyes met, hers large and round, a startling clear gray, and unwavering. Then her shoulders relaxed and she seemed to accept him, or at least she was resigned to his helping her. For a moment he took in her eyes, her clear pale skin, and the outline of her face. She had high cheekbones with a narrow nose and slightly pointed chin. Her lips were pressed together in a thin, pale line. Locks of light brown, almost blond hair escaped from her bonnet. He saw that she was not severe-looking at all.

"You stay right here," he said, trying to regather the composure that had suddenly left him. "I have to collect some things." He pried a narrow slat from the side of the wagon and broke it in two over his knee. Then he went to where he'd tethered his horse. He took a pocket knife from his trousers, opened the blade, and cut one of the leather reins from the bridle. The boards and the leather strap he lay in the wagon beside her hip.

"Ready?" he asked, standing in front of her.

She nodded, not daring to speak.

"All right. I'm going to pull on your arm until the bone slides back into place. That's the part that will hurt the most," he explained. "After that, it'll be all with the wind on our quarter and sailing by and large."

She smiled thinly and nodded again.

Charles turned his back to her and held her upper arm tightly between his own arm and his side, awkwardly aware of the fullness of her breast against his elbow. "You haven't told me your name," he said conversationally.

"I'm Penelope—" She gave a sharp piercing shriek as he pulled on her wrist, felt for the break and let the bone slide back into place. "Oh, damn, oh *damn!*" she cried, choking back tears.

"I'm very sorry I had to do that," Charles said, then added, "Are you all right?" He was still holding her arm as carefully and firmly as he could between his own. He could hear her breathing in gasps and felt her chest heaving against his arm. She had courage, he'd give her that.

"I think so," she said in a whisper. "Art thou done?"

"All except for the splint," he said, relaxing his grip and turning. He reached for one of his boards and held it under her forearm. "You didn't finish telling me your name," he continued, placing the other on top.

"Penelope Brown," she said, her voice stronger. "Who art thou?"

Charles took the leather strap and put one end between his teeth; the other he began to loop firmly around the boards, immobilizing the bones in her arm between them. "Charles Edgemont, from Tattenall," he said as he was tying the ends of the strap together. "My friends call me Charlie, and I need your bonnet."

"My bonnet? Why?" she said, her hand moving to the bow under her chin as if to protect it.

"It's either your bonnet or one of your petticoats," Charles said happily. "I need to make you a sling."

"Oh," she said, and her face reddened. She pulled one of the long straps and the bow came undone. "The bonnet, I think." She held it out to him as her hair slipped down around her shoulders.

Charles placed the bonnet under her arm and tied the long straps together over her shoulder, pushing some of her hair away to do so. The soft strands felt like silken spindrift against his fingers.

"Well, Miss Brown," he said clumsily, "if you tell me where you live, I'll take you home."

"My name is Penelope Brown, not Miss Brown," she said with a small smile. "And I live near Gatesheath, not a mile from here."

He saw that, with her hair softening the outline of her face and her mouth broken into a smile, that she was startlingly pretty, maybe beautiful. Charles stood silently staring until her eyes met his. "I'd best change the horses," he said, hastily looking away. "Yours will be all right given a little time, but I think it'd be better if mine pulled your cart for now." He retreated to busy himself with the horses. Finally, after some difficulty with his stallion, who apparently thought himself above pulling carts, he had the mare tethered behind the wagon and his horse hitched between the shafts. He returned to the back of the wagon and saw that she had been watching him, her expression softer than before. She smiled, her head cocked slightly to one side.

Unexpectedly, Penelope Brown reached out with her good arm and gently touched the dressing on the side of Charles's head. "Thou art injured," she said. "How camest thou by it?"

Reflexively Charles raised his hand to the bandage, and his fingers brushed against hers. "An accident at sea," he answered brusquely. "It's almost healed."

"Is that where thy expression, 'with the wind on our quarter,' cometh from?"

"The same," Charles said.

She looked at him curiously for a moment, then asked, "Wouldst thou help me down, please? I don't want to jump."

"Of course," Charles said, his awkwardness returning. He put his hands on her waist and set her gently on the ground. He saw she was tall for a girl, perhaps half a head shorter than he. She smiled up at him, and he quickly said, "Here, I'll help you up in the front."

This proved awkward. He lifted her by her waist up to the two-foot-high step, then supported her while she pulled herself onto the bench with her good arm. When Charles climbed up, he felt embarrassed about the intimacy of the contact between them and hardly dared look at her.

"Thank thee," she said at length. "Not for crashing my conveyance, doing injury to my horse, and breaking my arm, but for the gentle way thou looked after Maggie and for not being upset with me when I screamed and swore. I think thou art a Christian person."

Charles studied her profile out of the corner of his eye, trying not to be obvious. "I've seen worse," he said seriously, "much worse. You were very brave." He fell silent.

"The sun is almost down," she observed.

"Yes?" Charles said, wondering at the change of topic.

"Dost not thou think we should start? It's straight ahead and the first turning on the right."

"Oh, yes," he said, and quickly took the reins and flicked them. The stallion started forward.

After they had found the turning and were well along the lane to her home, she asked, "Doth thy horse have a name?"

"No," Charles answered. "I just bought him today. Do you have any ideas?"

She sat in thought. "What dost thou think of Pendle?"

At first Charles had been a little taken aback at her use of *thees* and *thous*. They were archaic pronouns that had long gone out of style in most of England, especially in the navy. But as she talked, he found he enjoyed the way she spoke. It suggested in his mind a certain intimacy between them. He assumed she spoke to everyone that way, though, and had no idea why. "Pendle?" Charles repeated. "Why Pendle?"

She gave a small laugh. "He's so large. When thou art mounting him thou couldst say thou wert climbing Pendle Hill." She smiled prettily at him.

Charles hadn't the least idea why anyone would name a horse after a small mountain in northern England, but he loved the sound of her when she was happy. He gallantly said, "Pendle it is." He flicked the horse's reins. "Git up, Pendle," and the stallion broke into a trot.

She started to laugh again and then stopped and said, "Oh, my arm hurts." After that she fell increasingly silent, leaning against him for support and shivering. He stopped the wagon, removed his jacket and wrapped it around her shoulders.

He hurried the horse as best he could while trying to minimize the jolts and rattles of the cart on the uneven dirt lane. Occasionally Penelope groaned and once cried out when a wheel hit a rock in the roadway.

It was becoming more dark than light, and it was difficult for Charles to see some of the smaller bumps and ruts.

"There," she said, pointing to a track on the left. He slowed to take the turn and walked the stallion up the lane toward a large stone house with lights showing on both floors. Several figures emerged from the doorway before Charles brought the wagon to a halt.

"Penny, is it thee?" a man called as the wagon neared.

"Yes, Father," the girl answered weakly.

"What is this?" the man said, seeing Charles's horse in the harness, and then, on seeing Charles, "Who art thou?"

Charles jumped to the ground and went around to help Penny from the cart. "Give me a hand, will you," he said to the man. "I'll lift her down to you. It's best to get her inside and warm as soon as possible."

"Of course," the man said. Charles climbed onto the cart step, lifted Penny with one arm under her thighs and the other behind her shoulders, and handed her down. Her father carried her into the house.

Alone in the near-dark, and chilly without his coat, Charles set about unhitching his horse. He got the one-reined bridle on and was carrying the saddle from the wagon bed when the door to the house opened and Penny's father and a young boy came out. The boy carried a lantern and Charles's jacket.

"May I know thy name?" the man said.

"Charles Edgemont, sir," Charles replied.

"Penelope said there was an accident. We are most grateful to thee for helping her."

Charles threw the saddle across the stallion's back and turned to the man. "It wasn't an accident like that, sir," he said. "It was my doing that caused it. Any help I was able to give should be seen in that light. I'm terribly sorry for what has happened, and will of course pay for any damages—doctor's bills, the injury to your mare, repairs to the cart, anything."

The man stood silently for a moment, then said, "I am George Brown, Penelope's father. This is my youngest child, Peter." The boy, perhaps fourteen, nodded and handed Charles his coat. The father continued, "It was lucky that thou knew how to set a broken bone. May I ask where thou learned such a thing?"

"I am an officer, a ship's commander in His Majesty's Navy," Charles replied. "I've seen plenty of broken bones."

"I imagine thou hast," the father said. "Still, not everyone would have done what thou did. We are grateful. Wouldst thou like something to eat? Penny hath gone to her room, but we would be pleased to fix something for thee."

Charles hesitated. "Thank you, no," he said. "I think it's better if I get home. I would like to pay a call tomorrow, if I may. To see how Miss Brown is, of course."

"Thou wouldst be welcome, I'm sure," George Brown said.

Charles bent under the horse, cinched the saddle, and, after waiting for the horse to exhale, pulled it tight. "There is one thing," he said.

"Yes?"

"May I borrow a small length of rope? I only have one rein at the moment."

CHARLES REACHED EDGEMONT Hall an hour later. He brushed down Pendle and put him in a stall with some fresh hay. He found his brother and sister in the dining room at their dinner.

"What took you so long?" John asked.

"Don't ask," Charles said with a broad smile on his face. He'd caught himself grinning all the way back from the Brown home, thinking about Penelope, the look of her eyes, the touch of her hair, and the sound of her laughter.

"Well, sit down and eat," Ellie said. "We set a place for you. And tell us why you're wearing that silly smile."

Charles sat and helped himself to the food. "You know Attwater and I went into Chester this morning," he began. It seemed like years ago. He told them about the matched mares and the carriage he'd bought, and hinted that there was a present for Ellie, at which point she jumped up and kissed him. "Attwater is bringing them, and whatever else he's bought, in the morning." He told them about the stallion that he'd ridden back on. They all agreed to go look at the animal after dinner.

"That still doesn't explain your smiling all over," Ellie insisted.

"Well," Charles said simply, "I crashed a woman's cart and broke her arm on the way home. I think she likes me. I'm to visit her tomorrow."

"You navy men certainly know how to get a woman's attention," John observed. "What's her name?"

"Penelope Brown," Charles said between forkfuls of potatoes and pork. "From over by Gatesheath."

"Oh, the Quaker Browns. I've met the father—what's his name? George, I think. He's all right, but I haven't much use for Quakers generally."

"Why not?" Charles asked. He knew about Quakers, of course; Philadelphia had been largely populated by them, and they were not uncommon in England. But he could remember little about their beliefs except that his father had praised them as honest businessmen and that they were derided in the navy as cowards for steadfastly refusing to fight.

"I don't want to speak ill of your new love, Charlie. But some say they're false Christians who think of themselves as better than other people. They can be very sharp with money. They won't swear to anything, not even in court, and they hold themselves apart from everyone else. They dress differently, and they talk differently. And, Charlie, they don't allow their women to marry anyone who isn't of their kind."

FOUR

ARLY THE NEXT MORNING, CHARLES RODE PENDLE TO
Bruxton to have a new rein fastened to his bridle. There were other
bridles hung on pegs in the stables at home, but he wanted to get out of
the house and away from anything cheerful or familiar. He had slept
poorly and rode in a black mood, alternately cursing his fate and reviling
himself for any thoughts he may have nurtured toward the girl. And
damn all Quakers and their haughty exclusions. Where did they get
the right to think they were so much better than anybody else? After
he'd done his business at the tackle maker's, his anger began to drift
into disappointment, then self-pity. He remembered the light in her
eyes, her soft hair, her *thee*s and *thou*s, her laughter, and most particularly
the closeness of her body when he set her arm and when he had helped
her into the wagon. The cruelty of it left him feeling abandoned and
depressed.

On the lane to the house he saw that Attwater had returned from
Chester with his train of horses and wagons. In no mood to talk with
anyone, Charles stopped Pendle a distance from the house and watched
as his brother walked around the carriage, even shaking its wheels, then
stood in front of the mares, stroking their necks and flanks. Suddenly he
saw the front door burst open and Ellie rush straight for the dappled
gelding. All in one motion she hugged its neck, kissed its muzzle, and, in
a very unladylike motion, threw herself sideways across its bare back,

struggling to a sitting position. From this viewpoint she looked around and spied Charles on his horse in the lane.

"Charlie, Charlie!" she called. "Come see!" She kicked her heels against the gelding in an effort to ride over to him, but, having no reins, the horse took three steps forward and stopped.

The cloud over Charles's head lightened fractionally in spite of himself. He smiled grimly, tapped Pendle's flanks, and walked the stallion up toward the house, stopping beside his sister. "Are you happy?" he said.

"Oh, yes," she answered, giving him a blinding smile. "Aren't you?"

Charles didn't answer. Instead he dismounted and out of curiosity went to the carriage to see what else Attwater had purchased in the city. He saw hundredweight bags each of barley, wheat, and rye flour, at least eight cured hams, several slabs of bacon, pigs' jowls, salted beef, a large box of coffee, two cases of wine, huge quantities of dried peas, and other bags and containers he would have to open in order to identify their contents. Apparently Attwater had bought everything any shopkeeper told him he might need, and Charles was confident that his steward had not the slightest idea how to prepare any of it. Attwater beamed with pride.

Ellie came up beside him and took his hand in hers. "What's the matter, Charlie?"

He looked at her and forced a smile. "Nothing's the matter."

"Don't be silly," Ellie persisted. "It's because of that girl you met yesterday, isn't it?"

"Of course not," he answered a little too quickly. Then, because she frowned at him, he said, "Maybe a little."

"Do you want to see her again?"

Charles hesitated. "Yes, but I think I'd better not."

"Do you love her?" Ellie's eyes never left his face.

The question jolted him. "Love's a strong word. Beside, you're too young to know about things like that."

"No I'm not," she asserted hotly. "Do you think about anyone or anything else?"

Charles stared at the ground. Did he love her? He'd only met her once, under unusual circumstances to be sure, but still only once. His heart ached at the thought of her. She had cared about him when she'd noticed his injury. Her touch was feather-soft, even while she had her own far worse pain from her broken arm. She'd shown real courage, and he sensed something direct and practical about her. He could love a woman like that. Maybe he did. Not that it mattered now. "Not very much else. Not recently," he finally admitted.

"Then go and see her. You said you would. John doesn't know everything. Go visit and see what happens." She squeezed his hand to emphasize her point, then added in a dreamy voice, "Love is so beautiful."

Charles considered this in silence. Maybe Ellie was right. He could just be paying a courteous visit to a person he'd accidentally injured. There was nothing wrong in that. What did he have to lose? He had an inspiration.

"I'll tell you what," he said, "I'll go tomorrow morning, if you'll come with me. Besides, I'd like to know what you think of her."

"Oh, I'd love that," Ellie said, glowing with pleasure. "We could ride our new horses. I'm naming mine Passion." Charles thought it a strange name for a gelding.

He and Ellie let the horses loose in the pasture. His sister went into the house and Charles cleared the stalls in the stables while John and Attwater unloaded the wagons. At lunch his brother announced that he had rehired the household cook and another of the maids. "And now I'll have to find a stableboy," he said with a mock frown. Turning to Charles, he added gravely, "I expect you to tell Attwater that he can't cook for us anymore."

In the afternoon Charles went into the parlor and put some wood on the fire. Pleasantly tired and in a better frame of mind, he sat in an armchair to think. He tried to set his thoughts on his new frigate and crew, the preparations he should make, and things he should check on. But he kept drifting back to Penelope, Penny, her clear gray eyes and soft, fawn-colored hair. He tried to imagine what she might say and what he should say when he visited her. While he was remembering the feel of her waist under his hands when he lifted her from the wagon, his head nodded to his chest and he slept.

SOMEWHERE FROM THE depths he heard a loud knock at the door and was aware that someone had gone to answer it. He was awake by the time Ellie came into the parlor, furiously, smoothing her dress and pushing at her hair. "It's for you," she said in a high state of anxiety, and promptly fled through the dining room and kitchen to the back stairs to her room. Charles found Stephen Winchester standing just inside the front door in a brand-new uniform of a lieutenant in the Royal Navy.

"By God, Stephen, you're a welcome sight," Charles said with genuine pleasure. "Come in, come in." He hadn't expected Winchester or Bevan to arrive for several weeks, perhaps a month, but he was pleased nonetheless.

"Hello, Commander Edgemont," Winchester said. "I'm sorry to intrude. You mentioned I could come to stay while we're waiting for the *Louisa*."

"Yes I did, and I meant it. You're more than welcome. When did the *Argonaut* arrive? Have you already visited your family?"

"I don't think I'll bother to go home," Winchester said sourly. "We landed in Plymouth four days ago. I came by coach as soon as I could and bought a horse in Chester. Lieutenant Bevan has gone on to Wales. He expects to be here in a month or so. He said for me to tell you that he still thinks you're God's punishment for all the navy's sins."

"The feeling is mutual," Charles said with a grin. "Did you see the *Louisa* while you were in Plymouth?" He was intensely interested in anything he could learn about his ship.

"Oh, yes. Lieutenant Bevan and I walked down to look at her. She's still in stocks on the beach. They're giving her a whole new bottom, copper sheathing and all."

They had barely seated themselves in the parlor before Ellie bounced in, slightly breathless. Charles noticed that her cheeks were scrubbed pink, her hair carefully brushed, and she had on a fresh dress that fit tightly over her bosom. "Your guest must be tired. May I get the two of you anything?" she said, looking straight at Winchester under lowered lashes.

The men stood and Charles introduced his newly made lieutenant to his sister. "Your servant, ma'am," Winchester said, bowing and eyeing her with barely disguised interest. She curtsied and bubbled, "Thank you, sir."

"Yes," Charles said loudly, to get Ellie's attention. "Please find Attwater and have him stable Stephen's horse. Then, if you would, bring us two glasses of sherry. I'm sure Attwater bought some. He bought everything else." Ellie looked at him sharply and Charles promptly said, "I meant three glasses of sherry, one a very small one." The instant she left the room Charles turned to Winchester. "I trust you will remember that she's my sister."

"Of course, sir," Winchester replied quickly, his eyes still fixed on the empty doorway.

At dinner, wonderfully prepared by the newly returned cook, Winchester was induced to relate his experiences during the battle of St. Vincent. He labored over the expression on Charles's face when he had told him he was now in command. "Rather like someone who had just walked into a post" was how he put it. John asked questions while Ellie sat silently, intently watching the lieutenant out of the corner of her eye. Charles studied the two with a growing sense of discomfort, noticing that Winchester frequently glanced in Ellie's direction, possibly due to the second fresh dress with a low, scooped neckline that she was now wearing. Winchester was handsome and quick-witted with an easy charm. That and a naval uniform could be devastating to women, Charles knew. On their night of celebration in Lisbon, even the professional dark-eyed Portuguese ladies competed for his attentions. Then Charles remembered the act over which the Portuguese ladies were competing to perform with Winchester. He resolved to keep his lieutenant and his sister where he could watch them as much as possible.

After dinner Charles asked Winchester if he had any other clothes. "I have some things in my kit," he answered, "and two more uniforms on order in Plymouth. Why?"

"Tomorrow morning Ellie and I are going to visit a woman whom I met, injured actually, on the road the other day. You're welcome to come along, but not in uniform." Not only was there safety in numbers, Charles thought, but it would enable him to keep an eye on the two nearly the whole day.

"Surely," Winchester said cheerfully, "but why the ordinary clothing?"

"She's a Quakeress. I don't think they approve of military men."

Winchester made a wry face and said, "They're a peculiar and obstinate people." To which Charles readily agreed.

The next morning, Charles, Ellie, and Winchester rode under low skies and a fresh westerly breeze along the back roads toward Gatesheath and the Brown home. The white dots of sheep and the black-and-white bulk of cattle were visible on the meadows, but Charles had little interest in them. Of the three, he was the only one seemingly in a hurry. Ellie and Winchester repeatedly lagged behind, riding side by side and talking animatedly to the extent that Charles had to occasionally halt Pendle impatiently in the roadway and wait for them to catch up. Finally they turned up the lane to the house, more or less together. In the daylight he saw that it was a substantial place, a large stone building with a much larger and well-kept millhouse behind. That explained the girl's finely made clothing: She was a prosperous miller's daughter.

As they neared the residence, a boy whom Charles recognized as Penny's younger brother, Peter, emerged from the doorway, looking back over his shoulder and nodding to someone inside. He hurried down the steps to meet Charles and the others. "Good day to thee," the boy said seriously. "May I take thy horses?"

Charles dismounted and handed Pendle's reins to him. "Is Mistress Brown at home?"

"Penny? Well, I think so. In just a moment, anyway," he answered, then he was distracted as Winchester handed his horse over. Winchester went around to help Ellie down, with somewhat more contact between the two of them than Charles thought absolutely necessary. "It's a nice day, isn't it?" Peter said conversationally, holding all three horses.

Charles looked at the glowering sky and felt a sprinkle of rain. "I've seen nicer," he said.

"Dost thou think it will rain?" the boy asked. Before Charles could respond, Peter glanced anxiously at the house. Apparently seeing some signal, he said, "Please, won't thou go in? I will put thy horses in the stables." The door opened before Charles knocked, and a pleasant-looking older woman said, "Come in, Charles Edgemont and friends. We were hoping thou might visit."

Charles introduced his companions: "My sister, Eleanor, and my friend, Stephen Winchester." The woman responded with a cheerful "Welcome one and all," and announced herself as Elizabeth Brown, Penelope's mother. She led them to a small sitting room in the back of the house.

Penny sat primly by a window, her injured arm in a proper sling across her chest. She appeared composed and self-assured, two things that at this moment Charles knew himself not to be. He stood nervously, not knowing what to say or do. Penny's mother said, "I will see to hot chocolate for everyone." Ellie promptly crossed the room, sat on the settee close beside Penny, and took her free hand. "I'm Ellie," she introduced herself volubly, "Charlie's sister. He's told me all about your meeting. Isn't it simply amazing how these things happen?"

Penny looked at the girl with amused eyes and laughed. "Our meeting?" she said. "I guess thou couldst call it a meeting. Thy brother hath a very forceful way of introducing himself."

"He never had much in the way of social graces," Ellie said conspiratorially, holding Penny's hand in both of hers. "He has to knock them over or no one will pay any attention to him."

Charles found a chair by the far wall and sat down while the two women talked. "Oh, I don't think so," Penny said, glancing in his direction. "He only needeth a little refinement, is all."

Seeing the direction of Penny's eyes, Ellie rose abruptly, looked at Winchester, and said, "Come, let's go look at the millpond."

"The millpond?" Winchester asked. "Why would anyone want to look at the millpond?"

"There might be ducks," Ellie said, pushing him toward the door.

Charles sat stiffly in his chair looking at Penny from across the room. He'd worked over in his mind a thousand things to say to her, and now none would come to him. "How is your arm?" finally bumbled out.

"Sometimes it pains me, but not as badly as before. The doctor came yesterday. I'm to take willowbark tea every few hours. He admired thy work with my splint."

"I'm glad," Charles said. He wished Ellie were still in the room.

"I don't like talking to thee over there." She indicated a chair adjacent to the settee. "Thou art too distant." Charles moved closer and sat silently.

"Why art thou so quiet?" she asked in a small voice. "Thou wert not so shy two days ago."

Charles managed a smile. "I haven't broken any of your bones yet today."

"I hope thou won't think that necessary." After an awkward pause she said seriously, "I looked for thee yesterday."

"Yes," he said, his floundering returning. "I—"

"Charles Edgemont," she said and touched his arm. It was the first time that day she'd used his name or touched him, and he stopped. "If I ask thee a difficult question, wilt thou give me a truthful answer?"

"I'll try."

"No, thou must promise."

"All right," he said at length. He knew what she was going to ask.

"Didst thou know I am a Quaker?"

Charles shook his head. "No, I didn't until later. My brother told me."

"Dost thou abide Quakers? Many don't."

"I have no quarrels with Quakers," he said carefully, "but I don't know very much about them. More important, I'm afraid that Quakers won't abide me."

"Because thou art a soldier in the navy?" she said.

Charles hesitated. *What was wrong with his being in the navy?* He knew that Quakers wouldn't fight; did that mean no one else could? "No," he said finally. "I mean because I'm not myself a member of your sect."

Penny said directly, "I am troubled by thee being in the navy and I will labor with thee about that another day. As for the other thing, it's God's will that's important more than the rules of religions."

"How do you know God's will?" Charles said doubtfully.

"If thou listens, God speaks to thee."

Charles considered this bit of wisdom more than a little mystifying. "God hasn't spoken to anyone since biblical times," he said, "and certainly not to me."

Penny smiled. "Yes, he does. Thou art not listening."

"I don't understand," Charles said. "Listen to what? A burning bush? A voice from the sky?"

"No, no. It's nothing like that," she explained patiently. "We Friends—the people of the world call us Quakers, but we call ourselves the Society of Friends—believe that God dwells in the heart of every person, man, woman, and child. If thou sit quietly and listens to what's inside, in thy heart and in thy conscience, God will speak to thee."

"That's incredible. If God speaks directly to ordinary people, then what are preachers for?" Charles began sarcastically. "And what does he say?" He was about to ask if God told her whether or not to receive calls from men who weren't Quakers, but realized that he had already gone too far.

Penny sat silently for a moment with a hurt look. "Dost thou truly wish to know, or dost thou wish to ridicule?" she asked.

Charles paused. He was unhappy with the direction the conversation was taking and knew he had already offended her. It didn't matter whether she thought God spoke to her or not. He only needed to know one thing, the one thing he could not ask directly: Was there, or was there not, any purpose for him to continue to call on her? "I want to know," he said carefully. "It doesn't mean that I will accept it, but I want to understand what you believe and what's important to you."

She nodded. "That is fair; I could not ask more. Sometimes God tells one what is right and what is wrong, what thou must do and what thou must not do. At other times he explains the meaning and importance of things. And sometimes he just brings one joy and contentment."

"So what God says, or what you think God says, is more important than what your preachers say," Charles persisted, trying for a clear answer to his central concern.

"We have no priests or preachers in the way you mean it," she said. "But yes, what God says is more important than what any man says, or any rules laid down by man—even the rules of religion."

Charles thought he understood this much of what she had told him: She thought herself free to make up her own mind about who she would see or marry. After that he felt more at ease, and they talked about other things. Rather, he mostly talked and she listened attentively. He told her about how and when he'd been sent to sea, the ships he'd served on and the places he'd been. He did not tell her about the battle at St. Vincent or the circumstances under which he'd been promoted to commander or the money he'd been awarded. He described his family home at Tattenall and his hopes of buying an estate of his own.

At one point a maid appeared with a tray bearing some biscuits and two cups of hot chocolate. Charles took the opportunity to ask the whereabouts of his sister and Winchester.

"Oh, they've gone out for a walk," the maid answered.

As soon as they were alone again, Penny said, "I like thy sister. I think she's a wonder."

"It was six years before I'd seen her last week. I hardly recognized her," Charles said with some warmth.

"But it's more than her personal beauty," Penny said, "although she has that in abundance. It's the joy within her that shines, and her openness and generosity."

A small cloud passed over Charles's face as he thought of Ellie and Winchester being "out for a walk," a worry that Penny's phrase about Ellie's generosity awakened in him.

"What?" Penny asked. "Art thou uneasy about thy sister?"

"Yes," Charles said, thankful to have someone to share his concerns with. "I'm not sure what to do—or not to do—about her and Stephen Winchester. She's very taken with him."

"Any woman would be. He's beautiful," Penelope said. "Hast thou spoken to her? Hast thou spoken to him? Dost thou trust them?"

"I have spoken to him, in a way. I haven't any idea what to say to her. And do I trust them? It's not a question of trust. It's a question of what I can imagine."

"Doth she have anyone to advise her?" Penny asked. "A relative or older friend?"

"There's only my brother John and me." He thought about his brother's evident lack of experience with women. "I don't think John would be of much help, either."

Penny nibbled on her lower lip, then said, "Would it be helpful if I conversed with her?"

"About what?" Charles asked.

"About womanly things," she answered promptly. "About things that are otherwise none of thy concern. And thou must discourse with Stephen Winchester in more clearly defined terms."

Charles was almost disappointed when Ellie and Winchester returned. Ellie looked radiantly happy and Winchester slightly perplexed. Charles guessed that Stephen had said something that Ellie had taken as a compliment but that he had meant as a suggestion. Whatever it was, Charles resolved to talk to his lieutenant at the earliest opportunity.

Penny motioned for Ellie to sit next to her, and Charles overheard her asking his sister to tea the next day. Then she leaned and whispered something in Ellie's ear, and both women laughed. On parting, Charles asked Penny if he could call on her again. "I hope thou wilt," she answered, "but not tomorrow."

Charles sent Attwater with Ellie in the carriage for her visit with Penny Brown the following day. After the noon meal he collected Winchester, and the two walked through the village to the abandoned Howell manor house, the old Tattenall Hall, so Charles could examine it a second time. In the beginning they talked about the *Louisa*, how work on her would be progressing at the Plymouth yards, and speculating about what duty she might be assigned to.

Walking around the house and examining its vine-covered exterior, Charles changed topics: "May I ask what your intentions are toward my sister?" he said directly.

Winchester cleared his throat and seemed to become absorbed with some architectural detail of the building's construction, perhaps a cornice on the gable end of the roof high above. "What do you mean?" he asked innocently.

"What do you think I mean?" Charles demanded. "The two of you goggle incessantly at each other like moonstruck . . . somethings. You're hardly ever out of each other's company."

"Well," Winchester looked uncomfortable, "I didn't think it was that obvious."

"Not *obvious*?" Charles said, almost angrily. "Look, I know she's pretty and—er, well—desirable, and that she's very attracted to you. She'd probably do anything for you if you asked her. What I want to know is, what are you thinking of asking her?"

"Oh," Winchester said. He swallowed hard and his eyes darted everywhere except at Charles. "I was thinking of asking her to marry me."

Charles stood, stunned. "Dear God help us," he muttered finally. He knew from direct experience that years at sea, punctuated by dalliances with mercenary ladies at various ports of call, did strange things to a man and his matrimonial inclinations. Many wealthy, even titled, officers had married barmaids or innkeeper's daughters, even actresses or prostitutes—virtually the first woman they met on shore who treated them half-decently. This problem did not apply to Charles himself, of course, since he was older and more experienced, but Winchester was obviously smitten. "Do you know what you're saying? You've only known her two days. She's only sixteen."

"Yes, sir," Winchester replied, the starch of defiance in his voice. "She's almost seventeen. My mother was fifteen when—"

"I don't care if your mother was still crawling on all fours," Charles growled. "We're talking about my sister here. And don't call me 'sir.' What would your father say?"

Winchester's voice roise. "I don't give a damn what my father says. And I'm sorry she's your sister, but you asked my intentions and I've told you. Besides, you're doing the same thing."

"The hell I am!" Charles snapped. "That's entirely different."

"How?" Winchester shot back. "How is it so different?"

"How is that different? How? Because—because I'm a commander and you're a lieutenant. That's how. I mean, I'm older than you. I'm wiser, too. It's clear as day." Charles heard the words as they came out of his mouth and realized how absurd they sounded. "Hell's fire," he said after a moment. "You'd be a lucky man."

"Yes, sir," Winchester replied, breathing hard.

"Oh, stop with the 'sirs,'" Charles said resignedly. "You're talking about becoming my brother-in-law."

"I didn't think about that," Winchester said, a grin on his face. "Maybe I'll reconsider."

"Have you spoken to Ellie about this?"

"Not directly," Winchester said seriously. "I made an allusion yesterday, something about her being the sunshine in the springtime of our lives together, but I'm not sure she caught my drift."

"God, you're poetical," Charles said. "Here are the standing orders," he went on, remembering Penny's instructions for him to be as clear as possible. "No—er, relations—without a priest having blessed it. And even so you'll have to talk to John first. He's her guardian."

———

THE FOLLOWING SEVERAL days passed in a blur of activity. Early the next morning a crew of builders showed up—carpenters, masons, thatchers, roofers, glaziers, painters—to begin the repair and refurbishing of Edgemont Hall. Soon the air was crowded with the ringing of hammers, the rasp of saws, and the chatter of workmen passing to and fro. At midmorning a coach and four arrived, the horses steaming from exertion. Two well-dressed men emerged, a very wide middle-aged accountant named Mr. Rhodes and a young, more naturally proportioned assistant named Mr. Smith. They had been dispatched by Thaddeus Edwards, Mr. Rhodes announced, in response to Captain Edgemont's inquiry about the purchase of the Howell estate. Mr. Rhodes and Mr. Smith took two full days, insisting Charles accompany them, investigating every aspect of the Howell buildings and property, as well as other available properties in the area. They also spent a day in Chester on the tax records at the Registry Office. In the end the accountant approved of the purchase of the estate in its entirety, mentioned a sum, and recommended acquiring a second property of about one thousand acres adjoining Edgemont Hall. This was to be joined with the family estate in return for giving Charles half-ownership of the whole, including forgiveness of the monies he had already lent his brother. "Mr. Edwards," Mr. Rhodes said confidentially, "feels very positively toward investing in agriculture at the moment and feels crop prices will rise significantly as the war with France progresses." Mr. Rhodes then offered his legal and financial expertise to bring the matter to completion.

Charles went to talk with his brother. They had a long discussion, eventually agreeing to the proposal for joint ownership of an expanded Edgemont estate, which John would manage. John also agreed to look after his brother's other property while Charles was at sea. With everything in place, Charles told Mr. Rhodes to make it so.

Around ten the next morning a navy courier arrived unexpectedly and asked to speak with Commander Charles Edgemont of His Majesty's Navy on official business. Attwater called him from the stables, where he was saddling Pendle; he was about to call on Penny to tell her about his new estates. When informed about the courier, Charles's heart sank. More than likely he was to deliver orders for Charles to report to Plymouth immediately, or at least sooner than expected, due to some emergency or another. He left the horse in its stall and, muttering obscenities to himself, went to meet the courier.

"Commander Edgemont, sir?" the man inquired as Charles approached.

"Yes," Charles answered.

"I'm sorry to intrude, sir, but Admiral Livingston—he's the port admiral at Liverpool—has asked to inquire as to your availability for a temporary command of not more than one month's duration. I am to return with your answer."

Charles relaxed. It was an offer he could refuse without incurring the displeasure of the Admiralty. "What sort of command?" he asked, although he already knew what answer he would give.

"The brig *Lomond,* sir, twelve guns. You'd perform duties as required by the local admiral in the Irish Sea for about one month while her usual commander recovers from an illness. You would be expected to report in a week's time."

This was easy. He could well imagine what the "duties as required" for a tiny brig would be: carrying dispatches and supplies to the larger warships on the Irish station, keeping a lookout for a French invasion fleet (there had been an unsuccessful attempt by the French to invade Ireland only months before), and suppressing the smugglers and privateers who abounded in the area. It might have been an interesting challenge at another time, but he had a larger and more powerful frigate awaiting him, and he was in any case involved in the much more engaging pursuit of Penny Brown. The privateers and smugglers would have to wait.

"Please convey my regrets to Admiral Livingston," Charles answered. "I am flattered by his offer, but family responsibilities require my attention here. I must decline."

"I see, sir," the courier responded evenly. "I will inform the admiral of your decision."

AS SOON AS the courier was given refreshment in the house and had departed, Charles returned to the stables, finished saddling Pendle, and left to call on Penny in an exuberant mood, full of the news and possibilities he was bursting to share with her. He was, he realized as the stallion trotted along, a made man: a substantial landowner, a ship's captain in demand, and, in every sense but one, set for life. The only things he lacked were a loving wife and a growing number of children at home.

As he trotted up the drive, he saw her kneeling on the ground by a flowerbed at the front of her father's house, pruning some rose bushes with her good arm. Charles called to her and waved. She put aside her shears, rose, dusted off her dress, straightened her bonnet, and stood waiting for him quietly.

Charles dismounted and tied Pendle to a post. "I have great news," he said. "I'm now a landowner, a real landowner. I've bought the old Howell place and more. You remember, I told you about it. We'll have to decide on a new name for the place. It has a beautiful large house. Imagine."

"I am happy for thee," she said, smiling, but not smiling as much as he would have expected.

"I want you to come and see it," he said. Then, sensing something had changed in her, the edge of his exuberance dulled. "It's beautiful, all hills and fields and trees . . . a stream . . ." His voice trailed off. "What's the matter?"

Penny rubbed the back of her hand across her forehead. Charles thought she looked unhappy. "I must discourse with thee," she said.

"Of course, we can talk anytime, about anything you like. But I want to show it to you," he persisted.

"I dare not," she answered.

"Oh, we can bring your mother or brother for a chaperone. That would be all right. Or I could bring Ellie."

"That is not the reason. We must discourse first."

"Discourse about what?" He felt disappointed by her lack of enthusiasm and a little put-upon. What about his grand news?

"We must discuss thy being a soldier in the navy." She said it with her feet planted firmly on the ground, facing him squarely, as if preparing to resist him.

"We talked about that already," he said, stiffening his back. "The navy is my life. I thought that was settled."

She shook her head. "No, that was not settled. I said that I would labor on it further with thee."

"What on earth does 'labor with' mean?"

"It means I will discuss, persuade, argue about it with thee. I told thee, I have difficulties with thy being in the navy."

"All right, all right," Charles said, raising his hands, trying to be reasonable. "What's wrong with my being in the navy? It's an honorable profession. I'm defending our country."

"It is a violent and destructive profession. When thou dost violence against other people, thou dost violence against God."

"No, I don't," Charles insisted. "I don't attack churches or priests. I fight for England against the French and her allies at sea."

"But the French, the Spanish, the Dutch, all of them are God's people," Penny insisted. "To do violence against any person is against God's law, 'Thou shalt not kill.'"

"Well, maybe the Dutch," Charles conceded. "But the French and Spanish are both Catholic . . ." He stopped, sensing that continuing this line of argument would resolve nothing. Instead he said, "Do you remember what you said to me the other day about listening to God?"

Penny nodded her head warily.

"God tells me I should be in the navy."

"God told you that?" she said incredulously.

"I didn't hear a voice saying, 'Charles, I want you to be in the navy.' But I am content being a naval officer, and my conscience is clear. I feel in my heart that I am doing the right thing."

He saw her expression harden. "So thou wilt not leave the navy?" she said.

"Oh, fine," Charles snapped. "This isn't fair. You're asking me to choose between two things I love—my commission and you."

Penny's eyes widened. "Didst thou say 'love'?"

"Care about," he hastily corrected himself. "I care about you. You know that."

She lowered her head so that the bonnet hid her face. "I have a tenderness for thee also," she said carefully. "That is why thy being a soldier is important. In addition to the other things, thou couldst be injured badly or killed. If thy profession is doing violence to others, it may also do violence to thy body or thy soul."

"If something were to happen to me, if we were . . . joined, you would be well cared for," he said.

"There are many things more important than wealth," she answered. Then she looked up and said, "Let us talk of other things."

Charles welcomed the opportunity to change the subject of their conversation. "About visiting my land?" he asked.

"No, I cannot," she said gently. "It would be a step. I cannot take steps now."

"If we can sit on that bench, I'll tell you about Ellie and Winchester," he said hopefully. They walked to a long wooden bench at the front of the house and sat, side by side, a little apart. Charles told her of his talk with Winchester and of Winchester's declared aspirations to marry his sister. Penny described almost word for word Ellie's visit and her own advices on appropriate female deportment with respect to ardent men, some of which they laughed about together.

"I don't think it's a bad match, thy sister and Stephen Winchester," Penny said at length. "I wish Ellie were a little older and that they could have had more time to get to know each other in a normal way. But she admires him greatly, and I think he would be a good and loving husband to her."

Charles carefully took her good hand and held it in his own. "Something similar might be said about you and me," he said softly.

Penny removed her hand from his and brushed it against his cheek. "I know," she said, her voice almost a whisper, "but it's not the same for thee and me. Thou art being true to thy beliefs about fighting and war, and I must be true to mine. Thou wouldn't want me otherwise, and I couldn't live with myself if I weren't."

"You can't mean that," he said, even though he was pretty sure now that she did.

"I mean," she said hesitantly, "that I don't see how we can . . . continue, with this between us."

Charles kicked at the dirt in the path and felt a heavy weight settle in his chest. It was bitterly ironic that two of the things that attracted him to her the most, her directness and independence, would keep them apart. He didn't trust himself to speak.

"I know it's not easy for thee," she said.

"Is that all?" he managed. "Is that the end? Because of my . . ." He left the thought unfinished.

She turned and faced him with tears on her cheeks. "Oh, Charles," she said, "I'm so sorry for thee. I understand thou had great plans. I don't know what to do. I don't think it can be." She was silent for a moment, then said, "I think we shouldn't see each other for a time. I want to be fair to thee. I don't want to keep thee hanging on false hopes."

"I see," Charles said, not really seeing at all. The sun had already set, he noticed, and it would be dark before he reached home. "I'd best be going," he said, not wanting to leave.

Penny nodded.

"Wilt thou ask Ellie to continue to visit me?" she said, wiping at her cheeks with her hand.

"I'll tell her," Charles said. There seemed to be nothing more to say, so he rose from the bench and started toward his horse. Penny followed close behind. Before he could put his foot in the stirrup, she took hold of his arm and turned him toward her.

"I want to thank thee," she said evenly. "Thou hast been a good friend to me. I want thee to know that I care deeply for thee and always will, no matter what happens between us."

"Thank you," Charles said, a feeling of loss enveloping him. He took her hand and kissed it lightly. "I'm sorry if I caused you any discomfort." With that he heaved himself onto Pendle's back. They exchanged terse good-byes and he trotted down the lane in the failing light. On the way home he decided that, if he left first thing in the morning, he could probably reach Liverpool in time to take command of the little brig before it was given to someone else.

FIVE

"**W**HICH SHIP, SIR?" THE STROKE OARSMAN ASKED AS Charles and Attwater settled uncomfortably in the riverboat's sternsheets, their sea chests wedged between the thwarts in front of their knees. A driving rain pelted the river's surface, with the wind blowing a small chop and driving the wet into every crevice and opening of Charles's boat cloak no matter how tightly he drew it around him. "The brig *Lomond,*" he replied.

"All right Bob, together now," the wherryman said to his companion on the opposite oar. "Remember what I said. Together means we both pull at the same time."

Bob, a thick-necked, dark-haired man who looked to be in his early thirties, nodded slowly, his eyes watching his companion's oar like a hawk, even though it was still shipped.

"The *Lomond,* she's upriver off Whitby," the stroke said, turning to Charles. "You'll have to give Bob here some leeway. Got hit on the head by a falling spar when we wuz messmates on the ol' *London.* Ain't been the same since. He wuz my best mate, though. I kind of looks after him."

"That's kind of you," Charles replied. "I'm sure he appreciates it." It had crossed his mind more than once that it was a harsh world for crippled or otherwise disabled seamen. They were a common sight in all the port towns, often missing limbs, or disfigured by scars or the pox, or wasted by some other disease. When no longer useful, they were simply discharged as unfit for service and left to be a burden on others or to fend for themselves. A few were reluctantly accepted onto parish poor rolls, some looked after by their families, if they could afford it. The rest died early, or became beggars or thieves. Bob was one of the lucky ones. The navy, for whom they had given their health, accepted no responsibility. For many, Charles thought, it would have been better if they'd been killed instead of injured.

"It's no trouble," the stroke said. "He pulls real good once you get him started." With that he unshipped his oar and shoved it against the jetty. As the boat fell off he said, "Now, Bob," and both men dipped their oars into the water. "Mind if'n I ask yer business on the *Lomond,* sir? If'n you don't mind my ask'n, that is." The boat moved into the current, well out of the crowded shipping channel. Although it was only early afternoon, the other ships anchored in the harbor were mere outlines in the downpour, the riverbanks and buildings beyond almost totally obscured.

"I'm her temporary commander," Charles answered, the wet and the cold wind off the water making him distinctly uncomfortable.

"Oooh," Bob intoned. It was the first sound Charles had heard him make and sounded deep and meaningful.

"I told you so," the stroke said to his mate a moment later, nodding significantly. "Didn't I tell you so?"

Charles and Attwater had left Edgemont Hall at first light the morning after Charles's conversation with Penny. They had driven in the carriage to the Liverpool port admiral's office, which they reached before noon. He had decided that taking up the command was the most sensible thing he could do. It would be his first real command, not counting his few days in charge of the battered *Argonaut,* and he thought that working with some other officer's trained and disciplined crew would be good practice before taking control of his own ship. He also hoped that a busy month at sea would keep him from brooding on the very painful subject of Penny Brown. She had cut him firmly adrift and it was time he found a new course. Only one thing worried him about leaving home— Stephen Winchester had declined to join him. Charles had requested, almost to the point of begging, that Winchester come along as a volunteer, but the lieutenant had steadfastly refused. In the end all he could do was to remind his lieutenant what he had said about priests and to instruct John to keep a very close eye on him and Ellie at all times. "Left to their own devices, they'd be like rabbits" were his exact words.

Although the port admiral was temporarily away from Liverpool, it was quickly arranged with the admiral's representative, one Captain Alphonse Dawson, that Charles should take command of the *Lomond* immediately. Dawson expressed surprise that Charles had arrived so soon; he hadn't been expected for a week or longer. The courier who had been sent to inquire as to his availability, and to whom Charles had refused the day before, had in fact not yet returned. As soon as the necessary orders were drawn up and signed, Charles and Attwater set off to find a riverboat to take them to his new ship.

"What do you mean, 'I told you so'?" Charles asked the stroke oarsman.

"Oh, sir, we shouldn't be talk'n about it. We'd be out of line, we would be," the waterman answered. Then, to his mate, "Bear a little to larboard. No, here, just ease yer oar a bit." Without a blush he said to Charles, "The *Lomond*'s capt'n, he's a sot. I know it for a fact. We rowed 'im to shore a week or two back. Shak'n like a loose jib too close to the wind, he was, and see'n things. Fit to be tied, he was." Nodding his head forward, he added, "That's her over there."

Charles peered through the falling rain, using his hand to shield his eyes, and made out the hull of a smallish brig anchored at the bow and stern about a cable and a half's length from shore. Her masts were indistinct against the backdrop of the land. From this distance she looked normal enough, but as they neared he began to notice details. Just under her taffrail the name LOMOND was carved in large block letters that had once been painted a brilliant gold. Now chipped and peeling, the lettering seemed to read ION NI. Both her masts were rigged but the yards were badly askew, hung at various angles fore and aft and tilted haphazardly to port or starboard. Several bumboats that normally ferried out local merchants selling all manner of goods, from clothing and tobacco to spirits and women, seemed to be more or less permanently tied up alongside.

By this time, rain or no rain, Charles and his boat were close enough that they should have been hailed by the watch on deck. No one seemed to be on deck and he heard no challenge. Charles began to suspect that all was not going to go as smoothly as he had hoped.

"She ain't exactly a smart ship, is she?" the stroke offered.

"Row around her. I want a closer look."

"It'll cost ye extra, sir," the stroke said, nudging Bob to lift his oar so he could swing the skiff to starboard. "Sixpence extra."

"All right."

"Each," he added.

"Fine," Charles muttered at the boatman.

As the small boat started along the side of the *Lomond*, Charles's dismay increased. The brig's sails were carelessly furled so that the huge folds bellied toward the deck as they filled with rainwater. The sail halyards and clew lines hung sloppily, poorly fastened or flapping in the wind, and some actually trailed overboard in the water alongside. As they passed under the bow, he could see that she had been a trim ship once, with fine lines, a little scrollwork on her bow, and a sharp cutwater. Now she had gone seedy from lack of paint and attention. On the port-side hammock netting clothing was hung out haphazardly, perhaps to dry before the rains had started.

It was at this point that a squeaky cry came from the ship, "Ahoy, what boat?" The high-pitched breaking voice reminded Charles of Billy Bowles from the old *Argonaut*.

"*Lomond!*" the stroke oar yelled back.

There was a silence before the someone on the deck said, "Just a moment." Charles thought it a strange reply to an announcement that the brig's commanding officer was about to come on board.

"Lay alongside. I'll climb up by the mizzen chains," Charles ordered.

"No, t'other way," the waterman said to Bob, and in a minute the wherry bumped against the *Lomond*'s side. Charles stood in the rocking craft and grabbed the heavy chains attached to a narrow platform on the ship's side and heaved himself up, then over the railing and onto the deck. He had discarded his boat cloak for the climb and the rain already began to soak through his new uniform coat. Almost immediately, a ship's boy, possibly twelve or thirteen, padded toward him. He was barefoot, clad in sodden oversized clothing, and incongruously carried a telescope almost as tall as he was on a strap over his shoulder.

"I told you to wait," the boy said indignantly.

"You call me 'sir,'" Charles answered. "You say, 'I told you to wait, *sir,*' and if you talk back to me again I'll have your behind striped. Now go below and fetch the lieutenant. Leave the glass by the binnacle." Charles waited, looking around him as the boy darted off, fuming at the sloppiness and disorder around him.

A disheveled and unshaven man in most of what might have been a British naval lieutenant's uniform appeared moments later, still tucking his shirt in as he came. Charles noted that they were about the same age and build, with the same short dark hair. He took an instant dislike to the unkempt lieutenant who could allow his ship to fall into such a state.

"I'm sorry, sir," the lieutenant said as he stopped in front of Charles. "Didn't expect you for another week at best. Be more presentable if we'd known."

"I should hope so," Charles answered, looking pointedly at the mess around him. In addition to the tangles of rope, the decks were filthy, there were overturned buckets, items of clothing, including women's clothing, and other equipment lying here and there. *Christ, Algerian slave galleys must be cleaner than this.* He looked at the officer more closely. His eyes were bleary and he swayed slightly but noticeably on his feet.

"Who are you?" Charles demanded.

"Tillman, sir. I'm the first lieutenant. I'm in charge while Commander Freemont is away."

"I'm in charge now," Charles snapped, his dismay turning to disgust. "My steward and sea chests are in a boat alongside. Have them brought aboard immediately. Pay the boatmen the going rate and two shillings extra."

"Yes, sir."

"Then have the women cleared off the ship and the spirits put under guard."

Tillman looked dismayed. "But, sir—"

"But what?" Charles snapped.

"Nothing, sir."

"As soon as the women are gone, call the ship's company aft and I'll read myself in. After that, we're going to put this ship in order."

"But, sir," Tillman interjected again.

The last thing Charles wanted to hear was an argument. An angry response was not far from his tongue. With an effort he restrained himself and said, "Yes, what?"

"Captain Freemont, our regular captain," Tillman sputtered on, "he let us have some time to relax a bit in port. He liked an efficient ship. He didn't care much how smart she was. All that polishing and flemished lines and all is a lot of foolery in his opinion. He often said, it's how well she—"

This was getting to be a longish speech and Charles seriously doubted that the *Lomond* was any more efficient than she was smart. "Captain Freemont is not among us at present," he broke in sharply. "Flemished lines are one thing, loose yards and guns are another. See to my steward and sea chests. Then the women. Then call the hands. Is that clear?"

"Yes, sir," the lieutenant responded, drawing himself up at the rebuke.

"I will be in my cabin. Have me called when the men are assembled." Charles turned to leave, then stopped and turned back. "And, Mr. Tillman, I do believe in a smart ship as well as an effective one. Including her officers."

"Yes, sir. I see, sir." The lieutenant was standing rigidly erect. He felt vaguely sorry for the man, but the *Lomond* in the condition she was in was an insult to the navy. If he was to accomplish anything during his brief command, things would have to change quickly. If that was hard on this lieutenant, then so be it. Charles took a moment to look over the masts, rigging, and deck again, grimaced, and then made his way aft toward the ladderway and the captain's cabin. He was looking for the key to Commander Freemont's desk when Attwater arrived with four seamen carrying their chests.

"Damnation," Charles swore, his frustration with the desk, the first lieutenant, and the deplorable state of the ship coming to the surface. "How do you open this thing?"

"'Ere, sir. Don't you fret none." The elderly steward reached up and felt along a ledge above the desk and almost immediately came down with a small black key. "That's where Captain Wood, 'e kept his key, sir. Hidden like, where no one couldn't find it."

"Thank you." Charles let out a long breath and some of the anger and disappointment seemed to leave him. "Arrange things as you see fit. When you have the time, ask the cook to make some coffee. He should probably make enough for the crew to have at dinner instead of their evening grog. I think they've had enough of that for now."

"That would be all of your stores, then," Attwater said indignantly. "We ain't had no time to buy any proper captain's stores. Coffee is all I brought. The cook, he won't have none."

"I'll send you into town to buy whatever you need, first chance," Charles promised. He realized that having the proper food and other little luxuries in hand was important to his steward, probably more important than it was to him. "In the meantime, give the coffee to the cook after you've finished unpacking."

While Attwater began to sort through their sea chests, Charles removed his hat and sword and hung them on pegs set into the bulkhead, then dropped heavily into the chair in front of the desk and unlocked the drawer. Inside he found the captain's log, the *Lomond*'s muster book, her punishment book, accounts, and the other official records that would tell him a lot about what kind of ship and crew he had inherited. With no appetite to examine them, he stared at the open drawer for a moment, thinking about what he already knew and what he should do about it. He was about to reach in and take out the ship's muster book when a sudden tumult of running feet, shouted orders, loud screams, and screeching obscenities erupted from the deck just above his head.

"Dear Mother of God, sir," Attwater exclaimed, "it's a mutiny." He rummaged frantically through Charles's sea chest. "I'll have your pistols in a minute."

Charles listened, trying to make some sense of the commotion. Then he grinned. "It's not a mutiny, it's the women. They've been asked to leave the ship. Apparently they don't like it. Just a dry jacket, Attwater. I think I'll go on deck."

The little brig was flush-decked, with no fore- or aftercastle, so Charles climbed the aft ladderway onto what served as her quarterdeck near the stern. He smiled broadly and almost laughed at the confused melee in progress midships. About a dozen seamen, under the command of a midshipman, were attempting to herd sixteen or eighteen women over the side and into the waiting boats. The women, clustered into several small knots of dubious femininity, were at least reluctant, if not openly rebellious. Charles heard a riot of shouted orders and answering obscenities and saw that not much progress was being made. "Now, Poll," he clearly heard a bosun's mate implore, "the new captain wants you off the ship. You have to go, it's orders." In answer he got, "I'm no Poll, you fucking whoremaster's bastard. And the captain can kiss my arse. I'm a free woman." From another corner came a loudly screeched, "Ye push me one more time, ye faggot, and I'll cut off yer balls and feed 'em to the fish." At least the rain was letting up.

Charles grinned and decided it was time he intervened personally to restore order using the authority and prestige of his uniform. He straightened his hat and started forward, then halted. One of the women around the midshipman lifted her bag and hit the unfortunate boy on the head with it. Then four of the women jumped on him, pulled him to the deck, kicking, scratching and punching, swearing loudly all the while.

Charles noticed someone standing near the ship's wheel almost doubled over in laughter at the spectacle. "You there," he ordered, "come here, please."

"Aye aye, sir?" the man said as he approached, struggling unsuccessfully to assume a serious demeanor. Charles saw that he wore a buff waistcoat under a black jacket. One of the warrant officers, he guessed.

"Who are you?" Charles asked abruptly.

"Wilson, sir, quartermaster. And might I inquire who you be?"

"Edgemont. I'm to be the temporary commander of this barge."

"I see, sir. Welcome aboard," Wilson said noncommittally.

"Yes," Charles answered, glancing toward the waist and seeing that the battle had now become general, with the few seamen still standing retreating toward the bow. "Are there any marines on board?"

"Aye, six, I think. Under Sergeant MacPherson."

Charles paused for a moment. It was time to end this, and end it quickly. "Fetch him and his men. Tell them to bring their muskets, loaded. And I want them in proper uniform."

Wilson looked at him in horror. "Loaded, sir? You're not going to . . ."

"That's none of your affair. Get them now, quick as you can."

The marines, more or less smart in their red coats, black hats, and clayed belts, arrived at a run up the ladderway soon after. Their officer, a tough-looking, bandy-legged Scot, ordered them into a line. His men presented arms and then shouldered them.

"Sergeant MacPherson, SIR!" the marine officer almost shouted. "The *Lomond*'s complement of Royal Marines all present and sober, SIR!"

Charles could tell at a glance that this last was not entirely true. Indeed, the sergeant himself looked somewhat under the weather. Still, it was the best he had at the moment. "Sergeant, I want you to take control of the deck and restore order immediately. Then you will assist those women off the ship. You may begin by firing a volley over the port rail."

"Aye aye, sir," MacPherson answered. Then, turning to his men, he snapped, "Left FACE! Shoulder ARMS! Aim high, boys, FIRE!"

The volley sounded like an explosion in a barrel, and Charles was pleased to see the mass writhing on the decks forward pause and look aft.

"Fix bayonets. Forward, MARCH."

The women, at least, began struggling to their feet. The seamen, looking sheepish and not that much the worse for wear, soon followed. To Charles's relief, the marines quickly cleared the deck. Presented with the threat of armed force, the women retreated with some indignity to their boats and were gone. The rain tapered away to a dull drizzle and the *Lomond*'s decks seemed unnaturally quiet despite the dozen or more seamen standing in the waist with the now-idle marines. Charles suddenly realized that they were all watching him with a mixture of curiosity and expectation.

"Pass the word for Lieutenant . . . er, Tillman," he said to Wilson. He then waited self-consciously, standing with this hands clasped behind his back and thinking about what he should do about the mess he found himself in. He was only the *Lomond*'s temporary commander—how much should he interfere with another man's ship? He knew the answer—as much as he thought was needed. Strangely, it made him feel a little easier. The condition the ship was in wasn't entirely the men's, or even the *Lomond*'s officers', fault. It was Freemont's. He'd set the tone and the expectations that his officers were to follow. Charles wondered how the man had kept his command so long.

To his relief, Tillman arrived promptly in a clean if wrinkled uniform and freshly shaved. There was a still-bleeding nick on his chin, as if to prove that he'd just done it. Charles softened marginally. Perhaps it was time to start on a fresh footing.

"You've cut yourself," he said by way of greeting.

"Yes, sir. I'm sorry, sir. I was in a hurry."

"It's all right, Mr. Tillman, I've done so myself under similar circumstances. You may assemble the hands aft. It's time I read myself in."

"Yes, sir," the lieutenant said automatically. He glanced sideways at Charles, as if surprised by the change in his temper since their last meeting.

"Bygones, Mr. Tillman. It's what we do next that matters. The hands please, sometime this week."

"All hands on deck!" Tillman immediately bellowed in a voice that Charles thought could probably be heard in Ireland. "All hands on deck by divisions, captain's orders!"

"That should do it," Charles observed.

"Sorry, sir. We don't have a drummer. Well, we do, but the drum is stove in."

"I'm shocked."

Charles watched with interest as the remainder of the crew staggered up the ladderways and groped toward their petty officers. Some were clearly drunk; others looked as if they had been sleeping it off. None seemed in a very lively condition. One by one the divisions were reported to the lieutenant in the time-honored formula as, "All present and sober."

"All present and counted, sir," Tillman said tactfully after the last report was received.

"Thank you," Charles said, and stepped forward to where he could be seen and heard more clearly. The fifty or sixty men gathered on the deck in front of him were the sorriest-looking he had ever seen. He didn't know the exact size of the *Lomond*'s complement yet, but that seemed about right. Without preamble he reached into his coat pocket, took out the orders he had been given, unfolded them, and read loudly and slowly. "To Commander Charles Edgemont, Esquire; hereby commander, His Majesty's brig *Lomond.* Sir, you are hereby requested and required to report onboard His Majesty's brig of war *Lomond,* presently moored in the River Mersey at Liverpool. You are directed to take temporary command of her until such time as you are relieved, *requiring all officers and company to behave with strict obedience to your orders.* You are also required to proceed pursuant to the General Printed Instructions and those orders you will receive on board from any superior officer of His Majesty's Service. *Nor you nor any of you may fail except at your peril.* Signed, Captain Alphonse Dawson, Acting Port Admiral, Liverpool."

When he finished reading, adding emphasis as he saw fit, every hand on the ship looked at least somewhat more sober than when he had begun. *And well they should,* he thought. By the act of reading his orders out loud, he had officially taken command of their ship and every one of their lives. He could with impunity order harsher punishments than the king could, up to and including death by hanging if he saw fit, all without a trial or a defense, or any chance of appeal to a higher court, or indeed any court. And the men knew nothing about him except his name and that it was not the same as their regular captain's.

He had considered making a short speech to introduce himself and explain how he intended to run the ship and what he expected of them in return. Most captains did. Some spoke of patriotism and calls to duty, others to honor and glory, and some gave frankly evangelical appeals to follow Christ and seek salvation. But Charles had rejected the idea almost immediately. Most of the men were too drunk to listen anyway. Instead of telling, he would show them.

He carefully refolded his orders and placed them back in his pocket. With every eye in the ship still fixed on him, focused or otherwise, he turned to Tillman and in a voice just loud enough to be overheard by the closest of the assembled seamen, he said, "I will inspect the ship before supper. I will only concern myself with the main and lower decks. I don't want any of the crew sent aloft in the state they're in. No food will be served to anyone on board, including the officers, until I am satisfied."

"But, sir—," Tillman interjected.

"My God, you say 'but, sir' a lot. What is it this time?"

"We can't, sir. It's too much. The *Lomond* hasn't had a proper cleaning in months. The captain thought, er, other things more important. There's too much to do. It would take all night."

Charles listened. It was probably sound advice. Belowdecks must be a shambles. He didn't want to ask the impossible, but he did want to drive home the point that he expected a clean and well-ordered ship, and the *Lomond* was going to become one whether Tillman or the crew liked it or not. "All right," he said, pulling Tillman aside and speaking in a softer voice, "I will make an inspection before supper. I'll overlook a lot, but I want to see progress made in putting this floating piggery in order. That itself will take some time, and I expect supper will be delayed an hour or so."

"Yes, sir. We can manage that with some effort."

"And one other thing. The crew is in bad enough condition. A good stint of hard work will help, but bullying won't. No starters or beatings. No punishments of any kind will be meted out. I want the officers to set an example, not browbeat them. If there are serious breaches of discipline, bring the offenders directly to me, and let them know I will be hard on them." It wouldn't hurt if the crew thought him strict or even harsh. He also wasn't worried that the officers would think him one of those captains who coddled the men at their expense. Everyone would know what kind of a commander he was within the next few days.

Tillman swallowed and gave a tentative, "Yes, sir."

"See to it," Charles said, nodding his dismissal. "Send the purser and cook aft. I'll be in my cabin."

The first thing he noticed on approaching his cabin door was the armed marine standing sentry outside. The man seemed reasonably sober and snapped to attention as Charles approached. At least Sergeant MacPherson had seen to that without having to be reminded. It was something.

"Coffee," he said to Attwater as he entered the cabin. "Three cups."

"Three, sir?"

"Yes, three, and quickly. I'm expecting the cook and purser momentarily and we're not serving any more spirits today."

The purser arrived first, a dour, plump man who was stone sober. He came carrying his ledger book. The cook, tall, thin, and missing his left arm from the elbow down, appeared red-nosed and unreasonably cheerful. Charles gave them each a mug of coffee, although he doubted the purser needed it.

"What's the state of the ship's provisions?" he asked without preamble.

"We've plenty, zur," the cook answered with an inappropriate grin. "Salt pork, salt beef, some still good. Plenty of biscuit, only a little weevily. Plenty of—"

"Any fresh meat?" Charles interrupted. "Beef, mutton, chicken, anything like that?"

"No, zur."

"Any vegetables? Flour for gravy?"

"Yes, zur. We've plenty of dried peas, sacks o' them. No flour, though. The rats got it all." The cook looked puzzled for a moment at the line of questioning, then added, "The rats don't like the peas much. Like little rocks, they are."

Charles turned to the purser. "Take one of the ship's boats with my steward, the cook, and his mates, if they're sober, into Liverpool. I want you to purchase sufficient fresh meat, vegetables, and flour for tonight's supper. Keep a full accounting for me to sign; I expect the Navy Board will want to question me about it later. Mr. Attwater will be doing his own purchasing."

The purser nodded expressionlessly. "But, zur," the cook protested, "even if we're as quick as can be I'll never have such a meal ready by the first dogwatch."

"Supper will be delayed. But be quick about it. I don't want the men to wait any longer than necessary. I'll give you an extra hour."

"What sort of a meal?" the purser asked.

"A hot, healthy meal with fresh meat, vegetables, potatoes, and gravy. Buy some fresh bread if you can. I want the food to be enjoyable as well as filling. I'm going to eat it myself, so it had better be as appealing as you can make it."

THE NEXT MORNING he sent the bosun, his mates, and all the topmen aloft to unfurl the sails so they could dry, square the yards, and put the rigging in proper order. The remainder were set to polishing the bright-work with brick dust and grinding the decks with holystones until they were white. In the afternoon, the bilge, which stank like a cesspool, was pumped dry. River water was pumped in and then out again several times. The effect was instantly noticeable, if not completely gratifying. Supper that evening consisted of the normal salted meat from casks, dried peas, and biscuit, with a carefully measured ration of spirits afterward.

On Charles's third day on board the *Lomond* he set the men to replacing chaffed lines and cables in the rigging at the direction of the bosun, and to general repairs under the supervision of the ship's carpenter. It was amazing how many little things had been neglected and needed attention. With the gunner in tow, he personally examined each of the six-pounder cannon and ordered several of the restraining tackles replaced as well as all the flints in the firing mechanisms. He then directed that the guns and their carriages be painted. Late in the afternoon, with his first lieutenant, he conducted a thorough inspection, from mast-tops to the hold. In the end he was satisfied and told Tillman so while they were standing near the base of the foremast, where he was sure his words would be overheard by a number of the crew. "You and the men have worked hard," he said. "She looks like a proper king's ship. You should be proud." It was certain that his words would be passed to every corner of the ship within minutes. Tillman looked relieved.

Charles was pleased with what had been accomplished thus far, but the test of a ship (Freemont was right about this much) was in how she performed, not what she looked like. He looked forward to receiving orders from the admiral and wondered why they hadn't been delivered yet.

The next day, to give them something to do, he exercised the men at changing sails and running the guns in and out. He couldn't order practice with shot and powder, of course. They were still anchored in the Mersey and the noise might panic the citizenry. No orders or communications of any kind arrived from the port admiral or anyone else.

Friday morning he sent Tillman in a boat to Liverpool to inquire as to the admiral's pleasure. Charles set the men to tarring the rigging, and, when that was done, blackening the masts.

"Nothing," Tillman reported on his return. "We're to be informed in due course."

Charles knew that he would only command the *Lomond* for a month, maybe less. Almost a week of that had already passed. He wanted to be at sea, hunting for privateers or serving as lookout against a French invasion fleet. There were said to be plenty of privateers in all seasons, and a French fleet had sailed boldly into the Irish Sea only a few months before with a large body of troops for the purpose of aiding the rebellion in Ireland. Only bad weather and ill-luck had prevented them from landing. In the absence of an enemy threat, even carrying dispatches or escorting a convoy would be agreeable. He didn't want to ride at anchor while all his work went for nothing and the men grew bored. In that case, he thought, he might as well invite the women back.

On Saturday, out of desperation, he turned the men to painting the hull. There was sufficient black paint in the bosun's stores for the task. He had the gunports and the strakes between them painted white. He even sent Attwater in one of the ship's boats to buy a pot of gold paint for the carved lettering on the stern and the scrollwork by the beak. When all was done, he had himself rowed around and thought the old girl looked rather sharp. On Sunday he led a religious service, which he had never done before, the burial service on board *Argonaut* excepted. He read long sections from the Bible. It seemed to bore everyone.

Charles found himself pleased with his ship and crew. The *Lomond* looked clean, even businesslike, and the men seemed in good spirits. Except for the watch, he left his officers and crew to their own devices for the rest of the day and decided to personally call on the port admiral the first thing in the morning.

SIX

NORTH OR SOUTH? THAT WAS THE QUESTION. IT WAS ONE of those imponderables that had no real answer. Still, it might be important. There could be a hundred privateers or smugglers in the southern half of the Irish Sea at this moment and none in the north. Or it might be the other way around. One never knew, or at least Charles was sure that *he* didn't know. And he didn't want to ask Tillman.

"The anchor's aweigh, sir," Tillman reported. Charles already knew, of course. He had been standing next to the lieutenant as the men heaved on the loudly clanking capstan to winch the brig's bower up from the muddy bottom of Dublin Bay and laboriously catted it home. The *Lomond's* bow was already falling off with the wind and turning toward the sea. The tide was on the ebb, the wind sufficient and steady from due west. He would sail in either direction he wished. Should it be north or south? The northern channel was the route of most shipping from North America. South was closer to the privateers' home ports in France and Spain.

"Thank you, Mr. Tillman. You may sheet home the foresail and jib. As soon as her head's around, set all the sail she'll carry. Lay a course to make the mouth of the bay and then steer . . . north."

Tillman looked at him in surprise. "North, sir? What about Liverpool?"

"North," Charles repeated firmly. "As if toward Belfast or Glasgow or

Scapa Flow. We will return to Liverpool in due time. First, I want to see if there's anything interesting to the north."

"Aye aye, sir," Tillman said. "North it is. But if you're thinking of hunting privateers, then I'd head south. They're thicker down that way, if you pardon my saying so, sir."

Charles cleared his throat while he digested this. Which was more important, covering up for his ignorance and insisting on continuing to the north, or giving Tillman the satisfaction of having seen through him? "Thank you," he said finally. "Once we clear the bay you may make to the south."

"Aye aye, sir," the lieutenant said, trying unsuccessfully to suppress a smile. "You mean as if toward Wexford or Penzance or Buenos Aires."

Charles laughed. "Exactly," he said.

Today was Saturday. On the previous Monday, Charles had gone to the port admiral's office in Liverpool to plead for orders, any orders. He had the sinking feeling that no one in the admiral's office had any plans whatsoever for the *Lomond* until Commander Freemont returned. Charles's temporary command was only to be a caretaker's job, a nanny to the ship to see that nothing bad happened in the interim. Not surprisingly, the port admiral was still unavailable when Charles called, and Captain Dawson had no orders for him. "Just sit easy and relax," he'd said. "Enjoy yourself. You've only a few more weeks before Freemont will be back." Charles did not want to sit back and relax and said so. He argued for something, some task to do, however small. Anything that would allow him to take the *Lomond* to sea. In the end Dawson relented and very reluctantly allowed that Charles could use the *Lomond* to ferry a newly appointed colonel in the Irish Guard, his horses and entourage, to Dublin. "Mind, you'll have to clean the old girl up a bit," Dawson added. "It's not my place to say, but Freemont keeps her in a shocking state."

"Of course," Charles agreed. "She'll be presentable. The colonel is prepared to board before tomorrow afternoon?"

"Oh, no. Certainly not. He's from a very important family. Nobility, in fact. I shouldn't think he'd consent to embark for a week or more. His Lordship hasn't even been informed that transport is available. I'll have to find a courier to inquire as to his pleasure. We're shorthanded as it is."

"As the ship's captain, I would be most pleased to contact the colonel myself," Charles offered.

Dawson pursed his lips while considering the offer. "If you wish, but tactfully, of course."

"Of course."

"After all, there's no hurry, is there? It's only a week over to Dublin and back. A nice, leisurely trip. It doesn't matter if you leave this week or next."

"Well," Charles answered carefully, "Commander Freemont may recover sooner than expected. I shouldn't want to keep him waiting for his ship any longer than necessary." This was such a bald lie that he wondered how he could have said it so easily. If it were up to him, he would keep *Lomond* until his own ship was ready, and Freemont could rot on the beach. He also didn't want to return to Cheshire any sooner than necessary. After his disappointment, he wasn't sure if he ever wanted to return. He was better off at sea. At sea something distracting, even interesting, might happen.

"That's very considerate of you," Dawson replied. "But I wouldn't worry too much over when you return. All in good time." Which were exactly the words Charles had hoped to hear.

After receiving his written orders, Charles went directly to the lodgings of his soon-to-be passenger. It proved to be an elegant brick house on the edge of Liverpool with extensive stables and manicured gardens. A uniformed butler answered his knock.

"Commander Edgemont to see Colonel Fitzhugh on military business," Charles announced. He was ushered into a parlor, where a rather short man in his early twenties with a very military bearing soon appeared. Charles thought he had aspiring aide-de-camp stamped all over him. "I have an urgent communication for your commanding officer, Colonel Fitzhugh," he said officiously. "I am required to deliver it personally."

"Then do so," the young man retorted. "I am Fitzhugh."

"Oh," Charles said, caught off guard. "I apologize. I thought—" Catching himself, he hurried on: "Sir, I command His Majesty's brig *Lomond*. I have orders to transport you and your party to Ireland and am hoping to do so with all possible dispatch. If it would be convenient, sir, for yourselves and your luggage to be dockside by noon tomorrow, we will sail on the afternoon tide."

The unlikely colonel stared unblinking for a long moment, whether in intense concentration or disbelief Charles couldn't tell. "Convenient?" he finally said. "What do you mean, if convenient? We've been waiting nearly a month for the damned navy to provide transport. I was about to hire my own ship to take us across at my own expense. You're damned right it's convenient. What's wrong with this afternoon's tide?"

Charles pulled his watch from his waistcoat pocket and looked at it. "There was nothing wrong with this afternoon's tide—if you could have had your company, equipment, and baggage ready about an hour and a half ago."

"And the next tide?"

"The next tide is at fourteen minutes past two in the morning," Charles answered.

"All right. When do you want us assembled?"

Fitzhugh and his party of nearly a dozen, with a small mountain of luggage and fully eighteen horses, assembled dockside at precisely the appointed time in the dead of night. The *Lomond* sailed on the tail of the tide for Ireland. It proved an uneventful if uncomfortable three days to Dublin in a seriously crowded ship against contrary winds, under intermittent rain, and with the horses secured on the foredeck, where they made an ungodly mess.

The crew, however, he found to be capable and good-humored as they went about their business. They took in and let out the sails with a minimum of fuss and hauled on the yards repeatedly as the *Lomond* tacked and tacked again battling to windward. Charles noted with satisfaction that the petty officers did not carry rope ends to "encourage" or threaten the men in their divisions. Only one seaman was presented to him for discipline, and that was for doing a jig on the end of the fore topgallant yardarm during a squall. The bosun's mate complained that the man was "endangering the king's property and must be punished." When Charles asked him to explain, the mate said that, "if 'e'd fell 'e could of landed on 'nuther seaman, or if 'e'd missed 'e could 'av kilt 'isself. Either way 'e was endangering the king's property." Charles awarded the offending seaman a stern lecture and a week on a half-ration of spirits, and everyone seemed satisfied.

He took a day in the harbor to hose off the decks and replenish the *Lomond*'s food, water, and firewood, then sailed again. Charles calculated that at the farthest margin he had two and a half weeks before the *Lomond* absolutely had to be back in Liverpool. His written orders were happily not explicit on this point and he intended to use every minute sailing the Irish Sea, looking for privateers or smugglers or whatever may come. The question he had not yet decided: Would he have better luck sailing north toward Belfast or south into St. George's Channel? In the end, with some assistance, he decided to sail south.

PRIVATEERS—PRIVATELY OWNED warships legally authorized to fight on their country's behalf by the contrivance of a letter of marque— were an all-too-common menace up and down the Irish Sea. Little better than semilegal pirates, they were usually small, fast craft designed for the twin purposes of capturing enemy commercial shipping and avoiding enemy warships. French, Dutch, and Spanish raiders, among others, prowled the waters in search of fat, slow British merchantmen and coastal traders. It was a potentially lucrative profession. A hull full of furs or tobacco from North America would bring far higher prices in trade-starved Amsterdam, Brest, or Bordeaux than in Liverpool, and the privateers didn't have to go through the inconvenience of paying for them.

By day Charles had the *Lomond* hug the verdant Irish coast, alive with the new greens of spring. He had lookouts posted in both masts and to port and starboard at the bow and stern. They looked carefully into every fishing village, inlet bay, and cove for ships that might be sheltered there: Bray, Greystones, Wicklow, wearing around Wicklow Head, Arklow, Kilmichael, Courtown, Riverchapel, and so on. Two hours before dusk, they would stand out to sea and run down any strange sails they spied. They spied many: fishing boats of all descriptions, coastal scows, large and small merchant vessels from twenty different countries, even "blackbirders," the dark, fast, foul-smelling slave ships hurrying to or from Africa, the Caribbean, or the United States with their precious and perishable cargos. Slavery constituted the single most important commodity on which Liverpool was said to have built its fortune.

Each even remotely promising bottom was boarded, its papers and hold inspected, and in every case sent on its way. Every master they encountered had proper papers showing they were British, allied, or neutral craft, and their cargo more or less matched the bill of lading. One or two Charles suspected were smugglers on their way to France or Spain, but he couldn't prove it, so he let them go.

On the sixth day out, cruising in the empty sea off Greenore Point, Charles reluctantly decided that he had just about stretched to the limit the time he could keep the *Lomond* at sea. A quick sail across St. George's Channel, then northward along the coast of Wales, stopping only to challenge the most suspicious craft, would take three or four days, wind permitting, and bring him back to Liverpool very nearly at the end of the promised month of his command. There would be questions, he knew, about taking nearly three weeks for a simple voyage to Dublin and back, but he could answer those. He'd broken no orders, he told himself, nor endangered any British shipping or other interests by his absence from port. Besides, no commander in these circumstances was likely to be disciplined for excessive zeal in searching for his country's enemies. Or at least he didn't think so. Still, it would go better if he had a prize or two to show, or at least could report that he had sighted and attempted to engage an enemy.

"Wear ship if you please, Mr. Tillman," he said, trying to keep any hint of disappointment out of his voice. "Make the course east by northeast."

"Aye aye, sir," Tillman answered. "It's too bad about the privateers, that we haven't found any, I mean. I'd have thought we'd do better."

"We're not home yet," Charles responded.

Tillman gave the orders for the wheel to be put over and the yards braced around. The *Lomond* heeled moderately as she turned on the calm blue sea, then righted when the wind came over her quarter.

"Deck there!" a cry came unexpectedly down from the fore masthead. "Sail off the port bow. Mebbe four, five leagues."

"What rig?" Charles called up, little interested now in some slaver or merchantman.

"Can't tell, sir," came the reply. "She's standing toward us. I can only see her t'gallants. They're in a line."

It was good work for a lookout to spot a ship at that distance. "Well done," Charles yelled back. "Let me know anything you see as she closes." Turning to Tillman, he said, "Take note of that man's name. I'd consider him for promotion if I were you."

Tillman nodded thoughtfully. "That's Wilkins. He has uncannily good eyes. He's already been promoted twice and twice disrated soon after. He has a penchant for sneaking young girls aboard and hiding them in the cable tier."

"Ah," Charles said.

The lookout on the foremast called down again. "She's signaling. Can't make it out yet. She's a frigate, I think."

This was something different. Signal flags meant another British warship. "Send the signals midshipman up into the rigging with a glass," he said to Tillman. Turning to Wilson by the wheel, he ordered, "Stand toward her. We'll see what this is about."

Charles stood by the weather rail in the bright sunshine, feeling the fresh wind and pondering what the approaching warship might want. He could see the distant speck of her upper sails, white against the deep blue sky. The signals midshipman should have been able to read her flags by now. Indeed, he saw the young man starting down from the tops with his glass pressed firmly under his arm.

"She's the *Foxhound,* sir, thirty-six. Captain Pierce," the boy reported. "Pass within hail, he asks."

"Thank you," Charles answered. "Acknowledge, then get aloft again and watch out for any further signals."

The distant specks slowly became a sleek gray-painted frigate wearing a full suit of tightly braced canvas. As the two ships came within hailing distance she put her helm down, turned cleanly into the wind and through it, all the while her sails braced around in perfect unison. As she settled on a parallel course, a figure on the *Foxhound*'s deck raised his speaking trumpet and called across. "*Lomond,* there, who's in command?"

Charles put his own speaking trumpet to his lips and yelled back. "Commander Edgemont, sir, job captain while Freemont is ill. We're on our way back to Liverpool."

"From where?" Pierce asked.

"Er, from Dublin, sir."

"Bit out of your way, aren't you? Get lost?" Charles could hear laughter from the *Foxhound*'s quarterdeck. Then Pierce called out, "Don't answer that, I can guess. When are you expected back in port?"

"A week ago, possibly," Charles answered. "Why?"

"There's a pair of French privateers hereabouts," Pierce replied. "I'm searching for 'em. Thought you might help."

"I've just been looking at the Irish coast from Dublin south. We found nothing."

"I thought that's why you were late," Pierce said with a chuckle. "How about this? You take your time sailing up the coast of Wales and I'll try further south. Keep a sharp lookout for anything suspicious. If they ask in Liverpool why you were delayed, you can say it was by my order. I'll note it in my log."

"Yes, sir," Charles responded. Then he added, "Thank you, sir." He saw Pierce gesture to his lieutenant to get under way. As the frigate's sails were braced around to catch the wind, Pierce called, "Good luck, Edgemont, and good hunting."

"The same to you, sir," Charles called back, then turned to Tillman to get under way. "Set course due east, if you please. We should raise the Welsh coast by nightfall. We'll heave to well offshore and look into Fishguard Bay first thing in the morning. Maybe our luck will change."

"Then north, sir, back to Liverpool?" There was a note of exasperation in Tillman's voice.

"Yes, north and home for you. The end of this command for me, and with likely nothing to show for it," Charles said a little bitterly. "But we may take our time. What's your hurry, anyway? Do you have a girl waiting for you?" He meant it as a joke, but Tillman blushed bright red. "My fiancée, sir, Mary—we're to be married this summer."

"Oh," Charles said. The mention of Mary made him think of Penny. He didn't want to be reminded of Penny and hadn't thought about her for days, or at least hours, and now there she was again. "I'm sorry, I didn't know," he said.

"Would it have made a difference if you had, sir?"

"Probably not," Charles answered.

"'ERE'S YOUR COFFEE, sir," Attwater's disembodied voice insisted. "It'll be dawn in 'alf an 'our. Come, sir, you asked to be wakened." Charles didn't want to wake up. He had been dreaming about Penny, a smiling, willing Penny. She was so close he could feel the warmth of her skin, the silken strands of her hair, smell her smell, hear her voice.

"Come, sir," Attwater's voice intruded. "Din't you not tell me to get you up?"

"Oh, all right," Charles managed, by degrees his dream and the sense of intimacy leaving him. "I'm awake."

"'Ere's your coffee. Your uniform is all laid out. Wind is moderate from the west. The 'ands will be at quarters as soon as they've finished their breakfast."

"Thank you," Charles said sleepily. Only the warmth of her nearness remained, and then that too dissipated. He took a sip of the proffered coffee.

On deck he saw that it was still entirely dark. Perhaps a shade lighter to the east, perhaps not. It was Charles's policy when at sea—indeed, it was the usual practice in almost all the navy, but apparently not on the *Lomond*—to greet each dawn with the ship cleared for action, the crew at their battle stations, the guns loaded and run out. This was a standard precaution in case the first light of day should reveal that an enemy warship had strayed into their vicinity unseen during the night. It was unlikely, Charles knew, and it had never happened in his thirteen years at sea. Still, it might one day, and he didn't want to have to explain how he'd lost his ship because he'd decided it best to let the men sleep in.

"Good morning," he said to Tillman. "Anything to report?"

The lieutenant touched his hat and replied, "Morning, sir. Nothing at all. Been as quiet as a graveyard. Be light soon."

The dawn was already starting and the outline of Strumble Head could just be seen to the east, the sea dark as ink beneath.

"The hands are at quarters?" Charles asked, just to fill the silence. He had already heard them clamoring up the ladderway after their breakfast, and if that weren't enough, the rumble of the carriage trucks as the guns were run out.

"Yes . . ." Tillman began.

"Deck, deck there," a call came from the foremast top, clear and loud in the morning air. "Ship off the starboard bow, I think. Might be two ships. Maybe seven, eight miles."

"What bearing?" Charles shouted back. "Can you see anything of their rigging?"

"Two points to starboard. And no, sir, it's too dark. I can only see the sticks. Might be three ships, sir."

They would know soon, Charles thought; the light was coming fast. "The sticks" meant bare masts with sails furled or brailed up. Two ships, possibly three, laid to during the night. It could be a small convoy of merchantmen sailing together, but Charles didn't think so. Merchantmen would more likely seek the comfort of a cove or bay—Fishguard Bay, just beyond the headlands, for example. "All the plain sail she'll carry, Mr. Tillman. Let's see what we have."

Men swarmed up the shrouds and out onto the yards, loosening the sails and letting them fall one by one. "Braces there," Charles heard Tillman shout, and in a quieter tone to the quartermaster, "Steer east by southeast." The canvas filled with loud snapping sounds and the *Lomond* began to surge ahead, sailing large, with the wind neat on her starboard quarter.

"It's three ships," the lookout shouted down over the noise of the wind in the taut rigging, the filling sails, and the straining yards. "Two cutters, it looks like, and a fat brig. The cutters are hoisting sail. You might see 'em from the deck soon. The brig's following."

The freshening wind and the current kicked up a small chop on the sea, more blue now as the sky lightened. The *Lomond* raced at an angle across the waves, throwing spray outward from her bow. Charles crossed to the binnacle for his glass, then back to the lee rail. He scanned the horizon as best he could dead ahead, at first finding nothing but empty sea against the dark loom of the Welsh coast. And then he saw them, two gaff-rigged single-masted ships with a brig between them, slicing across the wind to the south in an attempt to round Strumble Head. That answered one question. Any ships that hurriedly ran up their sails and set off at the sight of a warship in the Irish Sea were most likely no friends of Britain. And the brig, what was she, a third privateer or a prize? It was an important question: The *Lomond* could outgun the two cutters, but not all three if the brig were armed. They'd know soon enough.

"Run up the colors," he said to Tillman, "and keep to windward."

The *Lomond* churned south by southeast on a converging course with the officially unidentified but highly suspicious trio of ships. She had a much better point of sailing with the wind on her quarter. The distance closed quickly, and it soon became evident that they would be within range of even the *Lomond*'s six-pounders well before the other ships could clear the point. Within half an hour Charles, and everyone else on deck, could see the full set of the enemy's sails and not long after the tops of their hulls. He estimated they were less than five miles off.

"We're reaching on them," Tillman offered conversationally.

"Yes," Charles answered. The cutters in particular were not sailing across the wind anywhere near as quickly as he thought they could, while the brig was struggling unsuccessfully to keep up. "What do you make of them?" he asked, turning to the lieutenant. "Is the brig a warship or a prize?"

"Oh, a prize for certain, sir," Tillman said immediately. "True, she's pierced for guns, but she's beamy and Liverpool-built. Both cutters were built in French yards, I'll wager my pay on it. They'd fly without the brig."

Charles could see their hulls to the waterline now. What Tillman said made sense. "Do you think she's armed?"

"Probably a couple of popgun four-pounders on either side, I'd guess," Tillman answered, squinting across at the brig. "But she won't fight. She'll only have a prize crew big enough to sail her. Whoever commands those cutters must be too obstinate to give her up."

Charles thought about this for a moment in silence. What should he do when the cutters came within range? The brig he could have, but he didn't want her as a consolation prize. He wanted at least one of the privateers as well. More to the point, what would the cutters do when the *Lomond* was in a position to open fire? It was obvious to all that he would be on them long before they could weather the point. Why hadn't they left the brig behind already and fled?

Perhaps they weren't planning to flee. The two cutters and their captive were still about three miles away, downwind and slightly ahead of the *Lomond*. On their present course he judged they would come alongside the brig in about a half-hour's time.

"Alter course two points to windward, if you please, Mr. Tillman," Charles ordered. "We'll take a parallel course until we're well in front of them."

Tillman relayed his instructions to the quartermaster, then asked, "What are you thinking, sir?"

"I'm thinking that we can outsail that brig on any point of the wind. It's the cutters we need to worry about. If they let us get ahead of them, which they'll have to if they're going to stay with their prize, we'll drop down and squeeze them against the point or force them to fight."

Tillman looked at him, then back at the enemy ships. "They'll abandon her as soon as they see what we're up to," he said. "They have to."

"They might," Charles agreed. "But I want to see what they do. We get the brig either way. Maybe they'll do something foolish." He didn't really think the cutters would do anything foolish. He watched them closely as the *Lomond*'s sails were braced around and she settled on a nearly parallel course, about two miles to windward. They were easily reaching on the three craft. No, he corrected himself, the *Lomond* was overtaking the brig; the other two could shoot ahead whenever they chose to. Why hadn't they done so already? The *Lomond* would soon be in a position to run down on the cutters and open fire. He didn't think that the Frenchmen, with their lightly armed and thin-skinned craft, would risk a broadside-to-broadside pounding. Their strengths were quickness in the stays and lightning speed. No, if they chose to fight, they would do something unexpected—suddenly reverse course, or tack and try to take the weather gauge. And there were two of them, they might divide, one occupying Charles's ship while the other maneuvered to cross her bow or stern to rake him. Each of the cutters probably carried a larger crew than the *Lomond*. Given half an opportunity, one or the other would try to run alongside and board.

The *Lomond* was nearly abreast of the leading cutter. Charles wasn't sure what the privateers would do, but he knew they would do it soon. "Prepare to alter course to south by east, Mr. Tillman. Steer to close within long range of the leading cutter."

"Aye, aye, sir," Tillman responded, fairly alive with excitement now that the action was about to begin. The *Lomond* seemed to have every advantage.

"And Mr. Tillman, keep the hands at the braces; we may not stay our new course long."

"Yes, sir," Tillman answered, nodding his understanding. "Hands to the braces, lively there." To Wilson at the wheel he said, "Port your helm, steer south by east."

Charles felt the rudder ease and the ship settle onto an easier course, with the wind more over her stern as the yards came around. She quickly began to pick up speed, slicing across the chop diagonally toward a point some distance in front of the enemy and their prize, but still in position to retain the all-important weather gauge. He put his glass to his eye and watched intently for any sign of the privateers' reaction. He didn't have to wait long. Almost immediately, he saw the tiny figures of men on the shrouds of the leading privateer racing aloft to add more sail. Shifting the telescope to the second cutter, he watched her mainsail momentarily thrown into confusion as it swung hard around. The cutter tacked with incredible nimbleness, seeming to rotate on her keel, showing first the diminishing profile of her starboard side, then her stern, and finally her port side as she reversed course from south to north. Just for an instant Charles could read the name painted below her taffrail: *La Petite Claudette*. As soon as she had gathered way on her new course, she hauled her sails closer still and began to angle into the wind. The brig, he noted without surprise, continued on her own slow, now lonely course as before.

"We could run down and retake the prize," Tillman offered. "They've abandoned her."

"No," Charles said. "That's what they want us to do." The privateers' plans were clear. The brig was being offered as bait while the two cutters worked separately to windward. If the *Lomond* went for the brig, they would circle around and attack from either side, with the wind at their back. He surveyed the relative positions of the enemy ships. They were very fast, even faster than he had anticipated, and were already well on their way to taking the weather gauge. Not a moment was to be lost. "We will tack directly," he said, his throat feeling suddenly dry. "We will close with the northernmost cutter before she gets to windward of us."

Charles stood balanced on the balls of his feet with his hands clenched firmly behind his back as the orders were shouted, the yards pulled around and the helm spun hard over. Tacking into the wind was quicker but riskier than wearing. It was a gamble they had to take. His stomach muscles tensed as the *Lomond*'s bowsprit turned in a tight arc toward the wind, her bow kicking spray over the forward decking in fine white clouds. The rate of the turn slowed painfully the nearer she came to the wind. If she missed her stays and fell off, they would have to gather her back up and then wear around in the opposite direction. By then both cutters would already be well to windward.

The *Lomond* came into the eye of the wind and seemed to balance there with her sails aback, booming and pounding in confusion as if trying to make up their minds. Charles held his breath as the bow inched sluggishly across. "Hold her, hold her," he muttered, speaking more to himself than the quartermaster. Then she was across. "Braces there, tight up!" he shouted. Turning to the lieutenant, he said, "Keep her as close to the wind as she'll lie." Tillman grinned in response, his eyes wide with excitement.

Charles turned his attention to the *Claudette,* about a mile distant off the port bow. A large part of her copper bottom showed as she heeled well over, her mainsail pulled hard as a board and her cutwater kicking regular puffs of spray over her bows as she sliced seemingly effortlessly across the chop. She was a beautiful sight, a thoroughbred galloping over the waves, all purpose and urgency. The *Lomond* had little of her elegance and style, but Charles noted that his own deck was steeply enough canted as she heeled as to make it difficult to climb from starboard to port. Leaning on the lee rail for support, he studied the Frenchman closely. She was laying perhaps half a point closer to the wind than the *Lomond* and making better speed while doing it. Their courses were slowly converging, and Charles could almost see the point on the sea, as real as if it were marked in ink, where one ship would cross the bow of the other. It was vitally important that the crossing ship be the *Lomond.*

He looked over his shoulder and saw that the second privateer was well to the south, four or five miles at least, but had turned north and was pursuing at a furious pace across the wind. It all depended on which of the northernmost ships, *La Petite Claudette* or the *Lomond,* reached the imaginary spot in the ocean first, and which crossed the other's bow. If the Frenchman won, the *Lomond* would be forced to fall off the wind to bring its guns to bear and avoid being raked. If his ship wasn't crippled in the initial encounter, he would then have to deal with both cutters, both to windward, acting in concert. If properly handled, they would have every advantage. One at a time, he was confident the *Lomond*'s heavier broadside could defeat them. Both acting together, with one or the other of the nimble ships threatening his stem or stern, was not a prospect he relished.

His eyes were fixed on the *Claudette,* now even closer off the starboard bow. It would be close, by God, it would be close. He glanced upward at the rigging for what seemed like the hundredth time since the race began. Every yard was braced tight, every sail taut and hard. He saw no telltale flapping on their leading edges to indicate that she was too close to the wind, but there were tiny ripples that indicated she could go no further. There must be something he could do to improve her trim, to give her just one extra fathom of speed.

"I think we'll hit her midships," Tillman interjected, a certain awe in his voice. Charles had forgotten that the lieutenant was standing next to him by the rail. "Either that or she'll come and board us. Don't know why she doesn't lay off and run."

"For the same reason we don't," Charles answered. "She wants us, that's why. All she has to do is get to windward. When the other cutter catches up, one or the other will board and carry us by main force. Run out the port-side battery."

"The larboard guns, sir? You mean starboard. If we engage, she'll be to starboard."

"No, I mean port-side. Hauling their weight outboard will stiffen the ship a little and give the keel just a bit more bite. Every foot to windward will help. When that's done, have the starboard guns double shotted but not run out."

Tillman shouted the orders and the port guns were hauled laboriously up the steeply canted deck until they were snug against the bulwarks and secured in place. Charles bitterly wished he'd thought of it earlier. The ships were closing, almost within musket range. It did indeed look as if there would be a collision. One of them was going to crash into the side of the other, it was almost certain. What then? Both ships might lose their masts, more probably the frailer-built cutter. The Frenchman would probably try to board straightaway if he could. Was it a chance Charles was willing to take? Was it a chance the *Lomond* should take? He decided it wasn't. The odds would be better if he wore now to bring his guns to bear and hope to cripple the privateer. If that failed he would have to trust his luck in an open-sea fight against both cutters.

"It's no good," he said to Tillman. "Prepare to lay off. We'll try to rake her as we pass her stern."

"But, sir!" Tillman pleaded, "we can't. The Frenchie might still decide to turn away. We'd be giving up."

Charles turned to the lieutenant, prepared to order him to do what he was told, when something out of the corner of his eye caught his attention. The *Claudette*'s jibs and mainsheet began to shiver, then flog. She was only a half-cable's distance and either she had tried to turn a little closer to ensure she crossed the *Lomond*'s bow safely, or perhaps the *Lomond*'s twin pyramids of canvas had momentarily taken away her wind. Either way, the Frenchman was suddenly in disarray, her mainsail flailing and banging like cannons. "Good Lord, she's in irons. She's in irons!" Tillman shouted.

"Belay that order," Charles barked. "Wilson, lay off a point." To Tillman he said, "Run out the starboard guns and prepare to heave to."

The *La Petite Claudette*'s sails slapped in useless confusion as she lost way. She was momentarily almost dead in the water and out of control as her head began to fall off with the wind.

"Steady, boys, steady," he shouted to the men crouched at their guns. "We'll give her a broadside she won't soon forget."

The *Lomond* seemed to be racing down on her prey. The Frenchman continued to turn helplessly, her bow pushed by the wind. Now she was broadside to the waves, still turning, her stern showing. The *Lomond* would cross that stern at pistol range or less, fifty feet, no more.

"Back the fore mainsail," he shouted. Then, "Fire!"

The bark of the starboard six-pounders hurled the guns inboard on their carriages as one. Charles smiled to himself; compared to the old *Argonaut*'s thunderous broadside it wasn't much, but then they weren't dueling with two- and three-decked ships of the line. Thick gray-black smoke temporarily hid the *Claudette* from view except for her mast. A wild cheer broke out on the *Lomond's* decks.

"Silence! Reload," he ordered. "Canister on top of round shot."

Her backed mainsail acting as a brake, the *Lomond* slowed almost to a stop, drifting downwind on the cutter. As the smoke quickly blew clear, Charles could see the damage his guns had done. Several ragged holes just under her counter and—he looked closer to be sure—her rudder hanging uselessly at an awkward angle beneath. Her mast still stood and the mainsail began to fill. She could still flee downwind but had no hope of beating back until her rudder was repaired. The quicker gun crews were just now hauling the cannon back out, ready to fire.

"Fire as you bear," he ordered.

Orange flame stabbed across the gap. Above the smoke, he watched as the *Claudette's* mast teetered, then fell in a great arc over the side.

"That's done it," Tillman observed.

"Have the guns reloaded and run out," Charles said. "But don't fire them. We'll see if she strikes."

As the smoke cleared away, the French privateer lay dead in the water, rudderless, her mast half in the sea. A figure appeared at what was left of the taffrail shouting something in French and waving a French flag, which he promptly threw over the side.

Charles lifted his hat in salute across the span. "Send Sergeant MacPherson and his marines over to take command of her. Also the carpenter to survey her damage." He turned toward the rail and looked for the second privateer. She was barely a speck on the horizon, running southward with all sail set.

"She'll get away," Tillman said.

"Yes, but we still get the prize."

The *Lomond's* boats were lowered and the marines, the carpenter, and a half-dozen sailors went across to the crippled privateer. As soon as they were aboard and signaled that all was well, Charles directed that the *Lomond* come about and run down the captured merchant brig.

That night all three ships hove to while repairs were carried out on the cutter. Charles sent Tillman across to take command of the privateer along with a midshipman and six seamen. There was a short and heated discussion with the English master of the now-liberated brig *Ursula*, who would not understand that his ship was now a prize to the *Lomond* after being recaptured from the French, and was required to sail with the others to Liverpool to be condemned by the prize court.

"You didn't not do 'alf bad, all in all," Attwater observed as he was helping Charles prepare for bed.

"What do you mean?" Charles asked.

"I mean, sir, that you've captured two ships, even if one of 'em was English, and never a mark on the *Lomond*."

"Well, yes," he allowed, secretly pleased with the day's events. "But we'll be very late getting back to Liverpool. Captain Freemont will be furious."

IF COMMANDER NIGEL FREEMONT was furious, or even mildly perturbed, he concealed it well. Charles half-expected that the *Lomond*'s regular captain would be waiting in a small boat at the mouth of the Mersey, ready to storm aboard in righteous indignation at the length of time he had been kept waiting.

The *Lomond* and her two prizes sailed into the broad estuary on a bright Friday afternoon. All three ships dropped anchor off Whitby, at the *Lomond*'s previous anchorage of almost a month earlier. Charles immediately had a boat lowered into the water and sent a senior midshipman to the admiral's office in the port with the report of his encounter with the *La Petite Claudette*. There had been no small boat or irate captain waiting at the mouth of the river, nor did either appear that evening.

The following morning, Charles was discussing with Lieutenant Tillman arrangements for the transfer of the prisoners taken in the engagement when he overheard the midshipman of the watch shout, "Ahoy, what boat?" and the reply, "*Lomond*." Both men went to the entry port in the waist to greet the ship's rightful captain, Charles with some trepidation, Tillman without an apparent care in the world.

The figure that emerged up the sidesteps and onto the deck was a middle-aged man of average height with clear blue eyes and a somewhat distracted expression. Charles noted that he carried several thick books under his arm.

"Welcome back, sir," Tillman said, extending his hand. "I have the honor to present Commander Edgemont, who has very ably served as our temporary captain in your absence."

Charles and Freemont shook hands, then Freemont said, "Edgemont, Edgemont—weren't you somebody at St. Vincent?"

"Yes, I was second lieutenant aboard the *Argonaut*."

"Well, I see you've had a busy time here. Not worked our young lieutenant too hard, have you? I noticed all the fresh paint and such. And two prizes, my word. Still, no harm done. I want to thank you for your enthusiastic caretaking of my ship; I'm sure the crew enjoyed the change of routine. Now, if you will excuse me, I will retire to my cabin. I've finally obtained a copy of Herodotus's *Inquiry* in the Greek and can't wait to begin. Lieutenant Tillman will escort you to the side. Good day."

"Good day," Charles answered, half-bowing and touching his hat. As soon as Freeman had descended to his cabin, he turned to Tillman and said, "I guess that's that."

"I wouldn't take it personally, sir," Tillman answered. "That's the way he is. He loves his books. If I may say so, I've enjoyed serving with you, despite the beginning. It has been a bit of a change."

Charles decided to ask something that had been nagging at him almost since he first came on board. "Exactly what does the *Lomond* do when Freemont is in command?"

Tillman frowned. "Not very much," he said. "We sit at anchorage in the river at lot. Sometimes we sail out into the middle of the Irish Sea and heave to or sail up and down a bit. Then we come back and sit at anchorage some more."

"How can that be? Doesn't Freemont have orders, some regular mission, something he has to accomplish from time to time?"

"Well, you see," Tillman began, "Freemont is the third son of the earl of Connan in Ireland. The earl comes from a long line of sea captains, admirals, and such. He is also on friendly terms with the king and politically very important to the government. One older son died during the American War, commanding a frigate. The earl wanted one of his sons to carry on the family seafaring tradition, but he didn't want any more killed, so he worked out an arrangement. Captain Freemont gets to command a warship that can never be in any danger, or a danger to anyone else. He's not much of a commander, really. He likes a quiet ship with not too much work going on so he can read. He loves his books and his wine. Sometimes he likes the wine a little too much, so he has to go home and rest his liver now and again. When he's gone, I usually let the men have a little license with women and spirits. They have to be very quiet and mostly out of sight when he's on board. It wears on you after a while."

Charles shook his head in disbelief, then extended his hand. "If you ever think of transferring to a proper warship, I'd be pleased to have you serve with me again."

"Thank you, sir. I'll keep it in mind."

SEVEN

THE BROADSHEET OUTSIDE THE LIVERY SCREAMED, "Britons! Serve God, King and Country. Enlistments currently being accepted on board H.M. Frigate *Tempest*. Cash bonuses awarded for qualifying seamen. Set sail for Glory and Prize Money. All ratings accepted." Charles had seen hundreds of such posters in and around Liverpool, advertising for recruits for at least a dozen ships. The need was great. Almost every British warship sailed shorthanded; but the results from such advertisements as these, he knew, usually disappointed.

He and Attwater retrieved their horses and carriage from the livery early the next morning to begin the long drive back to Tattenall. Charles sat in the back in a contemplative frame of mind while his servant urged the horses along the crowded streets of Liverpool. Charles was, of course, pleased with the outcome of his time on board the *Lomond*. Not only had he established order and made the ship presentable, but he had notched a mark for himself by successfully engaging two privateers with their prize, capturing two of the ships. It was something to be proud of.

He idly noted the impressive bustle of the busy, largely commercial seaport as they passed. The scene was different from the streets of naval ports like Portsmouth or Plymouth. There were fewer naval officers to be seen in their blue uniforms fringed with gold, and far more merchant sailors, easily identified by their golden earrings, braided pigtails, or rolling, loping strides, a legacy of years at sea on pitching decks. The seamen of the King's Navy were rarely allowed to walk the streets of any port unattended for fear they would desert.

In addition to the broadsheets tacked to trees and lampposts seeking recruits, he had also seen evidence of the navy's more direct efforts to obtain men: patrols from the Impress Service—press gangs, in common parlance—trolling for the able but unwilling. He thought of the many iniquities in the means by which the Royal Navy supplied its ships with men and then kept them there. The press was one of the primary instruments and the worst, essentially arresting sailors on merchant ships in port or on the open seas and landsmen on the streets near their homes. It was a rotten, cruel system that brought the navy a steady stream of sullen malcontents, prone to become troublemakers. Charles didn't know of another method to keep the hundreds of warships the nation desperately required manned and at sea, but, in his opinion, better pay, better food, and less brutal punishments would be a start.

As they cleared the outskirts of the city, his mind turned to more pleasant things, the first of which was Penny Brown. Might she have changed her thinking while he was away? It had been more than a month, and it was said that absence makes the heart grow fonder. Should he call on her when he returned? He wanted to, badly. But he had better not. She had asked him not to for a time. How long was "a time"? Ellie might have some news or advice. She had become friends with Penny; she must know something.

Thinking of Ellie led him to contemplation of the relationship between his sister and Winchester. Charles grimaced. He was sure— almost sure—that the two were knowledgeable of each other in the biblical sense, or were at least quoting Scripture furiously. Maybe Winchester had proposed by now. That would make things a little better. But what about Penny? What did she know or think about Ellie and Winchester? Some women were likely to be a little peculiar when it came to intimate relations. Would she be shocked or understanding? What were the Quakers' attitudes about that sort of thing anyway? And so Charles's mind worked its way in meandering circles as Attwater encouraged the plodding horses along the deeply rutted roads toward home.

Late in the afternoon the pair of mares quickened their gait as they entered the familiar high street into Tattenall and soon after turned up the lane to Edgemont Hall. A freckled, redheaded boy of about fourteen, whom Charles did not recognize, came out from the stables to meet them.

"Who are ye?" the lad asked tartly. "And wha' d' ye want?"

"I am Charles Edgemont," Charles answered. "I live here. Who are you?"

"A'm Ezekiel Frith. A'm the new ostler."

"Pleased to meet you, Ezekiel. Help Mr. Attwater here take these sea chests into the house, if you please."

"A'm the ostler," the lad insisted with a touch of self-importance. "A don' heft chests."

"Well, Ostler Frith, I'd consider it a personal favor if you would make an exception in this case. I'm sure Mr. Attwater would appreciate it as well."

Just as the boy opened his mouth to say something potentially interesting about what Charles and Attwater might or might not appreciate, the door to the house opened and Charles's brother John came out. "Ah, Charles, welcome back. I see you've met Ezekiel."

"We were just discussing his moral dilemma in helping carry our chests into the house."

"See to it, please," John said. With a pout the boy went around to the side of the carriage, where Attwater added, "You only have to carry half. It ain't so hard."

"So, how did it go?" John asked as soon as they were alone. "Is England any safer from invasion by the French?"

"A little," Charles smiled, "I—"

"Oh, before I forget. You had a visitor about two weeks ago."

"Who?" Charles asked. His heart skipped a beat. "It wasn't Penny Brown, was it?"

"No, not Miss Brown. It was her father, George. He requested that you call on him as soon as you're back. Didn't say why, but he seemed unsettled."

Charles swore under his breath. What did Penny's father want? He hadn't done anything to his daughter. "I'll see him tomorrow," he said.

Inside the house, Ellie greeted Charles with an exuberant hug and a kiss on his cheek. "Have you spoken to Penny?" he asked directly.

"I saw her the day before yesterday. She's not been herself since you left," she said in a low voice. "I don't understand it exactly, but it's something to do with Quakers and soldiers, although I don't understand what soldiers have to do with it. It's sailormen in the navy, isn't it? There aren't any soldiers, are there? She did say that she hoped you were well."

"Yes, sailors; no soldiers," he said absently. "Where is Winchester? I haven't seen him yet."

Ellie's expression assumed a secretive air that also hinted at some inner joy. "He went home to visit his father. I expect him back in a day or two."

"His father, why?" Charles asked. "I didn't think he got along with his family."

"Oh, it's just something," she said mysteriously, her eyes shining. "You'll find out."

Charles looked at his sister in all her radiance and knew why his lieutenant had gone home to speak with his parents. *At least one of us is lucky in love,* he thought. "I can hardly wait," he said.

In the morning Charles rode to the Brown home in a sour mood. He didn't know why George Brown wanted to see him, but he could guess. He was also undecided about what he should say in return. He tried to be objective. How did he feel about Penny, really? They'd met only a few times. He couldn't be that attached to her, could he? He could say, if the father asked how he felt, that she was an agreeable girl, and that he was fond of her, but the differences in their backgrounds and religions would make any match between them unsuitable. He should say that, while he wished his daughter well, he had decided that his attentions must of necessity focus on the navy and his estate and that it would be unwise just now to be sidetracked by romance, particularly with a religious nonconformist. He could say honestly that she would be a hindrance to his career. Her father would have to agree with that.

He dismounted from Pendle in front of the mill beyond the house and with some trepidation walked inside. He found George Brown sitting at an uncluttered desk in a low-ceilinged office off to the side of the building. "Please, sit thee down," Penny's father said, half-rising and indicating a chair in front of the desk. "I thank thee for coming." Charles nodded and sat silently, waiting uneasily for the older man to speak his mind.

"What art thou about?" the miller said after a minute. "What dost thou require of my daughter?"

Charles had known the question would be asked in some form, but he didn't expect it to be put so directly. He avoided the older man's steady gaze as he tried to frame in his mind what he should say. The resolve he had built up earlier in the morning to put her behind him wavered, then vanished. He knew what he wanted. He was pretty sure that Penny at least liked him, but he didn't understand her reluctance. He didn't understand why she couldn't just put her religious scruples aside for him. Any normal woman would. Wives followed husbands, not the other way around. But she had once said something about how he should follow his heart, and he knew what his heart required. "I want to marry her," he said directly, looking her father in the eye. "I want your permission to ask her to be my wife."

"Art thou serious?" George Brown said, raising his eyebrows. "Dost thou, an officer in the King's Navy, wish to marry a Quaker woman? Why?"

"Because I love her," Charles said. The words, once begun, tumbled out. "Because I'm not happy when I can't be with her. She's all I think about. She . . . she brings joy into my life and I don't know how I'd live without her."

Penny's father appraised him thoughtfully. "I can well understand that," he said. "She brings those things into my life, and the lives of others, too." The older man took a breath. "I judge thee an agreeable man, Charles Edgemont. I think thee honest and direct and I think thee would be a caring husband to Penny. I am concerned about thy profession, but that is not for me to decide. Still, I do not think that thou fully grasps what thou art asking."

"There is nothing complicated about what I seek," Charles asserted.

"Then thou dost not fully know our Penny. We have raised her to be an independent being, one who knows her own mind." George Brown paused for a moment and shook his head as if in wonderment. "In this I sometimes feel we have been more successful than I ever desired. When she gets an idea into her head . . ." He left the thought unfinished, then said, "Penny is a person with a great strength in her convictions. She has been both a source of great joy to me and at times a challenge. She would be a trial to thee also," he said significantly. "More than thou might expect."

Charles did not know what to make of this, except for the fact that her father was attempting to discourage him. In any event, he felt he understood her perfectly well—or at least well enough. "Are you giving me permission to talk with her?" he said directly.

"My permission is not at issue," George Brown said with a sigh. "There is one additional concern that I must speak with thee about."

"What is that?"

"Thou must also understand Penny would pay a heavy price if she agreed to take thee to husband." Charles opened his mouth to object, but the older man stilled him with a wave of his hand. "She would be disowned by her religion, which she dearly loves. The members of our meeting have cherished and nurtured her from infancy, and to cut her off from them would be cruel. She told me that thou said once that she was asking thee to choose between two things thou loved. Understand that thou art asking the same of her. Now, I ask thee again, art thou certain what thou art about, Charles Edgemont, and what thou require of my daughter?"

Charles tried to digest Penny's father's words. Why did it have to be so complicated? If her religion was so important, that was all right with him. Religions were fine so long as they didn't actually interfere with your life. If she would only be reasonable, she would understand. Penny's father waited patiently for him to answer. Finally he said, "May I speak with her?"

"That is not for me to say," George Brown said firmly. "She agreed that I should explain these things to thee and I have done so. I will also relate to her what thou hast said. But hold no hope that she will alter her thinking." He paused for a moment, as if undecided, then continued. "I propose, Charles Edgemont, that thou put thy feelings aside and seek another woman to wed. One more in keeping with thy way of thinking." He said in a softer voice, "I am sorry for both of ye, but I see no other path."

Charles clung doggedly to what few rapidly fading shreds of hope he could find. "I will have to go to sea again soon, probably in a month or six weeks. Will you tell her that?"

George Brown's mouth hardened into a straight line. "I will tell her everything thou hast said. But do not expect her to seek thee out, Charles Edgemont. I would advise that thou cut the cord with a sharp knife and let the past be past. It would be best if thou didst not trouble thyself or my daughter further. Thy affection is difficult, painful to her . . . and unwelcome."

Charles rose, stung by the father's words. "Please tell Penny that I'm sorry. I never meant to distress her," he said, struggling to keep the bitterness out of his voice. "Tell her that I respect her choice. I won't bother her again."

He made his way slowly toward home, feeling abandoned and despondent at the finality of it. After a time he attempted to convince himself that it was all for the best. There would be other women, he was sure, who would be more than pleased to have him—beautiful, compliant women from more conventional families who would admire his career. The thought did little to ease the emptiness that had settled in his chest.

His mood lightened at the sight of Stephen Winchester's horse in the paddock by the stables. He gave Pendle to Ezekiel without a word and hurried into the house. He found John, Ellie, and Winchester in the parlor in the midst of being served sherry by the maid.

"Stephen, it's good to see you," he said warmly. "What took you to York? Ellie wouldn't tell me."

Ellie beamed what was possibly her biggest smile ever while Winchester stammered, "Well, sir, . . . I . . ." Then he broke into a broad grin.

"Better bring another glass, Constance," John said to the maid. To Charles he continued, "We're to have a new brother-in-law. I've given my blessing."

"Upon my word," Charles said, beaming. He took Winchester's hand and shook it warmly. "It's about time. I was beginning to worry."

OVER THE FOLLOWING week, Charles threw himself doggedly into overseeing the repairs and improvements to the manor house and estate that he'd purchased and preparing to go to sea in the *Louisa* whenever she would be ready. He made several trips into Chester to order stores and furnishings that he would take aboard. One day, while he was talking with the foremen supervising work on his house, it dawned on him that there would be no one to live in the place while he was away. Until recently he had hoped that Penny would stay there with numbers of servants and a growing collection of children—his children. Now all that had turned to ashes. That evening, still brooding on the subject, he asked Attwater if he had any family.

"Oh, yes, sir," Attwater said proudly. "There's Mrs. Attwater, and we have—" he counted on his fingers—"eleven children still living, most of them grown, though."

"You do?" Charles said in amazement. "Where do they live?"

"The missus and those that ain't set off rents a cottage down by Cheltenham, sir. Near Gloucester, like."

"What would you think of having them live in my house?" Charles asked. "For free, no rent. There's plenty of room, and they could look after it while we're away."

Attwater beamed with pleasure. "That would be wonderful, sir. I ain't seen my missus never in two years."

"Well, see to it quickly," Charles said. "You can take the carriage if you need to."

"Oh, no, sir," Attwater said quickly. "I'll just have someone write to them, like. The missus can have the parson read it to her."

"I'll write it for you, if you wish," Charles said. Then, thinking something was out of place, he asked, "How come you haven't gone to visit your family before now?"

Attwater eyed him steadily. "You ain't, haven't, given me no leave to, sir. Captain Wood, he did. But you ain't said nothing yet. I expected it was just a matter of time."

"But I didn't know . . ." Charles began. Then, Attwater's reasoning being beyond him, he changed his mind. "That was my fault, but bringing them to live here should help correct things. I apologize."

And there was Ellie's wedding to plan for. She and Winchester were scheduled to marry in the third week of April. Stephen arranged for a small ceremony at St. Michael's Church, halfway up Bridge Street in Chester, and promptly leased a modest house alongside the road just outside of Tattenall. He and Ellie seemed to be constantly together, surveying their home, shopping in Chester, or exploring the countryside in the carriage or on horseback.

Daniel Bevan arrived by hired coach from his family home near the fishing village of Rhyl in northern Wales on a sunny afternoon in the middle of April. "Well, Charlie," he greeted his friend with a grin, "anything interesting happen since we last met?" It took Charles late into the night and several bottles of wine to fill him in.

TWO DAYS BEFORE Ellie and Winchester's wedding, in the late afternoon, Charles and Bevan were occupying Winchester outdoors near the stables so that Ellie could have some time alone planning the finishing touches for her trousseau—or "trust-you," as Attwater liked to put it. Daniel Bevan was in the midst of explaining in explicit detail just what difficulties Winchester could expect on his wedding night (which mostly involved headaches, women's troubles, "not with *that* you aren't," and general lack of interest) when Charles started at the sight of a familiar gray mare with its cart racing up the lane. Penny Brown sat alone on the cart bench, snapping the reins and urging the clearly exhausted animal to greater effort. He ran to the drive in time to grab the horse's halter as she brought the cart to a halt. Penny was breathless and her face flushed. Somewhere she had lost her bonnet, and her hair hung in tangled curls around her face and shoulders.

"Please help me," she cried from the bench. "They've taken Peter!"

Charles went to help her down, and she stumbled against his chest. The contact with her seemed to burn into his flesh. "Who took him?" he asked. "When and where?"

"In Chester, this morning," she choked. "The soldiers in the navy took him by force and said he was to be one of them. He said he wouldn't, but they only laughed. And I said they couldn't have him, he was a Quaker. They only laughed more, and one of them touched me and tried to kiss me. It was horrible!"

So they're sweeping as far as Chester, Charles thought. *They must be in a terrible need for hands.* For a moment he thought of the press gangs he'd seen in Liverpool. "It will be all right," he said, trying to calm her. "We'll get him back." To Winchester and Bevan standing nearby he said, "If you're with me, then uniforms and swords."

Penny looked up. "Swords?" she said. "I want no bloodshed."

"No, of course not," Charles said reassuringly. "Only, well, swords are part of our uniform. They make it more official." He quickly followed the other two men into the house, yelled for Attwater to ready the carriage, and hurriedly changed. Outside, he approached Penny and said, "You go home. Leave the mare here and take Ellie's gelding. We'll bring Peter back safe and sound, I promise."

Winchester and Bevan emerged from the house as Attwater led the horses and carriage from the stables. "No," Penny said firmly, "I am coming with thee. He's my brother and I'm responsible."

"It's out of the question," Charles said directly. "It might be dangerous. I forbid it."

Penny eyed him through narrowed lids. "Dost thou?" she said evenly. Then she promptly turned, lifted her skirts, climbed into the carriage, and sat down, folding her arms defiantly across her chest.

Charles muttered something about headstrong women under his breath, which she heard but ignored, then climbed up and sat beside her. "Winchester," he growled, "you're junior, you drive." They rode almost the whole way in flinty silence.

They found the sweepings of the press gang where Charles thought they would be, huddled together in a pen out in the open on the old castle grounds. There seemed to be about thirty men and a few boys, frightened and miserable in the chilly night air. He saw an elderly midshipman and two seamen, armed with cudgels, sitting around a table with a lantern and several tankards on it. Charles jumped from the slowing carriage and approached the petty officer, buckling on his sword as he went.

"Who's in charge here?" he demanded as he neared the table.

"Bugger off, it's all legal," replied the midshipman, his back turned and raising his tankard to his lips.

"By God, you'll stand when you address me," Charles snapped.

The midshipman, well into his forties, pushed back his chair and stood. "Bugger off, I said," he snarled, turning. When he saw Charles's uniform and epaulette, he froze.

"You address me in that tone again, I'll see you swing for it," Charles threatened. "Where's your officer?"

"Yes, sir, I don't know, sir." The petty officer struggled to attention, swaying slightly on his feet.

Charles felt rather than saw Bevan and Winchester arrive to stand behind him. "What's your name and ship?"

"Withers, sir. The *Repulse,* sir."

"Have you been drinking, Mr. Withers? And what do you mean you don't know?"

"No, sir. And I just don't know where the lieutenant is. He went off with some doxy—er, woman—sir."

"That's dereliction of duty," Charles said. "I want to see the boys you've impressed."

"Why, sir?" Withers asked, clearly puzzled.

"Damn your eyes," Charles growled. "Don't you ever question my orders. But if you must know, I think you've taken a boy I've promised a midshipman's berth to on my own ship."

"Yes, sir," Withers said quickly. "I'm very sorry, sir. This way, sir."

As soon as the man opened the gate to the pen, Penny pushed through and ran into the group calling, "Peter! Peter!" When the boy stood up she waded into the crowd and pulled him away. As she shepherded her brother back out the gate, she passed Withers and hissed, "Thou foul lecherous beast."

Charles looked at the midshipman with renewed interest. He remembered Penny saying something about being touched. "Did you molest this woman when she protested your taking her brother?"

Withers swallowed hard. "T'were only in fun, sir."

"Lieutenant," Charles said to Bevan. "Put this man on report: insubordination, drunkenness, swearing, questioning orders, and attempted rape. I want him arrested and put under restraint the moment he sets foot on the *Repulse.* Send the report to Captain—"

Turning to the now-ashen Withers, he asked, "Who's your captain?"

"Jenkins, s-sir."

"—send your report to Captain Jenkins of the *Repulse* first thing in the morning."

"Aye aye, sir," Bevan responded, suppressing a grin and making a show of writing out the charges.

Returning to Withers, Charles added, "Consider yourself under arrest."

"But sir—" Withers pleaded.

Charles found himself beginning to enjoy browbeating the smarmy midshipman. He was considering threatening to hang the poor man right there in the street when he felt Penny's hand on his arm.

"What about all those others?" she said, nodding to the rest of the men collected by the press gang. "They've all been unfairly captured. Surely we can't leave them here."

Charles turned back to Withers. *Why not?* he thought. In for a penny, in for a pound. He smiled inwardly: in for a Penny . . . "Release the rest of these men you've pressed," he ordered. "Anyone who hasn't accepted the King's guinea." He heard Bevan clear his throat loudly, suggesting a warning that he was going too far.

"Why, sir?" Withers said, clearly aghast.

"Are you questioning me again? Because I suspect they've all been improperly impressed."

The disordered rush of cold and hungry men toward the open gate nearly knocked Charles over. Several swore at the petty officer as they passed, and two actually spit on him.

Bevan took the opportunity to pull Charles aside. "Are you quite finished?" he muttered under his breath. "You're sure you don't want to stroll over to the city jail and empty that as well? Perhaps you'd like to have the sheriff arrested."

Charles smiled in spite of himself. "No, you're right. We've gotten what we wanted. We can go."

While Bevan hurried Penny and her brother into the carriage, Charles left Withers in the custody of his two mates with orders that he be turned over to Captain Jenkins first thing in the morning. As he pulled himself up into the carriage, he turned to Peter, now wrapped in his sister's arms. "Are you hurt?" he asked the boy.

"Not much," Peter answered in a shaken voice.

Winchester snapped the reins and the carriage jerked forward. Once they were safely across the Dee bridge, Charles settled back and smiled. He had carefully neglected to mention his name or that of his ship. There would have been all hell to pay if he had done otherwise. Badgering the unfortunate petty officer, however enjoyable, was pointless, since he had probably done nothing illegal. On the other hand, ordering the release of the pressed men was highly irregular and Charles might have been severely reprimanded, even court-martialed.

"You like living dangerously, don't you, Charlie?" Bevan observed. Winchester remained studiously silent. Penny focused all her attentions on her younger brother.

They reached the Brown house in the early hours of the morning. Charles got down and walked the girl and her brother to the door. "I'll see that your horse and cart are returned in the morning," he said awkwardly. He wanted to say something more but didn't, afraid of the words that might come out.

Penny pushed Peter in through the doorway, then turned to Charles. "I don't know how to thank thee," she said softly.

"It's not necessary," Charles answered, his voice suddenly hoarse. He could feel her nearness in the dark. "It's all right." Steeling himself he added, "I only wanted to talk with you."

"I know," she said softly. "When dost thou leave for the sea?"

"In about ten days or two weeks, I think."

Penny paused significantly. "Wilt thou call on me before thou leaves?"

"I'd like that," Charles said. "May I see you after Ellie's wedding?"

"Isn't that tomorrow?"

Charles had to stop and think what day it was. "Yes, tomorrow morning in Chester," he said finally. "Won't you be there?"

"No. We are not to attend ceremonies presided over by priests, only Quaker ones."

"It's just the parson," Charles said. "It'll be a very small wedding."

"I don't know," she said in the darkness. "I'll think on it. I have caused scandal enough by being called on by a military man."

"Then I'll stop here on my way home."

"I will look for thee," she said, and slipped inside the doorway.

THE WEDDING PROCESSION to Chester was a joyous affair, with a radiant Ellie and a happily smiling Winchester in the carriage, hurriedly decked with wildflowers and ivy, driven by Attwater. Charles, John, and Bevan rode on horseback alongside. Across the Dee bridge and up the cobblestone street to the church, the couple was greeted with rude jeers and good-natured cheers by many of the passers-by. Inside, Charles was surprised to see Penny and her brother sitting in a pew near the back. On seeing him, she patted a space beside her, and he went there and sat down.

"I didn't think you were coming," he said.

"No one did," Penny answered with an impish smile. "Not even me until this morning."

The ceremony was simple and brief. When the parson closed his Bible and said, "You may kiss the bride," Charles noticed Penny take a handkerchief from her sleeve and dab her eyes. As soon as she decently could, Ellie rushed over and embraced her friend. "I'm so happy you came," she gushed, looking significantly from Penny to Charles and back again.

The procession went from the registry to a tavern down the street for the traditional wedding breakfast, where toasts were made and wedding cake eaten. It soon became increasingly obvious that Stephen and Ellie Winchester, unable to take their eyes and hands off each other, were anxious to be away. And as soon as they could politely do so, the newlyweds departed for home. In an aside to Charles, Daniel Bevan offered even money they didn't make it past the inn at Waverton.

Charles stood next to Penny in the street as the carriage pulled away. Peter stood beside Penny's cart, watching the two with a certain curiosity. John and Bevan had mounted their horses and were following the carriage. "Peter," Penny said, "wilt thou watch the cart for a moment longer?" She slipped her hand through Charles's arm and said, "May we walk a little?" They started slowly up the street—he in his best naval uniform, gold epaulette, and shining sword, and she in her plain brown Quaker dress and bonnet. Several passers-by stopped and stared.

"I was harsh to thee before," Penny said quietly. "I was trying not to pain thee."

"I know," Charles said. "Your father explained it to me. I don't think I understood before. I'm not sure I really do now."

"My father told me what thou said to him about . . . we two."

Charles stopped and faced her, still holding her arm. "I meant every word," he said.

"I don't want to talk about that now," she said, a gentle firmness in her voice, "but I would like thee to show me thy new house and lands, if thou still wishes to."

"I'd like that," Charles managed to say, his heart full. They arranged that Penny would call on the new Mrs. Eleanor Winchester at her husband's home outside Tattenall two days hence. Charles would meet her there in the morning and take her to see his properties. They walked a little further together until they became uncomfortable with people gawking at them and started back.

All the next morning Charles spent with the workmen at his manor house, trying to urge them along in the impossible hope that they might be finished before Penny arrived. Around noon, he noticed a uniformed courier riding up the drive on horseback.

"Good day," Charles said, his heart sinking, as the courier dismounted. "Orders already?"

"Yes, sir," he said, unstrapping the leather bag behind his saddle. "I have three, for Commander Edgemont and Lieutenants Bevan and Winchester."

"I'll sign for them," Charles said. "I'm Edgemont."

As the courier extracted the canvas envelopes, he said, "Have you heard the news, sir?"

"What news?"

"Spithead, the fleet anchorage at Portsmouth, the whole Channel fleet's mutinied. Sixteen ships of the line in all."

"The whole fleet?" Charles said in dismay. "My God, the Admiralty must be in an uproar."

"Yes, sir," the courier said, pocketing the receipt. His eyes darted left and right. "Begging your pardon, but if you ask me it's no surprise. It's not right the way some of the men are treated—years at sea, no shore leave, lousy food, beaten and cheated on board. I've spent my years before the mast in His Majesty's service, I know. I'm only surprised it hasn't happened before now. Anyway, everybody's orders are being pushed forward."

"Thank you," Charles said. The courier remounted, then tipped his hat and rode away. Mutiny was a desperate act, almost always punished by death. There had been a number of mutinies in individual ships over the years, but the whole Channel fleet? The Admiralty would have to take notice, and in Charles's opinion reform was long overdue. He hoped that something would come of it other than a mass of senseless hangings.

He sorted through the envelopes, pocketed two, and broke the seal on the third, which was addressed to "Charles Edgemont, Esq., hereby appointed Commander, H. M. Frigate *Louisa*." The first sentence was all he needed read: "Sir, You are hereby requested and required to report on board H.M. Frigate *Louisa,* presently moored at the Plymouth yards, not later than May 1, 1797."

Charles read the entire page through several times as if there might be some secret escape clause hidden in it, such as, "if convenient," or "conditions in your personal life permitting." The bald fact confronting him was that he had to be on the coach to Plymouth in two days' time, and he didn't know when he would return, if ever. He was ready, even eager to go to sea in every respect except one, and now there would be very little time to fix that. He thought about Penny's willingness to see his new house and lands. That would be a "step," she'd once said. And that meant that she must have softened her objections to his being in the military. He breathed a sigh. He wanted badly to come to some kind of agreement with her about their future before he left. Maybe it was still possible. He had one chance left, he decided. He would ask her to be his wife. She could say yes or no, but at least he would have asked. He worked late into the evening after supper laboriously writing out exactly what he wanted to say to her, and how, practicing and memorizing it.

THEY HAD AGREED to meet at the Winchesters' home after she had sufficient time to visit with Ellie. Charles guessed that ten in the morning would be about the right time for him to appear, but through anxiety and impatience he arrived in his carriage at nine-fifteen. He saw Penny's mare and cart standing in the street in front. Charles knocked on the door, which was almost immediately opened by a maid.

"Oh, Captain Edgemont," the maid said in an exasperated voice, "I am afraid Mr. and Mrs. Winchester have not yet come down." Charles had the impression from the tone of her voice that Stephen and Ellie had been confined upstairs pretty much since the moment they returned from their wedding two days before. "You are welcome to wait if you like, sir, but I don't think they'll be down anytime soon," she said. "Miss Brown's also just now arrived. I'm sorry, but I can't hold out much hope."

"I won't bother them, then," Charles said. "I'll just speak with Miss Brown, if I may." He entered to find Penny sitting stiffly in a stuffed chair in the parlor. He thought she looked distinctly uncomfortable.

"I'm sorry, miss," the maid said, turning to Penny, "but I don't think they'll be available for some time, not even if the house caught on fire."

Charles grinned at Penny. "Would you like to begin our tour?"

"Yes, please," she answered, rising and starting toward the door. As she passed the maid she said, "Please tell Eleanor Winchester that I am sorry she was . . . engaged, and that I hope to visit again when she is free."

"That will be tomorrow," Charles offered.

Once they were in the street, Penny said, "Tomorrow? Why tomorrow?"

"I've received my orders," Charles said seriously. "Bevan, Winchester, and I have to catch the coach to Plymouth tomorrow."

"So soon? I thought thou had longer." A flicker of concern crossed her face.

"Tomorrow," Charles repeated.

"Well, at least we have today," she said, brightening. "I am prepared to see thy lands, and I have brought us something to eat." She leaned into the back of her cart and came up with a blanket and a covered wicker basket that she put into the carriage. Charles unhitched Penny's mare and led her into Winchester's stable. They then set off in his carriage at a leisurely pace, Charles at the reins and Penny beside him.

As they drove along the narrow lanes between the fields, pastures, and hedgerows, he tried to explain what he knew of the traditional arrangements between the tenant farmers and the landowner, how the rents were apportioned and collected. She seemed very interested in these arrangements, and for many of her questions Charles had no answer. "You'll have to ask John about that," he repeated frequently. "He's to manage the place." In time, as the horse plodded along, she began to appreciate that it was a huge expanse of land including a great many small farms, woods, and pastures. "How much dost thou own?" she asked.

"There are two estates," Charles explained. "Each is about three thousand acres. I own all of one and half of the other."

"Four thousand five hundred acres?" Penny exclaimed, dismayed. "Thou art very substantial. More substantial than I ever imagined." She was silent for a time after that. Charles drove and chatted in a happy frame of mind. He felt comfortable and natural sitting beside her. Occasionally he glanced at her profile, her bright eyes and smiling lips. He could easily imagine a life with her as his wife and the mother of their children. He pictured her bustling around his house, sitting and talking with him at dinner, fussing affectionately over their offspring, sleeping beside him at night.

When the sun was as high as it would get, Charles asked if she were hungry.

"Yes," she answered, still distracted by the nearly incomprehensible extent of his holdings. "How large is it," she asked. "I mean, in miles?"

"I'll show you," Charles answered, and he pulled the carriage off the path onto a grassy meadow beneath a small knoll with a copse of trees at its summit. It was an isolated place with a few black-and-white dairy cows grazing nearby but no people or cottages in sight. He took the basket and blanket from the carriage and they started up the hill. The bright sun and its warmth bathed the countryside. Halfway up, Penny took off her bonnet and shook out her hair. Charles loved its soft color as it fell around her shoulders and down her back. At the summit, among the trees, he set down his things and stood beside her.

"Look," he said. Penny studied the expanse of land checkered with the new green of growing crops, pastures, and woods. Small thatched cottages and barns dotted the countryside as far as the eye could see, with several tiny hamlets and one larger village in the distance.

"It's grand," she said. "How far doth thy land go?"

"Almost to that steeple way over there," Charles said, pointing and brushing slightly against her as he did. "And in that direction to the stream. No, there, where that line of trees is." He turned her shoulders with his hands. "Down there is Tattenall, and do you see that house, the one with the trees around it?" The impressive structure stood out even from a mile away.

"Yes?" she said, a little in awe.

"That's my new house," Charles said, standing behind her, his hands still resting on her shoulders. "It could be our house."

Penny leaned lightly against him but said nothing.

He brushed his lips against her hair. She allowed herself to be nestled against him, and then his arms encircled her.

"Charles, please, no," she said firmly and removed herself from his embrace. She turned to face him. "I am willing to take steps, but not too many, and no large leaps."

"Penny," he said, frustration showing in his voice, "there isn't any more time. I told you, I leave—"

"I know," she said, stooping to pick up the blanket. "Here, help me with this." She handed him one end of the blanket and together they spread it on the grass. As he watched her open the basket and lay out its contents, his irritation left him. "Sit," she said and patted a place beside her.

Charles sat cross-legged on the blanket and surveyed her meal. There was cold beef, cheese, and dark bread laid out on wooden platters, some butter, two cups, and a stoppered container of cider that had been laid in over the winter. She handed him a knife and asked him to cut the bread while she poured out small measures of drink. Then she took the knife and sliced the meat and the cheese into perfect thin strips. Charles watched her hands as she worked—long, thin, and graceful. They ate for a time without speaking while he mentally rehearsed his prepared speech and attempted to find the courage to give it.

Penny broke the silence first. "Charles, may I ask thee a question?" she said. "It is only a question, not an accusation."

"Of course," he answered. "What?"

"Why dost thou remain in the navy? Surely if thou hast all this land and substance thou needst not."

His first thought was that she was going to "labor" with him over his profession again, but she had said it was not an accusation and her expression was open and earnest. In that light the question surprised him: He hadn't thought of his wealth and lands as an alternative to the navy. Why did he stay? It wasn't for the money. If Mr. Edwards was right, his wages as a commander in His Majesty's Navy would be small compared to the income from his estates. But he knew in his heart that he didn't want to leave, he couldn't, not now, anyway. "I wish there were an easy answer," he said at length.

"Please try," she said. "It's important to me."

Charles searched for a way to explain the complicated emotions that bound him to his profession. He decided to begin with his childhood. "When I was a boy, before I went to sea, my father often told me that a thing once begun needs to be finished. 'It's no good walking away from a job half-done,' he would say, 'not for the task and not for the man.'"

Penny nodded her head understandingly. "Pray continue," she said.

"I was sent into the navy at the age of twelve, shortly after my mother died." He remembered his tears at the thought of leaving home and his desperate unhappiness during his first years as a junior midshipman. "For almost thirteen years I have worked my way up on various ships of the line. I've studied sailing, gunnery, navigation, ships, and men, and experienced all of the elements of my trade except one."

"What was that?"

"I was never in a major ship-to-ship battle, with all the guns firing and us being fired upon. Never, that is, until just two weeks before I met you."

"Is that when thou wert injured?"

"Yes," Charles said, "in a manner of speaking." He reflexively touched his temple and could feel the scar where the wound had been.

"Then thou art finished. Thou hast done everything," she said hopefully, searching his eyes.

Charles returned her gaze steadily. "No, I'm not finished," he said. "First, there is the need to defeat revolutionary France. That task is far from complete." He saw a look of alarm come into her face and he hurried on. "There is a second reason I can't quit now."

"What?"

Charles took a deep breath and steeled himself. Up to this moment he had not confided what he was about to say to anyone, not even fully to himself. "It is possible that I am a coward."

"Thou?" Penny said incredulously. "I cannot believe—"

"It's true. During the battle I was scared, more than scared, terrified."

"But anyone would be," she persisted, "with cannons and guns banging all around. It must have been very dangerous. Were any killed?"

"More than a hundred died on the *Argonaut*," Charles said blankly. "I don't know about the Spanish; more, likely."

Penny's face turned ashen and she laid her hand on his. "Hundreds killed? And thou wounded? It must have been dreadful."

"Yes," he said flatly. "I have nightmares about it, terrifying dreams in which I can do nothing while others die horrible deaths. At times during the battle I was nearly paralyzed with fear." She opened her mouth to speak but he squeezed her hand and continued. "I have accepted a commission as a king's officer. Whatever you think about my profession, I cannot allow myself to be afraid in battle. You see, I must go on in the navy until I know for sure whether I am a coward or not. If I am, then I will quit the service as being unfit."

Penny sat silently beside him on the blanket for a moment, staring at her hand clasped in his larger, darker one. She raised her head and said, "And if thou finds that thou art not?"

Charles looked at her quickly, then looked away. "If I'm not a coward? Then . . . I don't know."

"I think I know," she said quietly, then fell silent again. "Thank thee for confiding in me," she said finally. "It cannot have been easy for thee and I understand better now. But having fear, even terrible fear, is not the same thing as being a coward. In the same way, bringing terror to others doth not make thee a hero. And I am sure of one thing, Charles Edgemont: Dreams or no dreams, thou art no coward."

"I thought you might like it better if I were," Charles said.

"Why?"

"Because, if I proved a coward, then I would leave the navy. I thought that would make you happy."

"Oh, no," she said quickly. "I do not want thee to leave because thou art afraid, and I do not want thee to leave because I wish it. I want thee to leave the navy because thou wishes it."

"That may not happen," Charles said.

"I know."

"And that's all right?"

Penny looked directly at him, meeting his eyes. "I don't know."

Charles thought about the question that he had promised himself he would ask. It didn't seem to be a very good time, but there wouldn't be any other. "This isn't what I thought we would be talking about today, cowards and heroes and the navy."

"What didst thou think we would discuss?"

"I think you know. Don't you?"

Penny lowered her head and said, "Yes, I know."

"Is it all right if we talk about it, even if it might involve big steps?"

"I am willing to talk about it," she said facing him, "but I might disappoint thee."

"That's fair," Charles said, and then with a deep intake of breath he began his carefully memorized speech. "Penelope Brown, you must know how I feel about you. I know this is difficult for you, but the fact is, my feelings are as they are, as you know they are. All I think about is you," he continued, "all during the day and at night—your face, your eyes, your words—everything about you fills my mind and my heart."

"Oh, Charles," she said, "that's beautiful. Thou art beautiful, but—"

"Just a minute," he said in an absurdly serious tone, "I'm not finished yet. I haven't gotten to the marriage part."

"Pray continue," she said, brushing at something on her cheek.

"I know I'm not very refined," he went on as if uninterrupted. "I'm not of your religion, and I don't understand it well. I know you don't approve of my profession as a soldier in the navy and that this is very important to you, as it should be. I would not ask you to change except in this one thing—to make an exception for me."

"Charles," she said softly.

"I'm almost done," he said, and she nodded for him to go on. "I want you to marry me and be the mother of our children and to live with me all our days. But I ask only this—that you will think seriously about marriage to me and that you will talk with your God about it. When you know in your heart what the answer is, then you will tell me yes or no, and I will be satisfied. Now I'm finished."

Penny did not answer him immediately. She sat silently on the blanket with her eyes closed and her hands folded softly in her lap. When she spoke she said, "May I call thee Charlie?"

"All my friends do," he answered.

She said, "Yes, I know. Thou told me on our first meeting." She sat still in her composed, serene way for a moment longer, then said, "I have a great fondness for thee too, Charlie, in the deepest part of my heart. If my conscience were clear I would marry thee tomorrow and long to be by thy side every minute. I already long for that, I want thee to know. But I am not clear. All my life I have been taught that war and violence are wrong and an insult to God. Now, in the stillness of silence, my heart pulls me to unite my life with a man who is a warrior, but my conscience says no. It is hard for me to know what is right."

"Is that because you would be disowned?" Charles asked.

"Oh, I will surely be disowned if I marry thee, but in a tender way," she said. "I would still be welcome to attend meeting for worship. No, what is hard for me now is to discern God's will, which I must surely follow."

"So what do we do?" he said.

Penny reached across and touched his cheek, tracing her fingers softly along the side of his face. "Thou art dear to me," she said. "I don't want to cause thee to suffer any longer than necessary. I will answer when thou returnest next from the sea."

"Thank you," Charles said, his heart full near to bursting. He took her hand and raised it, kissing her fingers. She leaned toward him and lightly brushed her lips across his cheek.

Late in the afternoon they repacked her basket and folded the blanket. They walked hand in hand down from the knoll, and in the carriage on the way back to Tattenall she sat very close to him while he drove. At the village he collected her mare and cart and tied it behind the carriage so that he could see her home. Ellie and Winchester came out to greet them, and Ellie gave a squeal of happiness on seeing them together and the expressions on their faces.

"Oh, Charlie, what have you done?" she said delightedly.

"I proposed marriage," he answered.

"How did it go?" Winchester asked.

"Don't know," Charles said happily, and he heard Penny laugh beside him.

EIGHT

CHARLES EDGEMONT CLIMBED DOWN FROM THE COACH
onto the worn cobbled surface of Millbay Road outside Plymouth
early in the evening, bone-tired after the long, jolting trip from Cheshire
and grateful to have his feet on solid ground. Daniel Bevan, Stephen
Winchester, and Timothy Attwater descended next, Bevan stretching
languorously while Winchester went to help Attwater as their luggage
was passed down. Plymouth had been the home port for the old *Argonaut* and Jervis's Mediterranean fleet, and all the men knew its haunts
well. "It's good to be home," Bevan said, yawning and rubbing his back-
side. "By Christ, I'm glad to be out of that carriage. Those things'll kill
you. Rattled to death, the papers will say."

Charles smiled in response while he looked up and down the street.
Something was out of place and for a moment he couldn't put his finger
on it. Then it came to him: While the street was not completely deserted,
he saw few of the warrants, commissioned officers, and other naval per-
sonnel that normally crowded the street sides and walkways. There was a
very small number of ships in the usually crowded naval anchorage in
the Hamoaze, most of them, judging by the state of their rigging, undergoing refit or repair.

"Look at that," Bevan said, directing his attention to two seventy-
fours with full sets of sail rounding Devil's Point in succession on their

way to the sound and the open sea. "Now that's beauty. Forget women—give me a ship of the line any day."

"You don't believe that," Charles said with a laugh.

"Well, no," Bevan allowed, scratching at the stubble in his chin. "I only said it in case some admiral might be listening."

Charles ran his palm across the stubble on his own cheeks. They had been two days in the coach and he was torn between the desire for a hot meal and a soft bed, or going out to see his new ship. A gravelly voice sounded at his elbow: "Tuppence to tote yer bag, Cap'n?"

He turned and saw a wiry one-armed man with a wheelbarrow standing beside him. The man had rigged a rope around the barrow's handles so he could lift it with his shoulders and steer it with his remaining arm. He knuckled his forehead as soon as Charles's eyes settled on him. He wore a golden earring and his hair was tied in a queue behind his head, which marked him as a veteran seaman. Charles noticed that there were about a half-dozen men with wheelbarrows or handcarts standing nearby. All of them were disfigured or maimed in some way. "I want to go to my ship," he said, coming to a decision. "There's a half-crown for you if you can find a carriage to take us there."

"And what ship would that be, sur?"

"The frigate *Louisa*."

"Ah," the porter said meaningfully. "I thought it might be something like that. Ye'll be her new captain, I'll wager. I heard ol' Jervie smiles on you 'cus of what ye did at St. Vincent."

Charles raised his eyebrows at the man's knowledge, but there must be a lot of scuttlebutt about the comings and goings of the fleet and the man had probably heard most of it. "Yes, I'm her new commander," he said. "Now, if you could help find us a carriage."

"I hear she's just had her twelves dropped into her," the porter continued, as if Charles hadn't spoken. "Ol' Grimsley, that would be the dock admiral, he's been paying close attention to her. More than usual. I'd be wary and check everything twice if I wus ye."

"Why's that?"

"Why's that? 'Cus Grimsley don't do nuttin' outa the goodness of his heart. I have a mate what does the port admiral's records. He sees the indents and all. My word, the stories he tells. Grimsley buys old and charges new, broke as good, and rotten as fine. Just ye check everything, is all I say."

"I will," Charles said quickly. "I appreciate your advice and I'll start as soon as I have a carriage to take me there."

"Easy as tying a bowline, sur," the porter said, and gave an ear-splitting whistle. An open coach pulled by two aging dobbins appeared from around a corner and plodded toward them.

After they had hoisted their sea chests aboard, Charles gave the one-armed porter a crown. "Where is she berthed?" he asked.

"In the Hamoaze," the porter answered, glancing at the coin and pocketing it quickly. "But don't expect much. She's a ways to go before she's ready for sea."

"You've been very helpful. What's your name?" Charles asked.

"Poole, Cap'n," the man said with a wide smile. "I was foretopman off the ol' *Caesar*. Lost my arm in ninety-four at the Glorious First 'o June."

"Must be hard on you."

"I ain't complaining, sur. I gets by. If there's anything I can do for ye, just ye ask for Jethro Poole. An' good luck with yer new command."

THE HIRED CARRIAGE deposited them at the gun wharf in the naval yard as the day's work wound down. While Bevan and the others unloaded their gear and paid off the driver, Charles walked out onto the dock to look for his ship. She was pointed out to him by a passing dock-worker, riding high in the water about two cable lengths' away in front of Torpoint. From what he could see at that distance, she had her masts stepped and her standing rigging, but no yards crossed. She seemed small compared to the *Argonaut* but was larger than the *Lomond*, probably a hundred-thirty feet along her gundeck, he guessed. Still, she had the raised fore- and afterdecks characteristic of frigates and a sturdy, seaworthy look about her. Charles surveyed the ship that would be his first real command and was unreasonably pleased.

"Perhaps we should board 'er, sir," Winchester said hesitantly, a sign that their relationship stood to change from that of brothers-in-law to that of commander and lieutenant. "Lieutenant Bevan has reserved a boat."

"Of course, Stephen," he said.

"*Louisa!*" Winchester shouted as the waterman hooked onto the ship's mainchains. This announcement of her commander's imminent presence on board was greeted by silence. There had been no challenge and no answering reply. For an instant Charles was reminded of his boarding of the disordered *Lomond* with her debauched crew. But everything looked reasonably shipshape this time, only unfinished and empty. He climbed up the sidesteps over the tumble-home, surveyed the empty maindeck, and swore under his breath. He saw no watch, no crew, no sign of any activity or human presence. The new masts stood without their yards or sails, like unadorned poles. The guns were in place, at least those on the maindeck, all housed and secured in neat lines on both sides in front of their ports. A glance told him that they were older models, scratched and rusted, salvaged out of some other ship. He swore again.

He started aft along the waist toward the raised quarterdeck and heard voices coming from the captain's cabin underneath. Ducking under the low doorway, he found four men sitting around a barrelhead, playing cards by the light of the galley windows behind them.

"Ahem," Charles noised loudly.

"Oh, m'God," one of the men, burly, muttonchopped, and balding, uttered as he jerked himself to his feet. The others followed as quickly as they could, one of them, a little taller than the others, loudly smacking his head against a deck beam as he did so. "Good evening, sir," another offered, while a third hurriedly collected the cards and stuffed them into his pocket.

"Please stand easy. I'm Edgemont, the new commander. Who are you?"

"Samuel Eliot, sir," the muttonchopped man said. "Ship's master."

Charles extended his hand. "Pleased to meet you." The introductions continued around the table: Davey Howell, the ship's carpenter, George George, gunner, and Matthew Lincoln, surgeon, still rubbing his skull.

"Where's the crew? And why is no watch being kept?"

"There ain't no crew and ain't no watch," Eliot said. "Apart from us there's four master's mates and a carpenter's mate. They've gone into the town for the evening. Ain't no one else."

Charles took his watch from his pocket and glanced at it. It was rapidly approaching suppertime. "Is there any food on board?"

"Only our own stores," the gunner offered. "You're welcome to share."

"Thank you, Mr. George," Charles said. "I promise to return the favor. You'll find two lieutenants and my steward on deck. Go introduce yourselves and work out who's to cook." As the men started to file out of the door, he remembered something important and added, "Pass the word for Timothy Attwater."

Standing in the middle of the almost bare captain's cabin, Charles told his steward to unpack their sea chests as best he could. Tomorrow Attwater could collect the furnishings and stores he'd purchased that were currently being held for him in the town. That would keep him busy for the time being and away from the galley stove.

Over dinner Charles asked Eliot about the general state of the ship and learned little that his eyes had not already told him. She had only a few of her warrant officers—no bosun, no purser, no quartermaster, no cook, sailmaker, cooper, or marines. Of course, she also had no crew. There were no stores from the victualling yard, no powder or shot, no yards, running rigging, or sails. And while the old twelve-pounder guns were secure on the maindeck, she still lacked the long nines for the quarterdeck. With a growing sense of alarm, he realized that the *Louisa* was far from being ready for sea. It would be almost impossible for him to meet the deadline laid down in his orders.

Charles went to bed, such as it was—a seaman's hammock slung from the beams of his sleeping cabin—in an unsettled and unhappy frame. He lay starkly awake for an hour as his mind drifted anxiously over all the many, many things that needed to be done before the *Louisa* would be ready to sail. In an effort to settle himself, he recalled his afternoon with Penny three days before, confiding his dreams and fears to her, and remembering her answers. Almost immediately he fell into deep and dreamless slumber.

Charles awoke late the next morning to the not-so-muffled sounds of heavy objects being dragged across the floor of his day cabin and his steward's high-pitched voice. "Avast there," he heard clearly. "Lift it quiet like or you'll wake the captain."

"Ain't he awake yet? Which it's nearly midmorning already," a surly voice answered, followed by a solid thump as something heavy was lowered clumsily onto the deckboards. "'At's the last of it, mate," a third voice said. Then he added hopefully, "That'll be three and sixpence for the delivery, and maybe a little something extra for the deliverymen, seeing as how nothing ain't damaged."

"Well I never," Attwater began, almost at the top of his voice. "What, there ain't nothing extra for—"

Charles rolled quickly out of his hammock and, still in his nightshirt, pushed aside the curtain to the day cabin. Except for the four twelve-pounder cannon and their carriages housed there, the large room had been empty the night before. Now in the bright light of the galley windows it seemed crowded with haphazardly placed crates and furnishings: a smallish desk, a largish table, eight chairs (six for the table, one for the desk, and one with arms for reading), a bookcase that would fold up into a box, and a cabinet. Attwater and two burly men stood amid the clutter.

"Now see what you've done," Attwater scolded the deliverymen. "You've gone and woke him." To Charles he said, "I'm sorry, sir, but these—"

"It's all right," Charles answered, pleased to see his furniture. "Give these men a shilling each for their effort, then start some hot water in the galley."

Half an hour later, washed, shaved, dressed in his best uniform, and with two cups of coffee in him, Charles sent Attwater to call the entire ship's company—all six of them, including his lieutenants—to the quarterdeck. As soon as everyone presented themselves he unfolded his orders and read them out loud, thus making himself officially commander of the *Louisa*. Having refolded the document and replaced it in his pocket, he turned back to them. "Our task now is to get this ship in all respects ready for sea as quickly as possible. We'll start with you, Mr. Eliot."

"Yes, sir."

"Go into Plymouth and collect the missing mates. Buy enough supplies in the town to last a week or so and then bring everyone and everything back on board at once. I'll pay for it, of course."

"Yes, sir."

"Mr. Howell, I want a complete report on all repairs and construction that still wants doing, and an itemized list of all carpenter's supplies needed before we sail on my desk by dinnertime."

"Aye aye, sir."

"Mr. George, every gun is to be fully inspected as to its fitness for duty. I want a full report to this effect and a list of the required shot, powder, and gunnery supplies. Lieutenant Winchester, you will draft a suitable handbill for recruiting crew members, especially topmen. I expect to review it with you after dinner and we'll have it printed tomorrow. Otherwise you will assist Lieutenant Bevan as he sees fit."

"Yes, sir."

Finally, Charles turned to Daniel Bevan, who had been watching him speculatively. "Lieutenant Bevan, you will schedule the watch officers, to include Mr. Winchester and myself when I am available. You will also organize the other officers, warrants, mates, midshipmen, crew, and any others as they come aboard. I suggest you begin immediately."

"Aye aye, Captain," Bevan responded easily. "May I inquire what you're to be doing?"

"I am going to call personally on the dockyard admiral to find out why the bloody hell this tub's in the unready state she's in."

"Good luck," Bevan said dryly. "It's possible you'll need it."

After the cabin had emptied, Charles sent Attwater on deck to hail a water taxi to carry him across to the dockyard. As the small open boat pulled across the nearly empty harbor, he remembered what the crippled seaman, Poole, had said about the dockyard admiral. Charles had heard stories about Admiral Arthur Grimsley—everyone had. He was said to be notoriously corrupt but with enough influence in high places that he couldn't be removed from his post. Charles remembered one lieutenant telling him a year or so earlier that his own captain was driven to apoplexy by the treatment he'd received at the Plymouth dockyard and how much it had cost him out of his own pocket in "gifts" and "inducements" to get it all put to rights. Shoddy workmanship and substandard materials seemed to be the normal way of doing business, unless a commander were willing to pay for the difference. It occurred to him that Grimsley almost certainly knew about St. Vincent and the Spanish warships he'd been awarded, and probably knew to the farthing how much prize money he'd collected. He had a sinking feeling that Grimsley would expect to receive a lot of it. On the other hand, Charles thought, perhaps Grimsley was a good fellow and would be eager to help. Maybe others, jealous of his position, spread false rumors to damage his reputation. That was common enough. Perhaps he would be pleased when Charles pointed the *Louisa*'s deficiencies out to him and soon have them put to right. And maybe, he thought again, the moon is made of blue cheese and faeries sprinkle sand in your eyes to help you sleep.

Charles paid the boatman, climbed the ladder up the side of the wharf, and went to the dockyard admiral's office. Inside, he was directed down a corridor to a door marked ADMIRAL COMMANDING, HIS MAJESTY'S DOCKYARD, PLYMOUTH.

A bent, white-haired secretary answered his knock and ushered Charles into a small anteroom and then disappeared through an inner door. Vice-Admiral of the Blue Sir Arthur Grimsley himself came out a moment later. Grimsley was a bandy-legged man of medium height with florid cheeks and an impressively protuberant belly that the elegant cut of his admiral's uniform could not conceal.

"Commander Edgemont, I'm honored, sir, honored," Grimsley greeted him, extending his hand. "All England applauds your heroic efforts at the Battle of St. Vincent. I've read all about it."

"You are too kind, sir," Charles answered, caught off-guard by the effusive greeting. "I only came to inquire about my ship."

Grimsley smiled broadly, half-turned, and slapped Charles on the back. "The *Louisa,* isn't it? A fine little ship, lovely. You'll make plenty of prize money with her, mark my words. I'll tell you all about her. But I am amiss. Come into my office. Port or sherry? We'll talk in more pleasant surroundings." He nodded to the secretary, who opened the door, and Charles followed the admiral with a growing sense of trepidation into the sumptuously furnished room with damask drapes framing the windows and brocade-covered chairs. "Let me see," Grimsley said, searching through some papers on his desk. "Ah, yes, the *Louisa.* She was built in eighty-five in the Brest yards—that's in France—and captured last June off Île-de-Groix. She's a very robustly built little ship for a French yard, if

I may say. What else?" He squinted at the paper and held it up to his nose. "Oh, yes. Seven hundred fifty tons' displacement, one hundred twenty eight feet on her maindeck, draws fifteen feet. A twelve-pounder frigate, of course, although she has nine-pounders on her fore- and after-castles instead of the usual sixes. A very, very sharp little frigate." They were seated and the wine poured out by a servant who seemed to have appeared from nowhere. "Now, tell me about St. Vincent," Grimsley continued affably. "I want to know everything, the signals from the flag-ship, Spanish maneuvers, *Argonaut's* role, everything."

This was not what Charles wanted to talk about and he wondered at Grimsley's attention. He had a sense that he should tread carefully. "There isn't much to tell, sir," he temporized, "that wasn't in the *Gazette.*"

"Nonsense," Grimsley retorted. "Don't be modest. Details, details. I want to know everything." He leaned forward confidentially. "For example, the little *Argonaut* being ordered to stand alone in front of the Spanish fleet like that. Old Johnny Jervis, the newly dubbed Lord St. Vincent, he ordered that, didn't he? It hardly seems the right thing, does it? I can well imagine you were furious when you received those orders. Heh?"

Charles sipped at his port to collect his thoughts. It seemed to him that Grimsley was not so interested in the battle itself as he was to see if Charles might be used as a weapon to discredit Admiral Jervis. "I was not commanding the *Argonaut* when those orders were issued by the flag-ship, sir," he answered, choosing his words carefully and hoping to stay well clear of whatever vendetta Grimsley had against Jervis.

Grimsley leaned further forward still, resting his hand on Charles's knee. "But you were on board; surely you had a reaction, an opinion? Jervis sacrificed your ship in a vain quest for his own glory, don't you think? You must have been angry at the folly, the stupidity of it."

This was too much for Charles. Not only was Grimsley insulting Admiral Jervis, but indirectly it was an insult against Charles himself, that he would rather hang back and protect his ship than engage the enemy. "No, sir," he said with some heat. "The *Argonaut* was the only battleship in a position to delay the Spaniards until the remainder of our line could engage. I'll admit that I was anxious, frightened even. I under-stood the odds. But in my opinion it was an act of courage for Admiral

Jervis to order her into such a position, knowing that she would surely be destroyed, not otherwise."

Grimsley straightened abruptly in his chair, his eyes turning cold and his mouth hardening. "So you're just another of Jervis's toadies, are you? I must say I'm disappointed." He paused for a moment, then continued in a barely interested tone. "You've come to inquire about your ship, have you?"

"I'm no one's toady," Charles answered, trying to control his temper. "But my orders require that she be ready for sea by—"

Grimsley cut him off. "I know what your orders say."

"Well, sir, she's not as far along as I would have hoped. She has no running rigging or sails. There's no crew, no stores, and she's missing much of her armament and all of her gunnery supplies. Shall I go on? I must insist that the *Louisa* be made complete as soon as possible."

Grimsley remained unmoved. "You don't make demands on me, Commander. You'll not get so much as a nail or a biscuit until I say so."

Charles would guess what that meant. It meant money. He also knew that a battle with this admiral was one he would certainly lose. And if he couldn't get *Louisa* ready for sea, his career would be finished almost before it had begun. He hated himself for the next words he uttered. "Surely we can deal with this problem like gentlemen, sir. Perhaps you can think of some way I can help the work along."

Arthur Grimsley leaned back in his chair, steepled his fingers in front of his chin, and focused on Charles. "You mean some kind of accommodation? Financially speaking, I mean."

"Well, yes, sir," Charles said, resigned to dealing with Grimsley on his own terms. "In a manner of speaking. I was thinking that a contribution, a sizeable contribution, would be in order for the extra work and effort it will take to have the *Louisa* made seaworthy; some token of appreciation for the dockyard hands and shipwrights. I would leave this sum for you to disburse as you think best, of course."

"I see," the admiral said, struggling unsuccessfully to suppress a smile. "Something to help the work along. That's very generous of you."

Charles nodded, gritting his teeth. "For the good of the service, sir."

"We're both gentlemen of the world," Grimsley offered graciously. "How large of a sum were you thinking of . . . ah . . . contributing?"

Charles had no idea as to the amount of money customary in common bribery. Too much might seem suspicious; too little might anger the admiral. He was fairly certain that whatever amount he offered would likely be negotiated upward. "I was thinking a hundred pounds would be generous."

Grimsley pushed his steepled fingers together in a gesture curiously like that of a man at prayer. "A hundred pounds would be more than generous if this were some small civilian boatyard. I don't think you appreciate how many hundreds of men it takes to refit a king's frigate. There are porters, laborers, carpenters, riggers, not to mention draftsmen and clerks, and many, many more."

"How many hundreds?" Charles asked.

"Five." The steepled fingers parted and lay themselves flat on the admiral's desktop.

Charles forced a smile while his insides churned. "I wasn't proposing to reward all of Plymouth and the surrounding counties," he said with a small laugh. "But I may go as high as two hundred."

The figure finally agreed to was three hundred pounds cash.

The admiral seemed pleased, if not overjoyed, and was now anxious for Charles to leave his office. "And the money will be delivered tomorrow morning?" he said, rising and nodding toward the door.

Charles couldn't bring himself to shake the offered hand. "As soon as my bank opens. When can I expect my crew on board?"

"These things can't be hurried," Grimsley said, his smile fading. "You'll have to see Cavendish. He'll take care of everything."

Captain Cavendish, Charles knew, was the dockyard superintendent, Grimsley's executive officer. It was said he did nothing without his superior's approval. "I am sorry, sir," Charles said. "I expected to have my crew before now. I'm afraid I'll be too busy now to call on my banker until the afternoon, or even the morning after."

"All right, all right, I'll send over what I can in the morning," Grimsley conceded. "We have a hundred or so in the receiving hulks." Charles breathed an inward sigh of relief. "For the rest of what you need, you'll have to see Cavendish."

Charles wanted to be certain that his ship would receive all the attention she required. He began, "The *Louisa* also needs—"

"Cavendish knows what she needs," Grimsley said almost brusquely. "Now, if you'll excuse me, I have other problems to attend to."

"You will tell Captain Cavendish to take care of *Louisa* immediately?"

"Cavendish will take care of you," Grimsley repeated, pointing at the doorway.

"Just one more thing," Charles pressed as he backed toward the door. "The *Louisa's* main armament, the twelve-pounders on her gundeck, look like they've come from the bottom of the sea."

Charles thought he saw a look of uncertainty touch Grimsley's face. "Oh, yes—er, I had newer ones set aside for you, but they had to be given to another captain," the admiral explained rather hurriedly. "I had no choice; it was an emergency. The ones you have just need to be cleaned up a bit. A touch of paint will do wonders."

Charles thought the answer perfectly satisfactory, but the tone in which it was delivered somewhat strained. He wondered how much some other unfortunate captain had paid for his guns. "I'm sure a coat of paint will do the trick, sir. Thank you again, and I'll be looking for my crew in the morning."

Alone in the hallway, Charles's first thought was to go somewhere and wash. He felt as if he had been dipped in filth, outrageously treated and personally insulted, and it angered him that there was no way he could strike back. After calming himself, he went in search of Captain Cavendish and found that the dockyard superintendent would be unavailable until the next morning.

Leaving the building, he walked to a nearby tavern, still thinking about his encounter with Grimsley and the *Louisa's* cannon. Inside the half-filled room, the casual talk among most of the naval officers was about Spithead and the mutiny and how it should be dealt with. A few voiced sympathy for the sailors and the conditions under which they lived and worked. The larger number favored hanging for the ringleaders and harsh punishment for the rest, even if it meant flogging every sailor in the fleet. "You have to have complete discipline," one senior captain argued hotly, "no compromises, no concessions. Otherwise, there'll be no end to what the buggers want."

Charles sat with a fellow commander recently returned from the Mediterranean who seemed relatively unconcerned about the plight of sailors' lives. "The French have a new general commanding their army in Italy," the man said, looking very serious. "In the past year he's had one victory after another—Castiglione, Bassano, Arcola, Rivoli, Mantua. He's beaten up the Austrians so badly they say the emperor will sue for peace any day."

"Imagine that," Charles said with other things on his mind and only vaguely aware of where those places were. He was fairly confident that land battles in the far-inland foothills of the Alps wouldn't affect him very much.

"He's young, only twenty-eight," the commander continued. "They say he's ruthless. A Corsican named Buonaparte, Napoleon Buonaparte."

It was the first time Charles had heard the name and he promptly put it out of his head.

AT THE FIRST bell in the forenoon watch the next morning Charles sat, finishing his breakfast of toasted bread, cheese, and hot coffee at his own table, on his own chair, in his own cabin, when he heard a small commotion on deck, quickly followed by a knock at his door. "Enter," he shouted.

Winchester's head appeared through the doorway. "Beg pardon, sir," he said, "but it appears our crew is here. At least I think so."

"I'm coming," Charles said, dropping his spoon and signaling to Attwater that he was finished. He threw on his uniform jacket, snatched up his hat and sword, and hurried to the quarterdeck.

"Starboard side," Bevan said, pointing over the rail. In the water Charles saw four lighters crowded with all manner of men—young, old, heavy, thin, happy, and morose. A few were experienced seamen by the looks of them, many were rustic yokels, and the rest scattered in between—clerks, failed tradesmen of various kinds, possibly a few dandies escaping paternity suits or other problems.

"Get them on board and read them in," Charles said cheerfully. "It'll take you all day to sort that lot out."

When Bevan merely grimaced Charles said, "I'm going to see the dockyard superintendent. I'll help you with the watch-bills when I get back." He didn't say that he would stop at his bank first to withdraw the money to pay off Grimsley. When he finally arrived at the dockyard superintendent's office, he was in a less happy mood.

CAPTAIN CAVENDISH TURNED out to be a decent if hopelessly over-worked man with gray hair rapidly turning white. "I will get to it as soon as I can," he said, tapping his finger on the sheaf of lists Charles had given him. "I can't promise when. We're terribly shorthanded."

"I have to have food and water immediately," Charles persisted. "I now have a crew to provide for."

Cavendish threw up his hands. "I can't possibly do it before tomor-row."

Charles leaned across the desk. "Do you at least have my ship's boats? A launch and cutter will do for now. I'll send a party to pick them up, and they can bring back enough supplies to tide us over."

"I'll agree to that if your men load the boats," Cavendish said.

"Agreed."

They talked about the rest of Charles's lists, item by item, and worked out a rough schedule for many of them: food and water the next day; the nine-pounder guns the day after; spars for yards early the next week; sails and cordage after that; and on and on.

Reasonably satisfied in the end, Charles rose to leave. "By the way," he said out of curiosity, "what ship took my new twelve-pounder guns?"

Cavendish looked at him strangely, "What ship? No ship. The admi-ral had ordered new guns from the Ordnance Board, but they were con-demned, something about defective casting. They were returned to the foundry only three days ago."

"Thank you," Charles said. He left Cavendish and walked thought-fully down to the wharf, where he signaled a waiting wherryman. He hastily scribbled a note and gave it to the man. "Take this to the *Louisa* and give it to Lieutenant Bevan. Wait a bit. He'll want to send a party back with you so he can collect our ship's boats."

The wherryman, a former sailor himself, knuckled his forehead and then pulled on his oars. Charles checked his purse, then hired a chaise and directed that he be taken to the coach station on Millbay Road. He found the one-armed seaman Poole sitting on his wheelbarrow by the doorway to a nearby inn.

"Mornin', Cap'n." Poole rose as Charles approached. "How do ye find yer new *Louisa*?"

"You've a good memory," Charles answered with a smile. "She's coming along." Getting straight to he point, he ventured, "You mentioned you have a friend doing the dockyard accounts?"

"Aye," Poole said cautiously. "Is there somethin' ye wants to know?"

Charles took him by his one arm and walked him a little away, where they wouldn't be overheard. "Yes," he said. "I want to know what happened to twenty-two new twelve-pounder cannon that were set aside for *Louisa*. They were apparently condemned as defective and returned. There's twenty pounds in it for you if you can find out what's happened to them and why. Fifty if you bring me the paperwork."

Poole whistled. "I might be able to do that, sur. I also know some boys in the ordnance yard. Don't know what it'll come to, though."

"I knew I could count on you," Charles said, opening his purse and counting out ten pounds. "This should get you started. And, Poole, not a word to anybody who might talk to the admiral."

"'Course not, sur," Poole replied.

THE NEXT TWO weeks passed in a flurry of barely controlled confusion. One hundred two hands, overwhelmingly raw landsmen, had been delivered by the lighters. The ship's requirement was one hundred seventy-five, not counting the marines. Charles sent Winchester, with two of the master's mates and the newly printed handbills, recruiting throughout the port and nearby towns and villages. Winchester had obviously labored long and hard over the wording and Charles was pleased with its understated appeal:

BRITONS!
HEARTS OF OAK!
Here is your opportunity to join
CAPTAIN CHARLES EDGEMONT, the **HERO of St. Vincent,**
and **HM Frigate LOUISA** to fight your country's enemies!
Captain Edgemont is renowned for
PRIZES taken and prize **MONEY** paid among his crews!
Steer to **GLORY!**
Sign on today while positions are still available.

No impressments, Charles told Winchester; but he could offer extra cash bonuses for experienced sailors. Charles would pay for it out of his own pocket.

The remainder of *Louisa*'s warrant officers arrived in ones and twos: George Black, the purser, a rail-thin, cadaverous-looking man; Keswick the bosun; the sailmaker, the cooper, the armorer, and Mr. Mahone the quartermaster. Several midshipmen ranging in age from ten to thirty-four also dribbled in, and on a Friday afternoon thirty red-coated marines and their sergeant arrived on board and were promptly marched to their quarters. All of the men had to be read in, entered in the ship's books, assigned to watches and stations (there were two watches, termed "starboard" and "port," and while *Louisa* was on active duty they would normally man the ship in alternating shifts). Each of them also had to be assigned a berthing space, twenty-eight inches by six feet where they could sling their hammock—two men assigned to each space, to be used by whichever was not on watch. Finding space was not yet a problem, since *Louisa* was still seriously undermanned, but with her full complement on board every inch would be at a premium.

As the stores were delivered they had to be inspected, counted and weighed, signed for and entered into innumerable ledger books before being stowed away. Each warrant officer had his own responsibility: the purser for the food, water, spirits, tobacco, and the like; the gunner for shot, powder, cartridges, and the equipment needed to work the cannon; the bosun for spare spars and canvas, paint, cordage, and cables. It all had to be stored with care in the hold, since the distribution of its weight would be of considerable importance to the handling of the ship at sea.

Late on a Saturday afternoon Mr. Cleaves, one of the master's mates, approached Charles on the quarterdeck and touched his hat. "There's a visitor asking for you, sir. I haven't allowed him on board—he's a bit disreputable-looking."

Charles couldn't think who it would be, then he remembered Poole. "Has he got one arm?"

"Yes, sir."

"Show him to my cabin. I'll be there in a minute."

Charles found Poole standing nervously in the middle of the room when he arrived.

"I got what ye wanted, sur," the porter said without preamble. "It were scary difficult."

"What did you find?" Charles asked.

"It's all here," Poole said, holding out a collection of papers. "The admiral had yer guns condemned and then had the navy buy 'em back again, good as new. Paid for twice, they were."

Charles took the papers and began to leaf through them—invoices, condemnation reports, more invoices. They were all signed by Grimsley. "Pocketing the difference?" he asked.

"Big difference," Poole said. "It's all there."

Charles unlocked a drawer to his desk and took out an envelope he'd put there earlier—it contained forty one-pound notes—and handed it over. He put the papers Poole had brought in its place and relocked the drawer. "Why was it 'scary difficult'?" he asked.

"I think they're on to me, sur," Poole said. "I had to steal them papers. If they catch me, no tellin' what they'll do."

Charles thought about this for a moment. "Care to sign on?" he asked. "We'll enter you under another name."

Poole's face brightened. "I loved the navy, sur, but I only got one arm now."

"Pass the word for Mr. Bevan," Charles shouted at the marine sentry outside his door, "and tell him to bring the ship's roster." To Poole he said, "Can you cook?"

WITHIN A FURTHER week, already past the deadline set in his orders, *Louisa* was nearly ready for sea. Her yards were up and rigged, all her guns in place, and her stores as complete as they were going to get. He had long since received his orders, carried by packet from London. *Louisa* was to proceed to Lisbon with all dispatch, there to join the Mediterranean fleet. He was to report directly to Admiral Jervis for disposition at his lordship's pleasure.

Winchester's recruiting efforts paid off better than Charles had any right to expect, netting sixteen experienced seamen, which had cost him dearly. That, together with the warrants, petty officers, and others that had shown up over the previous month, still left the ship forty-four hands short. Charles decided it was time to visit the dockyard admiral again. Actually, with the papers he'd acquired, he looked forward to it.

The next morning he dressed carefully and allowed Attwater to fuss over him while he ate his breakfast. When he heard the ship's bell ring twice, he called through the door to the marine sentry to have the ship's gig readied. Then he went to his desk, removed an addressed envelope containing an unsigned cover letter and the papers Poole had given him, and slid it into his jacket pocket. As the gig's crew pulled across the Hamoaze, he thought about Admiral Grimsley and what he might say to him.

Charles was disappointed to find the admiral away, so he went across the hall to see Captain Cavendish. The older man looked at him warily but gave him a warm enough greeting.

"Where's Grimsley?" Charles asked.

"At the Admiralty in London," Cavendish said with a sigh. "In front of a board of inquiry. Just between you and me, I'm afraid they haven't got enough on him. He expects to be back in a week or so."

"I'm sorry to have missed him," Charles said, speaking truthfully. "But I'm here on business."

"What do you need?" Cavendish said, looking pained.

"Forty-four experienced sailors—topmen, if you have them."

"I don't," Cavendish said, "God's truth. I have six able seamen pressed off a merchantman yesterday and a motley collection of sheriff's quotamen."

The sheriff's men, Charles knew, were the rawest landsmen, recently culled from the region's prisons and jails: poachers, vagrants, thieves, and other petty criminals. "I'll take them," he said without hesitation, "and be gone on the next tide."

Cavendish leaned back in his chair and smiled. "I envy you," he said, "just starting out on your first command. I wish I had mine to do over again."

Charles felt the bulky envelope in his pocket. "May I speak to you in confidence?" he said.

Cavendish nodded, looking at him curiously.

NINE

"WEIGH ANCHOR, MR. BEVAN. AS SOON AS WE CLEAR THE sound you may set a course to weather the Eddystone light" were the first seagoing instructions Charles uttered as *Louisa*'s commander, and he said them with as much gravity as he could summon. The *Louisa* was already one week past the time laid down in his orders for leaving harbor. Charles watched with silent displeasure, tending to alarm, as the crew, the preponderance for whom the term "inexperienced lubbers" might seem a compliment, were sent into the yards or to the capstan or the starboard braces for the delicate maneuvers that would sail *Louisa* slowly over her own anchor so that it could be pulled directly upward out of the ooze of the harbor bottom. At Bevan's shouts of "hands to the fore and mizzen topsails" and "man the larboard braces," some of the crew ran to the left, others to the right. A few started up the shrouds of the wrong masts. In the confusion of swearing petty officers and bewildered landsmen, a furious Lieutenant Bevan bellowed, "Belay! Silence fore and aft!"

The ship slowly fell silent and movement ceased except for those asking what "belay" and "fore and aft" meant. All eyes turned to the quarterdeck. Charles stood alone by the weather rail, trying to look unconcerned while Bevan fumed. He thought that the worst thing he could do would be to intervene. That would be taken as lack of faith in his officers, especially his first lieutenant. He also knew from experience that marshaling a new crew into a disciplined, efficient organization took time and patience, and neither he nor Bevan had ever seen a ship's company with such a high proportion of utterly inexperienced hands before.

"Petty officers, assemble your men by divisions on the deck," Bevan ordered in a disgusted tone. When the crew had sorted itself, after some directing and shoving, into the appropriate groups on different parts of the maindeck, Bevan sent the topmen into the rigging, then the waisters (the mostly landsmen whose station was in the waist of the ship) to haul on the braces, and finally those who were to man the capstan to their places. Step by step he paced them through the process until the anchor was up and catted home and the ship under way. There was some further confusion as *Louisa* cautiously wore at Devil's Point and tacked around Drake's Island at the entrance to the sound, but apart from the ship's almost coming ashore at the foot of Mount Batton, there were no major mishaps. They added sail at the approach to Penlee Point, and when the long rollers of the Atlantic came under *Louisa*'s hull Charles finally spoke. "Mr. Bevan, please call the hands aft. I wish to address them."

Charles watched the men assemble in the waist of the ship, then stepped to the forward rail of the quarterdeck. All chatter and idle conversation on the maindeck below ceased. Some of the crew he knew well: his midshipmen, the various warrant officers, the masters and their mates, mostly. Two or three he recognized from the old *Argonaut*. He hardly knew any of the rest of their names. A half-dozen were lascars, and there were several blackamoors. The experienced sailors he could easily identify by their clothing and casual, expectant attitudes. He guessed they were mostly wondering what kind of captain he would be—harsh, lenient, capable, petty, stupid. The others, far too many others, were watching him anxiously. To them he would be one more new face in a confusion of new faces, tasks, living arrangements, food, and punishments. The first few months on board could be very hard for new hands, seemingly without reason or coherence, and all with the almost unlimited power of the captain and his officers hanging over them.

Charles had already read to them the thirty-five Articles of War (which he was required to do by act of Parliament at least once a month) the previous Sunday. The articles laid out in explicit detail the activities prohibited on His Majesty's ships and their attendant punishments, usually flogging or death. Now he wanted to explain why they were on board, what was expected of them, what rewards might come their way, and hint at what type of captain he would be.

This would be the first time in his life Charles had addressed so many people, and he felt more nervous than he had expected to. "Our task is to defeat the French and her allies at sea wherever we meet them," he began in a slightly faltering voice, which he covered with a cough. "I have noticed that we are not yet ready to do this." A ripple of subdued laughter, mostly from the experienced seamen, spread across the deck as he had expected it would. Bevan moved to call for silence, but Charles stayed him. When the noise died away of its own accord, he continued. "I promise you that by the time we are called to action we will be ready to give England's enemies more than they bargain for." His apprehensions leaving him, he attempted a gesture, pointing at them. "If you follow orders and work hard I promise that *Louisa* will become among the best fighting frigates in His Majesty's Navy—and, it is to be hoped, the richest in prize money.

"Some of you have a lot to learn," he went on, much more easily now, with a broad sweep of his arm. "This is all new to many of you. There's no shame in that. Listen to your officers, follow their orders, and you will all become expert sailors and proud of your profession. It will be hard and you will make mistakes. All I ask is, don't make the same mistake twice."

The faces continued to stare at him expectantly until it was clear that he was finished. Then someone yelled "Three cheers for the captain!" Charles had taken Jonathan Cleaves, one of the master's mates, aside earlier and told him to yell that. Three indifferent "huzzas" followed from the waist of the ship. Charles waved his arms for silence. "Three cheers for the *Louisa* and her crew!" he shouted back, and the men broke into a series of uproarious shouts. With the noise still echoing across the deck, he turned to Bevan and said, "You may pipe the hands to dinner. Afterward we'll exercise them aloft."

"I WOULD BE pleased if you and Lieutenant Winchester would dine in my cabin this evening," Charles said to Bevan as they were standing on the quarterdeck, watching the topmen high in the topgallant yards practicing reefing the stiff new canvas. The more experienced were sure-footed and confident even at those dizzying heights. The newer hands, at least those new to the tops, inched their way along the footropes, clasping the thick yard as if their lives depended on it, which of course they did.

"I don't know, I'm sure, sir," Bevan answered, his eyes never leaving the men working above. "Such short notice. I'll have to consult my social secretary." Charles was about to respond when his lieutenant interjected, "There, that man there, third in on the starboard yard. He's no business being in the tops. He'll kill himself."

Charles saw the man Bevan pointed out frozen in place, clinging to the yard with his arms wrapped desperately around it. "Have someone bring him down," he said quietly. "We'll assign him somewhere else." Finding good topmen could be a hit-or-miss proposition. Some were naturals, adapting quickly to working far, far above the decks on the wildly swaying spars, some came to it slowly, and some never adjusted at all. He listened as Bevan ordered a bosun's mate into the shrouds to lead the man down—"and mind your bloody tongue, he's scared enough already."

"As to dinner," Charles said, bringing them back to the subject on his mind. "I will expect you both at the end of the second dogwatch."

"What's the occasion?" Bevan asked, turning serious.

"I'd like your impressions of the crew, what we have and how do we bring them along. I think that should do for starters." That was part of the reason, Charles knew, to discuss the ship's business in a more relaxed and convivial atmosphere. The other part was simply to have company. He was rapidly discovering that being a ship's captain was an exceedingly insular business. He answered to no one on board and the temptation to stand in splendid isolation, issuing orders from on high, was strong. Captain Wood had done that. Charles couldn't remember him inviting his lieutenants to dine more than once or twice on the *Argonaut*. But the more he had thought about it, the more he liked the idea of regular, possibly weekly meals with Bevan and Winchester. Not only would it help to keep him informed of the day-to-day goings-on aboard ship, but it would also keep boredom away. He might do something similar with the warrants—the master, purser, gunner, surgeon, bosun, and so on—though not weekly, perhaps monthly. It would help him to get to know them better, and they him. The same could be said of the midshipmen, although that was a less interesting prospect. Some of them were mere adolescents and they ate like wolves. Which reminded him that he had to assign someone to see to their education, the basics only: reading, writing, spherical geometry, and celestial navigation. The small *Louisa* had no schoolmaster. Maybe the sailing master would agree to take that on; Charles would have to ask him. And if he invited all of them to dine in his cabin, and on his stores, on a routine basis, they would be obliged to return the favor. It would be good to visit the wardroom again from time to time, he decided. He missed the arguments, humor, the pranks, and tall stories he had known there. Of course, it would all be somewhat subdued with the ship's captain present.

Dinner that evening, their first at sea in the *Louisa*, threatened to be a slow and awkward affair. It was as if neither Bevan nor Winchester knew how to relate to him as their captain when they were off the quarterdeck. Both lieutenants arrived wearing their best uniforms. Somewhat formal greetings were exchanged as Attwater took their hats and swords. "Wine before dinner?" Charles offered. "I have claret and port. I recommend the claret early in the voyage and that we don't start on the port until that runs out."

"Claret would be fine, sir," Bevan ventured.

Charles nodded to Attwater. Bevan's use of the term "sir," which sounded more or less natural on deck, jarred him, but he let it go. "I have a toast," he said as the wine was served. "To the *Louisa*, her officers and crew. May we all benefit from our experiences."

"Especially the crew," Bevan rejoined with a grimace. "God bless their lubberly, gaol-house ways."

"And may God help their officers," Winchester spoke. "We'll need it."

"No doubt," Charles said as he lifted his glass and then drank. "The question is, what do we do about it?"

"What do you mean, sir?" Winchester asked.

"He means, Stevie, my boy," Bevan answered, "how do we go about making this ragtag collection of misfits and criminals into the best frigate crew in His Majesty's Navy? Do we bring them along fast and spotty or slow and sure? Do we start with sail-handling or gunnery, or both at once? Am I right, Captain?"

At that moment Attwater coughed discreetly to indicate that their dinner was about to be served. Charles gestured to the table laden with cooked freshly butchered pork and recently harvested vegetable dishes, purchased only hours before leaving port. As soon as they were seated, he said, "That's exactly what I want to talk about. I have some ideas, but I'd like your thoughts."

The dinner went well, with a lively discussion about new crews and their training, mixing experienced seamen among the raw ones, even (something Winchester proposed) holding small "theoretical lectures" on the various aspects of ship management, sail handling, and gunnery, explaining why things were done the way they were. "Oh, posh," Bevan said of the suggestion, but Charles thought it worth trying.

"We're agreed, then," Charles said, consulting some notes he had scribbled as the after-dinner sherry was being poured out by a slightly tipsy Attwater. "We'll concentrate on sail handling first, with explanations. Gunnery after they can get the canvas up and down properly. I suppose we must simply pray that we run into no enemy warships early on."

"Agreed," Bevan answered, leaning back in his chair and rubbing his belly. "Now, if you've had enough of us telling you how to run your ship, I suggest Winchester toast the king. I have the middle watch." The toast to the king, always offered by the junior officer present and always given seated in the navy in deference to low shipboard deck beams, was the traditional signal for the evening's end.

"There's one more thing," Charles said, staying Winchester with his hand. "Most of the new men know nothing of life on board a ship of war. I don't want to rely on rope ends and punishments to force them along. A little yelling and some pushing is all right, but no beatings. Life will be hard enough on them for the next few weeks as it is."

"You're sure about that?" Bevan asked skeptically. "What if there's a mutiny?"

"There will be no mutiny if we do our jobs properly. I will deal with serious breaches of discipline personally, but pass the word to the bosun's mates to keep their starters in their pockets or they'll answer to me."

Bevan looked at him dubiously but Charles ignored him. Turning to Winchester, he said, "The toast, if you will."

"To King George," Winchester intoned, raising his glass. "Long may he reign."

DURING THE TWO weeks the *Louisa* took to sail from Plymouth to Lisbon, Bevan had the men swarming up and down the rigging for two hours each during the middle, forenoon, and afternoon watches, taking in, setting, and reefing sails, lowering yardarms to the deck and hoisting them back up again. They repeatedly wore and tacked the ship under differing conditions and combinations of sails, backed and filled, hove to, and every other maneuver that Charles and Bevan could think of. When the *Louisa* dropped anchor in the familiar confines of Lisbon harbor, she did so with almost credible proficiency.

"The flagship's signaling, sir," said Beechum, the signals midshipman. "Our number, '*Captain to report on board.*'"

"Call away my gig, Mr. Beechum, and have the mail sacks from Plymouth brought from my cabin." Attwater had laid out his best uniform coat and hat earlier in the morning, and Charles had changed soon after Cape Roxant had come into sight on the port bow.

"*Louisa,*" the coxswain called as the gig approached *Victory's* towering side. Charles mounted the sidesteps, four bosun's whistles shrieking the moment his head rose above the level of the deck. The flag lieutenant led him aft to a bench in the passageway outside Jervis's office. "Not a good day" was all he said, gesturing for Charles to sit. Charles waited for an hour before being called inside.

"You took your time getting here," the admiral said sharply when Charles entered. "I expected you more than a week ago." Jervis's stern face looked tired and not at all pleased about much of anything.

"I'm sorry, sir," Charles said quickly, standing at rigid attention in front of the desk. "I had trouble with the dockyard. I thought it best to see *Louisa* properly fitted out and provisioned."

"At Plymouth, weren't you?" Jervis said, his glare lightening marginally. "What was the problem? Did Admiral Grimsley want to sell your guns to you?"

"Something like that, sir."

"That man's a drogue anchor on the navy," Jervis said, frowning in displeasure. "If he didn't have so many high-placed friends, I'd have sunk him years ago."

"I'd be pleased to see that myself," Charles said, thinking of the papers he'd obtained illegally and sent to the Admiralty. "But that's only one of the reasons I'm late. The other is that I have a very raw crew. I took some time to familiarize them with the sails and rigging."

"I see," Jervis said. "Well, that can't be helped now. In the future I expect you to be more punctual."

"Yes, sir," Charles said, still standing.

"Sit, sit," the admiral said, gesturing to a chair. Then he opened a drawer in his desk, pulled out an envelope, and offered it to Charles. "These are your new orders. You may read them when you return to *Louisa,* but I'll give you the gist now. I'm sending you to join Captain Ecclesby in the frigate *Syrius,* which is patrolling off the northwest corner of Spain—roughly between Cape Finisterre and Cape Peñas. Your duties are to interdict shipping and generally interfere with Spanish communications in the area. The only sizable harbors are at Coruna and the naval facilities at Ferrol across the bay. The entrance to the bay is well fortified, so you'll have to exercise some common sense."

"Yes, sir," Charles said, guessing there was more to come. He didn't think it required two frigates to stand watch over such a small and isolated stretch of coastline.

"I'm told," Jervis continued, "that there is a heavy Spanish frigate undergoing repairs at Ferrol, but she's some way from being ready for sea. You'll need to maintain a steady eye on the yards there and keep me informed of what they're up to. Is that clear?"

"Yes, sir," Charles answered. Two English frigates—the *Syrius* he thought had thirty-six guns and the *Louisa* had twenty-eight—should be able to deal with a single Spanish frigate, heavy or not. "Where do I find Captain . . . er . . . Ecclesby?"

Jervis frowned. "You were to rendezvous with him off Finisterre today. Seeing as how you're late, you'll have to find him somewhere along the coast. And you'll have to hurry because *Syrius* is overdue for repairs and provisioning. As it is there will be just enough time for Ecclesby to show you the ropes and fill you in on the latest situation."

"Yes, sir," Charles said. There was nothing else he could say. He assumed the interview was over, but the older man leaned back and appraised his young commander over steepled fingers in a way that made Charles uneasy. "One more thing," Jervis said thoughtfully. "Young commanders always concern me. You lads sometimes do the damnedest things. My advice to you is, be careful. If faced with a superior force, use discretion. It is of infinitely more value to me just now than valor. The frigate in Ferrol mounts forty guns, eighteen-pounders. If you do have to confront her in two or three months, follow Ecclesby's lead. Perhaps the two of you can do something together. In other words, don't do anything unusually foolish. You've only just begun your career as a naval captain. I'd like to see it last for a while."

Charles assumed that the admiral was saying he had potential. "Thank you, sir," he said.

Jervis extended his hand and Charles rose from his chair to shake it. "You'd better get started while you still have the tide."

"BEAT TO QUARTERS, Mr. Bevan," Charles said, staring absently over the lee rail at the dark form of Cape Roxant, rapidly disappearing over the stern quarter.

"Have the marine drummer beat to quarters please, Mr. Beechum," Bevan ordered, looking quizzically at Charles. The very short, fourteen-year-old drummer in his scarlet jacket and white trousers marched stiffly to the fore of the quarterdeck and started a ponderous roll. Almost immediately hands appeared, rushing up the ladderways from below to take their battle stations.

Charles cleared his throat and spit over the railing. "It's about time we practiced with the guns." He had told Bevan the essence of his conversation with Jervis shortly after he'd set foot on board, including their intended rendezvous with Captain Ecclesby, their patrol area, and the half-repaired Spanish frigate in the Ferrol yard. Charles had never heard of a Captain George Ecclesby. When he'd asked Bevan about him, the lieutenant shook his head in response. Together they examined the most recent Navy List—more than six hundred names, ordered strictly by seniority, starting with Admiral of the Red and ending with the most junior commander—Charles himself was third from the bottom—and found

Ecclesby quite high up: high up enough to have been passed over several times for a larger command. It entered Charles's mind that the northwest coast of Spain might be a place where the navy hid its incompetent and inexperienced commanders to keep them out of harm's way.

When he was satisfied that the crew was all present and accounted for, and every man at his correct station, Charles said, "You may clear the ship for action, Mr. Bevan."

The shrill of the bosun's whistle and calls of "All hands clear for action" resounded along the *Louisa*'s decks as men raced in all directions to carry below everything not essential for battle. The temporary bulkheads in the officers' quarters were struck and stored in the hold along with their furnishings and sea chests, the galley fires put overboard, the courses hauled up and put in brails, the gundecks cleared, and sand spread on the decking around the guns to improve footing and absorb blood. Charles watched the operation carefully and noted a good deal of confusion, but not nearly as much as they had experienced leaving Plymouth Harbor.

"Ship cleared for action, sir," Lieutenant Winchester reported somewhat sourly to Bevan. Both Charles and Bevan were studying their watches. Bevan glanced momentarily at Charles and received a silent nod in return. Then he turned to Winchester, who had also noted the time on his own watch. "Thirty-two minutes," Bevan said. "I'll settle for twenty-seven minutes next time, but before a real fight they have to be able to do it in twenty. Have them put it all back and we'll try again."

"Aye aye, sir," Winchester responded with the smallest of grimaces. The courses were refurled, the bulkheads and officers' furnishings replaced, the galley fire relit, and in general the *Louisa* restored to her original condition.

"Clear for action, Mr. Bevan," Charles said. This time it took twenty-five minutes. After that he ordered that the ship's main armament of twelve-pounder long cannons be run out. Each of the now newly black-painted monsters was eight and a half feet long from muzzle to cascabel and together with its carriage weighed two tons. Charged with four pounds of powder, it would throw a 4.4-inch-diameter twelve-pound shot almost a mile before it first hit the water; at two hundred yards it could penetrate two feet of solid oak. Charles directed Winchester to have the guns run in and out a half-dozen times so that the gun captains could organize their crews and the newer hands would become accustomed to the sequence of actions involved in loading, firing, cleaning, and reloading them. After that he permitted them to fire several slow salvos with powder only so they might appreciate the recoil of the guns against their restraining ropes and become familiar with the noise and smoke. Finally, just before dinner, he allowed each crew to fire a single round shot just so they could witness the satisfying splash in the distance.

At the end of the day, after the excited and talkative hands had their dinner and their spirits, Charles retired to his cabin (now replaced as if it had never been disturbed). He sat at his table while Attwater brought him his supper. As it did most nights after he had finished reviewing the ship's ledgers and made the necessary entries in his log, his mind drifted to home and Cheshire and Penny Brown with a sense of longing. He enjoyed reliving the things he and Penny had talked about and done together. He especially savored the memory of their last day, her touch and the moist softness of her lips on his cheek. Sometimes he allowed himself to think about a future with her and what they might yet do together. He had not heard from her during the time the *Louisa* was still in Plymouth, nor did he expect to. Winchester, he knew, received multiple letters from Ellie with every packet. Ellie had mentioned several times that she continued to visit Penny, but that was all. In order to give him something to occupy his mind, and in the hopes of communicating at least indirectly with Penny (it would be highly improper to write to her directly—they weren't even engaged), he began a letter to his sister in the expectation that she would share it with her friend. He wrote a few paragraphs nearly every evening, mostly describing the day's events. Occasionally he would write of his feelings for Penny, that he missed her and hoped that she might think of him from time to time. The act of writing took some of his feelings of loneliness away.

He also thought about the changed and sometimes awkward relationship between himself and Daniel Bevan. They had been fast friends and nearly equals on the old *Argonaut*. Now their roles were different and rigidly defined by centuries of naval tradition. Charles felt awkward when Bevan saluted him or called him "sir," and he guessed that his friend felt the same. After thinking on this for some time, he decided that the *Louisa* could make some of her own traditions.

THE WATERS OFF Cape Finisterre, the westernmost point of Spain and a major landmark for Atlantic shipping, lay calm and nearly empty in the late-spring sunshine. A few dun-colored fishing boats could be seen in the distance around the shoaling waters at the base of the Finisterre promontory that jutted from the mountainous Galician shore, but no merchantmen or warships, and no sails on the distant horizon.

"Crosstrees, what do you see?" Charles shouted to the lookout stationed high in the mast.

"Naught, sir," came the reply, "'cept for them few fishing barks alee'ard."

The ship's bell rang four times—four bells in the forenoon watch. "Seems Ecclesby's gone on," Bevan said, stating the obvious. The *Louisa* glided slowly onward, creaking gently as she rolled under topsails and topgallants in a steady westerly breeze over the placid Atlantic swells.

"Yes," Charles answered absently, thinking of Penny and wishing he could share the beauty of the scene with her, the rugged Spanish mountainsides covered in the fresh green of spring cascading down to the deep blue of the sea. He reluctantly shifted his attention to the present. Should he order further gun practice? The gun crews were becoming more adept with the weapons, but were still slower from one broadside to the next than he liked. And God alone knew how accurate they would be—they had not as yet practiced with shotted guns against a target. But it was Sunday and he had worked his crew hard since leaving Plymouth. He decided to give them an easy day. He would also make one other small change in the *Louisa*'s social routine.

"Let's get the courses and royals on her, Daniel," Charles said casually, omitting the customary "Mr. Bevan" for the first time since he'd taken command of the ship. "Once we clear the headland, I want to steer east by northeast. We'll have a look into Coruna Bay before nightfall."

"Aye aye," Bevan said, giving Charles a sideways glance and a small smile.

THE CORUNA LIGHTHOUSE showed first. Kept dark during the war, it could be seen from fifteen miles away or more on a clear day, even from *Louisa*'s decks. It looked to be a very old stone tower indeed. Some said that it was built by the Romans when they ruled Galicia; others thought earlier, by the Phoenicians. Nearby, atop the bluffs that marked the southern entrance to the bay, sat a stark fort housing one of the batteries protecting against intruders. The fort was clearly marked on Charles's charts, as was a second battery on the Ferrol promontory at the northern entrance to the bay. The width of the mouth of the inlet and the distance between the forts was less than three miles, close enough for the forty-two-pounder cannon on both sides to pour down a deadly crossfire on anyone who dared try the passage.

In an inlet on the northern edge of Coruna Bay, behind the Ferrol fortifications, lay the Spanish naval shipyard. It was from this yard and the bay itself that Philip II's "Invincible Armada" sailed to invade England in 1588, and it was the city of Coruna that Drake captured and burned in retaliation a year later. With the sun low on the horizon lighting the hillsides in a warm glow, it was hard for Charles to imagine the now-empty roads as they must have been then, crowded with ships of war readying to make sail. The distant sounds of Coruna's church bells reached him from over the water, and he could just see the steeples behind the headlands and Coruna's whitewashed houses scattered like bread crumbs over the slopes. It looked tranquil—and would remain so, as long as he stayed out of range of the batteries in the forts.

The *Louisa* glided north by east across the mouth of the bay under shortened sails. In a few moments the lookout should be able to see into the naval yards.

"Do you see anything yet?" Charles shouted up to the top.

"Not yet, sir. Just a minute."

Charles waited, tapping his fingers absently on the lee rail. "Sir, I see one ship-rigged craft in the yards, just the one. A frigate, I think," the lookout reported. "There's some small coastal craft and a hulk or two. That's all." That was what Charles had expected, one half-repaired Spanish frigate. A gun sounded unexpectedly from the fort at the southern entrance to the bay. Charles turned in time to see its smoke drift lazily past the battlements. What was that for, he wondered. The *Louisa* was well out of range of either battery. He saw no telltale splash of a ball.

"Very well," Charles said to Bevan, "we've—"

"The frigate's dropped her sails!" the lookout shouted excitedly.

"What?" Charles said. He grabbed his telescope from its place by the mast and started up the mizzen shrouds to see for himself. At the platform at the mizzentop he steadied the glass on the entrance to the yards. He found her immediately, a large frigate with filling sails and a black hull, beating up against the wind. Charles snapped the telescope shut and turned to start back down, then he stopped and opened it again. There was something familiar about the ship. He studied her lines with his glass and it came to him. She was the *Santa Brigida,* the same ship that had cruelly raked the battered *Argonaut* at St. Vincent. "You son of a bitch," Charles muttered to himself.

"Shoals dead ahead," the lookout cried. He looked and could see the white line of surf among black rocks over the bow, about a mile distant. He had expected them. They were marked on his chart as "*Dientes del Diablo*"— the Devil's Teeth.

Back on the quarterdeck, he ordered to the quartermaster at the wheel, "Two points to windward please, Mr. Mahone." Turning to Bevan, he said, "Let's get the sails back on her, courses to topgallants and a full set of jibs." Charles knew there was little chance that any ship, especially a heavy frigate, coming out of Ferrol would overhaul them. Not only because the *Louisa* would show a clean pair of heels in light winds and moderate seas, but also because, with the wind west by northwest, the Spaniard would have to beat against it for several miles before she could round the reef and take up the *Louisa*'s wake in pursuit. Still, there was no point in taking chances.

BY NIGHTFALL THEY had watched the *Santa Brigida*'s sails sink below the horizon and by midnight had worn around Cape Ortegal and afterward changed heading to due east to sail along the southern rim of the Bay of Biscay in search of the *Syrius*. They found her the next morning hove to off Luarca.

Captain George Ecclesby was everything Charles expected and more, an old, tired man with unkempt hair, an unhealthy pallor, and a persistent cough. "Where in damnation have you been?" Ecclesby greeted him angrily. "I should have left weeks ago."

"I'm sorry," Charles began, trying to be contrite, "I came as soon as—"

"Doesn't matter," Ecclesby interrupted him. "You're more than welcome to this pestilent, godforsaken region. Good day to you."

"Good day?" Charles repeated. The *Louisa* had only just arrived. This wasn't how brother officers treated each other.

"Yes, good day. You're my replacement. I'm returning to England."

"But, but . . ." Charles didn't know where to begin. "What about the frigate at Ferrol?"

"Oh, she won't be ready for sea for months, years, if ever." A coughing fit seized the withered man. "Good day," he wheezed when he regained his voice.

"But she's out now," Charles persisted. "I saw her. She chased me."

"Not my problem," Ecclesby snapped, his patience with Charles apparently at an end. "Now get off my ship."

"Just a minute . . ." Charles began, his anger and alarm rising quickly to the surface.

"Sergeant of the marines! Show this gentleman over the side. Throw him over if necessary."

Charles had no sooner indignantly climbed down *Syrius*'s side into his gig than the larger frigate dropped her sails and started north. Soon after he returned to *Louisa*'s quarterdeck, she was nearly hull down and receding quickly.

For the next several days he exercised the hands at the guns with a new intensity. Charles ordered contests between the starboard and larboard gun crews to see who could fire off the most broadsides in a ten-minute interval, with an extra half-ration of spirits to the winners. He offered prizes from his own pocket to the crews that came closest to hitting a floating barrel at one hundred, two hundred, and four hundred yards. When he was at least partially satisfied with their performance, he began his assigned patrol toward Cape Peñas, sailing purposefully along the beautiful high-mountain coast with its great spurs and gorges running down to the sea. The "Costa Verde," this part of Spain was called, and for good reason, given its forest covered coasts and highlands. They looked into each of the numerous fishing villages and minor ports along the way. The only other boats they saw were small fishing vessels that scurried in all directions to give the *Louisa* a wide berth.

At Cape Peñas they brought the ship about and started the long beat against the wind back to the west. Off the port of Figueras, the lookout spotted a single brigantine merchantman, but it darted into the fjordlike harbor under the guns of a coastal battery before the *Louisa* could close on it.

SINCE HIS MEETING with Ecclesby, Charles had spent much of his time thinking about the *Santa Brigida*. Allowed to roam the seas, she was a menace to shipping. Huge amounts of critical British cargo sailed past Cape Finisterre on its way between England and Gibraltar. Most of Jervis's fleet was supplied that way. A single Spanish frigate could do untold damage, slipping out of the Ferrol yards to snatch up a fat transport or two and then running for shelter behind the forts guarding the bay. He would have to do something, but what? Fighting her on anything like even terms was out of the question. The *Santa Brigida* could throw more than twice the weight of metal as the *Louisa* in a single broadside. Yet there had to be some way he could gain an advantage. And there was the element of revenge for what she'd done to *Argonaut*. Charles's jaw clenched whenever he recalled the Spanish frigate's shot screaming the length of the defenseless ship's decks. One thing was clear: Jervis would have to be notified of the changed situation as soon as possible, and, until some opportunity presented itself, the *Louisa*'s responsibility was to dog the Spaniard wherever she went, to warn friendly shipping of her presence, and to strike if the opportunity arose. The question was how to inform Jervis without the *Louisa* deserting her station.

The afternoon the *Louisa* passed the entrance to Coruna Bay for the second time, Charles stood her far out to sea so as not to incite a chase. That evening Bevan and Winchester dined with him, as was their weekly custom. Over mutton, potatoes, and pease porridge, the three men talked easily about the progress of the crew and several small discipline problems that were easily dealt with. Over the sherry, Winchester brought up the subject that was on all their minds.

"What about the Spanish frigate in Ferrol?" he asked offhandedly.

Bevan leaned forward, his expression serious. "We'll need help, Charlie. She's too big. It's a pity that old bag Ecclesby shot off like that."

"Well, we need to inform Admiral Jervis in any event," Charles responded. "To do that we need a boat, any boat. Preferably a Spanish one."

The next morning they sailed south along the coast, examining each of the inlets and harbors with great care. They found what they were looking for well south of Cape Finisterre two days later—a small Spanish *guarda costa* lugger anchored in the Vigo estuary, under the guns of the fort at Bayona. The moment she was sighted, Charles had the *Louisa* come about and stand out to sea, well out of the sight of land. After nightfall, with a three-quarter moon showing intermittently through broken clouds, they crept back in. Charles had already written his report to Jervis about the *Santa Brigida* and the abrupt departure of the *Syrius,* stating that it was his intention to hamper the Spanish ship in any way possible until help or fresh instructions arrived. The report lay in a canvas satchel in his cabin along with the rest of the ship's mail.

The *guarda costa* lugger was only forty feet long and would have a crew of no more than a dozen, along with a few tiny four-pounders for armament. Some of the crew might even be sleeping on shore. The trick would be to board and subdue her in silence, cut her anchor cables, and get under way before the guns in the fort could react. The wind was in their favor, blowing moderately but steadily from the southwest. Charles's greatest worry was the moonlight—too much when it shined through gaps in the clouds and too unpredictable as to when and where it would. He also knew that delay would not necessarily bring a better opportunity.

The *Louisa* cautiously approached the Spanish shore as close as she dared along an uninhabited stretch of beach under a high bluff, four miles south of Bayona. The Spanish landmass rose as an impregnable wall of silent blackness in the night. The loudest sounds were the surf against the shore and the more distant cicadas in the treeline above. "Stay in the shadows as much as you can," Charles said to Winchester, who was preparing to climb down into the *Louisa*'s cutter, where sixteen of the crew were already assembled with cutlasses and axes.

"Yes, sir," Winchester answered tersely. They had gone over the plan several times already.

"If it goes badly, get out as fast as you can. We'll think of something else."

"Let him go, Charlie," Bevan said, putting his hand on Charles's shoulder. "He knows what to do."

Charles stepped back. "Good luck, Stephen," he said, intensely aware that he could be sending these men—including his brother-in-law—to their deaths, or years of miserable confinement in a Spanish prison. Stephen Winchester slipped over the side and into the cutter. Charles heard him say, "Let go all," and heard the oars dipping into the water. The cutter soon disappeared, indistinguishable against the black void of the shoreline.

Charles stared hard into the dark for a moment longer, then turned back to Bevan. "Put the ship on the larboard tack and let's get to our station." Bevan nodded to the bosun beside him, and in a minute the hands climbed silently into the rigging without the usual whistles or shouted orders. As the topgallants and topsails were crowded on one by one, *Louisa*'s head began to swing and he felt the ship gain way. They stood a little out to sea, then sailed north, approaching the shore again just out of cannon range on the other side of the fort, with luck undetected in the night. If something did go wrong—if a cry was raised or the fort opened fire—they would stand in and try to create a diversion so that Winchester and his men could escape. When they had worked out the plan the evening before, it had all seemed plausible. Now, staring over the railing into the darkness and straining his ears for any sound, Charles thought it possibly the most irresponsible, stupidest notion he had ever come up with.

A ray of moonlight pierced the clouds, briefly illuminating the fort on the headland. Snatching a glass, he could just make out the lugger still anchored where she had been the day before. Everything seemed deceptively quiet, peaceful, normal. A few dim lights from Bayona flickered in the distance, glittering off the wave tops. Time passed at a crawl. Charles's stomach muscles began to ache. He could see nothing. Maybe the cutter had gotten lost, he thought, or hit a reef and sunk, or been intercepted by a Spanish guard boat, or . . . Surely the cutter should have gotten there by now. He waited, drumming his fingers on the lee railing until he noticed it; then he balled his hand into a fist and jammed it into his pocket.

After an interminable time there was a noise, distant and insubstantial. A warning yell perhaps, or a cry for help. Then the clear sound of a musket being fired echoed across the water. That was bad—Winchester's men weren't armed with muskets. Almost immediately a bugle sounded its warning from the fort. The clouds over Bayona parted again and with his glass Charles saw that the lugger had set her sails and was moving. If he saw it, he was sure the gun crews in the fort could see it, too.

"We'll stand in. Prepare to fire, Daniel."

"All hands to set sail!" Bevan bellowed, there no longer being any reason for quiet. "Run out the larboard guns."

A bright flash from the fort lit the harbor for an instant, followed by three more almost simultaneously. The great bangs of the guns reached them an instant later. Charles couldn't see where the shots fell but he would be surprised if they could hit the tiny lugger on their first salvo. "Come about and fire," Charles ordered. The fort was out of range of *Louisa*'s twelve-pounders, but the muzzle flashes and noise would divert their attention.

The *Louisa* turned into the wind and the deafening crash of her broadside sounded, heeling her slightly with the guns' recoil. In the instant of light Charles saw the lugger, with the ship's cutter in tow, rounding the Bayona Point with all sail set.

"Time to go," Charles said quickly.

Bevan shouted out orders. *Louisa* dropped her courses and began to pick up speed. One gun, then two more, followed by a fourth spit yellow flame from the fort. The first three were well wide of them; the fourth threw up a towering geyser far too close to their port side. And then they were out of range.

Three-quarters of an hour later, the *Louisa* found the lugger near the place where they had left Winchester and the cutter.

"Any trouble?" Charles asked when Winchester climbed aboard.

"Not really, sir," the lieutenant replied. "One of them had a musket across his lap that went off when he woke up. We must have startled him. There were only four in the boat."

Charles saw no prisoners. "Where are they?" he asked.

"Two died," Winchester answered grimly. "Two jumped."

Charles noted splashes of blood on the young lieutenant's waistcoat and breeches. "I see," he said, then turned to the master's mate who was standing with four experienced seamen nearby. "Mr. Cleaves, check the lugger for food and water. When you're sure you have everything you'll need, take her to Lisbon." Charles handed him the satchel with the report he'd written for Jervis, his very long letter to Ellie, and the other mail the crew had ready to send home. "You're to take my report directly to the flagship. Tell them it's urgent. Then get back here with the admiral's reply as quick as you can. Most likely we'll be off Coruna somewhere."

"Aye aye, sir," Cleaves said, touching his forehead. The first hint of dawn began to lighten the clouds over the Spanish mainland. Charles felt unreasonably pleased with himself, although he struggled not to show it.

THE *LOUISA* SAILED north and took up a position about five miles outside the entrance to Coruna Bay. The *Santa Brigida*, they could see from the masthead, was still moored near the entrance to the naval yard with her yards crossed and sails furled. She made no effort to exit the bay and challenge them, however, and Charles wondered why. Perhaps, he thought, her stores were not complete, or she lacked a sufficient crew. Most intriguing to him was the thought that she might be short of powder and shot. In normal times the Ferrol yards would be supplied almost exclusively by sea. The roads of Galicia were notoriously poor, and in any event the tip of northwestern Spain was a long, long way from Madrid. Charles had no way of knowing how much of her ammunition the *Santa Brigida* may have used at St. Vincent, but it might have been a lot, or even nearly all. The task of transporting the tons of powder and shot overland by cart or pack mule would require a train of several hundred animals and months to accomplish. The Spanish, who were frequently casual about such things, probably wouldn't bother to try. And if the frigate only had a few broadsides to throw at him, then it was Charles's duty to somehow draw her out and destroy her. He would wait for instructions from Jervis, as he had promised in the report he'd sent to Lisbon. But that didn't mean he couldn't make a nuisance of himself to the Spanish and see how the frigate reacted.

A series of rain squalls and a violent August thunderstorm delayed his plans by forcing him to stand out to sea to avoid being blown against the lee shore or under the guns guarding the bay. Charles watched with satisfaction, however, as the hands repeatedly raced up the shrouds to shorten sail in the howling winds and heavy seas without mishap. They had become at least a competent crew during the few months they had been at sea. Now they only remained to be tested in a serious action with the guns.

As soon as the storm abated, he put his ship before the wind and stood her in toward Coruna. Before they reached sight of land the lookout called down: "Sail ho! Fine on the starboard bow."

"What can you make of her?" Charles shouted back. As yet, not even the approaching ship's topgallants were visible from the *Louisa*'s quarterdeck. After a moment the lookout reported, "A sloop of war. One of ours, I think."

"Show our number, Mr. Beechum, and the recognition signal." A tiny rectangle of gray canvas was just visible on the horizon to the south as *Louisa* rose on a swell. As she dipped into the trough, it disappeared.

"She's the *Speedy*, sir," Beechum reported, peering through his telescope at the little ship now frequently visible from *Louisa*'s decks. Beechum hurriedly consulted a book by the binnacle. "Fourteen-gun sloop, sir. Commander James Allenby." Signal flags shot up *Speedy*'s halyards. "He has dispatches for us, sir," he translated.

"Heave to, Daniel," Charles said, briefly wondering whether he or Commander Allenby were senior. He decided that the odds were in Allenby's favor.

The sloop turned into the wind twenty yards away and smartly dropped her sails. She had a boat in the water before she'd lost all her way. Charles watched as *Speedy*'s cutter, with a dozen men in her, struggled across the heavy sea to hook onto *Louisa*'s lee chains.

The commander's hat appeared above the rail as two of the *Louisa*'s bosun's mates piped him on board. Cleaves and the rest of the lugger's prize crew followed him up the side. "I'm very pleased to meet you, Captain Edgemont," Commander Allenby said, touching his hat and extending his hand. Commanders were addressed as "Captain" only as a courtesy and Charles returned the favor. "The pleasure is mine, Captain Allenby," he said, shaking his hand. "May I offer you some refreshment in my cabin?"

"Thank you, no," Allenby replied and held out a canvas satchel. "I've only time to return your prize crew and deliver your ship's mail. There are orders from Captain Elphinbottom in there, too."

"Who's Captain Elphinbottom?" Charles asked. "What happened to Admiral Jervis?"

"Oh, old Jervie's in London on business. Elphinbottom's handling things from Lisbon," Allenby said, making a gesture with his fist and thumb depicting a man drinking from a bottle. "He's a bit—ah—peculiar, if you ask me."

"Do you know about my situation here?" Charles asked, worried now that Jervis hadn't gotten his report. "Do you know if they plan to send me any reinforcements?"

"Not a word," Allenby replied. "Sorry." He turned and started for the rail. "I must be off. I've dispatches for the Admiralty in London."

"One thing," Charles asked out of curiosity, "which of us is senior?"

Commander Allenby grinned and touched his hat. "You are, sir, by almost a month. You're sixth from the bottom; I'm second."

"Only a few short steps to admiral," Charles said happily. "Good luck to you."

"Good luck to you, sir," Allenby said, and to the twitter of pipes descended over the side to his boat.

Charles took the satchel to his cabin and opened it, shuffling through the thirty or so envelopes until he found his orders from Elphinbottom and to his surprise a letter to him from Ellie. Without a qualm he opened his sister's letter first:

Tattenall

14 June 1797

My Dearest Brother,

I wish you and your friend Daniel Bevan and of course my dearest beloved husband Stevie could be here at home this time of year. Everything is green and the roses are all in bloom. John sends his best wishes and asks me to tell you that he will be writing about the management of your estates soon. He says for me to tell you everything is going well and he has reduced the rents on the crofts and there has been some good result from this, exactly what I forget. He asked me to tell you more but it's too complicated for me to remember right now.

I must tell you that Penny Brown (do you remember her? Ha ha.) and I visit together about once a week. She is such a wonderful, wise person, my closest and dearest friend in the whole world, after you and my darling sweetheart Stevie, of course. I even went to Quaker meeting (they call it meeting, not church) with her last Sunday. There was no minister or sermon or anything! Anyway, I subscribe to the *Gazette* now and Penny and I read it together as soon as it comes. We always look for some mention of the *Louisa* and her crew, but so far in vain. She said just the other day, after we read about some of the naval battles (I forget which ones), that she didn't realize that being in the navy was so dangerous. She asked me to convey to you her fondest thoughts and that she is still laboring with your suggestion.

So Charlie, you must do everything in your power to keep yourself and my husband, whom I love and adore more than anything, safe until he can return to me.

Hugs and kisses,
Ellie

Charles rifled through the mail satchel further, pulled out fully a dozen and a half letters from Ellie to Stephen, and set them aside. So Penny and Ellie met every week and talked about him. And they even read the *Gazette,* and Penny worried that he might be in danger. Charles smiled to himself. Penny's face appeared before him, and he could almost hear her voice, almost see her. Suddenly his heart ached and he wished he were home so they could walk and talk . . . Then with a start he remembered his orders from Lisbon and tore them open:

Commander Charles Edgemont,
HMS *Louisa*

Sir,

Admiral Sir John Jervis (Lord St. Vincent) being detained, it has fallen to me to respond to your request for instructions regarding the Spanish frigate *Santa Brigida*. You are hereby expressly requested and required to make every effort to prevent said frigate from departing her base at Ferrol providing that you do so without endangering your ship in any way. Further, if she does present, you are authorized and required to capture or destroy said frigate so long as this will be done with every assurance of success and minimal loss to His Majesty's Navy. You must do this with the resources currently at your disposal as no additional assistance is available.

You disregard these orders at your peril.

Your servant, &tc,
Gladwin Elphinbottom
Acting Fleet Captain, Lisbon

Charles threw the paper on his desk in disgust. "What does he expect me to do, sprinkle it with faerie dust?" he muttered to himself. He sat in deep contemplation at his desk for a time, all thoughts of Ellie and Penny gone from his head. "Pass the word for Lieutenants Bevan and Winchester," he growled loudly at the marine sentry outside his door.

"WHAT ARE WE going to do?" Bevan said after reading Elphinbottom's orders and passing them on to Winchester.

Charles frowned at the question. "I don't see that we have much choice," he said slowly. "First, we're low on stores and are going to have to leave to resupply soon anyway. Elphinbottom didn't mention anything about supplying us at sea. I'm not sure he realizes that ships at sea actually need to be supplied from time to time. Second, I doubt Ecclesby is returning anytime soon, if at all." Charles took a deep breath. "To answer your question, Daniel, I'm planning to engage the *Santa Brigida*, at least to damage her enough so that she won't be a threat for a while."

Bevan whistled softly. "And how do you plan to do that, Charlie?"

Charles told him. "If the wind holds, we do it tomorrow morning," he concluded. Bevan was not enthusiastic.

Then, remembering another duty he had, Charles picked up a three-inch-thick pile of letters from Ellie to Winchester and handed it to him.

TEN

"CLEAR THE SHIP FOR ACTION, DANIEL," CHARLES SAID. The ponderous headlands of Cape Prior, just a few miles north of Ferrol, were well within view from the quarterdeck. The sun rising over the Spanish highlands illuminated *Louisa's* sails with a golden glow that contrasted exquisitely with the clear blue of the cloudless early September sky and the deeper blue of the long Atlantic swells. The ship's wake stretched in a wavering line, like chalk on sapphire, as far as the eye could see.

It's going to be a beautiful day, he thought. The air had just a hint of the crispness of the coming autumn. The wind blew steadily for now from the southwest, but would probably diminish as the day wore on and the landmass heated up. He hoped to get his business done before that happened. He watched as a solitary bird, a tern, he decided, soared toward the foretopgallant masthead and lighted effortlessly on the truck at its very top. There it perched like some kind of talisman while the masthead swayed lazily in its great circle across the sky.

"The ship's cleared for action," Bevan reported, breaking into Charles's thoughts.

"How long did it take?"

"Nineteen minutes, near enough," Bevan answered. "Best so far."

Charles nodded his satisfaction. "You may put her on a starboard tack to weather the reef in front of Ferrol and then beat to quarters."

Charles didn't like to use the name for the reef on his charts: "*Dientes del Diablo.*" It sounded too foreboding, too melodramatic.

"Aye aye," Bevan responded, then turned to issue the orders.

The *Louisa* came about smartly and started south by southeast, leaning moderately as she sailed into the wind. "Reef ahead, four miles off the starboard bow," the lookout in the fore crosstrees called down. Charles could just see the white surf boiling over the black rocks from the quarterdeck. He felt his muscles tense at the thought of battle. He couldn't tell whether he was anticipating or dreading it. The little marine drummer began his roll, and the cry "All hands to quarters" sounded across the deck. With a flurry of scurrying feet, the men rushed up the ladderways to their battle stations. As *Louisa* skirted the reef about a mile to leeward, Charles turned to Eliot: "When we get to a point a mile south and west of the rocks, I want you to swing her head around and heave to under topsails. We'll wait there and see what happens."

"Aye aye, sir."

"Crosstrees," Charles yelled upward. "Can you see into the shipyard?"

"Yes, sir," the lookout called down. "I see the frigate. Her yards are crossed. She's moored just past the fort. There's a power of activity on her."

At the place on the sea Charles had indicated, the topmen once again rushed into the rigging while the waisters heaved on the braces. When Eliot shouted "Wear ship" and spun the wheel, the *Louisa* turned full circle. "Back the foretopsail," the master roared, and she lost what little way she had, becoming more or less stationary three miles from the mouth of Coruna Bay.

Charles climbed partway up the mizzenmast shrouds with his glass to better see his adversary and consider the position, its advantages and liabilities. He hoped to lure the *Santa Brigida* out of her protected anchorage. She would have a long slow tack into the wind to get at him, her course options limited by the Ferrol promontory and the reef on her starboard and the direction of the wind over her larboard bow quarter. From the time the Spanish frigate came into extreme range of *Louisa's* guns until she beat up enough to present her cannon at close range, his guns could get off five or six broadsides. If they were skillful or lucky enough to carry away a few yards or even a mast, they might cripple her so that *Louisa* could close, lay across the Spaniard's bow, and rake her till she sank or struck. If they weren't able to damage the *Santa Brigida* sufficiently during the time she would be unable to present her broadside . . . well, Charles didn't want to think about that. The Spaniard's more numerous eighteen-pounders could do a lot more damage a lot faster than *Louisa*'s twelves. Another liability seemed to be that *Louisa* was drifting with the wind and current toward the shore—and under the guns of the forts—more quickly than he had expected. It was something he would have to watch, but if he could induce the Spaniard to come out soon enough they should be all right. Satisfied, he climbed back down to the deck.

"Run up the colors," he said to Beechum. Almost immediately the Union Flag of Great Britain broke out above the taffrail at the stern. "Any movement?" he called up to the crosstrees.

"Naught, sir. She ain't moving."

"Run out the guns, Daniel, and fire one," Charles said. He was beginning to worry that the *Santa Brigida* would refuse battle. The firing of a gun in these circumstances was a calculated insult, a challenge to fight every bit as personal as a slap in the face. He was in effect calling the Spanish captain a coward if he stayed at his moorings behind the harbor's fortifications. The roar of the gun sounded, then echoed back from the mainland's heights.

Charles waited expectantly, hardly breathing.

"She's putting on sail!" the lookout shouted. "She's coming out!"

Charles could just see the tops of the frigate's masts moving on the other side of the promontory. They were lost from view as the *Santa Brigida* passed behind the fort, and soon her bow appeared as she emerged into the bay.

The fort looked closer to him than it had when *Louisa* first hove to. "Mr. Eliot, take a bearing on those two forts. I want to be notified directly when we are about to come within range."

"Yes, sir," the master replied. He passed the wheel to two of the mates and went to collect his transit.

Charles watched tensely as the frigate wore around Ferrol point and her masts slowly came into line, pendants standing out sideways at every masthead. She looked powerful and menacing, her black hull cutting meaningfully through the water. Doubts began to creep in that would not go away. What if he had miscalculated the wind or the tide or the Spaniard's speed, or made some other mistake in his planning, or overlooked some vital fact? What if *Louisa* lost the encounter and he was killed or captured? He would be written off as a failed commander, incompetent and stupid. They'd say he was promoted too young; that he was inept. What would Penny think? He might never see her again. Would she remember him? And his friends Bevan and Winchester, the entire crew, they all relied on his judgment. The image of young Billy Bowles being smashed to pulp by a cannonball on *Argonaut* flashed before his eyes. The same thing could happen to him, to any of them. And he was responsible. He remembered Jervis's words to him: ". . . be careful . . . use discretion . . . don't do anything unusually foolish." What could be more foolish than a twenty-eight-gun frigate with an inexperienced crew and captain challenging a veteran forty-gun ship of war? What if he had no idea what he was doing and no business doing it?

On the other hand, he considered as he tried to force some order on his thoughts, he had the weather gauge, and he would get his broadsides before the *Santa Brigida* could respond with anything but her bow-chasers. That was advantage enough. Charles felt his fingers tapping against his thigh. He clasped his hands firmly behind his back and began pacing deliberately up and down the quarterdeck, only occasionally glancing over the railing at his opponent. In this way he hoped the crew might see how confident and unconcerned he was.

The *Santa Brigida* emerged from the mouth of the bay with all her sails set, from topgallants to courses. She was close-hauled, her canvas stretched drum tight, and heeled well over, running as close to the wind as she could lie. She seemed to inch toward them, and Charles supposed that *Louisa's* leeway was inching her toward the enemy frigate as well. Both ships would be uncomfortably close to the reef when it began. The *Santa Brigida* looked to be about a mile away.

"What do you think?" Charles said to Bevan.

"A few minutes," Bevan said, intently studying the slowly approaching opponent. "Then it might be worth a try."

"Try a shot anyway," Charles said.

Bevan crossed to one of the nine-pounder gun crews on the quarter-deck and talked for a minute with the gun captain. Together they removed the quoins for maximum elevation and spent a little time making sure the cannon was laid directly at its target. Both men stepped to the side. Charles heard Bevan say, "On the up roll," and then, as *Louisa's* side slowly rose on the swell, "Fire."

The gun barked and leapt backward in a cloud of smoke. Every eye looked for the fall of the shot. The telltale splash came on line and fifty yards short. That was close enough. Bevan looked at Charles, who nodded wordlessly in return. The lieutenant then walked forward to the quarterdeck rail and called down to Winchester commanding the twelve-pounders on the maindeck. "Fire on my command."

Charles heard Winchester's "Aye aye, sir" come from the waist. A shrieking noise passed through *Louisa's* rigging, and a hole appeared in the mainsail. He saw the smoke billowing across the *Santa Brigida's* bow before he heard the sound of the report.

"You may fire when ready, Daniel," Charles said.

Bevan balanced on the balls of his feet, measuring *Louisa's* roll. The deck slowly canted back. "Fire!" he yelled, and immediately the ship's side erupted in flame and smoke in a thunderous roar.

"Sponge out," Charles heard the midshipman in charge of the quarterdeck guns order. He strained through the smoke to mark the fall of the shot and saw that many fell short, but at least some were alongside. He saw no signs of damage.

"Load with cartridge," the midshipman yelled.

"Load with shot. Wad your shot."

The *Santa Brigida* gave off another puff of smoke and a ball tore through *Louisa's* rigging, severing a topmast shroud. "Splice that," Bevan shouted at someone.

"Ram home," the midshipman ordered.

Bevan stood, measuring the roll. "On my command. Fire!"

The *Louisa* bellowed out another cloud of gray acrid smoke and Charles felt the recoil of the guns through the deck. He saw splashes all around the Spaniard. There must have been some hits. The frigate was less than a thousand yards distant and still advancing.

"Fire at will," Charles ordered. The next broadside was a rolling thunder as the quicker gun crews fired before the more deliberate. A hole appeared in the *Santa Brigida*'s foretopsail in line with her mast, but he saw no serious damage. Some of the other shots were long, others short, and most were wide, a few well wide.

"Cease fire!" Charles shouted angrily. The ship fell silent except for the scream of a passing Spanish ball. He stepped to the forward rail and yelled, "*Aim* your guns for Christ's sake," at the top of his voice. "You're shooting all over the goddamned place. Resume firing."

The next salvo rained shot all around the Spaniard in a relatively tight pattern, and in the closing distance between the two ships he clearly saw several stays part and her foretopmast crack and sway. Still she came on—six hundred yards, five-fifty. The Spanish captain had courage to endure this. The frigate fired its bowchasers again, and Charles heard a crash forward and an unearthly scream as a ball struck someone. He looked quickly over the stem to check on the reef and saw that it was much closer; not close enough to cause immediate concern, but he wouldn't have much more time.

"Beg yer pardon, sir," a voice said at his shoulder. Charles turned and saw it was Eliot. "You told me to say when we was nearly in range of the fort."

"Yes?"

"We're nearly in range of the fort, sir."

"Thank you," Charles responded, his words drowned out by the explosion of *Louisa*'s guns. This time he saw several hits and the jib-boom split, throwing the frigate's jib and foretopmast staysail into confusion. The *Santa Brigida* immediately lost way, turned into the wind and, at four hundred yards, presented her broadside.

"Set all plain sail, Daniel," Charles said quickly. "Pile on sails, it's time to leave." As Bevan raised his hand to his mouth to shout out orders, the Spaniard fired. Round shot shrieked and howled across *Louisa*'s decks, thudding into her hull and sending up geysers in the water all around. A gun in the waist overturned, a yard overhead cracked with a splintering crash, and several gaps appeared in the railing. The hands rushed aloft to loose the tethered canvas. The *Louisa* slowly gathered way as her head fell off with the wind. Charles's eyes riveted on the reef, now very close on the starboard bow. He clearly saw the jagged rocks, which did indeed look like the Devil's own teeth when one saw them close up. He heard the *Santa Brigida* fire again, but didn't turn to look.

"Helm hard over!" he yelled at Eliot.

"It is hard over, sir," Eliot responded, anxiety in his voice.

The black stones seemed to race toward them, white surf boiling at their base. They looked like some unholy monster from the deep, baring its fangs and rising to swallow its prey. It would be close, too close.

The whole ship heard and felt the grinding scrape of her hull against granite. And then they were past. Charles saw several shiny sheets of copper flashing in the tossing surf as they sailed on and felt his heart pounding in his breast. He looked to see what had become of the Spanish warship. With relief he noted that she had gone about and was limping back toward Ferrol.

Bevan had *Louisa*'s guns housed and secured, her bulwarks and other furnishings replaced. The ship's bell struck seven times; it was just 11:30 in the morning. Once again the sky was a perfect blue and the seas running a gentle swell. The winds became variable and intermittent, soon to die away altogether. It was a stunningly beautiful day.

"How badly are we damaged?" Charles asked as Bevan emerged from belowdecks, where he had been conferring with the carpenter.

"All in all, not badly," Bevan answered. "There's some small damage above the waterline. The only real problems are the snapped main topsail yard and a few strakes stove in under the hold midships. It's nothing that the pumps can't handle, but it would be best to be taken care of in a yard."

"Dead and injured?" Charles asked.

"Four injured, one serious," Bevan said. "A landsman named Gates lost a leg. We got off a lot better than we . . . than you had any right to expect."

"Nonsense," Charles said with a straight face, "it was perfect planning."

"Sure it was," said Bevan grinned dubiously. "The best that can be said is that we haven't sunk."

"We hurt her, Daniel," Charles said seriously. "For now, that's enough." To change the subject, he said, "You may pipe the hands to dinner, and as soon as there's any wind we'll make for Portsmouth for supplies and to have her bottom fixed."

"Why Portsmouth, Charlie?" Bevan asked. "Why not Gibraltar?"

Charles cleared his throat. "Portsmouth is a little closer, and the wind favors it," he said finally. "That's in case anybody asks. Just between you and me," he met Bevan's eyes, "Admiral Jervis is likely to want to talk to me if we go to Gibraltar. He may not like what we've just done with the Spanish frigate, and he's apt to change my orders. If we go to Portsmouth he won't find out for a while. We have further business with the *Santa Brigida*."

ST. CATHERINE'S POINT on the southern tip of the Isle of Wight showed first, a tiny speck off the port bow. Soon the *Louisa* was sailing large past the Foreland and into Spithead, where she dropped her best bower as near to the entrance to Portsmouth Harbor as the pilot would let her.

Charles was preparing to climb down into his gig to call on the Portsmouth dockyard admiral's office when Winchester approached diffidently and touched his hat. "How long do you think we'll be in harbor, sir?" he asked.

"I won't know until after I talk to the admiral," Charles answered. "As short a time as possible. A few weeks, I should think. Why?"

"May I have leave to go home, sir? I'd like to visit Ellie. I could be back in plenty of time."

Charles had to think for a moment. He was sure that Winchester wanted very badly to see Ellie, but it just couldn't be done. He only had two lieutenants, and he needed both to oversee the repairs and manage the men and the resupplying of the ship. "No," he said. "I'm sorry."

Winchester's face fell.

"But, I'll tell you what I'll do. You send for her and put her up in a good inn. I'll give you permission to sleep on shore." While the young lieutenant considered this, he added, "I'd like to see her, too. And, you can show her the ship. Ellie's never been on a ship—she'd love it."

"Do you think that would be all right?" Winchester said doubtfully. "I mean, she'd have to travel a long way and all."

"I think it would be fine," Charles said. "We can send Attwater along to accompany her if you like."

"I think it would be better if she brought a maid," Winchester said soberly.

"Good, then it's settled." Charles promptly climbed over the side into the waiting gig.

Charles called on the port admiral's office and was directed to the captain superintendent of the dockyard. The man, one Thomas Bradley, was a kindly, slow-thinking gentleman with an open and friendly face who was more than happy to help but would not be hurried. He greeted Charles at nine-thirty in the morning with, "Madeira or sherry, sir?" His answer to every question seemed to be a sympathetic nod and "We'll get to it just as soon as we can."

Returning to the *Louisa* in a frustrated and slightly tipsy state, Charles found Bevan waiting for him as he climbed on board. "The men are requesting permission for wives and sweethearts, Charlie," he said with a sour face. Since naval crews were almost never allowed shore leave while in an English port (for fear of desertion), it was a long-established custom to allow "wives and sweethearts" on board. Which were wives, which were sweethearts, and which were professional sweethearts of the moment one never knew—and, if a captain were wise, never asked. Charles shrugged his assent and went to his cabin. When he emerged a few hours later, the maindeck was crawling with drunken whores and sailors (the liquor having been smuggled on board by the women), many of whom were doing their business between the guns.

Charles retreated forthwith to the quarterdeck, followed closely by a pleasantly plump young woman with curly brown hair, a cheerful freckled face, and a turned-up nose. She was apparently ambitious, with higher aspirations than common sailors. When he stopped at his usual place by the starboard rail, she stepped in front of him, lifted her blouse to show her breasts, and said, "Fancy a fuck, Admiral?"

"Thank you, no," Charles replied. He yelled, "Sergeant at arms! Show this young woman back to the maindeck and post guards on both ladderways. I want no unauthorized visitors on my quarterdeck."

"My name's Molly, Admiral," the girl called as she was being led away. "You just ask for me." Then, to the two marines pushing her along, she shouted, "Hey! Watch your hands, you short-peckered, ball-less faggots." The last thing Charles heard was her asking her escorts, "Do either of you want a knob job? Five shillings. All right, three." The only bearable thing about this, Charles thought, was that sooner or later the men would run out of money and the women would go away.

For the next several days Charles made regular visits to Captain Bradley's office. "No," Bradley explained patiently to one of Charles's many pleas and suggestions, "it's no good loading her victuals or powder and shot first. She's got to be beached to fix her bottom, and she has to be empty to do that."

"When will that be?" Charles had asked.

"Just as soon as we can get to it," came the answer.

After four days in port, Charles noticed that Winchester was becoming increasingly distracted. Early that afternoon the lieutenant asked if he could have leave to meet the coach from Gloucester—the one that Ellie would most likely arrive on. Charles agreed, but Winchester returned in the evening empty-handed. The next day there was a similar request and a similar result. At the lieutenant's third request in as many days Charles not only agreed, but, thinking it was the earliest coach that she might actually arrive on, suggested that he come along. He would enjoy seeing his sister, but most of all he wanted to hear what she had to tell him about Penny.

They took the *Louisa*'s gig to the point, then hired a carriage to take them up High Street to the George on Cambridge Road. The George was a tony inn with comfortable private rooms and a large public dining area catering to post captains, admirals, and their families. The two men lounged against the wall of the inn waiting for the Gloucester coach— Charles relaxed and in no hurry, Winchester in a high state of anxiety. Within a half-hour, to much honking of its horn, a coach-and-six clattered down the busy street and pulled to a stop in front of the inn. Winchester rushed forward to see if his wife was on board, while Charles hung back, not wanting to intrude on their reunion. He was therefore astonished when he saw that the first person to exit the coach was a Quaker woman in a plain brown dress and gray bonnet. He watched, rooted in place and his heart pounding, as Penny Brown lifted the front of her skirt with one hand and started down the steps placed in front of the coach door. She looked elegant, even dainty in her simple, modest clothing, and altogether beautiful. At the bottom of the steps she turned back to help Ellie descend.

Winchester arrived at the coach just as his wife stepped onto the street. Charles saw him say something to Penny and point in Charles's direction before he and Ellie embraced. Charles started hesitantly forward, awkward and unprepared. Penny's eyes soon picked him out, and she smiled with recognition, waiting as he approached.

"Good day to thee, Charles Edgemont," she said, smiling brightly, her face radiant.

Charles stopped three feet in front of her, opened his mouth hoping to say something eloquent, but the best he could come up with was, "Penny? I didn't expect . . ."

"Art thou not pleased I came?" she said, a shadow of doubt crossing her face.

He took a deep breath to regain his bearings. "No. Yes. I'm pleased." He stumbled over the words. "I'm delighted, overwhelmed. I'm surprised. I didn't know you were coming."

"I told thee that I would," she said tersely.

Charles racked his brain but came up with nothing. He was fairly certain that she had never said she would visit him in Portsmouth or anywhere else.

"Charlie, Charlie!" Ellie cried, having disentangled herself from Winchester. She hugged Charles's arm and exuberantly kissed his cheek. "Do you see who I brought? Isn't it wonderful? And Penny told me she has an answer for you. I asked and asked, but she wouldn't say what it was. Isn't it wonderful?"

"Oh," Charles said. He remembered that Penny had promised an answer to his proposal that they marry when he returned from the sea. He had to say something to explain his mistake. "You see," he said brightly, "I'm not really back."

"But thou art in England," Penny said, looking perplexed and a little embarrassed.

"Well, yes. In a manner of speaking. But, you see, we're only in port for . . ." he began, feeling that somehow he'd gotten off on the wrong tack and everything had become jumbled and confused. This wasn't what he wanted to be talking with her about at all. He stopped in mid-sentence, the essence of his sister's words finally penetrating. "You have an answer for me?"

Penny lowered her eyes and nodded. "Yes, but not here," she said. "There are too many people."

"An answer to my proposal?" Charles persisted, wanting to be absolutely sure that he understood correctly.

"Yes, to thy proposal." She glanced uncertainly at the crowd of people in the street, some of whom were looking curiously at them.

Charles stared into her eyes, oblivious to the world around him. "To marry?" he asked, anxious to nail down the last shred of doubt.

"Yes," Penny said in exasperation, "to marry. And to marry *thee*, before thou asks that question. I have come with a solution to thy proposal for marriage between thee and me. But if thou wishes to hear it, we must go somewhere less public."

"Of course," Charles said, noticing increasing numbers of people dawdling around them. He took her arm and quickly led her to a less crowded place on the side of the road. "Penelope Brown," he said very seriously, taking her hand and dropping to one knee. "Will you . . . can we . . . may I have your hand in marriage?" A number of the more curious passers-by had followed them to the side of the street to watch the unusual spectacle of a naval officer complete with sword and uniform in the obvious process of asking to marry a Quaker woman.

Penny glared at the faces gathering around them, then shrugged in resignation. She took his hand in both of hers and knelt in the dirt in front of him. "I have decided my answer," she said in a whisper that, though intended to give them a measure of privacy, only caused some of the onlookers to lean closer. "I am very tender toward thee, Charlie. I would willingly go anywhere with thee, even to marriage."

He bent forward to kiss her when he heard an onlooker say, "Oh, good on you, miss." Someone clapped his hands and applause broke out around them. Charles was startled to see twenty or thirty people smiling and clapping heartily. The two immediately stood. Penny stared in embarrassed defiance while Charles raised his hat and waved it in happy victory to the crowd. She quickly grabbed his arm and pulled him away to go in search of Ellie and Winchester and her luggage.

ROOMS WERE ARRANGED at the George, one for Ellie and Winchester and another, smaller one for Penny. She would not allow Charles to pay for it. "It might give thee ideas," she said firmly. That evening the four dined together in the public room. If Penny felt awkward or out of place in her plain clothing among the more gaily dressed admirals' and captains' wives, she did not show it. Midway through the meal she asked, "I was hoping that Ellie and I might visit thy naval craft."

"Oh yes," Ellie chimed in, "I'd love to see where my Stevie lives when he's away from me."

Winchester stared in dismay, first at his wife, then at Charles. "The women," he mouthed. "Wives and sweethearts."

"I'll arrange it for tomorrow," Charles answered with studied nonchalance. "Wives and sweethearts are permitted on board while we are in port, of course, so you may have company." Penny and Ellie looked pleased, while Winchester slumped in his chair like a slowly sinking ship.

After dinner, and after Charles had suitably said good night to Penny, he returned to the *Louisa* alone. It was arranged that he would call for her and the Winchesters in the morning. As soon as he climbed aboard, he quickly surveyed the maindeck with its huddled, exhausted couples between the guns, and women's clothing hung out on lines to dry in the night air. Well, he knew what to do about that, he thought. He had allowed the women on board, and he could order them off. He had done it before. He would have Bevan do it.

Charles found Daniel Bevan in what served as the officers' wardroom, sharing a bottle of wine with the industrious half-dressed Molly (Eliot had the watch, such as it was), and put it to him directly. "Daniel, I want the whores off this ship first thing in the morning."

Molly looked offended; Bevan kicked out a chair for Charles to sit in and pushed the wine bottle toward him. "Aye aye," Bevan said, "which are the wives and sweethearts and which the whores?"

"I'm a sweetheart," Molly chirped, "Daniel's."

"Aren't they all?" Charles asked, ignoring the girl.

"Not me," she insisted.

"I think some of them are actual wives," Bevan said.

"And actual sweethearts," said Molly.

"Then throw the rest of them off the ship," Charles said.

"Mrs. Winchester will be visiting, I presume?" Bevan asked. "The men won't like having their women taken away. Can't she look from the shore?"

"No, she can't," Charles said. "I have agreed to allow her and Penny to visit the ship."

"Who's Penny?" Molly asked, interested.

"My fiancée," Charles answered.

"Oh my, and congratulations. In that case I suppose we'll have to do something," Bevan agreed.

"Yes, but what?"

"Will you be, you know, doing the jig with her on board?" Molly asked with an understanding smile.

"No," Charles said in annoyance.

"Then if it's only for a little while," she offered, "why don't we have all the girls play at wives and sweethearts while she's here? You know, proper-like."

"I thought that's what they were doing," Charles said.

Molly laughed. "I mean proper-like, with no jigging," she said. "I'll fix it for you."

Bevan gave Charles an amused, questioning look. "That should be interesting," he said.

"It'll work fine, I promise," Molly insisted, and looked to Bevan for support.

"It would amuse the crew," Bevan offered.

Against his better judgment, Charles took the path of least resistance. "All right," he said, "but the laundry has to come down and no jigging. And no knob jobs either," he added, just to be clear.

"Speaking of knob jobs, Admiral," Molly offered brightly. Bevan gave her a warning glance and shook his head.

"What?" Molly protested. "He ain't married yet."

The next morning Charles left the *Louisa* amid a general bustle of cleaning, straightening, and the taking down of dried clothing. "Try and get them to dress a little more modestly," he said to Bevan, nodding at some of the women down on all fours scrubbing the deck with their skirts hoisted up and their breasts swaying freely under loose blouses. Molly, meanwhile, bubbled around the deck talking to women and sailors alike. Charles shivered, then climbed down over the railing to his gig.

He collected Penny, Stephen, and Ellie at the George, and, taking as much time as he could, escorted them to the ship. A bosun's chair had been rigged from the lower mainmast yard to sway the two women up. Charles and Winchester climbed up the side ladder. The scene that greeted them was somewhat unusual.

The decks were immaculately clean, the brightwork gleamed, all the lines were neatly flaked, and there was no sign of laundry anywhere (except for a sleeve protruding from the muzzle of one gun, Charles noted). Numerous couples were strolling purposefully arm in arm along the maindeck, a scene of happy if somewhat formal domesticity, while those of the crew who didn't have "wives" looked on seriously. Charles mentally compared the scene to the rhythmic heaving of naked buttocks between the guns of only a day or two before and was thankful. The men were dressed in their best uniforms and ribboned hats, the women at least better attired than before. Many were wearing sailors' jerseys over their blouses, and a few had ducks from the purser's slops under torn skirts. Some had applied liberal quantities of fresh make up.

Bevan and Molly were standing arm-in-arm on the quarterdeck, looking every inch the committed couple, when Charles and the others arrived. As Penny was lowered onto the deck, Charles saw Molly say something to Bevan and give him a push. The two descended the gangway together as if to greet invited guests. The sailors on deck tipped their hats with a serious, "How d' ye do Cap'n, Lieutenant, Missus," while the women attempted some form of curtsy. Charles had no idea how to reply, so he touched his hat and nodded wordlessly in return. Winchester looked stunned. Penny and Ellie responded with gracious, "Fine, thank yous," and "Pleased to meet thees."

Molly dragged Bevan over to them and curtsied rather too deeply, revealing almost all of her breasts. "Welcome to the *Louisa,*" she said effusively. "Ain't Daniel and I pleased you could visit."

"Thank you," Penny said, dipping more modestly in return and looking around her, trying to take it all in. "Which are the wives and which are the sweethearts?" she asked too innocently.

"Them here are husband and wife," Molly said, introducing the nearest couple. "Them's Ned and Catherine, er, Jones. Over here," pointing to another pair, "is Bob and Anne Smith. And that's Bill and Betty Brown." Charles winced.

"Oh, I'm a Brown," Penny said cheerfully. "Where art thou from?" She received blank stares in response. Penny turned to another twosome, a fifty-years-plus seaman holding a sixteen-year-old waif by the waist. "Who art thou?" she asked.

"Oh, them's sweethearts," Molly said hurriedly. "Like a pair of doves, they are." She took Bevan's arm and squeezed it against her side, "Daniel and me, we're—"

"Good friends," Bevan interjected.

"Yes, darlin'," Molly said, and kissed him hard on the mouth.

At this Charles took Penny's arm and said, "Come on, I'd better show you around."

"Is it always like this?" she asked as they started toward the quarterdeck.

"Hardly ever," Charles said.

"They aren't all real wives and sweethearts, are they?"

"Hardly any."

They climbed to the quarterdeck, and to change the subject he showed her the ship's wheel and the compass in its binnacle, and explained how they worked. They watched as the sandglass ran to empty and was turned, and he let her ring the ship's bell seven times. He pointed up into the masts and described their parts and names, and the names of all the sails. Penny stared in wonder.

"It's very complicated, isn't it?" she said.

"Yes, I guess so," Charles said. "It takes a while to learn it all."

"Can we go down, to the . . . lower floors?" she asked.

"I dare not." Charles grinned. "I don't think all of the wives are on deck."

Penny looked thoughtful. "Do all these women go to sea with thee?"

"No, none of them," Charles said. "They're only allowed in port."

"Thou—all of thy men—must get lonely while thou art at sea."

"Yes," Charles said reluctantly. He could guess the next question.

"Hast thou been with women like these?"

Charles looked directly at her. "On occasion," he said. "Not since I met you."

"Good," she said and hugged his arm. "Now I want to see thy cannons."

He led her to the railing and showed her one of the great guns. "This is a nine-pounder," he explained, "it fires a nine-pound iron ball. The guns on the main deck are twelve-pounders."

She studied the huge black thing for some seconds and looked at the rows of similar guns lining the bulwarks, but said nothing.

"All of this must be difficult for you," Charles said.

Penny shook her head. "No," she said seriously. "I want to know as much about thy profession and thy life at sea as I can. It doesn't mean that I approve or disapprove of what thou dost. I want to know so that I can be a good and understanding wife to thee."

Charles leaned and kissed her cheek, and she smiled brightly at him. Just then the ship's bell rang eight times. "It's noon," he said, "Attwater will have a meal set for us in my cabin. I've invited Stephen and Ellie and Daniel Bevan."

"And Molly?" Penny asked.

"No, I didn't invite Molly."

"Do," she said, "she'll be hurt otherwise."

"But she's a prostitute."

"It doesn't matter," she said firmly. Charles sighed and sent a master's mate with instructions to politely invite Molly to his cabin for dinner.

The meal was carefully prepared in the galley and ostentatiously served by Attwater and several assistants he cobbled from the crew in Charles's crowded cabin.

Talk around the table tended to ships and voyages and life at sea, with Penny and Ellie asking questions and the men giving elaborate, nautical answers. After a time, Charles noticed that Molly was sitting primly, ill at ease, without participating at all in the conversation. He said, "Molly, tell us where you're from."

The girl blushed and stared down at her food, "Oh, I ain't important, sir. But my folks was from Bremley, close on Basingstoke, before they lost their land."

"Is that when thou came to Portsmouth?" Penny asked, turning to the girl.

"Yes, miss, six months past."

After that Penny made sure that Molly was included in the conversation, awkward though it might be for the girl. When the meal concluded, Penny whispered something in Bevan's ear, and Charles saw his lieutenant nod in response. As Bevan and Molly and Stephen and Ellie rose from the table, Penny put her hand on Charles's arm to keep him behind.

"I want to do something for her," she said.

"Do you want me to give her some money?" Charles said. "I think she's made quite a bit already."

"No, I want thee to give her employment on thy estate in Tattenall," Penny said seriously. "Thou canst afford it, and she will fit in well with the others in thy house."

"With Attwater's family?" Charles said. His steward had kept him informed about his family's occupation of Charles's house, but he knew virtually nothing about what kind of people they were.

"Yes, they are a little peculiar, but very loving. I want thee to send her there."

"Why?" Charles asked.

"Because she is intelligent, creative, and hardworking. I'm sure she arranged this whole performance about wives and sweethearts for Ellie's and my benefit. And, if she stays too long living as she is, she will surely take ill and die."

"Well, maybe," Charles said.

"If thou art worried about thy pocketbook," Penny said sternly, "she is young and pretty and with a new start will soon find a husband of her own. She won't be on thy hands for long."

The idea of employing anyone, especially a prostitute, so as to give them a new start on life was a novel one to Charles, and it took a little while for him to get used to it. "What would she do?" he asked.

Penny pulled Charles close and kissed him. "I love thee," she said. "We'll have to ask her."

Outside on deck, they found Molly and Bevan standing by the starboard rail. Molly's eyes were ringed with red and her cheeks wet. Clearly she had been crying. Penny went to stand beside her and touched her arm. "Charles Edgemont wishes to speak with thee," she said.

Molly rubbed at her eyes and looked at Charles. "Penny and I were wondering if you would be interested in a job, for wages, on my property in Cheshire," he said. "You'll have meals and a place to live and I'll pay you ten shillings—" Penny looked at him sharply—"a pound a month." That was more than generous, Charles thought.

"And I would be doing what?" Molly asked, her mouth hardening.

"What dost thou know to do?" Penny asked.

"You know," Molly said grimly.

"Dost thou know anything else? Canst thou keep a garden?" Penny persisted, "or tend animals?"

"My pa was a shepherd," she said, a look of relief on her face.

"You could work in the stables and help with my horses," Charles offered.

"Oh, I love horses," Molly said. "They're grand animals."

"Then it's done," said Charles. "I'll put you on the coach tomorrow with some money and a letter to my brother."

"Wait," Molly said. "I don't know. Why are you doing this?"

"It's honest employment," Charles said. "No jigging, I promise."

Penny glanced at Charles very strangely, then turned to the girl. "It's because I asked him to," she said in a kindly voice. "Thou canst start afresh. Perhaps thou will meet a boy. Thou canst do whatever thou likes." Molly still hesitated, so Penny went on, "I will be nearby, and Ellie Winchester. We can visit. Charles Edgemont and Daniel Bevan will also be there sometimes."

Molly glanced up at Bevan, who nodded to her. "Thank you," she said seriously. "Wouldn't I be pleased to help you out with your animals." Bevan led her a little distance away, and Charles saw him talking to her earnestly.

Winchester and Ellie had gone on. Charles had chairs brought up on the quarterdeck, and he and Penny sat and talked of inconsequential things, watching the sun set over the masts in the Solent.

In the midst of the sunset, a lieutenant arrived from the dockyard superintendent's office with word that there was space for the *Louisa* to be beached in two days' time. Tomorrow she could be warped to the number-three wharf and unloaded of her stores and armament. Her crew would be temporarily transferred to a receiving hulk in the harbor. Officers should find their own accommodations on shore. Her repairs should be complete after three days' work; the guns would be restored the day after and then she would be reprovisioned. The *Louisa* would be ready to sail in as little as a week.

Attwater brought them something cold to eat on deck, and after that Charles took Penny back to her inn. They had a long, lingering good-night embrace in the hired chase between the point and the George.

As Charles was walking with her to the entrance of the inn, Penny asked, "What's 'jigging'?"

"I'm told it's a kind of folk dance," he said very seriously.

IN THE MORNING Charles sent Molly off with one of the midshipmen to collect her belongings and board the coach that would take her to Cheshire. He gave her a letter he had written to his brother and sufficient money for the journey. The remaining women were then taken ashore in the ship's cutter amid much wailing and tearful farewells.

Around midmorning a dockyard pilot arrived and the *Louisa* was carefully towed into the harbor and warped alongside her assigned quay. The rest of the day was spent hoisting her guns out and emptying her hold. In the evening the crew were transported under armed marine escort to the mastless hulk of an ancient three-decker tied up just outside Gosport, which would confine them in fetid squalor until they were needed again.

Well after dark Charles and Attwater made their way to the George, where Charles had reserved rooms. Bevan boarded at the less expensive Swan and Anchor nearby, while the midshipmen and warrant officers found other lodgings. Charles called on Penny while his steward unpacked, and the two had a quiet dinner in the public room. They agreed to meet late the next morning after he had seen the *Louisa* hauled up on dry land.

He rose before dawn and walked to the dockyard. The operation of beaching a ship, even one as small as the *Louisa,* was a tricky business.

Charles watched anxiously as, at almost high tide and in the first light of day, she was carefully kedged into position over two heavy wooden rails beginning well under water and extending onto the land. Just as the tide started to turn, she was winched up the rails and heavy wooden shoring placed under the curve of her hull to hold her upright. High and dry, Charles could easily see the gouge along her side. A long strip of copper sheets was torn completely away, the edges of those above and below were crumpled and torn, and the splintered planking underneath clearly visible. Charles walked down to the beach among the workmen to study her at close range. He made his way around the hull, examining the copper sheeting and looking for other problems.

Returning to where he started, he recognized Daniel Bevan standing with his hands on his hips and looking at the damaged strakes.

"Isn't this a bit early for you to be up?" Charles said, by way of announcing his presence. "Or are you just finishing a late night?"

"Aha," Bevan answered, pointing at the tear, "where'd you learn to steer a boat, in the Alps?"

"I rely on my officers to do that," Charles answered. "Good officers are hard to find."

Turning serious, Bevan said, "That was a near thing, Charlie. Another foot to starboard and we might have sunk."

"We'll be more careful next time."

"You're still set on trying the frigate again?"

Charles paused, glanced around the shipyard, then met Bevan's eyes. "I'm going to sink her, Daniel," he said in a matter-of-fact tone.

"Because of what she did at St. Vincent?"

Charles nodded. "We just have to start a little further from the rocks."

"You're daft" was Bevan's opinion.

Charles walked back to the George in a chipper mood, happy in the bright fall sunshine and full of anticipation at seeing Penny, even though he'd been with her less than twelve hours before. He thought about the girl, Molly, and about her dropping into prostitution when her parents lost their land. He wondered at Penny's not being repelled by Molly's profession. Yet she was concerned about his profession, he knew, even though she'd agreed to marry him. He needed to ask her why she had changed her mind. That, and she'd said she loved him. He felt himself a very lucky man.

Charles asked the proprietor of the George where he could hire a carriage and horses for the day. He also requested a basket dinner for two and a blanket that he could borrow. The innkeeper immediately sent a boy running to have a phaeton with two horses brought from the livery.

Charles then sent one of the innkeeper's daughters to Penny's room to announce his presence. The girl returned to say that he should go up. Penny opened her door to his knock and invited him to wait while she collected her bonnet and a shawl. Charles loved the look of her, and her hair, its colors and fullness when it fell about her shoulders, and before she could turn away he took her in his arms and kissed her. Penny returned his kisses for a moment, then gently pried herself away.

"Thou art as bad as those sailormen on thy ship," she said, her face somewhat flushed.

"Worse," Charles said. "You'll see."

"I don't doubt it," she said and brushed her fingers against his cheek.

Downstairs they collected the basket Charles had ordered and were directed to the covered coach with its driver waiting out front. Charles helped Penny onto the back bench, spoke to the driver, then climbed up himself. The journey ended two miles later on the open hillside in front of Southsea Castle, overlooking the several score warships anchored at Spithead.

Charles spread the blanket and they both sat down in the warmth of the noonday sun with the strong scent of salt in the sea air.

"Oh, my," said Penny, "I never dreamed there were so many ships all in one place."

"This is a major anchorage," Charles explained. "Plymouth and the Mole by London are two others. There are dozens of smaller ones elsewhere in England and around the world."

"I never knew there were so many," she repeated.

"Look, that's a first-rate," Charles told her, pointing at a man of war that stood out for its size from the others. "She's the *Royal Sovereign,* a hundred guns. Just past her is the *Témeraire,* ninety-eight. The other big ones are mostly seventy-fours—*Conqueror, Defiance, Leviathan,* and a lot I can't name."

"What's that little one, there?" Penny asked.

"That's a brig," Charles said. "You can tell because it's square-rigged but only has two masts. And that one with a single mast is a cutter."

"They're smaller than the *Louisa,* aren't they?"

"The cutter's probably about half as large," Charles said. "They're fine sailers, though."

"So many," she said in wonder and stared at the sea of ships. Presently she began to explore the contents of their dinner basket. She came up with half a loaf of bread, cheese, a goose-liver spread, two pasties, napkins, and a bottle of French wine from Bordeaux. "You made a much more elegant picnic than I did."

"I didn't make it," Charles answered, "I bought it."

They ate for a time and looked at the ships. Whenever one was entering or leaving the anchorage she would ask what it was.

"That one's a galliot," Charles said of the latest to enter, "a merchantman from Denmark, probably. That next one is a snow." Penny had removed her bonnet and he watched as she attended to her food while the breeze whispered through her hair, gently stirring the tips and loose strands.

"Penny?" he said as she was finishing her pasty.

"Yes?" she answered, her eyes darting at him and then back to the ships.

"When I first talked about marriage, you said that you couldn't abide my profession. What changed?"

She was silent for a moment as she wiped her mouth with a napkin and brushed at the crumbs on her lap. "I was attracted to thee the first day," she said. "I also thought about marriage soon after. I told thee that I was brought up to believe that war and violence are wrong. I still believe this very strongly. And thy profession is still difficult for me."

Charles nodded his understanding and reached for her hand.

"I promised thee after thy suggestion that we marry that I would think and pray and seek guidance from God. I did this," she said earnestly. "I labored very hard with my heart and my mind."

"Yes?" Charles said.

Penny looked at him tenderly and touched his lips with her finger-tips. "I believe this to be true, Charlie, that God brought thee into my life for a purpose. I think thou art meant to be a challenge to my beliefs in order to strengthen them. In addition to being a husband to me, I believe that God wants thou to be a teacher also, so that I may see the world as other men see it and so that I may understand it better, even if I do not agree."

"What about my career?" Charles asked. "What about my being in the navy? How do you feel about that?"

"For myself, I wish thy career was more peaceful and less dangerous," she said carefully. "And I wish that thou wouldst not be gone at sea for so long. But thy career is for thee to decide. I will honor thy decision. I will not labor with thee longer on it."

"Thank you," Charles said.

"Perhaps I will labor with thee on other things," she said pertly.

Charles chuckled. "I'm sure you will." He lay back on the blanket, pulling her down beside him. They lay together in each other's arms for some time without words. Charles felt warm and secure with her beside him and her breath on his cheek, at peace with himself and the world. His mind wandered over the ups and downs, joys and difficulties to be overcome, that would be their lives together. For some reason he thought of Molly.

"There's going to be a lot of that, isn't there?" he said sleepily.

"A lot of what?"

"A lot of Mollies—wayward women, beggar children, foundling infants."

"Only until all the problems and inequities of the world are ended," she said happily and kissed his chin.

"Fine," Charles mumbled and drifted into sleep.

When he awoke he saw Penny asleep beside him, her head resting on his arm. He moved slightly and her eyes flickered open.

"I am very tender toward thee," he whispered, mimicking what she had said when he proposed, and she snuggled closer to him.

"How shall we be married?" she mumbled, her voice still thick with sleep.

"How do you mean?" he asked lazily. "In a church, of course. I was thinking of St. John's at the New Gate by Chester. It's a beautiful old place and the parson was an acquaintance of my father's. I could inquire about Chester Cathedral if you like."

Penny's eyes opened wide and she pushed herself up on one elbow. "I cannot be married in a church by a hireling priest," she announced abruptly. There was alarm in her voice.

Charles sat up and stroked her hand to reassure her. "Why not?"

"Because, because . . . Oh, thou dost not understand! Because God does not bide in buildings made by the hand of man, despite their pretentious spires and their paid clergy. And God does not speak through those hireling priests!"

Charles struggled to digest this latest roadblock to their union. "What then, a Quaker marriage in one of your meetinghouses?"

"Thank thee," she said thoughtfully, "but we cannot. My meeting, any meeting, will not sanction my marriage to you, much less celebrate it. No, we must find another way."

"What other way? There is no other way," Charles sputtered, his voice rising in timbre. "We could go to Scotland. They'll marry anyone. But it's still by a clergyman, only the Church of Scotland. It would be much easier in a local church. We could avoid all the traveling."

"I cannot marry thee in a church in Scotland or elsewhere," she repeated as she sat upright. "It's unchristian."

Charles's mouth worked as he tried to fathom the opposition between church and Christianity. Finally he said, "How, then? Do you want to go abroad? I'm told they permit civil ceremonies in Rhode Island."

Her eyes grew thoughtful and she fell silent, her mouth in a firm line. "There must be another way," she said at length.

"Not in England, there isn't," he said quickly. "It's either in front of a clergyman or nothing."

"Would it be possible to stand before a clergyman in a place other than a church?"

Charles noted her use of the term "clergyman" in place of her usual "priest," which she generally used with the same inflection that others did with "pederast" or "procurer." He took it as an offer of compromise.

"It might be possible," he said carefully. "It would cost something extra, of course. Something for the parson's trouble."

"How much extra?"

"I don't rightly know," Charles answered. "Twenty-five or fifty pounds perhaps. A trifle."

"It is less dear to marry in a chapel?"

"I should think so, yes. It's the normal way of doing things. It's what they're accustomed to."

"All right," Penny said as if the words were being dragged from her by horses. "In a small chapel, by a priest, with a very inexpensive ceremony."

"Thank you," Charles answered. "I will write to the vicar at St. Alban's in Tattenall. That should serve."

DURING THE REMAINDER of their time in Portsmouth they were only able to see each other sporadically, usually at dinner. Charles needed to be with the *Louisa,* watching the work done on her and seeing if he could get one or two other small changes made at the same time. Almost all of one day he was busy at the dockyard superintendent's office signing invoices. At the victualling yard he prepared requests for stores. At the ordnance yard he was informed that the *Louisa*'s armament was to be augmented by four snub-nosed thirty-two-pounder carronades, two each for the fore- and aftercastles. The carronades were brutally powerful short-range weapons mounted on traversable slides rather than carriages, and did not count against the *Louisa*'s rating of twenty-eight guns. He eagerly agreed to it and the paperwork took a good part of that day.

The last two days in port passed in a rush of activity that lasted from before dawn to well after dark for Charles and everyone else connected with the *Louisa.* As soon as she was kedged back into the water, a long patch of bright new copper over the repair to her hull, her crew was transported back on board. The wharf at the victualling yard was next for a long day of sorting, inspecting, positioning, and repositioning the ninety tons of water casks, sixty tons of provisions, and thirty tons of fuel that would provide drink and food for her crew at normal rations for ninety days. That night Charles staggered back to the George for a late supper with Penny, then returned to his cabin on board his ship to collapse into exhausted sleep.

The next morning, the *Louisa* transferred to the gun wharf, where her twelve-pounders, nine-pounders, and four new carronades were swayed aboard one by one, delicately lowered into position, and secured. Only then were the nearly fifty tons of shot, hundredweight barrels of powder, and other ordnance stores brought aboard and stowed away. *Louisa* slowly returned to her normal routine at anchor, ready to sail on the morning tide.

Charles spent his last evening with Penny in a small parlor at the inn. He had arranged for a special dinner for the two of them to celebrate together in private, but instead ate in strained conversation with many long, awkward silences.

"When thou next returns, will we have sufficient time to marry?" Penny asked at one point.

"I'll request leave," Charles answered. "I don't know what Jervis will say." He was thinking that if he disposed of the *Santa Brigida,* leave was much more likely to be granted than otherwise. But he had carefully avoided mentioning anything about the Spanish frigate to her, and he wasn't about to bring the subject up on their last day together.

"Thou wilt write to me?" Penny said.

"Every day," Charles answered. "But I don't have many opportunities for posting my letters."

"I know," she said, "like thou didst with Ellie. I will write to thee of my love also."

After very hard and repeated good-byes, Charles made his solitary way back to his ship.

AT FOUR BELLS in the morning watch in the first tentative light of day, the *Louisa* swung her bow with the turning tide and started toward the harbor mouth and the broader waters of Spithead beyond. As they eased past the point, Bevan nudged Charles and called to Winchester, gesturing to port.

Charles looked and saw Penny and Ellie standing among a half-dozen others in the half-light, waving handkerchiefs. He waved back, his heart breaking. As the *Louisa* nosed into the Spithead channel, he said to no one in particular, "All normal sail and set a course to weather Ushant."

ELEVEN

THE *LOUISA* BEAT DOWN PAST CAPE PRIOR ON OCTOBER 7, 1797, under double-reefed topgallants. The wind shrieked through the rigging in capricious gusts, sweeping cold rain in sheets across the decks. Charles stood, wet and uncomfortable, in his tarpaulin rain gear on the quarterdeck, his feet wide apart and his legs compensating unconsciously for the movement of the ship. He could just make out the *Dientes del Diablo,* a surging froth of white surf against the steel-gray seas, transforming into billowing towers of spray as the Atlantic rollers crashed down on the rocks at metered intervals. "Beechum!" he shouted to the signals midshipman huddled in the lee of the binnacle fifteen yards away.

"Yes, sir?" the boy answered after hurrying to him.

"Run up the foremast and report back what the lookout sees," Charles ordered. There would be no shouting back and forth to the tops in this weather.

"Yes, sir," the boy said, and glanced dubiously at the upper masts oscillating wildly as the ship crested a large wave at an oblique angle, corkscrewed, and started down into the trough.

"Tell him I want to know the whereabouts of the Spanish frigate and anything else he sees in the Ferrol yards."

"Yes, sir." The midshipman repeated his instructions: "Report back to you the location of the frigate and other activity in the yards."

"Very good. Get along." The boy departed.

"Any guesses?" Charles said, turning to Bevan.

The lieutenant shrugged almost imperceptibly under his bulky oil-skin. "Difficult to say. Depends on how badly we hurt her and whether or not they have the parts on hand for repairs."

"I'm betting they don't," Charles said. "I'll bet she's still moored in the yards."

"You always were an optimist," Bevan replied dryly.

The *Louisa* rose on another wave, crested, corkscrewed, and slid downward, then repeated the cycle and started over again, green water crashing over her bow each time she rose. Almost against his will his eyes were drawn back to the reef, nearly fine on the starboard beam, a maelstrom of exploding foam. Charles saw Beechum climbing cautiously back down the foremast ratlines.

"The lookout says that the frigate is tied up alongside a wharf in the yard, sir," the boy reported breathlessly. "He thinks she may have her foremast out of her. He says it's hard to tell in this weather."

"Thank you," Charles said. "Back up you go and report anything important."

He had spent a great deal of time thinking about the Spanish frigate during the five weeks since their last meeting, wondering or guessing how badly she might have been damaged. Now it seemed possible that her lower foremast had been more seriously wounded than he had thought; seriously enough that it needed to be replaced. If the Ferrol yards had a replacement lower mast section, they would have done the work already. Since they apparently did not have a suitable timber available, one would have to be ordered. Such a request would probably be sent overland and word would only just now be reaching Madrid that it was required. There would be some urgency about it, Charles knew; the potential for damage to British shipping that a heavy frigate could make was great. The only source for such a made-up spar, three feet in diameter and some seventy-five feet long, would be one of the other major Spanish naval yards at Cádiz or Cartagena. A transport from Cádiz was the best bet. Anything from Cartagena would require passing through the many British warships around Gibraltar. Supply by road across Castile and the Galician mountains was almost unthinkable, especially at this time of year, when the dirt tracks would be a morass. In all probability the Spanish authorities would try to slip a transport laden with naval stores, including the mast sections, past the blockade at Cádiz. That wouldn't be too difficult at night and in the right weather conditions. If Charles were the captain of such a ship, he would immediately stand well out to sea to avoid the naval traffic along the Portuguese coast and make a dash into Coruna Bay from the northwest, with the prevailing winds on his quarter.

He decided he had seen enough. With high seas and nightfall coming on, his next priority was plenty of distance between the *Louisa* and the lee shore, especially the reef. "Wear ship and get us some sea room," he said to Bevan, "ample sea room."

For the next several weeks, the *Louisa* sailed a regular pattern from Ferrol to Cape Finisterre, northward to a point about thirty miles northwest of the mouth of the bay, then to Cape Ortegal and back to her starting point off Ferrol. In this way Charles could note any progress on repairs to the *Santa Brigida* every four or five days and was in a good position to intercept whatever enemy shipping rounded the northwest Spanish coast or attempted to enter Ferrol.

The routine of sailing in a large triangle soon became tedious. Almost all the merchantmen they ran down on were British or Portuguese. The rest proved to be from some neutral country: two from Sweden, three from the United States, and one from Russia. The Americans were, to a man, Charles thought, unreasonably indignant about being stopped on the high seas by a British warship and having their papers examined. Nor was there any change in the *Santa Brigida*. She remained tied alongside a wharf in Ferrol, absent her foremast. The weather varied between heavily overcast with periodic squalls and beautiful, fresh fall days when it was a pleasure to be on deck. The wooded mountainsides of Spain slowly turned brown, forecasting the coming winter. To relieve the monotony, Charles exercised the hands at the guns regularly, especially the new carronades.

Toward the end of October, as the *Louisa* was nearing its turning point well out to sea from the entrance to Coruna Bay, the lookout called out, "Sail fine on the port bow."

"How far?" Charles yelled.

"Mebbe fifteen miles," the lookout shouted back.

"What do you make of her?"

"I think she's a polacre, sir. I can only see her from the topsails upward."

"What's her course?"

"South by east, sir. Straight for Ferrol."

"Show the colors and run up to her, Daniel," Charles said.

The polacre hauled her wind almost as soon as the *Louisa* turned in her direction. She was cut off from running before the wind or toward land and had no other point of sailing in which she had any hope of outrunning the British frigate. She turned south, but in a half-hearted way, and as soon as she was in range of *Louisa*'s guns she ran up the Spanish flag and promptly hauled it down again.

The transport's captain abjectly bemoaned his ill luck at being captured by tilting back a bottle of Madeira. As its contents were already mostly drained, Charles thought it was a project he must have begun soon after he'd seen *Louisa*'s sails. Her cargo, interestingly, consisted mostly of powder and shot—eighteen-pound shot—as well as turpentine, pitch, and other naval supplies, but no spars. After removing some of the powder to use in practicing his own guns, Charles detached the senior master's mate and six seamen to take her to Gibraltar along with *Louisa*'s mail (including his own letter to Penny) and a report to Admiral Jervis on the *Santa Brigida*'s situation and his activities.

Four days later, the *Louisa* reached Cape Finisterre and came into the wind to start the northward leg of her triangular patrol. The blocks squealed loudly as the yards braced around, and the sails snapped with sounds like musket shots as the canvas slatted, then filled.

"Sail ho!" yelled the lookout. "No, two sails, three!"

"Where away?" Charles called.

"Due north, sir," the lookout shouted. "I see five sail, six. They're ours, sir. One of them is the *Royal Sovereign*."

"Make the recognition signal and our number," Charles said to Bevan. It had to be a squadron from Portsmouth sailing south to join the Mediterranean fleet. He remembered pointing out the hundred-gun *Royal Sovereign* to Penny from under the walls of the Southsea Castle. What was that: a month, two months ago? It seemed like a lifetime.

There were nine men of war, their sails easily visible from the *Louisa*'s quarterdeck now. Charles made out four ships of the line, all seventy-fours, in addition to the towering three-decker, as well as three frigates on the wings and a small sloop of war. "*Sovereign*'s signaling, sir," reported the signal's midshipman. " 'Send boat, mail on board,' it says."

"Acknowledge, Mr. Beechum," Charles said to the midshipman. To Winchester standing nearby he said, "Hoist out the launch and collect our mail from the flagship. Look lively—I doubt they'll even slow down."

Winchester returned a half-hour later and carried the mail satchel up to the quarterdeck while the launch was being hoisted inboard. "There's good news," he said, handing over the bag. "Admiral Duncan met the Dutch at Camperdown in the first part of October. Captured eight ships of the line and two frigates."

"How about that," Charles said absently, opening the satchel. He rifled around amongst the two dozen or so letters until he found what he was looking for, an envelope addressed to him in a neat schoolgirlish hand from "Penelope Brown, Gatesheath, Cheshire." There was also a larger Admiralty envelope for him from Jervis. He handed the satchel to Winchester with the words, "Here, most of that's for you. See that the rest is delivered." Then he turned the quarterdeck over to Bevan and went below to his cabin. He opened Penny's letter first.

Ninth Month 30, 1797

My Dearest,

I have only just returned home from Portsmouth and already I miss thee terribly. Our return journey was a sad one both for thy sister and me (she sorrows at being apart from her love, as do I). During our travels home she told me about thy experience at St. Vincent, which thou hast never fully told me. I worry constantly about the danger thou art in.

Molly Bridges is settled with the Attwaters in thy grand house in Tattenall. I think she is happy there. She speaks often of Daniel Bevan and I think she admires him. Molly dotes on thy horse, Pendle, and spoils him unmercifully.

I have told my parents of our engagement. My father is pleased;

I think he likes thee as a man. My mother is concerned about thy profession and my being disowned. I have not spoken to my meeting as yet but will this First Day.

I have nothing more to say than my love, so I will say it. I am exceedingly tender toward thee, Charles Edgemont. I am thy,

Penny

Charles read the letter though several times, then folded it carefully and placed it in his shirt pocket next to his heart. The second envelope he opened more warily. It was written after *Louisa*'s encounter with the *Santa Brigida* but before Jervis would have heard about it.

1 September, 1797
HMS *Victory*

Commander Edgemont,

I have been informed of your observations concerning the Spanish Frigate *Santa Brigida* and of Captain Ecclesby's return to England. I have also been informed that Captain Ecclesby has become temporarily indisposed due to ill health. I am most sorry that I am unable at this time to find a replacement to assist you.

You are hereby directed and required to do your utmost to protect British and allied shipping from the depredations of said frigate. As to how you accomplish this I can only rely on your judgment. I strongly advise that you avoid direct confrontation if possible, but as the commander on the scene you must make that decision and be responsible for its outcome.

Your servant, &c.,
Sir John Jervis,
Earl St. Vincent,
Admiral Commanding, Mediterranean Fleet

Well, that wasn't so bad, Charles thought. It was what he was already doing, sort of.

DECEMBER BEGAN AS a month of squalls and gales and unrelenting rain. On the third of December the *Louisa* lay hove to under storm sails well off the mouth of Coruna Bay. The wind screamed across the Atlantic from the southwest, driving the rain in sheets and whipping the sea into heaving white-capped mountains, the scud blowing horizontally from crest to crest. It was not a day Charles would have expected any shipping to attempt Ferrol.

"Beggin yer pardon, sur," a topman named Jones shouted in Charles's ear. Jones had been posted as lookout in the maintop.

"What is it?" Charles shouted back, raising his voice to be heard in the roaring wind.

"I seen a sail alee'ard, sur. Making for Coruna, like."

"Are you sure?" Charles asked.

"Yus, sur. I seen him plain as day. Ship-rigged, under triple-reefed topgallants, he wus."

"Thank you," Charles said. "Get back to your station. I'll send someone up to relay messages."

"Daniel, put on what sail she'll carry," he yelled through cupped hands. "Steer for Ferrol. Some fool's trying to make the bay."

Bevan nodded and yelled orders through his speaking trumpet. Seamen made for the shrouds as the *Louisa's* bow swung with the wind. High above on the wildly undulating yards, the topmen struggled to shake out a reef in the topgallants and set close-reefed topsails. Soon the ship was plunging pell-mell across the rollers, her bow disappearing in a cascade of spray as she nosed into each new wave.

As the *Louisa* crested a mountainous swell, Charles saw a tiny oblong of canvas off the larboard bow. At the second and third crests it grew progressively larger, and soon the vessel's hull was regularly visible, the mountains of Spain looming indistinctly in the distance.

"Christ, she's making a lot of sail," Bevan observed.

He gauged the distances. The Coruna lighthouse was just visible five or six miles away, and soon so would be the forts on either side of the entrance to the bay. *Louisa* stood a little more than a half-mile behind the ship and was closing. It would be a near thing, Charles decided, as to whether they could overhaul her before she reached the protection of the forts.

"She's shaken out a reef in her maintopsail," Bevan said in amazement. "The captain's crazy. It'll carry away."

Charles watched the transport plunge madly over the heaving gray sea. The *Louisa* had closed: a quarter-mile, maybe less. He could see the flags standing straight out on both forts and to port he watched the rollers dissolving into towering explosions as they crashed down onto the unmovable black fangs of the reef.

"I think the bloody fool is going to make it," Bevan said. Every eye watched as the Spaniard raced at perilous speed, burying her bow in green water at every crest, now almost level with the Coruna headland.

Charles was about to order the *Louisa* to reduce sail and give up the chase when some fluke in the wind off the headland caught the transport aback. She faltered, leaning almost to her port rail. He clearly saw a vertical split appear on her overtaut main topsail. The canvas immediately vanished, the wind shredding it to rags. Increased pressure on the Spaniard's foresail threw her head before the wind like a vane and in an instant she had lost any chance of weathering the headland.

Everyone on *Louisa*'s deck watched in fascination and despair as the vessel made a desperate attempt for the narrow inlet to the Ferrol yards. A second wind eddy tossed her bow to port. Unbalanced without her mainsail, her rudder was slow, too slow. For a moment it looked as though she would run straight onto the rocks under the fort. The Spaniard fought for her life now, trying to claw clear of the Ferrol promontory and scratch her way back out to sea. She just cleared the headland under the Ferrol fortress, racing before the wind, and plunged helplessly for the waiting reef. Charles watched, horrified, as a white-capped wave picked the transport up and up, and heaved her bodily onto the rocks. The ship vanished in an enormous eruption of foam. As the water ebbed off the rocks, the vessel reappeared amid the stones, mastless and broken. He saw a few men clinging to the mast stumps or pieces of railing, but it was hopeless for their ship and hopeless for them. The next roller crashed with a roar, thankfully hiding the scene. As the froth receded there were fewer men to be seen, and the ship's bowsprit and part of her bow had been carried away. The rest, Charles was sure, would follow within the hour, a few of her crew clinging miserably to the wreckage to the bitter end.

"Reduce sail," Charles said in a shaken voice. "Take in the mainsails and reef the topgallants. Take her back out." It would be lunacy to attempt a rescue from the windward in these seas and under the guns of the fort.

THE *LOUISA* SPENT the night hove to five miles off Cape Prior and let the storm blow itself out. In the chill gray dawn of the next morning Charles was called from his breakfast by a messenger requesting his presence on the quarterdeck.

"What is it, Daniel?" he said, buttoning his jacket as he arrived.

Bevan pointed over the starboard rail and there, bobbing in the swells, was an open boat not much larger than a ship's gig. It had an oar lashed upright midships with what looked like a white shirt blowing from it.

"Close on her and let's see what we have." Charles thought it might be a few crewmen from yesterday's transport, but for the life of him he couldn't think how anyone might have survived. As the *Louisa* glided alongside, he saw the figures of eight men huddled in the bottom of the craft. One, the one who had evidently taken off his shirt to tie to the oar, was wearing a ragged blue jacket over his bare chest. He was a young man, Charles saw, no more than nineteen or twenty, with stubble on his face and disheveled hair. Charles was surprised to hear him announce in plain English, "I am a king's officer. Where's the officer of the watch?"

"I am the ship's commander," Charles called down. "We'll have you on board in a moment." To Bevan he said, "Rig a sling to hoist those men on deck. And send someone for blankets and something hot for them to drink."

"AND YOU ARE, sir?" Charles asked the young Englishman sitting at the table in Charles's cabin, clutching a mug of steaming coffee laced with rum.

"Lieutenant Horatio Hornblower, sir, of the *Indefatigable*. I've been a prisoner in Ferrol since February last." He was a little taller than Charles, bone thin, with dark hair and alert brown eyes.

"And how did you come to be in a small boat with a bunch of Spaniards in the midst of an Atlantic gale?" Charles asked. The young man told of his organizing an attempt from Ferrol to save at least some of the crew on the reef after the vessel had struck. The others in the open boat were all Spanish, three from Ferrol and four rescued off the reef. It was a truly heroic deed, Charles thought, although Hornblower described it in matter-of-fact, self-deprecating terms.

". . . and afterward the wind blew us north up the coast to where you found us this morning," he concluded.

"I am pleased to have found you," Charles said. "I can always use another officer, at least until we return to Portsmouth."

Hornblower's expression deadened. "I'm sorry, sir. I can't."

"Why not?"

"I'm on parole. I've given my word that I'll return."

"Oh," Charles said. "I'm sorry."

"No more than I am, sir," Hornblower said with a forced smile.

Charles wondered if he had a woman in the town. "Of course, but there's no hurry. You can eat and sleep on board tonight. I think Winchester can give you a proper lieutenant's uniform. He's about your size. I'll return you and the others to Ferrol under a flag of truce tomorrow." After Hornblower left for fresh clothing and hot food, Charles shook his head. Woman or no woman, and parole or no parole, he was fairly certain that he would be hard-pressed to voluntarily return to captivity under similar circumstances.

The next morning dawned sunny and relatively calm. The *Louisa* beat south, back to the mouth of the bay and just out of range of the guns in the forts. Charles had the cutter hoisted over the side. As the Spaniards were climbing down, he took Hornblower aside. "Is there anyone you'd like me to write to in England for you?"

"I have no one, sir," the young lieutenant answered.

"I'll inform the Admiralty of your situation, then," Charles said, feeling very sorry for the boy, and held out his hand.

"Thank you, sir," said Hornblower, shaking it. Then he reluctantly descended into the cutter.

Winchester came last, carrying a white flag that he fixed to the cutter's bow. "All pull," he said, and the boat started toward a small jetty at the base of the Ferrol fort. The cutter returned, minus its passengers, an hour later with a case of the local wine, a gift from Ferrol's commander.

THE *LOUISA* RESUMED her regular course, southwest to Finisterre, then wore sharply northward. When they next looked into Ferrol five days later, Charles got a nasty shock. The lookout reported a brig in the naval yard that wasn't there before, and the Spanish were in the process of hoisting a lower foremast section off her deck. From then onward he had the patrol shortened to Cape Prior in the north and the Sisargas Islands to the west so that he could look into the naval yard every day. Christmas came and went, observed by a more elaborate meal than usual, but with the same weevily biscuit, leathery pickled beef, roast potatoes nearly gone completely bad (the *Louisa* was nearing time for resupply), and an extra ration of spirits. When it was apparent that the *Santa Brigida* would be ready for sea in a matter of days, if not hours, Charles hove to five miles off the mouth of the bay—well away from the reef—and waited.

The *Louisa* sat outside Coruna Bay for three days, watching as the *Santa Brigida*'s rigging was completed and her stores taken aboard. Charles used some of the time to practice with the guns, running them in and out repeatedly, and firing powder broadsides. He wanted to exercise the crew and keep them sharp. He also wanted the Spanish to know that he was ready and eager to fight. The weather grew increasingly cold and overcast, with steady if moderate winds from the south.

The morning of January 1, 1798, began with rain mixed with heavy wet snow, then turned entirely to snow, which soon coated the decks and rigging. A quiet settled around the ship, the loudest noises being the muffled slap of the waves against her hull and the creaking of the blocks in the rigging.

"Sir, sir! She's moving!" came an excited shout down from the main crosstrees.

"What do you see?" Charles called up.

"I'm not sure, sir. It's hard to make out," the lookout yelled. "But I think I see sails in the yard. Yes, sir, I see 'em. She's headed out."

Charles strained his eyes to leeward. He could just make out the vague outlines of the forts on the headlands, but even with a glass the falling snow blurred any attempt to make out details on the water's surface. "Get the slush cleared off the decks," he said to Bevan. "Let the cook keep the galley lit; otherwise, clear for action."

After a short time Charles thought he saw something moving on the water, just clearing the Ferrol promontory. Slowly it grew more distinct, the darker shape of a ship's hull as it rounded the point. There was something unreal about the scene, its quiet and softness in the white air.

"Cleared for action," Bevan reported. Charles guessed that it would be an hour at least before the Spanish frigate came within range of *Louisa*'s guns. "Feed the hands below, then we'll douse the galley and beat to quarters," he said.

Charles stood on the quarterdeck by the lee rail and watched as the *Santa Brigida* slowly approached, a ghost ship against a pale background. She was well past the Ferrol headlands and would soon clear the reef. At about two miles distant, the line of her masts shifted to the left.

"She's trying to reach on us," Bevan said. "She'd like to get ahead downwind, then tack and cross our bows."

Charles nodded. "Get some way on. I want to stay about a cable's length ahead. But not so far as our guns won't bear." The two ships assumed slowly converging courses, both edging cautiously closer with the wind behind them. The distance narrowed: a mile, three-quarters, a half. "Run out the guns," Charles said, his eyes never leaving the opponent. He remembered St. Vincent, the beaten *Argonaut* being raked again and again. He remembered young Billy Bowles, his body shattered by one of the Spaniard's round shot. He itched for the thing to begin.

The *Santa Brigida* fired her broadside at four hundred yards. Charles heard and felt one ball strike the hull, the rest plunging into the water alongside or astern. The frigate was still closing on them but was about a half a cable's length behind.

"Wait," Charles said. "A little closer." He mentally counted off how long it would take the enemy to reload.

"Eliot," he barked to the master at the ship's wheel. "On my command, starboard your helm two points. After we fire, straighten her out again."

"Aye aye, sir," the master answered.

"Ready, Daniel?" Charles said. "You may fire as the guns bear."

Charles's count reached sixty seconds. "Now," he said to Eliot. The *Louisa* swung to the starboard, her guns easily sighting on the Spanish frigate.

"Fire!" yelled Bevan. Water boiled up around the *Santa Brigida*. Gaps appeared in her railing and holes in a few of the lower sails.

"Straighten her out," Charles shouted. He glanced at the gun crews swarming over their weapons, sponging out and ramming home cartridges.

The maneuver had cost *Louisa* some of her headway, and the Spaniard's bow was almost even with her stern and a hundred yards to starboard. With a powerful roar the frigate fired again, but with her bow still angled at closing the distance with the *Louisa,* many of her shots churned up the water in the English ship's wake. A few told, however, severing a mizzen stay and one sweeping across the quarterdeck, killing a midshipman and a carronade gunner.

Charles studied the distance between the ships and calculated. "Reloaded?" he asked Bevan.

"Just now," Bevan answered.

"Hard astarboard," Charles ordered Eliot. To Bevan, he said, "We'll rake her as we pass. I want every shot to count."

The *Louisa* darted into the path of the Spaniard, clearing her bowsprit by a scant twenty yards.

"As you bear," Bevan yelled, "Fire!"

Shot after shot crashed into the frigate's bow, opening gaping holes in her hull. The foremost section of the *Santa Brigida*'s bowsprit caught momentarily in the *Louisa*'s aft rigging, tearing the mizzen topsail before catching on the mast and snapping off. Up to now it had been the *Louisa*'s starboard battery engaged with the *Santa Brigida*'s port side. The tables turned when the *Louisa* crossed over and they were on parallel courses, so close that the two ships' yardarms almost touched, midships to midships. Both ships' previously unused batteries fired together in a deafening blast, cannonballs and flaming wads spewing across both decks. Gaps appeared in *Louisa*'s larboard rail, and a gun reared up and twisted backward off its carriage, crashing to the deck. One of the nine-pounders on the quarterdeck overturned, its port dissolving into a ragged four-foot gap in the bulwark. There were screams and cries in the smoke, and unmoving bodies lay like so much scattered cordwood. The too-familiar smells of burnt powder and fresh blood curdled the air.

Charles stood by the port rail, almost close enough to speak to the *Santa Brigida*'s captain. He watched interestedly as his opposite, the same thin wiry man with a large mustache he remembered, ran back and forth on his quarterdeck, gesturing and yelling excitedly. Momentarily their eyes met, and Charles immediately doffed his hat and bowed deeply in a gesture that might be interpreted as comradely respect or utter contempt. The Spaniard instantly looked away, ignoring him completely. As Charles leaned against the railing something tugged momentarily on the sleeve of his jacket and knocked his left hand away. He glanced irritably to see who might be trying to get his attention, saw no one, then saw two neat holes in the cuff of his sleeve and blood running down onto the back of his hand. For the first time he noticed Spanish soldiers in the frigate's rigging, priming and loading their muskets, aiming and firing down onto *Louisa*'s decks. His own marines were doing the same thing from *Louisa*'s tops and railings. Charles picked out one soldier in particular on the Spaniard's mizzen top who had just lowered his weapon and was preparing to reload. He glared furiously at the man for a few seconds, then walked a few paces to a group of six marines by the quarterdeck rail, pointed out the offending Spanish soldier, and said, "Shoot him." The marines fired as one and the man fell twisting to the deck below.

The *Louisa* fired her next broadside well before the Spanish frigate. As the smoke blew clear, Charles saw new holes and gaps in the Spaniard's hull.

"Are the starboard guns loaded?" he asked Bevan.

"Aye."

"Back the mainsail."

"Hands to the braces," Bevan yelled. The *Louisa* immediately lost way. The *Santa Brigida*'s broadside, when it came, hit the *Louisa*'s bow, chopping off part of the bowsprit or splashing into the water in front of her. As the Spanish frigate's stern pulled ahead, Charles called, "Hard to port."

"Man the starboard battery," Bevan shouted. The starboard guns went off in twos and threes as *Louisa* glided past the *Santa Brigida*'s stern, repeatedly smashing the gallery and aftercabin windows and sending shot after shot the length of her decks.

"There, you son of a bitch," Charles muttered to himself. "See how you like it."

The *Louisa* turned back on her course, parallel to the Spaniard but fifty yards behind. He watched with some trepidation as the *Santa*

Brigida's yards braced around and could see her rudder pivot on its pintles. She turned, a black hull belching flame and smoke as she crossed *Louisa*'s bows. The *Louisa* staggered under the blows. Her foremast tilted awkwardly to starboard, then fell in a great sweep into the sea.

"Clear that wreckage," Bevan shouted forward.

"Port-side guns," Charles yelled. The two ships had once again switched sides and were once more midships to midships. With the *Louisa*'s foremast by the board there would be no more maneuvering. "Fire at will," he called.

The *Louisa*'s guns spoke first in a ragged roar. The *Santa Brigida*'s mainmast swayed and, snapping stays like strings, pitched forward, taking the foretopmast with it. The Spaniard's guns answered, but with less authority and determination, Charles thought. Four, five, maybe six of her starboard battery were either unmanned or overturned. He saw blood running from her scuppers in long vertical lines down to the sea. His own ship, Charles knew, was in hardly better condition. There were overturned guns and missing crews both port and starboard, numerous bodies sprawled on the decks, and streams of bright-red blood expanding as the *Louisa* pitched and rolled.

What guns were still operational on both ships fired without pattern or command, a continuous confusion of explosions interrupted by odd periods of expectant silence. The rest of *Louisa*'s bowsprit was shot off at the beak to trail in the water alongside. Slowly the lower section of the Spaniard's foremast, the one that had just been mounted, toppled into the water. The periods of silence between gun blasts grew longer. Without sails for effective steerage, the two ships drifted slowly apart. A last half-hearted salvo from the *Santa Brigida* at four hundred yards cracked *Louisa*'s main topmast. Charles watched, entranced, as the huge spar swayed and then started downward, directly over him. For an instant it didn't register that he was in danger. When he realized that he was about to be crushed he started to run, stumbled over the barrel of an overturned carronade, and fell heavily, pain shooting through his ankle. The monstrous mast dropped onto the quarterdeck taffrail with a splintering crash, coming to rest about two feet from Charles's head. He lay on his back on the deck, staring wide-eyed at it, scarcely breathing.

"You're just a magnet for things falling out of the sky, aren't you?" Bevan said as he took Charles under the arms and helped him to a sitting position. "Are you hurt?"

Charles surveyed himself. He had a dull pain in his left wrist that made it difficult for him to move his fingers, and a sharp one in his right ankle. "I'm fine," he said, but when he tried to stand he found he couldn't. "Where's the Spaniard?"

"Leeward and well astern," Bevan said, and reading Charles's mind added, "There's no way we can close her. We don't have the sails."

"Hell, we almost had her," Charles said.

"Sure," Bevan answered, "if the declared winner is whichever ship touches the seabed last."

WHEN LINCOLN, THE ship's surgeon, examined Charles, he determined that a musket ball had grazed the radius bone in his arm, just above the wrist. Charles had also broken a bone in his ankle, almost certainly when he tripped over the carronade. Neither injury was serious; both would be painful and Charles would have to stay off his feet for a time, then walk with a crutch for a few weeks after that.

The *Louisa* had suffered worse. Thirty-three of her crew were dead, nearly seventy wounded, twenty-seven seriously. Aside from the damage to the masts, both sides of her hull and her bow had been holed repeatedly, several times below the waterline. Sails were fothered under her bottom and jury-rigged masts were set up during the night. In the morning, there being no sign of the *Santa Brigida, Louisa* began her long struggle home.

Charles insisted that Bevan join him for a cold breakfast and hot coffee in his cabin after they had gotten under way.

"It's going to take a long time for the yard to get her put back to rights," he observed ruefully.

"Months," Bevan agreed. "But it will take the Spaniard longer. And look at the bright side, Charlie. You'll have time to be married."

TWELVE

THE *LOUISA* ARRIVED AT SPITHEAD AND THE ENTRANCE TO Portsmouth harbor after two weeks of battling contrary winds and the nearly continuous clanking of her pumps. Her badly battered hull and jury-rigging attracted considerable attention from the officers and crews of the other warships in the anchorage, some of whom cheered or waved as she slipped slowly to her moorings. The diminished and exhausted crew acknowledged the first few greetings, then proudly ignored the rest. They were all veterans now; they had experienced real battle and survived. Of her original complement of a hundred seventy-five seamen, *Louisa* now had one hundred three effective and twenty-seven not sufficiently recovered from injuries to resume their duties.

Charles stood, leaning heavily on the quarterdeck lee rail for support, watching the warships as they passed. His mind drifted haphazardly over the engagement with the Spanish frigate, the *Louisa,* her crew, and Penny. They were the same subjects and very much the same thoughts that had occupied him for the past fortnight. He was pleased with the conduct of the battle but unhappy about its outcome. His ship had fought well, both outmaneuvering and, for her size, outgunning the better-armed and heavier opponent. If, with a little luck, they had done more damage to the *Santa Brigida*'s rigging earlier, the outcome could have been decisive. Of course, as Bevan had pointed out, if the *Louisa* had suffered more damage to her masts sooner they would all be dead or prisoners in Ferrol now.

No matter how Charles analyzed it, the *Louisa* was simply out-gunned. With the addition of her thirty-two-pounder carronades she fired a broadside of two hundred thirty-nine pounds of iron to the Spaniard's three hundred twenty-four. Another pair of carronades on the quarterdeck might make the odds more acceptable—perhaps in place of two of the long nines. More and larger guns would help, he knew, but were not the only consideration. The *Louisa's* crew had performed admirably during the struggle, far better than he would have expected from the ragtag collection of seamen, landsmen, and former prisoners he'd started with. They had handled the sails and braces flawlessly and fired off four broadsides to the *Santa Brigida's* three. Still, it hadn't been enough. But with another carronade, he mused, and if they could fire her guns just a little faster, or aim for the Spaniard's gundeck to slow her rate of fire . . . There had to be a way; he just had to find it.

And there was Penny, his beautiful, tender, loving Penny. She was never far from his heart. He ached to see her again, talk to her, make her laugh, make her his wife. She would be upset that he'd been hurt, but he could explain that. The wrist injury was painful but superficial. His broken ankle had been an accident—it could have happened to anybody who happened to trip over a cannon left carelessly in their path. It would only be a matter of how he explained it to her.

"Deck!" the lookout in the foremast rigging called down. "The flagship's in the roads."

Charles could see the towering bulk of the *Victory* anchored in the roadstead, and his mind shifted to a whole new line of thought: What would Jervis say about his activities? It was an altogether less attractive prospect than reuniting with Penny. As soon as *Louisa* dropped anchor, he took the report he'd written and hobbled to the ship's side, where he allowed himself to be lowered in a bosun's chair into his gig. He also had to be hoisted, at considerable cost to his dignity, onto the flagship's maindeck.

"I'm very sorry, sir," the flag lieutenant said after greeting him, "but the admiral is ashore. If you'd care to wait . . . " He looked at Charles, who had one arm in a sling across his chest and stood with the aid of a crutch, then glanced at the battered *Louisa* clearly visible over the starboard rail. "Oh, never mind, he'll be anxious to see you. You'd best go directly to the dockyard admiral's office."

Charles thanked the lieutenant and handed over his report. Once lowered back into his gig, he ordered that he be taken to the naval yard.

He had to allow himself to be carried up the dockside ladder, slung over the shoulder of one of his larger crewmen like so many potatoes, his hat, sword, and crutch carried by another.

"We'll be happy to wait for you, sir," the coxswain offered delicately. "It might be difficult like if you tried climbing down into a wherry."

"Thank you, I'd appreciate it," Charles said. "I'll try to be as quick as I can." He pulled at his uniform to straighten it as best he could, set his hat firmly on his head, tucked his crutch under his arm, and hobbled off with what little of his dignity remained.

He was not in a happy frame of mind when a nattily dressed lieutenant stopped him near the door to the port admiral's office and said, "The admiral is in a meeting and cannot be disturbed."

"I don't want to see the port admiral, I want to see Admiral Jervis," Charles replied. "Commander Edgemont of the *Louisa*. Tell him I'm here."

"I'm sorry, sir, you'll have to wait. The admirals cannot be disturbed."

"Tell Jervis I'm here anyway," Charles snapped, "or I'll do it myself."

The aide hesitated, glancing at the dark cast of Charles's face. "All right," he said reluctantly, "but I'm not responsible." The lieutenant rapped on the door and stuck his head in. "There is a commander outside who insists on seeing his Lordship, Admiral Jervis, immediately. I've told him to wait," Charles heard him say.

The office door opened wide and Jervis himself stepped out. "Are you looking for me, Commander Edgemont?"

"Yes, sir," Charles answered, standing as erectly as he could.

"This man insisted on interrupting your meeting, Your Lordship," the aide began indignantly.

"And quite rightly so," Jervis growled. "In the future if one of my officers wants to see me, you let him in. Do you understand?"

"Yes, sir. But—"

"No buts. And bring a chair for the commander." He opened the door wide and gestured for Charles to enter. "This is Admiral Dorchester, the commander of His Majesty's dockyard in Portsmouth," Jervis said. "And this is Commander Charles Edgemont of the *Louisa*, one of our promising young frigate captains." Charles found himself uneasy in the presence of the two senior admirals in their blue uniform coats, heavy with gold braid and epaulettes.

Dorchester, a dignified gray-haired figure with a friendly smile, rose from behind his desk. "I'm honored, Commander," he said, shaking Charles's good hand. "What on earth has happened to you?"

The aide appeared with a chair and placed it behind Charles, who awkwardly lowered himself into it. "We had an engagement with the Spanish frigate just outside Ferrol, sir. I'm afraid that the *Louisa* is rather seriously damaged."

Jervis's face darkened. "The result?" he said tersely.

"Inconclusive, sir," Charles said, then, seeing Jervis's concern, he quickly added, "The *Santa Brigida* is at least as badly damaged as we are. Neither of us had any standing rigging toward the end and we drifted apart. In the morning she had disappeared. Made her way back to the Ferrol yards, I suppose. It's all in my report on board the *Victory*, sir."

"You took on a forty-gun frigate and fought her to a standstill?" Jervis's eyebrows rose.

"Yes, sir," Charles answered. "But we paid for it dearly."

"How long do you think the Spaniard's repairs will take?" Jervis asked.

Charles paused for a moment to consider. "It's hard to say, sir. The Ferrol yards don't seem to be very well supplied. Requisitions for mast sections and other material will have to be sent overland to Madrid. It might be four or five months, or even more. I'd say three to be on the windward side. They'll have to replace a goodly number of her crew as well."

"How badly damaged is the *Louisa*?" Dorchester asked.

"We've only jury-rigged masts," Charles said matter-of-factly. "The bowsprit's gone and the hull's taken a pretty pounding."

"And your crew?"

"We've forty-five seamen and twelve marines killed. I expect another sixteen will have to be invalided out."

Jervis turned to Dorchester. "I'd consider it a personal favor, Admiral, if you would see to it that the *Louisa* is repaired as quickly as possible. It's vital to the navy that she is made ready for sea before the Spaniard."

Dorchester smiled wryly and rifled some papers piled on his desk. "It seems that it's vital to complete every repair and refit as quickly as possible. We'll need a thorough inspection first, of course. Then we'll know what's required. If it's not too bad, I'd say two months ought to be possible."

"If it will be that long, sir," Charles said carefully, "might my officers and myself take leave while the *Louisa* is laid up? I'd like to go home to tend to my injuries. I also have some personal business to attend to."

"I suppose you'd better," Jervis answered. "The crew can be looked after on one of the hulks while you're away. I'll see to it in the morning."

Charles hadn't thought of how his crew would be cared for. He hated the idea that his men, men he'd trained and come to rely on, and who had risked their lives to do his bidding, would be confined for two months in an airless, stinking hulk under guard. Worse, few of them would be left when the time came, he knew, since other captains with urgent needs and greater seniority would find ways for Charles's seamen to end up on their ships. But what could he do about it? He knew he couldn't ask that they be given leave, and he couldn't confront the *Santa Brigida* when the time came with a raw crew. An idea came to him, a dangerous, radical idea. An idea that he liked better and better the more he thought about it. "Thank you, sir," he said.

"Do you have any other requests?" Jervis asked, signaling that his forbearance of Charles's interruption of his meeting was coming to an end.

"Just one small thing, sir," Charles said. "Would it be possible to cut two additional gunports on the *Louisa*'s maindeck? There's room forward. I would like to shift two of the nine-pounders down to the gundeck and replace them with thirty-two-pound carronades on the quarterdeck. They'd give us more punch in a close fight."

Jervis looked to the dockyard admiral, who nodded. "It might be possible," Dorchester said. "I'll have the ordnance yard look into it while your ship is laid up. If they feel the *Louisa* can manage the extra weight and stresses, then we'll do it."

"Thank you, sir," Charles said.

"Is there anything else?" Jervis asked, a touch of impatience showing.

"No, sir," Charles said with a disarming smile. "I'm sorry to have interrupted your meeting." With a slightly exaggerated show of difficulty he pushed himself upright and out of his chair. "It was an honor to meet you, Admiral," he said to Dorchester. Without thinking, he added, "I must say that it's been a greater pleasure doing business with you than it was with Admiral Grimsley in Plymouth."

Jervis gave Charles a curious look and rose abruptly from his seat. "I'll see you out," he said unexpectedly.

"Oh, that's not necessary, sir," Charles said. "I can see myself out."

"I'll see you out," Jervis repeated in a tone that encouraged no argument, taking Charles's arm and steering him toward the door. "I'll be back in a moment," he said over his shoulder.

In the hallway outside, Jervis stopped and said, "What do you know about Admiral Grimsley and his dealings in Plymouth?"

Charles devoutly wished he had never brought the subject up. He knew Jervis and Grimsley had been bitter enemies for years. He also knew that he had solicited the theft of some incriminating documents of Grimsley's and sent them anonymously to the Admiralty. He did not know the outcome of their investigations, but he guessed that the penalty for stealing Admiralty documents would be severe. Charles felt he was treading in deep waters. "I'm not sure what you mean, sir," he said.

Jervis looked at him sharply. "I mean, did you forward any papers to the Admiralty regarding a shipment of twelve-pounder cannons? Cannons, I might add, that were once intended for the *Louisa.*"

Charles felt distinctly uncomfortable under the admiral's gaze. "Me, sir? What's become of Admiral Grimsley, anyway?"

"He finally retired under something of a cloud, thank God," Jervis said, his deep eyes studying Charles's face. After a moment he added, "All right, I'll accept your claim of innocence for now. But I'd like to shake the hand of the man who sent those papers."

"It might depend on how they were come by," Charles said, meeting Jervis's eyes.

"Not on my watch it doesn't," the admiral answered, a look of understanding showing on his face. "You mentioned some personal business," he went on, quickly changing the subject. "May I ask what it is?"

"I'm to be married, sir."

The fleet admiral was silent for a moment, then put his hand on Charles's shoulder. "So that's why you want leave," he said gruffly. "I don't approve of my junior officers marrying. It distracts their attention from the service. But I suppose I am obligated to wish you and your intended well. You must introduce her to me when the opportunity arises."

"Thank you, sir," Charles said, "I'll be sure to," thinking that a meeting between Penny and Jervis was something that should be avoided at any cost.

"I also want to congratulate you on your business with the Spanish frigate, and . . . ah . . . any other services you may have performed on behalf of the navy, strictly legal or otherwise."

"Thank you, sir," Charles said. With a firm handshake, Jervis sent him on his way and returned to Dorchester's office, closing the door behind him.

Charles hurried as fast as his one good leg and crutch would carry him back to his gig by the quayside. "To the *Louisa*," he said to the coxswain after he had been manhandled down into the craft, "and pull hard. There's no time to lose."

As soon as he was back onboard he called for Bevan and Winchester. "Daniel, I want you to hire a lugger or brig, anything large enough to transport a hundred and thirty men around the Lizard to Chester." Turning to Winchester, he said, "We need water and provisions for the same number for a week or more. Buy it in the port and arrange that it be loaded this afternoon, this evening at the latest."

The two lieutenants stared at him without comprehension. "May I ask why?" Bevan said.

"We're going to sail home," Charles said nonchalantly, "and apart from the ship's standing officers I'm taking the crew with me. We leave after dark."

THE TWO-HUNDRED-TON barque *Maryanne* rounded Point of Ayr in the Irish Sea and entered the broad estuary of the River Dee five days later, having experienced largely favorable winds and moderate weather. With the brown mountains of Wales to starboard and the flat woodlands of Cheshire's Wirral Peninsula port-side, the *Maryanne* proceeded as far upriver as was navigable in the early-morning mist. Chester had been an important seaport during the time Rome ruled Britain. The Dee estuary had silted up badly during the Middle Ages, however, and the *Maryanne* tied up dockside at the small port of Connah's Quay a few miles west of the city.

Charles sent Bevan and Black, the purser, each with a small party of sailors, into the town. He and Winchester supervised the transfer of the remainder of the *Louisa*'s crew and their hammocks, duffel bags, and sea chests, including the wounded, to shore. Bevan was to hire whatever horse-and-wagon teams were available; Black was to arrange the purchase of beef, pork, vegetables, cheese, beer, and so on to feed them for a month. They could buy more later. By midmorning a train of four heavy wagons pulled by teams of horses was assembled in a small square just inside the Watergate in Chester's walls. Two were loaded with the wounded (attended by Lincoln, the surgeon); the remainder were filled with casks, boxes, and bags of foodstuffs and the sailors' gear.

The Chester townsfolk, who think of themselves as a fairly sophisticated lot, stared curiously as the wagons set off for the Dee Bridge accompanied by nearly a hundred sailors on foot and a small herd of cattle and swine. Almost immediately there was more animated and suggestive conversation between the sailors and certain young women they encountered along the roadway than Charles liked. He ordered the petty officers to organize the men by divisions, to remind them that they were still under orders, and to encourage a sense of decorum.

Charles rode on the bench of the leading wagon driven by Tom York, an able seaman who was clearly more at home reefing a sail than managing a team of drays. Once over the bridge and into the countryside, the procession began to spread out, slowed by the meandering livestock. He ordered several halts for everyone to regroup and for the small bands of seamen who had run off excitedly in pursuit of escaped sows or errant bullocks to be gathered back up. By noon they were nearing Hatton and the turnoff that led past Gatesheath to Tattenall. It was also time to think about feeding the men. Charles decided that the grounds of the Brown household would be the perfect place to stop and prepare their dinner. After all, Penny might be there.

Charles's heart quickened as his heavily laden wagon splashed through the same stream he had raced across on Pendle the day he had bought him. As they lumbered around the bend, he stared at the place where he had overturned Penny's cart and then set her broken arm. Soon the procession turned off the road and began its way up the drive to the Brown home. Too late, Charles hoped it wouldn't inconvenience them.

Peter saw them first, an army of sailors, wagons, cattle, and pigs strung out along the drive and far down the road. Charles watched as the boy shouted something excitedly to the house and then ran to see who it was descending on his property. Seeing Charles, the boy stopped and waved. "Greetings to thee, Charles Edgemont," he called out. "What art thou about?"

"Hello, Peter," Charles said, signaling to York to stop the wagon. "I was hoping to use your land to prepare a meal for my men. Would you tell your father that we're here . . . and your sister?"

The boy nodded, spun on his heel, and ran toward the mill. Charles's heart seemed to stop when he saw Penny come from the house and with a wave start toward them. She had pulled a long cloak over her dress and the January wind pulled at the edges of her bonnet. She looked altogether lovely. "Let's go," he said to York. "Stop when we reach the woman."

The sailor managed to start the horses forward, only to stop a few paces later, when Penny caught up to them. Charles moved to jump down from the wagon seat. York put a hand on his arm and restrained him. "Mind y'er ankle, sur," he said. Charles sat nervously and waited.

"Hello, Penny," he said from his perch atop the wagon.

"Oh, Charles," Penny said, seeing his sling. "What hath happened to thy arm?"

"It's nothing," he said reassuringly. "Nothing's broken. Look, I can move it." He flapped his damaged arm like a chicken's wing.

Penny looked at him suspiciously. "Why dost thou not descend?"

Charles thought of three different excuses all at the same time, none of them satisfactory. "I can't," he said finally. "I've broken my ankle."

"I'll get ye down, sur," York offered. "Just a minute." The seaman jumped from the wagon and whistled shrilly for some of his mates.

Penny's face turned ashen as a half-dozen men lifted Charles bodily from the wagon and set him gently on the ground. York proudly handed Charles his crutch. "This isn't as bad as it looks," Charles said hurriedly as he hobbled toward her. "I wasn't shot in the leg. I tripped over a cannon and broke it by accident. It could have happened to anybody."

"Thou wert shot in thy arm?" she asked, her eyes narrowing.

"Well, as a matter of fact . . ." Charles began.

"It were a big battle, ma'am," York interjected enthusiastically, trying to be helpful. "You should have seen it. Lots of people were injured worse. Y'er Captain Edgemont was lucky."

Penny smiled sweetly at York. "Were any killed?" she asked.

"Oh, my word—ouch!" York cut short when Charles rapped him sharply on the shin with his crutch.

"I'll talk to you about it later," Charles said. "I'll tell you the whole story, I promise."

She took his good arm and moved close to him. "I am pleased to see thee," she said. "Tell me the truth. Art thou badly injured?"

"No, I'm not, really," Charles said. "I have a minor wound to my wrist that will soon heal, and I broke a bone in my ankle when I tripped and fell." When she turned her face up to look into his he said, "That's the truth." Then he kissed her.

"We will talk of this later," she said, blushing, conscious of the men standing around and watching them. She asked, "Is this thy navy?"

"My crew, yes," he said. Then on an inspiration he added, "I brought them to attend our wedding."

"Didst thou really?" she said in amazement.

"Well, partly," he answered.

Soon they were joined by her mother and father, Bevan and Winchester, and a growing circle of curious sailors.

"I was hoping that we might use your land to prepare dinner for my men," Charles said to George Brown. "We're on our way from Chester to Tattenall. We've brought our own food."

George Brown nodded, "That would be fine. Thou art welcome to any firewood thou needs and water from the well."

"We would gladly feed thee all," Elizabeth Brown said, looking in wonder around her, "but I think we haven't enough food."

"Thank you," Charles said, "we can prepare our own meal. I'll send some people over later in the week to replace any firewood or whatever else we use." Just then, one of the larger wagons, attempting to turn at the end of the drive, drove against the corner of a fence in front of the house and knocked it flat. In a torrent of blasphemy one of the younger midshipmen yelled at the seaman driving the wagon, who in turn swore loudly at his team of horses.

"And we'll repair any damage," Charles said. Turning to Bevan, he added, "Get them organized, will you? One cooking fire for each division. Let them prepare whatever they want. And get them to watch their language."

"What about the wounded?" Bevan asked.

"Wounded? What wounded?" Penny exclaimed.

Charles turned to Penny and said seriously, "We have twenty-seven wounded men in those wagons over there. They are being looked after by the ship's surgeon. Some of them are in very serious condition and some have lost limbs. I didn't have the heart to leave them in Portsmouth. I thought they would have a better chance of recovery at Tattenall. We'll feed them along with the others."

"I want to see them," Penny said.

"It's not very pretty," Charles continued confidently. "Certainly not a place for a woman." Due to the intimacy involved, very few women ever attended to sick or injured men. Those who did were generally considered to be little better than harlots.

Penny looked at him sharply. "Dost thou imagine life for women is always pretty things?"

"Well,—no," Charles said. "But—"

Penny called to her mother.

Very soon thereafter Charles reluctantly followed Penny, and George and Elizabeth Brown, to the wagons with the wounded. He found Lincoln inside the second, bending over one of his patients and changing a dressing over the stump of the man's arm. Without a word Elizabeth Brown hoisted her skirts and climbed up into the wagon, followed closely by her daughter.

The surgeon looked startled at the appearance of the two women. "What are you doing here?" he demanded.

Elizabeth Brown knelt next to a groaning man with a large bandage around his chest. "Which are the most serious?" she asked Lincoln over her shoulder.

"You shouldn't be here, ma'am," Lincoln insisted. "These are sick men."

"I can see that," Penny's mother said brusquely. "Which are the sickest?"

Lincoln looked to Charles in frustration. "Sir," he protested.

"Answer her questions," Charles said. "I think she means to help."

The surgeon turned back to the older woman with a shrug. "There are six in this wagon and three in the other," he said respectfully. "They're the worst."

Elizabeth Brown turned to Charles. "Wouldst thou please have thy men carry those nine into the house? Penny will show them where." To her husband she said: "Send Peter to fetch Joseph Willard immediately. After he calls on the doctor, he is to go to the Worrall and Clayton farms. Have them bring their wagons and bedding. Surely each of us can care for three of these poor creatures."

Peter soon galloped off on horseback, and while Lincoln was supervising the transfer, Charles spoke to Penny's father. "I don't understand," he said. "I thought Quakers didn't abide fighting men."

The older man looked at Charles seriously. "It's the fighting we don't abide. These men are each one God's creatures and deserve our care. It wouldn't matter if they were English or French."

"At least I can pay for the doctor's visits and any expenses to you in keeping them."

"I thank thee," George Brown said. "Joseph Willard will charge nothing for his services in this case, nor will the Worralls or Claytons for food and board. We do this for love of God, not profit."

"I see. Thank you. I am most grateful."

As the last of the stretchers was being carefully lifted out of the wagon, Charles turned to see Penny returning, tight-lipped, pale, and clearly agitated. He knew what she would be upset about and decided that it was something they were going to have to deal with sooner or later. "Come into the house," she said brusquely. "I must converse with thee."

He followed dutifully as she led him to the doorway, opened it, and stood aside without speaking as he hobbled through. Charles felt he could cut the silence with a knife.

"Charles Edgemont, see what thou hast done," she said, her anger spilling out as soon as she had closed the door loudly behind her.

"I didn't do it," he said defensively. "The Spanish did."

"Yes, but thou wert a willing conspirator," she said furiously. "If thou and thy warship were not there, thou wouldst not have been set upon, and these poor men would still be whole."

Charles faced her squarely. "I was not set upon," he said evenly. "I gave the order to attack the Spanish warship. A warship, I might add, considerably larger than the *Louisa*. I saw an opportunity to defeat her and I took it. This is my duty, the thing that I do. If I have another such opportunity I will do the same again."

Penny stared at him for a long moment, her face pale and strained. "I do not like war," she said at last. "Thou can see what it does."

"Yes," Charles said, "I don't like war either. Hardly anyone does. But sometimes it is necessary."

"No, Charlie, it is not." There was an intensity in her tone that he had never heard before. "Oh, the men of the world always speak of war as necessary and heroic and honorable. But it is never thus. War is murder, cruelty, and greed, bloodlust and thievery. Why are all the women ravaged after a battle? Why are all the goods and chattels looted? War is not noble. War is man's lowest instinct. It is butchery, arrogance, and lust, and nothing more."

Taken aback by her outburst, Charles raised his voice. "You must remember that France declared war on England. Surely we are entitled to defend ourselves."

"In God's love, Charlie," her outrage building, she almost shouted, "we are the same people. It doesn't matter who declared first. If they hadn't we would have the very next day. England and France have had one war after another this past century and longer. All this violence has yielded nothing, only death and widows and cripples and orphans and poverty. A hundred years ago we fought against the French long and hard because we could not agree on who would be the king of Spain. Imagine," she exclaimed, "English blood over the king of Spain. Then there was war and war and war with Spain herself. For what? A few islands.

Then more war with France. And the so-called Seven Years War; and the American War; and now this war against the Republic of France because their people overthrew a vile and stupid king—their king, not ours. Still we fight and fight and murder and slaughter without end. I ask you, what good has come of all this war? What good at all?"

Charles stood, stunned and mute. She was not entirely wrong, he thought, if one looked at it her way. He knew he could argue with none of it, not in any terms that would pacify her. And he had a greater worry as he watched the anger in her face, one that terrified him. "Does this change our . . . plans?" he said in a very soft voice.

Her breath still came rapidly, but her eyes softened. "No," she spoke in more measured tones, "I am not angry with thee. I am angry at the world. I have long known who thou art and have resigned to it." Looking firmly up into his eyes, she added, "But if thou comes home to me dead, Charlie, I will be angry with thee forever."

He pulled her to him and put his arms around her. "I'm very sorry," he whispered. "I'm sorry to have distressed you. I wouldn't cause you pain for the world." They stood together for some minutes, close together and alone in the hallway while he felt her breathing slowly return to normal.

Soon after, she led him to the parlor at the back of the house, helped him out of his coat, and set him down at a table. She left to go into the kitchen and, after a moment, came back with a tray containing two bowls of steaming stew, one rather larger than the other, and bread and butter. Once the food was arranged on the table she sat opposite him.

There was something more he wanted to know; something he had never fully understood. "Penny," he asked, reaching for her hand, "why are you resigned to me? Why do you put up with my ways?"

She met his gaze and answered seriously: "Because thou art kind, Charlie; I fear too kind for thy profession. I saw it immediately when thou tended my horse and set my arm. That is why I love thee. I am sorry for thee and what thou feels thou must do, and I pray that it will not always be thus." Then she smiled brightly at him and gave a small laugh. "There is that, and also because thou art not frightened by me. All the others have been."

"I can well imagine," he said, thinking of something entirely different and gently rubbing his thumb in small circles on the palm of her hand.

She instantly met his eyes and pulled her hand away. "Oh, thou art a challenge to me," she said, slightly flushed. "What am I to do with thee?"

"If you give me a little time, I may come up with an idea or two," he said with a grin.

He felt her shoe rub against his calf. "Thou art impertinent," she said without expression and promptly changed the subject. "How long before thou returns to the sea?"

Charles hesitated. "Two months, maybe longer. It depends on how long it takes the dockyard to repair my ship."

"And thy injuries?"

"My injuries will be healed before then. Lincoln says I should be able to use my wrist in about a week and put some weight on my foot a little after that."

"I would like Joseph Willard to look at thee while he's here."

"All right." Charles put down his fork. "I'd like for us to be married, if you're still willing."

"I am," she said, touching his hand. "When wouldst thou wish to have the ceremony?"

"As soon as possible," Charles said seriously. "I'd like for us to be able to spend as much time together as we can." He held her hand tightly in his.

"I want that also," she said softly. "But there is planning to do. People will have to be invited. I need a dress fit for a wedding. And you must speak with my mother and father. They know, but thou must make thy intentions direct."

"Of course," Charles said, trying to arrange the details in his mind. "I would still like it to be soon. I want to be with you," he added huskily. "We can talk to your parents this afternoon."

Penny lowered her eyes and nodded.

Charles heard someone clear his throat and looked up to see Bevan standing in the doorway. "I'm sorry to interrupt," he said, looking from Charles to Penny, "really sorry. Your servant, ma'am. The men have eaten. They're cleaning up. Do you want us to wait for you?"

"No," Charles said. "Just leave York and one of the wagons. Get the men settled in at Tattenall as best you can. I'll be over later."

"All right," Bevan said and turned to leave.

"Daniel," Charles said hurriedly, "don't leave without congratulating us. It's official."

"I feared as much," Bevan said, crossing the room and kissing Penny on the cheek. "Good luck. You, miss, in particular will need it. And you, Charlie," he continued, shaking Charles's hand, "if luck were cows there wouldn't be anywhere to step."

Penny rose and hugged Bevan. "Thou art a good friend, Daniel Bevan," she said. "Take York and the wagon. I will bring Charlie home this evening."

Bevan bowed. "This evening, then."

The remainder of the afternoon passed quickly. Joseph Willard, the Quaker doctor, soon arrived. Charles thought him a pompous and graveyard-serious middle-aged man. The doctor carefully examined each of the wounded men, removing their dressings, questioning them about their injuries and pains, prescribing medicines, and reapplying poultices and wrappings. "I will assume responsibility for tending these men, but I expect your surgeon to call on me when he is free," Willard said.

Charles was introduced to the Worrall and Clayton families, who arrived with their carriages and older children to take their share of the more seriously injured away. With Penny at his side, he spoke briefly with each of the men before they were moved, explaining quietly what was being done for them and how they should behave. The three most critically injured, who were to stay with the Browns, were moved carefully into an upstairs room.

A short while later, Dr. Willard found Charles and Penny in the parlor. "Thou may return when I call thee, Penelope Brown," he said sternly. As soon as they were alone, he sat Charles on a chair and frowned at him. "I do not approve of military officers and military affairs," he said. "Look what thou hast caused."

"Yes," Charles said in a clipped tone; he had had this argument already.

Willard sighed. "Take off thy shirt," he said. After a period of bending, poking, and stretching Charles's injuries, the doctor grudgingly pronounced him reasonably fit. "Thou canst do without the sling," he said. "Thou mayest use thy wrist gently; much of the strength in it will return in time. Thou mayest also begin to put a little weight on thy ankle, but not so much that it pains thee. Continue to use a cane or crutch for another week or two."

Charles said, "Thank you for all you've done. I'd like to pay you for your services."

Willard appraised him sourly. "I will not accept money for tending to the navy's injured. I do not approve of what they do."

"I see," Charles said tersely.

"As for thee," the doctor continued, "I understand thou art to marry our Penny."

"Yes," Charles said, wondering what was next.

"My wife brought that girl into this world. I have been her doctor all her life and I expect thee to make sure she is content in it." Charles started to say something, but Willard went on. "I also expect to continue to be her physician and thy children's. I suppose, for efficiency, that will make thee my patient also, as distasteful as that may be. On this basis I will charge thee one pound, ten shillings for this visit."

Charles paid him.

Penny entered the room as soon as the doctor opened the door. She found Charles fumbling to redo the buttons of his shirt and, brushing his hands away, she fastened them for him. The touch of her fingers on his bare skin thrilled him. "Thou wilt have to tuck thy shirttails in thyself," she said primly. Charles pulled her onto his lap and kissed her. She kissed him back for a moment, then pulled her face away. "My parents are waiting for us to speak to them," she said, her eyes shining. "There will be plenty of time for kissing later."

"Do you promise?" Charles said, but she had gotten to her feet. He pushed himself upright, and, balanced on one foot, managed to get most of his shirttails down into his trousers. She studied him, straightened his collar, and brushed her fingers through his hair. "That will have to suffice," she said finally. After he'd collected his crutch she led him to a larger parlor in the front of the house, more formally furnished. George and Elizabeth Brown sat on a sofa with Peter fidgeting expectantly on a chair nearby.

Penny took Charles's arm and stood close beside him in the middle of the room. "Thou speakest first," she whispered in his ear.

"Your daughter and I wish to marry," he said directly. "We seek your blessing."

George Brown smiled broadly; Penny's mother did not. "When?" Elizabeth Brown asked.

"As soon as it can be arranged," Charles answered. "Within the week, I hope."

Penny's father rose from the sofa. "If the two of ye are decided on this, then congratulations to ye both," he said, shaking Charles's hand and then hugging his daughter.

Elizabeth Brown remained on the sofa. "Art thou truly fixed in this?" she said to Penny.

Penny said firmly, "Yes, Mother. We have spoken about it already."

George Brown sat down beside his wife and put his hand on her arm. He talked to her in very low tones and patted her hand affectionately. Elizabeth looked undecided, then resigned. She rose and stood in front of Charles. "I welcome thee with small misgivings," she said. "Penny is my youngest daughter and very special. I let her go reluctantly." She kissed Charles's cheek and then Penny's. "I do wish thee joy," she said, dry-eyed.

CHARLES STAYED FOR supper with the Browns, eating a simple country meal and answering when spoken to. Mostly he watched his soon-to-be wife with a mixture of anticipation and wonder. Penny talked distractedly with her parents and brother about the unusual events of the day and her plans for the wedding. At the end of the meal, she announced that it was time for her to take Charles back to Tattenall. She had promised Daniel Bevan she would do so, she explained.

"But it's nearly dark," George Brown said, a look of alarm spreading across his face. His eyes darted from his daughter to Charles, who tried to look unconcerned and said nothing. "I will take him in the cart myself."

"No," Penny said firmly. "I said I should, and I shall."

"But it will be very late. How wilt thou get home?"

"I can spend the night at Ellie Winchester's," Penny said quickly, looking desperately to her mother.

"No," George Brown said, his voice rising. "I won't have it. I forbid—"

"George!" Elizabeth said, rising from her chair. "I need thee in the kitchen."

When the two came back a few moments later, Penny's mother said, "Make sure thou hast something warm to sleep in." George Brown looked at Charles and started to speak, changed his mind, and fell unhappily silent.

Penny and Charles sat side by side on the bench of her cart under a crisp January moon as Penny's mare, Maggie, trotted along the roadway, her nostrils streaming puffs of mist into the cold air.

"What do you think your mother said in the kitchen?" Charles asked as the cart rattled along.

Penny, the reins in her hands, stared at the road ahead. "I have heard there is some question as to whether my oldest brother, Thomas, was conceived before or after their wedding. It apparently caused quite a scandal at the time. My uncle Seth sometimes still teases about it."

"Oh," Charles said. "I'd never have guessed."

Penny turned her head and looked at him. "We must be cautious that no such thing happens to us."

"Of course not." He reached over with his uninjured hand, took the reins, and pulled Maggie to a halt. Then he took Penny in his arms and kissed her. "You can't conceive by kissing," he said.

"Only ideas," Penny answered between his kisses. As they kissed some more, Charles's free hand wandered over her outer clothing to places where it normally would have no business going. When his fingers turned their attention to the hooks on her cloak, she pushed the hand away. "No," she said. "And we cannot sit out here in the road all night. We'll freeze to death. Or by thy plan at least I shall."

Charles took the reins and snapped the mare into motion. The cart soon clattered through Tattenall in the still darkness and up the drive to Charles's grand new house. The building was dark except for a single candle in a window near the door. He drove the mare to the stables, where they climbed down, Penny helping Charles and handing him his crutch. They unhitched Maggie together and led her to the stable entrance. Charles lit a lantern that hung there. He pulled back the heavy door and was greeted with the sound of snoring from the darkness within. Holding up the lantern, they saw the forms of a dozen or more seamen in various postures of sleep on piles of hay or in hammocks slung from posts. Charles closed the door while Penny led her horse to the paddock.

They walked hand in hand back to the house, Penny holding a small bag she had brought with her. Inside were similar sounds of sleeping men—many sleeping men. Charles took the guttering candle from the windowsill and shone it around. Every room he looked into seemed mostly empty of furniture and occupied by sailors curled on the floor, snoring sonorously.

"Now what?" Charles said softly.

"Where is thy bedchamber?" Penny whispered.

"I don't know. I've never stayed here. It wasn't finished when I left."

A flickering candle appeared at the end of the hall from the direction of the kitchen. The welcome form of Timothy Attwater in a sleeping cap and long nightshirt padded toward them holding a lighted candle.

"Oh, it's you, sir," he said loudly, his voice ringing in the hallway. Nodding to Penny he said, "Good evening, miss."

"Are there any empty rooms?" Charles asked, trying to forestall any sociable chattiness.

"Oh, yes, sir," Attwater answered, yawning. "I kept your room free. There's a made-up bed and all." He glanced knowingly at Penny. "A big bed, sir."

"I need two rooms," Charles said sternly. "One for Miss Brown."

The steward rubbed at the stubble on his chin. "Ain't another one, sir. Ain't one that ain't full."

"What about at the Winchesters' house, or my brother's?"

"Don't think so, sir," Attwater said, the corners of his mouth twitching. Charles suspected that his steward was enjoying his role as dispenser of bad news. "The midshipmen and warrants is with Lieutenant Winchester. The rest of the wounded have pretty well filled up your brother's house."

"All right," Charles said. "Penny—Miss Brown—can sleep in my room. Find me a sofa or a table, anything I can lie on."

Attwater smiled as if appreciating the delicacy of the situation. "Ain't no empty tables, sir. Lessen I throw somebody off."

Penny put her hand on Charles's arm. "Show us Charles's chamber," she said to Attwater. "We'll manage."

"This way, sir, miss," the steward said, leading with his candle. He opened a doorway at the top of the stairs, entered, and lit an oil lamp on a chest of drawers inside. "It's all fixed for you."

"Oh, my," Penny said. Inside the room was a spacious bed made up with a man's nightshirt laid across it, the chest, and a single wooden chair.

"I'll sleep on the floor," Charles said.

"Don't be silly," Penny said. "We're adults. We just need to have an understanding." To Attwater she said, "Thank thee. Thou mayest return to thy sleep." Charles heard his steward cackle with laughter as he padded back down the stairs.

"Thou must wait outside," Penny said, removing her bonnet and reaching to undo her cloak. "I will call thee in a moment."

Charles waited in the hall until he heard her voice. She lay on the bed with the covers pulled up to her chin, her hair fanned over the pillow. He sat down on the side of the bed. "Where do I change?" he said hoarsely, as if something were caught in his throat.

"Put out the light," she said. "Thou canst change in the dark."

Charles blew out the lamp, stripped, and pulled the nightshirt over his head. He slipped carefully into the bed beside her. "Are you sure this is all right?"

"I expect thee to be a gentleman."

"I expect you to be a lady," Charles answered and reached for her hand under the covers. He felt her foot tentatively touch his leg. Then her toenails scraped slowly down the side of his calf. He stretched across for her waist and tickled, to which she squealed loudly, then quickly put her finger to his lips and whispered, "Shhhh."

CHARLES WOKE IN the first light of dawn to find Penny cuddled against him, her cheek resting against his shoulder, breathing softly on his neck. He carefully pushed a little of her hair aside and watched her sleep. After a time one eye flickered open, clear gray with hints of tan around the edges of the iris. He kissed her nose and said, "You were no lady."

"And thou wert no gentleman," she answered. She stretched languorously and rolled half on his chest, her fingers toying with the buttons on his nightshirt.

Much later Charles awoke a second time to find himself alone, the bed still warm beside him. He rose reluctantly, dressed, and splashed some water from a bowl on the bureau onto his face. He found Penny, Attwater, and a number of his sailors along with an older woman and two younger ones he didn't recognize in the kitchen, preparing what seemed to be a very large container of oatmeal on the woodstove. Charles was introduced to Mrs. Attwater and two of her daughters, Daisy and Rose. All three glanced knowingly from Charles to Penny and smiled.

A little later that morning Charles took Penny in the carriage into Tattenall to inquire after the arrangements for their wedding at the old St. Alban's Church in the village. Charles had written to the rector, William Weddlestone, A.M., from Plymouth soon after Penny had accepted his proposal. He had as yet received no reply, which wasn't surprising given that he had been at sea almost the entire time. Still, the banns should have been long since posted and other arrangements put into train. It only remained, he expected, to fix a date when the vicar would be available. The sooner the better.

The two sat, mostly silent, side-by-side on the bench as the carriage and horses clattered into the village, turning almost immediately past the old sandstone church into the drive to the rectory. He descended gingerly, hitching the horses to a post in front of the house. They walked— Charles was relying on his cane less each day—to the heavy doorway in what seemed strained silence. Glancing at Penny, he saw that her lips were pursed in a tight line and her eyes fixed straight ahead.

"It will be all right," he said, and lifted the heavy door knocker. "You'll see."

A housekeeper answered the knock. Charles announced himself and Miss Brown, and they were shown into a comfortably furnished parlor with highly polished oak paneling. The Reverend Weddlestone, Rector of St. Alban's, entered soon afterward. Charles noted that he was a youngish man, perhaps in his mid-thirties, with a thin face, receding hair, and well-tailored clothing.

"I am Charles Edgemont of Tattenall and this is Penelope Brown of Gatesheath," he said by way of introductions, extending his hand. "I wrote to you earlier of our plans to marry."

"Ah, the naval officer," Weddlestone answered, a guarded look about his eyes that was not what Charles would have expected. He did not acknowledge the offered hand.

"I have received no reply to my letter," Charles pushed on. "I was hoping we could set a date for the ceremony."

"When, pray tell," Weddlestone answered distantly.

"As soon as possible," Charles said, put off by the man's lack of warmth, or even common courtesy. "I shall have to return to the sea in a few weeks or a month."

Weddlestone focused on something outside the room's only window. "I cannot marry you at any time," he said under his breath.

"I beg your pardon?"

"I cannot perform the ceremony," the rector said in a stronger voice. "I'm sorry."

Charles thought there must be some mistake. "Why not? I wrote—"

"I made inquiries," Weddlestone said, more boldly now. "Mistress Brown is a nonconformist, a Quaker. I do not hold with such heathen views; they are anathema to the very being of the Church. I cannot, will not marry nonbelievers." He spat out the words "nonconformist" and "Quaker" as if they were synonymous with "Satan" or "Beelzebub."

Charles felt Penny stiffen beside him and saw her glare at the priest, the color draining from her face. "Thou false Christian," she began. "Thou pretentious priest. I would not have thy—"

"Penny," Charles said quickly, "there has been a small misunderstanding. The Reverend and I need to speak in confidence for a moment. If you would step into the garden, I'll join you there as quickly as I can."

She looked at him with narrowed eyes, further elaborations on Weddlestone's spiritual views not far from her lips. When he added, "Please," she made her way wordlessly to the door, closing it loudly behind her.

Alone with Weddlestone, Charles paused and looked around the comfortable room. "You have a nice living here in Tattenall," he said off-handedly. "What's it bring you, two hundred fifty, three hundred pounds a year? Quite a plum for a man your age. You've made inquiries; you must know who I am, do you not?"

Weddlestone nodded warily. "You've purchased the old Tattenall Hall."

"Yes," Charles said. "I own the entirety of it and also a half-interest in the Edgemont lands." He paused. "To be clear, I own almost all of your living and my brother owns a good deal of the rest." Before Weddlestone could reply, he went on, "You are a courageous man. It must be hard to refuse a wounded naval officer the chance to marry the woman he loves; particularly one who controls your employment. I respect that."

"I mean nothing personal against you," the rector said, meeting Charles's eyes. "I have read about your accomplishments in battle. But a Quaker? They are the bane of the country, worse even than Ranters or Presbyterians; a stubborn, hard, unchristian people."

"Penny can be as stubborn as any woman," Charles said with a smile. "But I assure you that she is neither hard nor unchristian. You do know that the moment we are married she will no longer be a member of their society."

"Do you mean that she will convert?"

"I don't know about that. She will be disowned by her religion. Her view toward your Church will most likely be determined by the nature of her relationship with yourself. So far you haven't made a very favorable impression."

"I see," Weddlestone said, letting his breath out slowly. "You are certain that she will no longer follow her previous religion?"

"She will certainly be disowned," Charles said, choosing his words carefully.

"Well, that changes everything." The rector smiled tentatively. "I see no reason why you should not be wed. What date would you like?"

"Saturday."

"Saturday? I can't possibly—"

"Saturday," Charles repeated firmly. "A very small, very simple, very brief ceremony on Saturday morning. No choirs or music or anything like that. I wrote to you about this in plenty of time. I'm sure you can arrange to postdate the banns and do anything else that might need fixing. Saturday."

OUTSIDE, HE FOUND Penny sitting tensely on a bench in the garden with her hands folded tightly in her lap and clutching a handkerchief. "It's all agreed," he said with forced cheerfulness. "Saturday morning."

"The priest has agreed to the ceremony?" She looked both incredulous and angry. "Charlie, I cannot—"

"No, no," he said reassuringly, lowering himself onto the bench and taking her hands in his own. "It's settled. Everything is fixed. It will be fine, you'll see. He's looking forward to the ceremony. It was only a small misunderstanding."

"A misunderstanding? A small misunderstanding?" She tried to pull her hands away but he tightened his grip. "What misunderstanding could that pompous, arrogant, uncaring, heathenous priest have had? I cannot—" She stopped in midsentence, her chest heaving. He could see that she was on the verge of tears. She stared down at their hands in her lap and then up into Charles's face. After a deep breath, she said, "What misunderstanding?"

"I only had to explain to him some of the practices of Quakers," Charles answered almost proudly. "Now he sees things differently."

"*Thou* explained the practices of Quakers?"

"Yes," Charles continued, speaking rapidly. "Also, I don't think he truly appreciated the extent to which I control his livelihood."

"Thou threatened the priest?"

"I did not. I educated him. And please call him a minister, vicar, or rector. I don't think he likes being called a priest."

Penny sat silently on the bench, staring fixedly at her lap again and nibbling on her lower lip for a moment in deep concentration, as if attempting to digest what he had said and trying to decide whether it answered her objections.

"You see, it's all right now," Charles offered hopefully. He studied her carefully as her expression by degrees softened. He patted her hand reassuringly.

Abruptly her brow furrowed and she turned to face him. "Saturday?" she exclaimed in alarm. "That's only five days! How couldst thou arrange it for Saturday? I must return home at once."

"You're going back to Gatesheath?" Charles asked. He had assumed, to the extent he had thought about it at all, that they would carry on more or less as before, with the additional requirement of showing up at the church on Saturday morning. He saw now that he was wrong.

"I must. Only five days!" she said, clearly distracted. "What didst thou expect?"

Charles chose not to answer that question. Instead he said, "Will I see you at all?"

"Not before Saturday." Seeing that he was unhappy, she turned and stroked his cheek. "I will see thee on the morning of our marriage," she said. "And every day after that until thou returns to the sea. Now take me back to my cart."

CHARLES AWOKE EACH of the following mornings knowing that he would not find Penny in the bed next to him but feeling for her under the covers anyway. Mostly he kept himself busy with trips into Chester (where Ellie told him he had to buy a new suit of clothes for the ceremony; his naval uniform would not do) and other errands. The temptation to stop by the Brown house on his way home each time was almost overwhelming. On Friday, the day before his wedding, Charles awoke feeling listless, ill-tempered, and anxious. He knew he had no more preparations to make, no errands to run, nothing at all to do. He argued with Attwater about his breakfast and snapped at two of his crewmen for capering loudly in the hallway. By midmorning he wanted someone to talk to; anyone would do. Stephen and Ellie Winchester were not at home and the maid who answered the door either didn't know or wouldn't say where they'd gone. Bevan he found beyond the stables amid a clamor of hammers and saws and stacks of lumber. He was apparently supervising a number of the midshipmen and about half of the crew in erecting a long wooden shelter.

"What's this?" Charles asked.

"It's quarters for the crew, Charlie," Bevan said, turning toward him. "We thought it might be a good idea to get the men out of the house before Miss Brown comes. Frankly, you don't need the competition."

Charles tried to think. "Whose idea was this?"

"Winchester's and mine, if I recall," Bevan said doubtfully, "or possibly Mrs. Winchester suggested it."

"Where'd the lumber come from?" Charles asked.

"You're just a barrel full of questions, aren't you?" Bevan said. "But if you must know, Winchester had it delivered yesterday. It was supposed to be the day before, in which case this would all have been a surprise, but they were late. So, tomorrow, look surprised."

"All right, I'll look surprised," Charles said. "Where are the Winchesters?"

"Can't say," Bevan answered.

"Can't say, or don't know?"

"Can't say."

"Are they planning any other surprises?"

"Can't say." Bevan looked at him and grinned. "I'm awfully busy just now, Charlie. Molly's in the stables, why don't you talk to her?"

"Is Molly involved in this?" Charles said, aghast.

"Can't . . . well, yes."

Charles was no longer listless or anxious. He was now alarmed. He started toward the stables and noticed smaller groups of seamen busily cleaning out underbrush, raking the lawns and drive, repairing fences, and generally tidying the place up, and wondered who had thought of that. He found Molly Bridges, with her back turned to him, in the stables, currying Pendle. He noticed a half-dozen black horses he didn't recognize in adjoining stalls. Of his chestnut mares for the carriage, and the carriage itself, for that matter, he saw nothing.

"Hello, Molly," Charles said. "What's going on?"

The girl turned with a jerk. "Oh, shit!" she said, then covered her mouth with her hands. "I'm sorry, Admiral," she said quickly. "Old habits."

With all his time with Penny and other things, Charles had hardly seen Molly since he'd returned to Tattenall. He was pleased that she looked healthier, more rosy-cheeked, much more modestly dressed, and perhaps a little more sedate.

"Where are my mares and my carriage?" Charles asked, feeling a little bewildered. "I'll need them tomorrow."

Molly bit her lip. "I ain't supposed to say, sir, but they're at your brother's stable. It's all arranged."

"What's all arranged?"

"I ain't supposed to say."

"How am I to pick up Penny?" Charles asked with alarm.

"It's all arranged," Molly said desperately. "You're to ride on Pendle here. I'm to make him beautiful for you."

"What about Penny?"

"I ain't supposed to say," she said. "It ain't my part."

"All right," Charles said, sensing that events were out of his control. There was only one nagging question. "There isn't any playacting with wives and sweethearts, is there?"

"Oh, no, sir." She beamed. "We couldn't do that twice; she'd catch on for sure."

Charles limped directly back to his house, yelled for Attwater, and went to his room. He didn't blink an eye when he saw that there was now a carpet on the floor, curtains in the windows, a small table with two chairs, and a large armoire.

"Yes, sir?" Attwater said, poking his head in the door.

"Bring me something to eat and a good book."

"A good book, sir?"

"Any book, damn it."

CHARLES WAS ALREADY awake when Attwater knocked at his door the next morning. His steward entered with a candle in one hand and a mug of coffee in the other. "It's your wedding day, sir," Attwater said, as if he was afraid Charles might have forgotten.

"Thank you," Charles said. He sat up, took the mug, and sipped.

"There's a tub for you in the kitchen," Attwater said. "Hot water to bathe in. If you'll follow me."

Charles sipped some more of his coffee, then climbed out of the bed. He found his slippers and cane and hobbled down the hallway after his servant. The kitchen was brightly lit and in the middle of it stood a large half-barrel full of steaming water. Mrs. Attwater and her two daughters were just lifting a heavy cast-iron pot onto the stove to heat some more.

"If I may have your nightshirt, sir," Attwater said.

Charles glanced at the three women, all watching him speculatively. "Tell them to turn around," he said. The water was hot enough to be uncomfortable, relaxing, and stimulating all at the same time. He scrubbed himself with soap and a stiff brush, then leaned back as Attwater shaved him. "There, sir. You look fit to be a groom."

Attwater took Charles's new suit of clothing from the armoire and laid it out on the bed along with a clean shirt and other items of his dress. At seven-thirty, Bevan, Winchester, and his brother John, all smartly attired in civilian clothing, arrived to find Charles finishing his breakfast in the dining room. "Time to go, Charlie," Bevan announced. "We're here to see that you don't run off on the way to church."

"And Penny?" Charles asked.

"She'll be there," Bevan said. "Unless she comes to her senses."

Attwater brought Charles his coat and helped him into it. "Good luck, sir," he said gravely. "The matrimonial state can be a wonderful thing."

"Thank you," Charles said. The four men went outside where Pendle and three other horses stood saddled and waiting. They mounted and started briskly off. Charles noticed Winchester frequently checking his watch.

After the short ride into the village and up to the church, he was surprised to see two of his crew, uniformed in new blue jackets, white breeches, and black lacquered straw hats with the word LOUISA embroidered on the bands. The sailors stepped smartly forward, saluted, and held the horses' bridles while the party dismounted.

"We wait," said Bevan. Winchester checked his watch. John looked idly around. Charles wondered what was next.

Around the corner six matched black horses appeared, their iron shoes clattering loudly on the hard-packed street. They were formed in a column of twos ridden by sailors in uniforms matching those of the men who had held their horses. Two carriages, decked in pine boughs and ivy garlands, followed behind, driven by similarly liveried sailors. Charles saw that the first contained Penny and her parents, the second Ellie, Molly, and Peter.

He watched in near amazement as the sailors on horseback dismounted in unison and smartly formed a corridor from the leading carriage for Penny to pass through. All else faded from his view as Penny was handed down onto the street. She looked stunningly fresh and beautiful, he thought, as she gave the sailor helping her a dazzling smile. He noticed that she wore a pale gray satin dress under her cloak and small curls protruded just so from the edges of her bonnet. Her eyes glistened over cheeks tinted pink from the cold.

"Charlie," she called as she hurried forward. Slipping her arm in his, she beamed at him and said, "Didst thou arrange all this?"

"Not me," Charles answered with a grin. "You'll have to find someone else to blame." Two sailors opened the church doors wide and Charles and Penny passed inside.

The ceremony turned out to be not as simple and brief as Charles had anticipated. Evidently having resolved to make the best of the unfortunate situation he found himself in, the Reverend Weddlestone spoke at length, almost waxing poetical, about the sanctity, beauty, and importance of marriage, and all the fruits thereof (sex excepted). He next launched into several prolonged quotations from the Book of Common Prayer before getting down to the actual business at hand. Charles heard, or at least attended to, almost none of it. He was aware only of the rigid gaze and labored breathing of the woman standing beside him, and was almost startled when Weddlestone held forward a Bible and intoned, "Do you, Commander Charles Algernon Edgemont, Esquire, take this woman, Miss Penelope Hanna Brown, to be your lawfully wedded wife, to love and honor, in sickness and in health, for better or for worse, for as long as you both shall live?"

"I do," Charles said, laying his hand on the book.

"Do you, Penelope Hannah Brown—"

Penny laid her hand over Charles's. "Yes," she said.

Weddlestone continued as if uninterrupted: "—promise to take Commander Charles Algernon Edgemont as your lawfully wedded husband—"

"Yes," Penny repeated insistently.

The reverend doggedly, and Charles thought rather foolishly, persevered. "—to love, honor, and obey in all things, in sickness and in health, so long as you both shall live?"

Penny looked sharply up at Weddlestone.

Charles sighed in resignation.

"Thou didst not require obedience of my husband," Penny said acidly.

Weddlestone's eyebrows arched, his lips pursed in anticipation of a response.

Charles turned immediately to Penny. "I promise to be your humble and obedient servant," he said under his breath. "Please just answer so we can be done with it."

"All right," Penny managed toward Weddlestone between clenched teeth.

"Say, 'I do,'" insisted Weddlestone.

"All right, I do."

"Then by the power vested in me by the Holy See of England and the One True Church in Cheshire, I pronounce you man and wife."

Charles turned her forcibly away from the minister before she could reply and pulled her toward him. "Mrs. Edgemont," he said, taking her in his arms. At that moment, for several reasons, it seemed astonishing to him that this woman had agreed to join her life to his.

Penny hesitated for a moment, then, to his great relief, her eyes met his. "Good morning to thee, my love," she whispered back and they kissed.

Outside Charles saw that a sizable crowd had gathered to see what all the sailors and carriages were about. A midshipman shouted, "Three cheers for the happy couple!" and the whole street joined in the huzzas.

Some enthusiastic soul in the street shouted out, "Kiss the bride!" A chorus started up: "Kiss! Kiss! Kiss the bride!"

Penny looked at Charles, her face now flushed with excitement or embarrassment, and they did.

They paraded back to their house with the mounted sailors in the fore, Charles and Penny in their carriage, followed by the second carriage, and John, Winchester, and Bevan on horseback behind. Charles watched in renewed surprise as they turned into the drive. Seamen lined the way, waving their hats and cheering as they passed. He noticed that most of the injured crewmen were among them, some standing, others in chairs, and a few being held up on stretchers. The lawn was crowded with people he guessed were his crofters or just local villagers. A steer and a boar turned on spits near the front of the house, and tables piled with food and drink were set up on the grass.

"Oh, Charlie," Penny said, waving back with one hand and clutching his arm tightly with the other, "it's too much. I don't know any of these people." Still, her eyes were shining and there was an absurdly large smile on her face. "Oh, I see some of my friends!" she exclaimed. "There are the Howells and Joshua and Mary Worrall and their children, and the Claytons."

Charles climbed down from the carriage and took Penny's hand as she followed. They walked back to the second carriage, where Penny embraced her parents, Ellie, Molly, and even Peter. Charles was promptly kissed by Elizabeth Brown and embraced by her husband. The crowd closed around them and he kissed Penny again to robust cheers. Soon Penny was pulled away by some of her friends and Charles found himself with Daniel Bevan and Stephen Winchester. "Did you two organize all this?" he asked.

"Not me, I was just following orders," Bevan answered.

"It was mostly Ellie's idea," Winchester said defensively.

"Do you think she invited enough people?" Charles said.

"I think it's everyone Ellie's ever met and then some," he said, a little in awe. "She can be very enthusiastic."

"Come with me, both of you," Charles said. "I want to say thank you and I want to include my sister." The three men started through the crowd toward Ellie, where she was talking with Molly.

"Charlie, Charlie!" she cried as soon as she saw him approaching and rushed forward. "Isn't it wonderful! I'm so happy for you." She exuberantly kissed his cheeks, almost jumping with pleasure. "And for Penny, too, of course. Isn't it wonderful?"

"I wanted to thank you for all you've done," Charles said seriously, kissing her cheeks in return, "and Stephen and Daniel too, and Molly." He shook the two men's hands and bussed Molly carefully on the cheek. "I don't know how I can repay you."

"Oh, Charlie," Ellie sobbed, grabbing Winchester's arm with sudden tears streaming down her cheeks. "It's so beautiful. You're just perfect for each other. Isn't that right, Stevie?"

Winchester nodded dutifully in agreement.

"Damnation," Bevan breathed. Charles glanced at his lieutenant and saw him staring at something in the distance. He followed Bevan's gaze and saw a lone horseman in the uniform of a naval courier trotting up the drive. The courier stopped beside a group of sailors and bent in his saddle, as if asking directions. Charles's heart sank as he watched a man point in his direction.

"Commander Edgemont?" the courier asked after dismounting.

"I'm Edgemont," Charles said.

"I'm sorry to interrupt the festivities, sir. I have orders for you."

With a rising sense of dread, Charles signed for the Admiralty envelope. "You're welcome to stay for something to eat," he said.

"Thank you, sir. What's all this in celebration of?"

"My marriage."

"I am sorry, sir."

Charles walked a little away and opened the envelope, his expression hardening as he read:

> To Commander Charles Edgemont
> of HM Frigate *Louisa*
>
> Sir,
>
> You are hereby requested and required to report at your earliest possible opportunity onboard HM Frigate *Louisa along with her officers and crew.* Said *Louisa* is to be found in a restored state and ready for sea at the Portsmouth Naval Yards. You are further required to report to the Portsmouth Dockyard Admiral's Office immediately on arrival for receipt of further orders.
>
> Nor you, nor any of you may fail in the strictest and most immediate execution of these orders except at your peril.
>
>> Your servant,
> > Arthur Dorchester,
> > Admiral, Portsmouth Naval Yard

"What does it say, Charlie?" Bevan asked.

"You know what it says, Daniel." Charles tried to keep the bile out of his voice. "Send one of the midshipmen on horseback to tell the *Maryanne* to prepare. Pass the word to muster the men at first light.

We sail for Portsmouth in the morning. They've fixed *Louisa* in record time."

"I'm very sorry," Bevan said.

"Yes," Charles answered.

He leaned on his cane and looked around him until he found Penny talking animatedly with some of her friends. He studied the blush of her cheeks, the brightness of her eyes, the happiness on her face. Reluctantly he moved toward her.

"I have to speak to you in the house," he said as soon as he caught her attention.

"In a minute, Charlie," she said. Then she saw the dismay in his expression. "Excuse us," she said to her friends, took his arm, and walked with him toward their home.

"What is it?" she asked as soon as they were inside.

Charles led her into the parlor and they sat down. "I've orders to return to the *Louisa*," he said solemnly.

"When?"

"We leave at dawn."

"Oh, Charlie, thou and I have just begun."

"I know," Charles said slowly. "I feel so badly for you."

"When wilt thou return?"

Charles sat silent, staring at the floor. "I don't know," he said at last.

Penny reached for his hands and held them between her own. "We have this day," she said. "And whatever time God gives us in the rest of our days."

THIRTEEN

THE BARQUE *MARYANNE* MADE HER WAY UP THE SOLENT and into Portsmouth Harbor on a clear cold morning with the tide still making and a moderate westerly breeze blowing a small chop across the anchorage. Charles picked out the *Louisa* among the crowd of naval ships as soon as they passed the point. She rode high in the water with all new masts, her yards crossed and a fresh coat of dark-gray paint on her hull. She looked more new than repaired, although, if he looked carefully, he could just see the joints in her strakes where damage from the *Santa Brigida*'s broadsides had been patched over.

Charles leaned on the *Maryanne*'s port rail to take some of the weight off his injured ankle. He had given up the use of his cane several days earlier, but still walked with a small limp. It was more of a dull ache than an actual pain, but it became bothersome when he spent too much time on his feet. "If you would be so good as to lay her close alongside," he said to the *Maryanne*'s master. "And thank you for a pleasant and speedy passage."

The barque came to about ten fathoms from the *Louisa* and dropped anchors fore and aft. "Get a boat in the water," Charles said to Bevan.

"What boat?" the familiar voice of Samuel Eliot called out as *Maryanne*'s jolly boat approached the *Louisa*'s side. Eliot, Howell the carpenter, Keswick the bosun, and George the gunner and their mates had stayed on the ship to oversee the repairs.

"*Louisa*," Bevan called back as they hooked onto the ship's main-chains. "How be you, Mr. Eliot? Did you miss us?"

"Not likely, Mr. Bevan," Eliot called back with a chuckle.

Charles climbed the entry ladder first, favoring his ankle, and was greeted by the twittering pipes of two of the bosun's mates as he stepped on deck.

"Welcome aboard, Captain," Eliot said warmly. "It's good to have you back."

"You have to call him 'Mr. Captain,'" Bevan said, stepping through the entryway. "He's gotten married, you know. Yes, he's not his own man anymore. Now he answers to a higher and infinitely more attractive authority."

"Really, sir?" said Eliot. "Congratulations. I wouldn't have thought there was time for it. You've only been gone a month or so."

"I'd expected to be home a bit longer," Charles said, "but thank you anyway."

"Seems someone was careless about informing the Spanish of our esteemed commander's plans," Bevan offered, "or they might have suspended the war for a time in consideration."

Charles looked carefully around him at the decks, masts, rigging, and all the other details that made the ship function. Everything seemed to be clean, newly painted, and generally shipshape. If he hadn't known, he could hardly tell which parts were original and which had been repaired or replaced. "The dockyard certainly worked quickly," he said. "What kind of a job did they do?"

"You'll get a full report from Davey Howell, but they worked on her in double shifts from dawn till dusk. On my word, I've never seen a yard make such an effort. To my eye it seems they did a workmanlike job, though."

Charles counted the twelve-pounder cannon lined up along the maindeck. With satisfaction he saw that there were twelve on each side, one more than there had been before. "They've added another pair of carronades?" he asked.

"Aye, on the quarterdeck. There was a great deal of discussion about it. In the end they took away two of the nine-pounders and replaced them with twelves on the maindeck forward. The carronades are where the nines were."

Charles nodded his approval. To Bevan he said, "Get the cutter in the water and bring the crew across. As soon as that's started, lower the gig. I've orders to call on the dockyard admiral."

After changing into his best uniform and hat, and with a boat cloak wrapped tightly against the cold, Charles climbed down the *Louisa*'s side to the waiting gig. He timed his jump carefully, landing mostly on his good leg, and made his way to the sternsheets, where he sat down.

"Let go all," Williams the coxswain ordered to the four hands at the oars, and the small boat started toward the wharf ladderway.

"Do ye need help getting up the side, sir?" his coxswain offered as they arrived.

Remembering his last visit, when he was carried up slung over the shoulder of one of his crew, he smiled and said, "No thank you, Williams. I can manage this time."

"Do you desire us to wait for you, sir?"

Charles shook his head. "Thank you, no. I don't know how long I'll be. I'll hire a boat to take me back." He climbed the ladder, consciously favoring his ankle, trying to hide his limp as he crossed the quay, and entered the long stone building housing the Portsmouth port admiral's office.

"IN A MOMENT; the admiral hasn't had his coffee yet," the dockyard lieutenant said—the same aide who had tried to prevent Charles from seeing Jervis on his previous visit.

"I'll wait," Charles said. He did not feel himself pressed for time, and in any event was not as sure of his ground with Dorchester as he would have been with Jervis. "Please inform the admiral that I'm waiting." With that he sat on a wooden chair in the hallway and crossed his almost-healed leg over his good one. Ten minutes later, the aide reemerged and ushered Charles through the door.

"Good morning, Commander Edgemont," Dorchester said, rising and extending his hand. "Coffee or tea?"

"Coffee, sir," Charles said, shook the offered hand, and felt for the chair behind him. Once Dorchester was seated he sat down.

"How are your injuries?" the admiral asked, searching distractedly through a large stack of papers on his desk.

"Much better, thank you, sir," Charles answered.

"And the personal business you had to attend to? Jervis—er, Lord St. Vincent—told me you were to be married." Not waiting for an answer, he said, "Ah, yes, here it is," and pulled an envelope from the stack.

"Completed satisfactorily, sir," Charles said.

"Eh, what?" Dorchester said, evidently having momentarily forgotten his question. Then, remembering, "Oh, yes, good. Capital thing, marriage. Don't agree with the admiral at all about that one. He doesn't like his officers married—thinks it makes them cautious, averse to taking risks."

"Yes, sir," Charles said noncommittally. An elderly seaman brought in his coffee and placed it on a small adjacent table.

Dorchester extended his hand with the envelope, then paused and frowned. "I must say something about your absconding with *Louisa*'s crew."

"I thought the change would do them good," Charles said quickly, and braced himself for a stern reprimand.

"I'm sure it would," Dorchester said gruffly, "but think of the discipline. You must have had men running at every opportunity. How many did you lose?"

"I had no deserters, sir. We had very little trouble with discipline; nothing that couldn't be handled. The only men left behind were the most seriously injured and disabled, amputees mostly."

"No deserters?" Dorchester said, skepticism showing on his face.

"No, sir, not one."

"Still, it's highly irregular, highly," he said, his tone softening. He handed Charles the extended envelope. "But there's nothing explicit in the regulations about it, I checked. I'll let it go this time. Don't do it again."

"Yes, sir," Charles said, breathing easier. He broke the seal on his orders and, scanning the handwriting, noted that the *Louisa* was to return to Ferrol to watch over the Spanish frigate and impede her in any way he could. There was more, but he didn't have time to read all of it.

"On his return to Gibraltar," Dorchester continued, "His Lordship looked into Ferrol and found your *Santa Brigida* to be advanced in her repairs. He sent word back to me immediately to make *Louisa* our highest priority, with a note requesting that I see to it personally. In deference to his Lordship, I have done so, including the addition to her armament you requested. I think you'll find the work satisfactory."

"It seems well done," Charles said earnestly. "I appreciate the time and effort you've put into it."

Dorchester smiled his acknowledgment, then lifted his hand to indicate that he wasn't finished. "I'm to tell you that His Lordship is also urgently seeking a second frigate to assist in dealing with the *Santa Brigida* once and for all. There is something about this in your orders, and I believe Captain Hillard's *Thalis* will be available shortly. Hillard will have more detailed orders and an extra complement of marines. I am told a cutting-out expedition is contemplated."

Charles's heart sank. Hillard, he knew, was a post captain well up the first third of the Navy List, and as such would have overall command of any engagement. He would never have admitted it, but he didn't want some other commander giving orders and taking credit for what Charles considered to be his own personal fight.

"His Lordship feels strongly," Dorchester emphasized, "that, in the short term, containing the Spanish frigate in Ferrol is of the highest importance. In no event should she be allowed to run free. The damage she could do to British shipping is simply too great."

"I understand, sir," Charles said, anxious now to return to his ship and put to sea. "Is *Louisa* provisioned?"

"That will be done this afternoon."

"My crew is seriously under its complement," Charles said. "Our casualties from the previous battle have not been replaced."

"I am aware of that, Commander," Dorchester said, frowning. "How could they have been? We didn't know where to send them." Satisfied that he had driven home his point, he asked, "How many do you need?"

"We are short sixty-five seamen, sir."

The admiral looked for another paper in the pile on his desk. Finding what he wanted, he studied it and said, "I can provide you with forty."

"Experienced seamen, sir?"

"Commander Edgemont," Dorchester said sternly, "you will have to make do with whatever is available. After all, you might get it in your head to take them to see St. Paul's or to enjoy the waters at Bath next."

"Yes, sir. Thank you, sir," Charles said.

THE LOUISA SAILED directly from Portsmouth on the evening tide the next day, sorting out her crew and practicing at her guns as she went. They sighted the familiar outline of Cape Ortegal on the northwest corner of Spain late in the afternoon in the second week in February. A heavy fog along the coast forced them to stand out to sea during the night. They had turned back toward land that morning only after the wind freshened moderately from just west of south and blew the mist away. The Louisa made landfall again off Cape Villano, had worn, and now approached Ferrol from the southwest on easy seas with long undulating swells and a light but steady wind on its larboard quarter.

Charles leaned against the lee quarterdeck rail next to Daniel Bevan, listening to the breeze whisper through the rigging and the gentle groan of the timbers as the ship slowly rolled over the easy sea. He stared absently at the distant gray mass of the passing Galician mountains, wondering about the Santa Brigida, how far along her repairs really were, and where the timbers and supplies had come from with which to repair her. Perhaps the Spanish authorities had decided to restock the Ferrol yards for use as a fully functioning naval base once again. In any event, he would soon know; the entrance to Coruna Bay should almost be in sight from the masthead.

"Deck!" the lookout in the foremast crosstrees shouted. "There's a ship in the entrance to the bay."

"What bearing?" Charles called up.

"Two points to starboard, sir, maybe fifteen miles afar."

"What heading?"

"She's tacking to the east, out to sea, like." There was a pause. "I recognize her t'gallants. She's the Spanish frigate, sir! The same as we fought before."

"Do you want to stand out again?" Bevan said, a trace of anxiety in his voice. "We'll want the searoom."

Charles thought for a moment. "Crosstrees," he yelled. "Is she in or out of the bay?"

"Almost out, sir. She's just under the fort," came the reply.

He gauged the wind on his cheek and stared hard at the outline of the distant mountains.

"No," Charles said to Bevan, coming to a tentative decision. "We'll run straight down large on her and see what we have. We can stand out later if we want to."

Within two bells the *Santa Brigida*'s topgallants were visible from *Louisa*'s quarterdeck—white specks outlined against the darker bulk of the land. The spots slowly grew and assumed an oblong shape, slivers of her topsails appearing beneath them.

"She's making slow going," Bevan observed. The distant sails seemed hardly to be moving.

"Yes," Charles said, more to himself than his lieutenant. "There's not much wind, and what there is isn't in her favor." His mind raced, trying to calculate the advantages and liabilities of his position. "Clear the ship for action, Daniel."

Bevan looked at him with alarm. "You're not going to fight her in the mouth of the bay?"

"I don't know yet," Charles said quietly, his eyes still fixed on the Spaniard's sails. "I need a better picture. In the meantime, clear the ship for action. We'll beat to quarters in half an hour."

Bevan muttered something unintelligible under his breath and gave the order.

Charles left the quarterdeck and made his way to the foremast shrouds with his glass. He climbed slowly, finally reaching the high platform at the crosstrees with his ankle aching and short of breath.

"Mornin,' Cap'n," the lookout greeted him, sliding over to one side to make room.

"Good morning," Charles said, and lowered himself gingerly down to a sitting position, his back to the mast. "What's your name?" he asked.

"Connley, sur, topman," the lookout answered.

From high in the rigging Charles could see the entire land- and seascape spread before him—the entrance to the bay, the forts, the white froth of the reef, and the frigate now about seven miles away. The *Santa*

Brigida was close-hauled, about as near to the wind as she could lie, and had just cleared the promontory that marked the far end of the mouth of the bay. Raising the glass to his eye, he saw her sails ripple, indicating that she was having difficulty with the wind eddies off the headlands. Charles watched his enemy closely for about ten minutes, studying her progress and her relationship to the features of the land and sea.

"Where do you think she'll be in, say, forty-five minutes, Connley?" Charles asked.

"'Bout two and a half, maybe three miles out from the fort, I'd say, sir. She won't have cleared the reef," the lookout replied.

"That's what I think, too. Thank you for making space for me."

"Yer welcome, sir. Did you see what you was looking for?"

"I did," Charles answered.

"Are we goin' to fight her again, sir?"

"Yes, and we're going to have her this time," he said, turning on the narrow perch. "It's a sure wager." He felt for a foothold with his shoe and started his laborious descent to the deck.

"Hang out the studding sails, Daniel," Charles said, returning to the quarterdeck. "I want more speed; every fathom counts."

Bevan slowly exhaled, expressing a displeasure that he clearly did not want to voice openly. "Aye aye, Captain."

The *Louisa* bore slowly down on the Spanish frigate in the light air, her bow wave small curls of white and her wake an uneven trail across the swells. At four miles the *Santa Brigida* was fully visible, two and a half miles outside the Ferrol headlands, the black bulk of her hull emphasized by the white surf on the reef another mile or so beyond. As they watched, the Spaniard hove to, took in all but her topgallants, laid one against the mast, and waited broadside-on for the approaching smaller British frigate.

Charles nodded appreciatively. The *Santa Brigida's* captain had little choice but to back her sails and wait. She couldn't turn away without sailing onto the reef and couldn't lie anywhere near close enough to the wind to stand toward him. If the frigate had stayed on her halting course westward, the *Louisa* could have timed her approach, laid off the Spaniard's bow at the end of the reef, and raked her repeatedly. By heaving to she was demanding a broadside-to-broadside fight. In fact, her only options were to heave to and fight it out or reverse course and return to the bay. Charles didn't think the Spanish captain had the courage to turn tail and run—it would be his pride as well as the knowledge that he had the larger, better-armed ship that forced him to gamble he could pummel the *Louisa* into submission before drifting down onto the reef. It was a reasonable assumption except for one thing, Charles considered: After the first few broadsides in this wind, the *Santa Brigida* wouldn't be able to see him.

"This is crazy, Charlie," Bevan said nervously. "We can't maneuver here. She'll batter us."

Charles pulled his eyes away from the Spanish frigate to look at his lieutenant and friend. "I don't intend to maneuver, Daniel. Her captain thinks what you think—that he can beat us in a straight gun-to-gun fight. But he can't, not today. Lay us alongside at fifty yards, just off her bow quarter, and get every stitch of sail off her except for the fore and mizzen topsails. We'll back and fill, same as the Spaniard."

"All right, Charlie," Bevan said, resigned.

Charles glanced at the black-hulled ship, now less than a mile away. There was still a little time before it would begin. He forced himself to relax and stifled his fingers before they could start tapping on the rail. After a moment he started forward, carefully made his way down the ladderway to the gundeck, and limped to a central spot forward of the mainmast. The gun crews fell silent one by one as they noticed his presence.

"You know we're going to fight the Spanish frigate again," he said in a loud voice so all around could hear. "I promise you we'll beat her if we keep our heads. I expect you to run your guns in and out as quick as you can, but *aim* them. Lay every shot true for her gundeck. If you can't see her hull in the smoke, look for her masts. They'll tell you where she lies." He saw heads nod in comprehension.

"Three cheers for the *Louisa*!" Charles shouted, and loud huzzas followed. "Three cheers for her crew!" They were still cheering when he saw the Spaniard's gunports open and the black muzzles of her cannon run out.

"Pass the word for my steward," Charles said to Midshipman Beechum after hurrying as best he could back to the quarterdeck. "Tell him I want my best uniform coat and hat."

At three hundred yards the *Santa Brigida* fired a ragged broadside, gray-black smoke hiding her then drifting lazily with the breeze back over her decks. Balls splashed in the sea all around; one hit the *Louisa*'s bow with a crash, transmitting its impact through the frame of the ship.

"He should have waited until we were closer," Charles said to no one in particular. He pulled out his watch and noted the time. Turning to Bevan, he said, "Start taking the sails off her and run out the starboard battery."

Charles moved to the forward rail of the quarterdeck and called down to Winchester on the gundeck, "We're going to come about. Fire as you bear."

"Yes, sir," Winchester shouted back.

Satisfied that he'd done everything that could be done, Charles made his way to the larboard rail, leaned back against it, and looked at his watch again. Attwater arrived and helped him change coats, fussing nervously at invisible dust on the lapel as he did so.

"I hope you know what yer doing, sir," he said tensely. "She's got an awful big bite."

"I hope so, too."

At seventy-five yards he looked to the quartermaster at the wheel and said, "Port your helm, hard over." The unneeded sails were already being furled at lightning speed. Bevan yelled, "Back the main topgallant" to the men on the braces.

Louisa lost way as her head swung to port. Her broadside came a fraction before the *Santa Brigida*'s, the sounds of the combined guns at close range deafening in their thunderous roar. Charles felt the deck cant with the cannons' recoil and shudder as a number of the heavy Spanish balls pounded the *Louisa*'s hull. A section of the bulwark exploded inward by the number-eight gun in the waist, killing or maiming four of its crew.

"Get those men below and replace them," Charles ordered.

"Sponge out! Load with cartridge!" a young gunnery midshipman on the quarterdeck was shouting at the top of his lungs, but Charles saw that most of the gun crews were ahead of him.

"Home!" he heard one gun captain call, signaling that a powder cartridge had been pushed fully in. Charles watched as the shot and wad were forced into the muzzle and quickly rammed tight. The gun crew heaved on the rope tackle and the gun, trucks squealing shrilly, came up with a thud against the ship's side. The sharper bark of the quarterdeck carronades sounded first. They were quicker to reload and run out on their slides than the heavier nine- and twelve-pounders.

"Clear!" the gun captain yelled as he yanked on the lanyard. The black beast exploded its charge, expelling a ball of orange flame, and lurched viciously back against its restraints. A rolling crescendo of explosions followed as the *Louisa*'s second broadside fired.

Charles looked for damage on the Spanish frigate, but the smoke from his guns drifted toward her on the easy wind, obscuring much of his vision. This satisfied him. The *Santa Brigida* spoke a moment later, the flash of her guns just visible here and there through the deepening haze. Shot screamed across the decks, tearing new holes in the lee rail, upsetting a gun, and sending up fountains of water where cannonballs aimed low found the sea. "Detail some men to replace any damaged guns with those from the port-side battery," he said to Bevan.

Charles stared hard at the fort on the Ferrol promontory, trying to line its flagstaff with some landmark inland that he could remember later so he could judge *Louisa*'s leeway. The carronades fired nearly together, followed after a moment by most of the cannon in a rolling blast, then the last and slowest of the guns manned by newer hands. He saw a yard fall from the *Santa Brigida*'s rigging, the masts from her tops up being the only part of the Spanish ship he could see above the smoke. Both ships were soon firing nearly blind through the almost impenetrable cloud. But it was worse for the Spaniard, Charles knew. She had her own gunsmoke as well as the *Louisa*'s drifting slowly across her decks.

A loud crash forward accompanied by anguished screams told him that another of the twelve-pounders on the gundeck had been hit and dismounted from its carriage. A shot shrieked across the quarterdeck close enough that Charles could feel its passage. The ship's bell gave a last clank, and when he looked the belfry had disappeared.

"Warm work, Charlie," Bevan observed.

"Yes."

Almost immediately the *Louisa* loosed her own increasingly drawn-out cannonade, and, after an eerie quiet punctuated only by the sounds of shouting sailors and the marines firing their small arms from the tops, the carronades and then the long guns fired again before the Spaniard answered. Four rounds to their three, and maybe five for the carronades, Charles thought—only marginally better than before.

CANNON FIRE SOON became general from both ships, without rhythm or meter, as the guns were loaded and emptied as fast as the crews could work them. Now and again, Spanish balls crashed savagely against the *Louisa*'s hull, reverberating throughout the ship. He couldn't be sure of the toll from the *Louisa*'s fire, but he saw splashes in the water all around from the Spaniard's efforts, including a goodly number that had been fired well high and landed in the sea a half a mile or more beyond. A more concentrated burst than usual came from the *Santa Brigida* and Charles watched as wooden blocks and pulleys clattered loudly to the deck, followed by silent snakes of rope.

"They're aiming for our masts," Bevan offered.

"Maybe, but I doubt they can see our masts, or anything else of us," Charles answered. "It's just luck. If they send enough balls, they're bound to hit something." The pall of cannon smoke hung like an impenetrable fog from the sea surface almost to the lower yards, and the *Louisa* belched flame and ball into it over and over again.

Charles looked back at the Ferrol fort. He saw a puff from a cannon disappear in the wind, and someone was frantically running the Spanish flag up and down on its staff. He smiled grimly. He knew what the fort was trying to communicate to the *Santa Brigida*'s captain. The reef would be as invisible as the *Louisa* in the heavy fog of spent gunpowder drifting onto and past the frigate. He doubted the Spanish captain was thinking about the reef now, or that he could see the signal.

From the position of the Spaniard's masts, Charles saw that the distance between the two ships had gradually increased as the heavier frigate had drifted further to leeward than the *Louisa*. "Bring the yards around and close the gap," he said to Bevan. "I don't want too much space between us." He looked again at the Ferrol fort, checking for the position of the landmark he had picked out earlier.

The incessant crash of cannons seemed to continue interminably; the Spaniard began to exact a toll with its repeated strikes to the *Louisa*'s masts, hulls, and men. Another gun upset, a twelve-pounder in the

(279)

waist, and then a carronade on the quarterdeck reared backward with a loud clang as a ball struck its muzzle. Charles didn't want to lose any of his carronades. "Get that gun remounted or replace it with one from the port-side battery," he ordered, then saw that it was already being done. The topgallant mast snapped at its cap and came twisting down with its yard, through the stays and shrouds to land almost gently on the deck.

He heard a loud rending crack and saw the *Santa Brigida*'s entire foremast swing in a wide arc toward the sea, pulling the main top and topgallant masts with it. Ragged cheers broke out among the sweating gun crews on the *Louisa*'s decks.

"Silence," Bevan bellowed. "Tend to your business."

Whether from attrition or exhaustion or both, the gunfire on the Spanish frigate gradually began to slow to arhythmic bursts with lengthening silences in between. The *Louisa*'s own rate of fire wasn't as intense as when they began, but it was noticeably stronger than the *Santa Brigida*'s. The breeze picked up and the murk of gunsmoke slowly lightened, allowing Charles to see occasional glimpses of his opponent. Her sides were battered, with numerous upended muzzles. In places two, three, and—just aft of midships—four of her gunports were beaten into one. Strings of rigging trailed limply in the water.

The Spaniard's hull, deprived of the leverage of her foremast and most of her mainmast, rolled noticeably in the gentle swells. Still she fired from this gun and that as her few remaining gun crews reloaded them and heaved the beasts out against their bulwarks, but it was clear that the fight had gone out of her. Even with the clearing of the smoke, her guns were poorly aimed, firing high or short as she rolled.

Charles checked the Ferrol headland and then looked at the Spanish frigate again, cocking his head and listening.

"She's done, Daniel," Charles said.

A crash of three guns fired nearly together from the *Santa Brigida*. The *Louisa*'s foretopmast cracked and swayed down, hanging by its stays.

"Not yet, she isn't," Bevan said.

"Yes, she is. Listen."

During a silence between the firing cannons, Bevan listened. "I don't hear anything," he said. "Her guns have slacked off, but she hasn't struck."

"Not that," Charles said. "Listen to the surf, the reef."

Bevan stood silent for a moment as a wave broke on the rocks close behind the battered frigate. Both men heard it clearly. "Oh, God," he said.

Charles paused to consider that he had finally defeated the *Santa Brigida*. Her masts and hull were broken and battered and so many of her cannon were unserviceable that she was virtually disarmed. He had in his hands the means to avenge the brutal punishment the *Argonaut* had received from her guns at St. Vincent. But he felt little of the satisfaction he thought he would. He could sink her now if he wanted to. He could continue to pour shot after shot into her almost unprotected hull, or he could simply order the *Louisa* to put on sail and leave. For the Spanish frigate there was no escape. The reef was too close. Without her masts, she had no hope of clawing clear. If he wanted to, Charles could even order the *Louisa* to linger nearby, to discourage any boats from shore from coming out to take off the survivors. Even in this moderate sea, it would all be over in a few hours: The *Santa Brigida* would slowly break her bottom against the rocks, fill with water, and sink.

"What are you going to do, Charlie?" Bevan asked, reading his thoughts.

Charles watched the wiry Spanish captain with the mustache running back and forth on his quarterdeck, calling out orders, exhorting, trying to get the most from his dispirited crew. The man showed determination to fight to the end and no awareness of the all-too-rapidly approaching rocks.

"Cease firing," Charles said. "Get me a speaking trumpet." The *Louisa* fell eerily silent.

"*Señor Capitán, Señor Capitán*," Charles yelled through the trumpet. No one on the Spanish frigate noticed and she fired two more guns, one striking the *Louisa*'s hull. "*Señor Capitán, Santa Brigida!*" Charles screamed as loud as he could.

The man looked up quizzically. Charles saw that his uniform and face were stained with powder smoke and there was blood from a cut on his cheek. "Strike," Charles yelled. "Strike your colors."

A gun went off on the *Santa Brigida;* Charles watched gratefully as her captain gestured for silence, then cupped his hand to his ear. "*Qué?*" he shouted back.

"Is there anyone on board who speaks Spanish?" Charles asked Bevan.

"Beechum, I think."

"Fetch him." To the Spanish captain Charles shouted, "Surrender, strike, give up! For Christ's sake, the reef's behind you!"

The Spanish captain shouted something back. Charles had no idea what he'd said.

Beechum arrived. "Do you speak Spanish?" Charles asked.

"Some, sir. My nanny was Castilian," the midshipman answered.

"Ask him to strike. Do it politely," Charles said, handing Beechum the speaking trumpet.

The midshipman puckered his lips in concentration, then shouted, *"Háganos el favor de rendirse Usted."*

The Spanish captain clearly understood, frowned, and waved his hands in a gesture of dismissal.

"What did you say?" Charles asked.

"I asked him to please do us the courtesy of surrendering," Beechum said.

"That was polite," Bevan observed.

Charles grabbed the trumpet back and raised it to his lips. "Behind you, behind you! *Dientes del Diablo!*" he screamed.

Someone on the *Santa Brigida* understood him and looked around. Charles could hear the shouts of warning and dismay among the crew. He was right when he'd guessed that the reef would be invisible and forgotten in the heat of battle. The Spanish captain looked behind him in time to see a churning cauldron of foam as a swell washed over the black rocks. He turned back to Charles with a look of horror on his face.

"Get a cable to her, Daniel. We'll take her in tow."

"Aye aye," Bevan said and hurried off to organize the work.

"Keswick," Charles called to the bosun standing near the wheel. "Get as many hands as you can aloft to repair the rigging. We're going to need all the sail we can carry."

"What's the word for surrender?" Charles asked Beechum. "Just the word."

"Rendición, sir," Beechum said.

A lead line had already been heaved across to the Spanish ship, whose remaining crew were pulling it in as fast as they could. The small line would be attached to a larger rope, which would be tied to a cablet, eventually connecting to the anchor cable with which the *Louisa* would try to drag the *Santa Brigida* to safety.

"*Rendición?*" Charles shouted across at the *Santa Brigida*'s captain. "*Rendición?*"

"*Sí, sí. Rendición,*" the captain called back, gesturing his surrender with his hands and calling for someone to haul down the Spanish flag from its place above the taffrail.

Charles turned back to Bevan. "Send Winchester over with the marines and as many seamen as he thinks necessary to take possession of her."

The cable was passed with some urgency and fastened securely to *Louisa*'s bitts. She took the strain as gently as Eliot could manage, given her wounded masts and stays. Slowly they pulled the *Santa Brigida* clear and then several miles out to sea, where they hove to in order to carry out repairs to both ships.

THE SETTING SUN painted the underbellies of the clouds in spectacular hues of orange and gold to the horizon. Charles felt content and blissfully tired; there were only a few more things he had to see to. He found an intact section of the weather rail and leaned on it, enjoying the sunset and wishing Penny could be with him to share it. He felt Bevan's presence on the rail beside him. "What day is it?" Charles asked idly.

"February fourteenth, seventeen hundred and ninety-eight," Bevan answered.

"One year to the day," Charles observed, remembering their first meeting with the *Santa Brigida* at Cape St. Vincent.

"That's true," Bevan said dryly. "But, far more importantly, it's a day you'd better write to your wife. I'm told they expect such things on St. Valentine's Day."

"Beg your pardon, sirs," said Midshipman Beechum, "but Captain Manuel de Santa María de la Valencia is here to surrender his sword. He insisted, sir."

"Show him aft and stay to translate," Charles said.

The Spanish captain loped across the deck purposefully toward them, bowed to Charles with a flourish, said something lengthy to Beechum, and held his sword out in front of him.

"He says you are a most worthy opponent," Beechum summarized. "He is honored to surrender his sword to a man such as yourself. He said more, sir, much more, but that's the gist of it."

Charles bowed equally deeply in return. "Tell him he can keep his sword. Tell him . . . hell, tell him all the proper things he said to me, with the necessary embellishments and niceties. Invite him to dinner in my cabin this evening so that he can meet my officers. Tell him I'd be honored. You come, too. I want to propose an exchange of prisoners—he and his men for the British held captive in Ferrol."

He had wanted to add: "Tell him he'd needlessly murdered young Billy Bowles a year ago this day," but he didn't. That was over now.

LATE THAT NIGHT, after the dinner was concluded and the cabin cleared, he sat down with quill, ink, and paper to write a letter to his wife. In it he told her of his love and how she was constantly in his mind and in his heart, how much he longed to be with her, ending it with, "And I captured a Spanish ship today . . ."

Born into a military family and raised as a Quaker, JAY WORRALL grew up on a number of continents around the world, in Africa and Europe as well as the United States. During the Vietnam War he worked with refugees in the central highlands of that country and afterward taught English in Japan. Later, he worked in developing innovative and humane prison programs, policies, and administrations. He has also been a carpenter. Married and the very proud father of five sons, he currently lives and writes in Pennsylvania.

ABOUT THE TYPE

This book was set in Garamond, a typeface originally designed by the Parisian type cutter Claude
Garamond (1480–1561). This version of Garamond was modeled on a 1592 specimen sheet from
the Egenolff-Berner foundry, which was produced
from types assumed to have been brought to
Frankfurt by the punch cutter Jacques Sabon
(d. 1580).

Claude Garamond's distinguished romans
and italics first appeared in *Opera Ciceronis* in
1543–44. The Garamond types are clear, open, and
elegant.